Deadline for
Death

Deadline for
Death

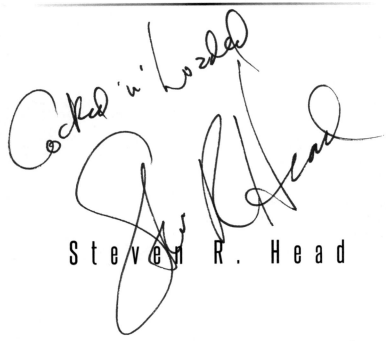

Steven R. Head

iUniverse

DEADLINE FOR DEATH

This is a work of fiction. All of the characters, names, incidents, organizations, and dialogue in this novel are either the products of the author's imagination or are used fictitiously.

iUniverse books may be ordered through booksellers or by contacting:

iUniverse LLC
1663 Liberty Drive
Bloomington, IN 47403
www.iuniverse.com
1-800-Authors (1-800-288-4677)

ISBN: 978-1-4917-4110-8 (sc)
ISBN: 978-1-4917-4112-2 (hc)
ISBN: 978-1-4917-4111-5 (e)

Library of Congress Control Number: 2014913113

Printed in the United States of America.

iUniverse rev. date: 08/06/2014

DEDICATION

This book is dedicated to my parents, Dean and Joan Head. Their decision to leave behind family and the familiar in the mid-1950s introduced me to the distinctive character and culture of Fremont County, Wyoming.

ACKNOWLEDGMENTS

This book would not have been possible without the support and encouragement of Kandra Hahn. Ms. Hahn also shared her knowledge of period fashions. Every author should have the good fortune of a friendship with an archivist—in my case John Irwin. Mr. Irwin's willingness to review drafts, respond to specific queries, and pep talk this project to the finish line was essential.

Doug Kucera suggested the use of a Parker shotgun along with general firearms background material. Don Arp Jr. made recommendations and performed research on the different handguns contained in this book. Any errors or inaccuracies concerning firearms in this book are the result of my failure to grasp key details. Mr. Arp also provided insight into the daily reality of rural law enforcement officers.

The work of the editorial and production staff of IUniverse has been invaluable to the shaping and completion of this work.

Day 1

September 2, 1952
Tuesday
(Day after Labor Day)

CHAPTER 1

Tribal Police officer Tom Masin may not have seen the car in the no-man's land between Highway 26 and the cabin fifty yards from the road without the almost full moon. The howl of tires on pavement subsided as he switched from gas to brake pedal. As the newest officer of the Wind River Indian Reservation Tribal Police Force, he had been volunteered to represent the agency at a meeting in Casper, Wyoming. The decision to set out before 4:00 am was driven by his fear of being late rather than specific orders from his captain.

Masin pulled the Army surplus Willys Jeep onto the shoulder fifteen feet from the mailbox at the end of the lane, slid off the seat with a flashlight, stood quietly and studied the terrain. He searched for movement and saw only the moonlit shapes and shadows of rabbit brush and sage, the car, and the small building. In six hours this scene would be sun-bleached, the same shapes monochrome with tiny shadows in pale hues. Masin liked the delicate tones of night views even though this one smelled of danger.

He pushed the switch of the flashlight to on as he approached the entry point of the lane. The tire tracks on top showed the car came from the east, probably Riverton. Fresh prints on top of the tire treads of a single individual pushing a bicycle from the car left a broken trail in the dirt of a tire path. He compared the length of a boot print to his own.

Masin set out toward the car a good yard beyond the lane, alert for movement ahead, and stopped every few yards to scan for more tracks but only found the single set. Near the rear of the car, through the broad rear windows, he could see the head of a figure in the driver's seat. Masin stopped and flashed light into the gap of the partially open trunk lid, likely location of the bicycle walked back to the road, and saw nothing of interest.

He inched around to the passenger side and noticed the rear windows wrap around in four distinct segments. Masin flashed the light into the back seat and saw bulky bags behind the driver side seat. He switched off the flashlight and let the moon illuminate the scene. Stepping forward to just behind the passenger door, he found neither boot prints on the loose sandy soil nor a companion in the passenger seat. He retreated behind the car and watched for movement in the car and from the cabin.

Masin moved to the driver side and focused the flashlight beam on the rolled up driver's window, taking care to leave the foot prints heading back to the highway undisturbed. The driver's chin rested on his chest, perhaps asleep. Standing behind the door, he tapped the flashlight against the window with his left hand, ready to retreat and draw his handgun if needed. No response. He tapped again. Still nothing.

Before taking a closer look at the driver he flashed around the ground, looking for footprints going toward the cabin but found none. Masin stepped closer and examined the face—the driver looked white, not Indian. The man appeared injured or dead, and he could do little in either circumstance. He knew it was best not to disturb the body if it was an injury.

Stepping to his left, away from the car, Masin checked for tire tracks leading to the cabin. The dirt on the driver's side path ahead of the car was undisturbed, dust and wind having filled in any tire tracks from an earlier visit. There was no reason to believe the cabin was occupied.

Masin hurried back to the road, taking care not to obscure the foot prints, slipped into the Jeep and drove east to the Riverton airport. The pay telephone booth outside the Sky Club was the quickest way to contact the local law officers. The Tribal Police budget could not afford two-way radio equipment, not to mention repair of the busted low gear in the Jeep. He dialed zero, identified himself, and asked the operator to send a Fremont County Sheriff's officer to the location of the car.

Driving back to the scene he questioned whether the man and car were on reservation land. Since the driver was not an Indian, turning it over to the County authorities made sense. The action could open him to ridicule from Tribal Council members, but Captain Latrell was likely to support his decision. The history of interagency squabbles between the Wind River Tribal Police and Fremont County Sheriff over issues of jurisdiction was piled high with conflict. This did not appear to be a situation worthy of a fresh skirmish.

As he waited for a sheriff to arrive Masin inspected the boot prints. Cowboy boots. No distinctive heel or sole markings. Masin walked ten yards in both directions along the side of the paved roadway but failed to find similar prints or bicycle tire tracks on either side. Sitting in the Jeep he made notes in a pad with a silver spiral wire along the top. Time, approximate location, license number, condition of the vehicle, bicycle tire tracks, approximate length of the boot print, along with the action taken.

Masin stood beside the Jeep when the headlights approached. A Fremont County Sheriff's car pulled into the entry point of the dirt road. The driver flashed his mounted spotlight on the vehicle down the lane. The car had appeared a yellow color in his flashlight beam, now it looked off-white. A stout man got out and pulled on a cowboy hat, looking over the roof of his patrol car.

"Deputy Sheriff Bud Yost. What we got here, chief?"

Masin felt the bite of sarcasm but resisted trading insults. He had learned not to play another man's game in the Army, and the value of appearing indifferent. Masin identified himself. "Car off the road. Man inside."

The deputy sat back in his car and drove to the other vehicle, covering the tire and bicycle tracks and foot prints. Masin feared the sheriff might destroy any clues they could offer and decided to assume the role of silent Indian as he followed down the roadway on foot. In his mind this was now a sheriff's department problem.

The deputy looked into the car and opened the door, placing the back of his hand against the driver's face. "This man's dead. Skin's cold."

Masin kept his distance, not wanting to get any closer to the dead man than necessary.

The deputy hitched the gun belt beneath his round belly. "Help me check for identification?"

Masin took a step to the side and away from the car. Even a boarding-school Indian knew to avoid contact with the dead.

The deputy turned and frowned. "Guess you people don't like gettin' too close to the dead, superstition and all."

Masin watched as the deputy pulled a wallet from the back pants pocket of the driver, toppling the dead man's upper body onto the passenger side. He took a step back, wanting even more distance.

"Corky Freeman." The deputy tossed the wallet to Masin. "Verify the amount of cash so we won't be accused of stealin' from the dead or somethin'."

Masin inspected the Wyoming drivers license and memorized the name and address. He counted out sixteen dollars in bills and handed the wallet to the deputy when he approached.

"I'm gonna call this in. Get somebody out for the body and a tow truck for the car. You got any ideas what happened?"

Masin shook his head no.

"Looks to me like some freak one-car accident. Maybe some medical condition. Guess it was his night to die or somethin'."

Masin looked expressionless at the deputy, disgusted at how casually the man made up a story about the dead driver. If the rest of the sheriff's department was like this deputy, they were not going to solve many crimes, since this deputy could not even recognize a suspicious death.

Masin was ready to move along to his meeting miles away. "Need me for anything? I've got a meeting in Casper."

"Nah, chief, I've got it from here."

Before starting the Jeep, Masin entered the name and address of the dead man in his notebook, along with "Deputy Bud Yost", followed by "or somthin'" and "one-car accident." He carefully pulled onto the highway and thought about needing a healing ceremony.

CHAPTER 2

Wilson Dodge hummed the melody to "In the Mood" as he walked along Main Street, past the Ben Franklin 5 & 10 and Missy Frank's Dress Shop, on the way to the Atomic Café. He liked the tempo of the big-band tune for walking, and the chill of the still-dark morning after Labor Day made his strides a fraction faster than normal.

The Atomic, formerly the Round-Up Café, faced the Third and Main Street intersection in downtown Riverton. A sign with neon yellow letters and three green neon arcs moving from left to right around a red center angled from the building's corner. Wil preferred the Round-Up's painted cowboy atop a horse twirling a neon lariat, but it was a new age.

No matter the time of day or season, walking into the windowless Atomic reminded Wil of entering a cave. Step-up booths surrounded the rectangular room, and tight alleys snaked around tables for two, four, and eight in the middle ground. The low-wattage string-pull lamps of the booths added little to the green and yellow neon light from recessed coves bouncing off the ceiling into the smoky air. The only bright light came from the kitchen service bay at the rear.

The smell of frying bacon and coffee met him at the door, and a haze of cigarette smoke patted him on the back as he passed the booths and tables en route to the counter. The tan-colored porcelain mug filled with hot coffee was absent at his customary stool, a consequence of his arriving an hour early.

New yellow plastic covered the stool Wil had occupied beside his father, Clayton Dodge, since grade school. In the interim period,

Wil had graduated from the University of Michigan, and Clayton had died.

Wil gave a nod to Rose, the waitress, and confirmed his standard order. Just like Wil's stool, Rose played her part in the history and ritual at the Round-Up turned Atomic. Little had changed about her except a darker shade of red had snuck into Rose's hair, and wrinkles had formed at the corners of her eyes. Of the habits Wil had established since returning to Riverton, breakfast evoked the fondest memories. But Riverton had changed, and so had he.

The young man who had come home to assume his father's duties as editor of the *Riverton Wrangler* looked similar to the naïve boy who had left for college in August of 1945, with his plans of attending seminary. Wil had been the kid who had helped out at the newspaper and at church throughout high school, and he had done little to change that perception.

Rose set silverware and a coffee mug in front of him and filled the latter. "Didn't know you're a fisherman."

He picked up the spoon and glanced at her. "I'm not."

"Doesn't look like you've been up all night with a new girlfriend. So if you're not after worms, why so early, Sam?"

Since his return to Riverton, Rose had started assigning him a different name each day, and it had taken most of a week before he had begun playing along. She had different rituals with the regulars, but the name game appeared to belong solely to him. "Thanks for asking, Olive. Two days of work to do in one. The paper goes out on Thursday, holiday or not. I might keep Sam. Does it suit me?"

"Mmm, maybe in ten years."

Rose spun, grabbed a pair of plates from the service window, and charged into the maze of tables. Wil wondered where he would be in ten years and whether the girlfriend Rose imagined would be making his breakfast, unlike his father's wife. But that would require finding a girl to date, and his dance card had contained only a handful of entries during the past year.

The returning graduate of Riverton High and the University of Michigan had expected few problems picking a spouse. Wil could name a half dozen gals he had dated in high school and just as many others who had interested him. Ramona, his mother, had encouraged him to use Ann Arbor as a hunting ground for a wife. The coeds at Michigan had shared little with the tomboyish western girls he knew and liked.

Rose set a plate of fried eggs, bacon, and fried potatoes in front of him. "Meatloaf's the special, if you make it back. It'll go quick. I can save your spot tomorrow if this is the new time."

"Back to normal tomorrow, Olive."

Wil had hoped to find his hometown the same as he had left it, including a selection of local women for his wife. But most of his classmates were married, and those who were still single did not interest him. Just as he had looked for tomboys at college, now he sought a polished and educated single women, a rare commodity in Fremont County.

One reason for his failure to find a suitable mate was the pressure of learning a new job. After a year in the role of editor, he had developed the full range of skills for the role, except for a weekly editorial. All the ideas that had bubbled for editorials on the drive from Chicago to Wyoming evaporated under the pressure of producing a weekly regional newspaper. Wil kept telling himself that next week he would write an opinion piece. Next week had yet to arrive.

Wil stood, leaving half the potatoes on his plate and a pile of change on the counter. He swallowed the last bit of coffee and headed out of the Atomic for the newspaper office and his list of chores—a front-page article on the Labor Day rally, composed but unwritten; scraps of submitted social news that needed sorting and editing; and photos to go with an unwritten page-3 piece on the first day of school at Jefferson Elementary, an assignment Corky, the photographer, would fit in along with his layout duties.

Streetlights illuminated Main as he escaped the warm and smoky Atomic Café for the crisp chill of September. Wil raised the collar on his wool jacket, and the thud of his cowboy boots accompanied the reflections in store windows as he marched toward the *Wrangler* office.

+ + +

Wil relished the thirty minutes of quiet before the crew of printers arrived to start the daylong cacophony of multiple printing presses. The distinct sound of typebars snapping against paper punctuated the silence as the Labor Day story moved from his thoughts onto the page. Without the background rhythm of a press, the end-of-line ping of the Underwood echoed in the open front office of the newspaper. The staccato of characters on paper filled the page as it inched through the typewriter.

He was near the halfway point on the article on the rally when the sound of the front door opening broke his concentration. His office companion, Geri Murphy, would not arrive until after 8:00 a.m. with the morning mail from the post office. And Corky Freeman, photographer and layout assistant, always ran late. Glancing over his shoulder, Wil saw a khaki uniform shirt and gold star. A silver Stetson tipped back to reveal sheriff's deputy Albert Nelson approaching the front counter.

"Wil, I got some bad news for ya. There's been an accident."

Wil tried to imagine the sort of accident that would bring a deputy to the *Wrangler* before sunrise.

"There's no good way to say this. Your man Corky, he's dead. The tribal boys found him off the road on 26, out past the airport." The deputy maintained eye contact. "One-car accident. Maybe he fell asleep, or there was an animal."

"One car ..." Wil heard the words but could not connect them. Corky had just turned twenty-two a month earlier. How could he be dead?

"Yup. We got the call around four this morning. Bud went out."

"You said dead, right? Not in the hospital, but ..."

"'Fraid so. We was hoping you could come identify him."

Stand, Wil thought, but his legs ignored the command.

"And do you know anything about his folks? He's not from around here."

Corky had promised to take Wil over the mountains to his family farm in Idaho and a supposed "better view" of the Tetons.

They had just talked about it the day before as they covered the Labor Day rally in City Park.

Wil rolled his chair near Geri's desk and the drawer with employee files. He copied the name, address, and telephone number of Corky's parents in Idaho. Wil handed the paper to Albert. "You're sure it's him?"

"That's why we want you to take a look."

Wil hoped it was a mistake. He still wanted to teach and go places with Corky.

"I can drive you to the morgue, at the hospital, if you need me to."

Wil stood, rolled the chair back toward his desk, and moved through the wooden spring-assisted half door of the office area. "I'm good to drive."

+ + +

Until that morning, Wil had no reason to care about the location of the morgue in the almost new Memorial Hospital. The only other death of someone close had been that of his father, Clayton Dodge, over a year ago. By the time Wil had arrived from Chicago, the mortuary viewing, funeral, and burial were compressed into less than twenty-four hours. As he entered the hospital, Wil wondered whether Clayton had spent any time in the hospital morgue. He took the stairs to the lower level, where "Store Room," "Maintenance," and "Laundry" joined "Morgue" on a wall-mounted directional sign.

As he walked down the ceramic tile and concrete block corridor, Wil kept telling himself it was all a mistake. The dead person would not be Corky but some other young man. He would go back to the office to find Corky goofing around in the darkroom.

Deputy Albert Nelson stood waiting at the door to the morgue. As he approached, Wil thought Albert looked the part of a movie lawman with the five-pointed gold star on his uniform shirt, the six-shooter holstered at his hip, and his solid six-foot frame. Albert's narrow, angular facial features reminded Wil of Dick Tracy, although others mentioned the deputy's similarity to movie actor Randolph Scott. Wil did not see the resemblance.

Albert opened and held the door as fluorescent brightness filled the hallway, and a blend of alcohol, ammonia, and iodine caused Wil to cover his nose just two steps into the room.

A white sheet was stretched over the top of a gurney, and Albert pulled the covering back. Seeing Corky's features brought on nausea. Wil turned his head away and inhaled a deep breath, wincing from the ammonia fumes. After holding his nose and squeezing his eyes shut for a moment, he opened them again and looked back at the figure, at the smooth forehead, unbroken pointed-tip nose, and strong chin. No mistake about it—this was Corky. Wil looked at Albert and nodded his head up and down. The deputy moved to cover the exposed face, until Wil held up his hand.

Wil had expected to see bruising and dried blood on his face, but there was neither. He pulled the sheet down to uncover Corky's chest and then exposed the smooth light-colored skin of his belly. No bruise marks. Wil leaned forward for a closer look and then made eye contact with Albert and asked a silent question. The deputy ignored it.

Speaking in a whisper, Wil repeated his inquiry aloud. "How did he die?"

"Not sure. You'll have to ask Ray Winslow. He's coroner now."

Slowly tracking from the bare belly up to the neck and face and down again, Wil felt a shiver along his spine. "No bruising on his face, neck, or chest. No sign of blood … How does a one-car accident kill a person without any sign of blood?"

Deputy Nelson shrugged. "Don't know. Maybe broke his neck."

Wil tried to make sense of what the deputy said but could not. A fatal one-car accident should involve cuts and bruises.

Wil looked on as Albert covered the supine Corky. He wanted another deep breath but was afraid to inhale the antiseptic air again. "I'm not talking as a newspaper man now, but as a close friend. Can you let me know the cause of death?"

"I'll ask Sheriff Farmer to give you a call."

"Thanks, Albert."

Albert opened the door, walked through, and turned back toward Wil. "People call me Al now, like they call you Wil, instead of Wilson or Dodger."

A surge of anger filled Wil at being corrected. What did it matter if the deputy was called Albert or Al? Corky was dead! That was what mattered. Wil instantly felt ashamed. Albert was not his equal, but there was little reason not to be civil. The deputy was just doing his job.

Wil moved past Albert and down the hallway. "Deputy."

Once outside the hospital, Wil ambled to his Chevrolet pickup. The sun- and sage-scented air calmed him as he drew deep breaths while crossing the small paved parking area. He stepped up onto the running board and into the cab and closed his eyes. The image of Corky's masklike face from the morgue imposed itself on the dark visual field.

A similar mental image of his father, lying in the coffin, plunged him into sadness. The unexpected death of Clayton had led to Wil's return to Riverton, to take charge of the newspaper. The challenges of the new role had helped fill his time but not his thoughts. The grieving process could not be denied. Corky's death opened the fragile scar tissue of the wound.

CHAPTER 3

Geraldine "Geri" Murphy shook a Lucky Strike from the pack and saw at least three more tucked inside. Four sharp taps on the glass-covered desktop compressed the tobacco. "Wil, where the hell are you?" Sparking a slim silver lighter, she drew smoke on her second office cigarette; the first casualty rested alone in the square clear glass ashtray. One of her personal rules involved starting the day with a clean ashtray.

The mail from the Labor Day weekend was already sorted into piles of bills, payments, legal notices, and "everything else." The last category always dominated, made up of handwritten notes on an array of topics—bridge club results, visiting guests, children at college or in military service, and other social news. Together with Wil, she would finish sorting each missive into wire baskets by town and divide up the baskets to type paragraphs for the weekly edition.

When her second call to Wil's apartment went unanswered, she began opening bills, releasing her frustration on the unsuspecting envelopes as she ripped open the tops. Geri stubbed out the second cigarette. "Damn it, Wil, where are you?" For that matter, where was Corky?

When Wil opened the office's front door, she froze, sensing something very wrong. Head bent forward, shoulders rounded, Wil pushed aside the spring-hinged wooden half door into the work area, turned his chair to face her, and plopped down. He looked into her eyes and then away. "Can I have a cigarette?"

The only other time Wil, a nonsmoker, had asked for a cigarette was when she questioned him about his girlfriend in Chicago. Geri wondered what could match the emotional pain of that rejection. She picked up the pack, shook a pair from the opening, lit both, and handed him one. Wil's hand shook as he took a quick drag.

"Corky was in a car accident."

Geri held her breath, waiting.

"He's dead. I don't know how else …"

Geri felt the first tear run down her cheek, and through watery eyes, she watched as a cloud of smoke engulfed his lowered head. Sorrow pushed aside the temper tantrum she had been nurturing. "I don't like it one damn bit."

Wil nodded his agreement.

+ + +

"I need to tell Bernie so he can make room on the front page. Have we got a photo of Corky?"

Geri angled her head toward Wil. "It's Bernie's haircut day. And we need to wrap up the town news. There's a big new batch."

Wil looked at the two piles of opened and unopened letters. "Can we do what's already sorted and then add the rest if there's time?"

Geri stood, nested the wire baskets with sorted letters for Wil's usual group of towns, and set them on his desk.

"I'll need a quote from a friend of Corky's—"

Geri swiveled toward Wil. "Gordon Blakeslee, camera club. He might have a head shot. Get going on those letters."

Listening to the taps on paper, Wil wished he could throw himself into work like Geri, setting aside feelings of shock and loss. She carried the deaths of her parents, her husband, her boss Clayton, and probably more in her heart. He supposed growing older gave a person control over those emotions.

A call to his uncle Dallas, an article on Corky's death, and the last part of the Labor Day ceremony in City Park delayed Wil from starting his share of the social news. At 9:30 a.m. Wil called his mother, Ramona Dodge, the official publisher of the *Riverton*

Wrangler, a title that had more to do with her ownership of shares of the corporation than any actual duties.

"Dodge residence." Wil recognized Ramona's practiced formality.

"Mother, have you been listening to the radio? Corky Freeman, our photographer, was found dead in his car, out west of town."

"How tragic. What happened?"

"The sheriff is saying single-car accident. I had to … to identify the body."

"I would not have been able to do that." Wil heard her take a heavy drag from a cigarette.

"I just wanted you to know so it wouldn't come as a surprise if someone called."

"Should I cancel the house party for Bob tomorrow?"

Bob Thornton, a recent widower and city council candidate, was dating Wil's mother. Ramona had agreed to host a campaign house party for Bob and had invited her friends. Wil understood her need for companionship, part of moving beyond Clayton's death. But Bob was not the kind of man Wil wanted to see as Ramona's second husband.

Wil thought of the response she had given when he questioned the propriety of dating Bob after Clayton's death: "It's 1952, not 1892. No black around the doorway and a year of black dresses." Although the comeback applied here, the triumph of parroting her words felt juvenile. He told her to go ahead with the party.

"Five thirty-ish. Be sure to dress up. No blue jeans."

Wil took a stack of letters from the top basket. "I know. I know. Call me if you need anything."

"Could you come for a cocktail after work?"

"It'll be after dark. I need to get the layout reworked with Bernie and do some chores."

"I'll have cold cuts and cheese."

"Sounds good. See you then." Wil set the telephone handpiece on the cradle.

Geri swiveled in her chair toward Wil, a cigarette clamped between her lips. "How'd Ramona take the news?"

"It didn't involve her, so pretty good."

"I'm sure she's sad in her own way."

"Kind of you to defend her, but we both know you've got more stories than anyone of Ramona's indifference to things not about her. I might be a close second ..."

Geri spun away and started typing, meaning it was time to get back to work.

CHAPTER 4

Impatient to get to Riverton, Fremont County sheriff Grayson Farmer downshifted and then accelerated through the hard turn on the way out of Hudson, one of several small towns scattered around sprawling Fremont County. Midway between Lander and Riverton, this one-dog town's principal distinction revolved around two popular restaurants.

Hudson's other defining feature was the second story cathouse over one of those restaurants. Hudson could not claim a monopoly on ladies-of-the-evening establishments in Fremont County, though, and since the county attorney refused to prosecute, the sheriff's department could do little. Grayson harbored no sense of moral outrage on the subject.

The decision to drive to Riverton from Lander had been made just before 5:00 a.m., when the courthouse switchboard operator phoned the sheriff's living quarters next to the jail. As the only man in the courthouse after hours, Grayson had learned to expect early morning calls that had more to do with maintenance than law enforcement. Today had been different.

The 9:00 a.m. KOVE news on the car radio began with the familiar lead-in: "It's a beautiful day in Lander." Grayson turned up the volume and listened to the first radio report naming Corky Freeman as the fatality of an early morning car crash. An hour earlier, Grayson had placed the long-distance call to the sheriff in Bonneville County, Idaho, asking his counterpart to notify Freeman's parents. Grayson switched off the AM radio.

Grayson had decided to investigate personally after hearing the details of a one-car accident from Deputy Bud Yost. Any death of a young person deserved his attention, especially just two months before the election. The report from Deputy Albert Nelson on the condition of the dead body created questions about the accuracy of the car accident description, confirming the need for personal involvement.

The sudden death of Sheriff Homer Yost from a liver problem had pushed Grayson from chief deputy in Lander to complete the remaining term as sheriff six years earlier, and nephew Bud Yost was a carryover from Homer's team. Bud's pattern of laziness and poor judgment had proved to be a disappointment to his uncle Homer, an assessment shared by Grayson. If Grayson was reelected, one of his first actions was going to be firing Bud.

The squawk of the dispatcher to a road crew on the shared countywide radio system shoved Grayson's thoughts from Bud and the election back to Corky Freeman and his connection to the Dodge family. Dallas Dodge owned a piece of the *Riverton Wrangler*, along with a number of other Fremont County businesses. Grayson would need to make a courtesy call on Dodge as part of his investigation.

County attorneys and law enforcement officers across the state had been manhandled in courtrooms by attorney Dallas Dodge. In spite of Grayson's plan to avoid confrontation with the man, mistakes by the sheriff's department had been exploited three times under his leadership to get charges dismissed for clients of Dodge. Grayson wished he had an excuse not to visit the lawyer or to delay it, to skip the guaranteed intimidation. But the investigation required the interview, no matter how demoralizing.

The second angle of the Dodge family involved the newspaper. The *Wrangler* rarely endorsed a candidate for elected office, but the new editor and nephew of Dallas might change that policy. Investigating the death of a newspaper employee could easily turn adversarial. With Freeman's death, the Dodge family had become a scorpion with twin stingers.

"Sheriff 1 to Base, have North Deputy 1 meet me at the accident scene in ten minutes. Over."

+ + +

Grayson pulled his black and white Ford radio car behind Deputy Nelson's older-model Ford with matching paint job on the north shoulder of Highway 26. Nelson crossed from the opposite side of the road as Grayson set the parking brake and turned on the rotating red roof-mounted light. He moved out of the car and closed the door. "What we got?"

"Far as I can tell, the tribal cop who called this in stopped about five yards from the entrance here." Nelson pointed to a single-lane dirt pathway flanked by ground-hugging grass tufts and brush, leading to a cabin at least fifty yards down the lane.

Nelson led the way across the pavement. "There's a set of boot tracks a yard or so into the weeds, away from the tire path, where the tribal probably walked to the car. But you can see there's all these tire tracks on top going in and out."

Grayson stopped, squatted, and looked at the different tire treads and widths. "This is how you found it?"

"When I got here, whoever took the body to the morgue was gone, and the tow truck was hooking up the Studebaker. Bud was sitting in the car, smoking. No road flares."

Grayson rose and looked west and then east, up and down the highway. "Show me where the car was."

Nelson took the left rut while Grayson followed in the right, noting the layering of tire tread patterns. Grayson's scanned the dirt lane until they reaching an area where grass tufts and rabbit brush had been trampled down, at least four different shoe and boot patterns recorded on the sandy ground.

Grayson stopped to inspect the area, right palm on the grip of his holstered revolver. "Car damaged?"

Nelson pushed the brim of his Stetson up with an index finger and scanned the area. "Not that I saw. No oil spots or leaks where the car was parked. I'd bet a dollar the car could've been driven back to Thurlow's."

"Bud's one-car accident don't work. You see any clues here? An' what about the tribal officer?"

Nelson moved dirt around with the pointed toe of his cowboy boot. "No clues. The tribal was gone when I got here. Bud said something about a powwow in Casper. Name's Masin."

"I hate going to the tribals. But there's no choice. Talk with this Masin." Grayson's impulse was to drive to Bud's house and fire him for mishandling the scene. But even though it was the right thing to do, Grayson could not risk giving Homer's nephew a reason to help his opponent in the general election, Wyoming highway patrolman Larry Jacobsen.

"I'll meet with Masin. What else you want me to do?"

The timing of this unexplained death, two months before the general election, could not be worse. If Winslow determined this a death due to suspicious causes, the voters would forget if he solved it too quickly. But if he failed to make an arrest before voting day, then everyone would talk of his shortcomings.

"Winslow's not said yet, but this is a suspicious death. Don't mean there was foul play. But we've got to make sure. I'll look at the car and talk to Dallas Dodge. See what he knows. You go to where Freeman lived. See what you can. Meet back at the station."

+ + +

Nelson had accurately described the Studebaker—no body damage and nothing to suggest a mechanical problem. Grayson started the car, revved the engine, and rocked back and forth to check the brakes. He found nothing suspicious inside the car, just camera equipment.

Grayson drove through town to Dodge's office. Unlike the other attorneys with offices in commercial buildings on Main or Federal, Dodge had adapted a large family residence for his practice on North First Street. The log cabin atop a river rock foundation with a matching chimney dominated the corner.

Grayson took a deep breath before mounting the porch steps to the law office. He could count his number of visits to this office on one hand, and two of those had involved holiday socials. The expensive furnishings had intimidated Grayson then, and today would probably be no different. He caught his reflection in the glass windowpanes and saw a frightened man as he opened the front door. A large Indian blanket hung behind the desk of the secretary, dwarfing the petite middle-aged woman.

"Sheriff Farmer, welcome. How are you this fine morning?" Even though the gray-haired secretary stood no more than five feet tall, her voice carried as well as any church choir soloist in the county.

"Well, thank you. Mr. Dodge, is he in?"

The creak of floorboards suggested movement, followed by the baritone voice of Dallas Dodge. "Virginia, did I hear Grayson Farmer's voice?" The attorney entered the room and glided his stout five-foot-six frame to a stop. Dodge wore a western-cut white shirt and black pants, and a bolo tie with a silver dollar–sized turquoise stone to complete his outfit. "Sheriff, what brings you to town?"

"Corky Freeman. From the newspaper."

Dodge motioned Grayson to follow along to his office and instructed Virginia to bring coffee. Framed photographs of Dodge and area politicians and businessmen lined the wall of the hallway, another display of power and influence. Just past the entry to a library and meeting room, the corridor opened into a large office complete with fireplace. An oversized mahogany-colored desk with two stuffed red-leather visitor chairs filled a corner of the room. Dodge took his position behind the desk and pointed Grayson to a chair.

Nothing in Dodge's reaction to Freeman's name indicated that it meant anything to him or that he even knew of the boy's death. "We found Mr. Freeman dead in his car, out on Highway 26 this morning." Grayson waited for a reaction but only received a nod. "We're investigating. Anything you can tell me?"

Dodge worked his jaw, as if chewing on something. "Even though I have an interest in the *Wrangler*, I am not familiar with this employee. In fact, I cannot say if Clayton or Wilson hired the man, or even the scope of his duties. I do know he was not one of my clients. How did you say he died?"

"Didn't. That's part of the investigation."

"Excuse me, gentlemen." Virginia set onto the desk a polished silver tray with a matching shiny coffeepot, white china cups and saucers, a cream pitcher and sugar bowl, spoons, and a plate of cookies. Using both hands, she poured out two cups of coffee and left the room.

"I can assure you the newspaper staff and my office will help in any way we can. If you have any difficulty with the fellas at the *Wrangler*, please let me know. Help yourself, Sheriff." Dodge lightened his cup with cream, stirred the added sugar, and lifted the saucer and cup.

Grayson took the other cup and saucer and held them. "Thanks. Anything might help us. Friends? Enemies? Trouble at the newspaper? Or elsewhere?"

Dodge lifted his cup to his mouth, silently sipping the coffee. "As I said, I do not know the man, and my knowledge of the details of the newspaper comes from my nephew, Wilson. I have no recollection of problems with Mr. Freeman."

Grayson felt awkward, with coffee in hand but no wish to drink it and with no other questions to ask the attorney. He studied Dodge's face with the broken nose and oiled dark hair combed straight back. The attorney made no secret of the origin of the nose bump; he had acquired it playing as a fullback for the University of Michigan. The attorney showed no sign of discomfort from the silence. "Sorry to bother you. Wanted to make sure."

Dodge lowered the saucer and cup to the desktop. "No bother, Sheriff. I appreciate the notification. If I discover something, I'll contact you." Dodge worked his jaw for a moment. "How is the election coming? Is Jacobsen going to be a problem for you?"

"Larry's Republican. Ike'll do good here. It'll be close."

"I've seen your newspaper ad. Same as last time. You might want to freshen it up."

"Good advice." Grayson placed the still-full cup and saucer back on the silver tray.

"If I hear anything about Freeman, as I said, I'll contact you. And I hope you will be able to give me reports on your investigation from time to time."

Grayson forced a smile, stood, and excused himself. As he walked to the patrol car, Grayson questioned whether any of Dodge's answers were true. Grayson was certain Dodge knew about the Freeman death before his arrival, in spite of the lawyer's claim of ignorance. And more than curiosity had caused mention of the election. Grayson thought there was an implied threat, though not one he could name.

The oddest part of the meeting was Dodge's request for reports on the investigation. Grayson had no intention of running like a schoolboy to Dodge, and he expected the same restraint from his deputies. He needed to keep a lid on the details. That meant leaving Bud out of the investigation and telling Nelson to keep his mouth shut.

The who, how, and why of Corky Freeman's death needed an answer, and as sheriff, he needed to investigate. It was the job of Raymond Winslow, coroner, to determine the cause of death. But this case might benefit from a medical examination of the victim. A call to Dr. Owen would be a smart move.

Even if Winslow labeled the death a murder, certain limits could be applied when important people shared an interest. And people like Dallas Dodge could find a way to define those limits. Since taking the office of sheriff, Grayson had learned that nothing was as simple as it appeared. To date his survival in this job had meant knowing his place. This was not the time to be a rebel.

+ + +

Standing behind his desk, Dallas held out his empty coffee cup for a refill. "Virginia, he did not drink your coffee, but I'll have some more."

Virginia filled the extended cup, using both hands as she leaned over his desk. "It was not fresh. And those cookies are from last week."

"What is your impression of our sheriff? Would you vote for him?"

"I did last election and haven't decided about this one. Gray Farmer's a tense man. Before you came out, his hands were in a fist. White knuckles. I think he's afraid of you."

Dallas frowned before adding cream and sugar to his coffee.

Virginia balanced the silver platter on the edge of the desk. "I doubt if Gray could have swallowed if he had taken a sip of coffee."

"That is an astute observation. We shall call it the Virginia Response and keep track of it. I wonder if it applies to alcohol. Sloshing a little whiskey around in your mouth may relax the muscles. What do you think?" Dallas angled his head and smirked.

Virginia lifted the tray as if ready to leave. "I think drinking coffee is better for you than drinking whiskey. And stop making fun of me."

Dallas enjoyed teasing his secretary, aware of her support of temperance. "I am doing no such thing. I'm serious about the Virginia Response and intend to use the test, routinely."

Virginia pursed her lips and stared at him.

"I counted the number of his sentences with more than five words. Only one. Our sheriff clearly is not a member of Toastmasters."

Virginia turned and walked toward the hallway, stopped, and half-turned back toward her boss. "Will you want any more of this coffee?"

"No, thank you."

The spring of the high-backed desk chair stretched as Dallas sat and leaned back, a short metallic groan offered in protest. Dallas rocked back, coaxing more chirps. He had known about the death of Corky Freeman before the sheriff's visit, having received a telephone call from his nephew, Wilson. But Dallas could not have picked Freeman out of a group of three strangers. Perhaps the young man's death justified posthumous inspection.

Virginia's observation rang true. Gray Farmer had acted afraid, and for good reason. The sheriff's chances of reelection were fifty-fifty at best, and he did not appear to have any suspects for this suspicious death. Frightened men, Dallas knew, could behave unpredictably.

CHAPTER 5

Gordon Blakeslee, Corky's close friends from the camera club, lived a block west of Broadway in a cozy house he had shared with his wife, Ruth. Geri had sent Ruth's obituary to Wil at college in Ann Arbor, along with her weekly letter and assortment of clippings. The letters from Geri had outnumbered those from Clayton and Ramona combined. Between her babysitting at the office, the constant correction of his grammar into high school, and her mailings during college, Wil had viewed Geri as his mother as much as Ramona.

Gordon's yard was in fair shape for a Riverton lawn in September with yellow spots and patches of grassless dirt. The low amount of rainfall and high cost of water for sprinkling meant the early June grass had taken a beating by September. Ruth's flower beds had disappeared, a sign Gordon had let things go after her death.

Wil had not visited Gordon since returning to Riverton, but he knew the man had retired as an engineer from one of the federal agencies with offices in Fremont County. When Gordon answered the door, Wil thought the lines of the older man's face and fragile appearance aged him beyond his years. Wil was saddened to see the physical decline of the man who had tutored him on the fine points of a press camera during high school.

"Come in, Wilson. Terrible about Corky. You know Pudgie." Gordon's yellow lab, standing at his master's side, worked his tail in a greeting. Gordon invited Wil to take a chair. "I'm having a cocktail. Care to join me?"

"No, thanks. Some water and a little ice, if it's not a bother." Wil disapproved of drinking this early in the day. He wondered if the cause of Gordon's physical deterioration might be drinking in the morning.

Wil took the glass of water and noted Gordon's tumbler dark with whiskey and a single ice cube. After he repeated Deputy Nelson's one-car accident story, Wil asked whether Gordon knew of a reason Corky might be out on the road past the airport, toward Kinnear and on to Dubois, so early.

Gordon looked at the wall, his toe tapping to the beat of the song on the radio in the kitchen. "Hmm. Can't think of a reason."

Pudgie set his jaw on Wil's thigh, eyes pleading for a rub or scratch. "I'm working on an article for Thursday about Corky and hoped I could quote you. You and Corky were good friends."

"Corky Freeman was my best friend and the star pupil in the Blakeslee School of Photography. He's got a good eye and always had a notebook. Film type, shutter speed, aperture opening, date, time—all that."

Wil opened his notebook and wrote down the "School of Photography" comment.

Gordon took a sip of his whiskey. "He might have a girlfriend out that way."

Wil scratched behind the dog's ears, evoking a groan. "Did he have a photography project going?"

"Don't think so. Why?"

Wil made an entry in his notebook as Pudgie repositioned himself at Gordon's feet. "Just curious. I'm trying to add details for the story on his death."

"Corky was a careful boy. I never saw him have more than one drink ... well, two beers. And he drove like Ruthie, slow and steady—unless he fell asleep at the wheel. Is that what happened?"

"I wish I knew, Gordon. It's kind of a mystery."

Gordon took a sip. "A mystery, huh? A little like your dad's death."

"How's that?"

Gordon leaned forward and closed his eyes. "Never was a reason given for his death. Just talk. What'd he die from?"

Wil wished he could answer that question even more than the one about Corky. "I don't know, exactly. Anything else you want to tell me about Corky, for the article?"

Gordon sipped his drink and looked up at the ceiling. "He was a darned good kid. I'm going to miss him. Terrible thing when a boy dies like that, especially here in Riverton. A person understands it with those boys dying in Korea, fighting the Communists."

Wil closed his notebook and struggled with what to say next.

Gordon slid to the edge of his chair and set his drink on the coffee table. "So do you know how Corky died?"

Wil glanced at Gordon, curious about the repetition of the question, and moved to the edge of his chair. Pudgie sat up onto his front paws.

Gordon tapped his fist on his left thigh. "Boysen Dam. He was working on that for the paper. Borrowed some of my equipment—telephoto lenses."

The mention of Boysen Dam caught Wil by surprise; he was unaware of any newspaper project on it. "Did he show you any of those photos?"

"Don't think so. Corky could be secretive."

"True enough." Wil wondered why Corky had not shared the photos with him either.

Gordon stood, Pudgie following. "I suppose his parents want him buried over in Idaho. I'd like to have some kind of funeral service here, for his friends in Riverton. Do you think they'd object?"

Wil rose to his feet, took a last sip of water, and gave the glass to Gordon. "Not at all, Gordon. They might even want to meet some of his friends. Geri has their telephone number if you need it, although it would be a long-distance call."

Gordon set the water glass on a windowsill and promised to arrange a funeral service. Wil agreed to hold a spot on the front page to announce it. Gordon extended an open invitation for the afternoon cocktail hour as Wil took the sidewalk to his pickup.

+ + +

Geri had completed over half the typing of items from Arapahoe when Ramona entered the front office of the *Wrangler*. Visits to the office from the wife, now widow, of Clayton Dodge were rarer than a hot day in January. Ramona was the last person Geri had expected to see that morning.

"What a lovely outfit, Ramona. Your hat is delightful." A small burnt orange number with velvet accents and matching veiling sat at a rakish angle to the right of her forehead. The contrast between the stylish hat and the black pageboy haircut reinforced Ramona's reputation as fashion royalty in Fremont County.

"Thank you, Geri. Is Wilson around? I hope this Corky business has not upset him."

"He's out but should be back soon. Have a seat and let me look at the rest of you." Geri pulled open the half door and pointed to Wil's office chair before going to the coffeepot.

"I like the length of that skirt, Geri. It should keep your legs warm on cold days."

"Hems are moving lower. Where did you get those darling pumps?" Whenever Geri spotted Ramona about town, the woman's wardrobe appeared ripped from the fashion magazines. But then Ramona never put on a pound, so if she was not buying food, she must have money for dresses and hats and shoes. Ramona possessed the sort of beauty that raised eyebrows and turned the heads of men of a certain age but did not stop traffic.

"When Wilson was still in Chicago, I picked up this pair in brown suede, and a pair in black just like them, at Marshall Fields. The next time you are in Chicago, you must go there."

Ramona talked like Geri could just pick up and go to Chicago when and as she pleased. The woman lived in her own world, but Geri already knew that. "They go perfectly with the gold suit."

"We have such a short season to wear suede shoes."

Geri set a mug of coffee for Ramona on Wil's desk before taking her seat. "It's past Labor Day, so your timing is good."

Ramona pulled a cigarette case from her beige purse. "I like fall but almost hate leaving the house in winter. Snow and ice and high heels are not a good mix."

Geri wheeled her chair close to Ramona and flicked her lighter for the widow and then for herself.

Ramona inhaled and blew a stream of smoke to her left. "Since it is just we girls, how do you think Wilson is doing?"

Geri dumped the ashtray in the trash, wanting it clean for her guest. "He does a good job for the paper. There's still room for improvement, but better than expected. Why?"

Ramona took a short puff and exhaled. "I think Wilson is trying to find his place in Riverton. The town has changed since he was in high school, although I wonder if he has. I worry about him."

Geri lacked insight into what the woman expected of her son. He had walked away from a graduate program at the University of Chicago to take over the paper after Clay's death. "I'm not sure what you mean."

Ramona stretched her chin forward, the sort of exercise women her age did out of habit. "For a twenty-five-year-old man who has been to college, he acts immature. I know he had more dates in high school than now. He should be thinking of a wife and children."

Geri agreed with her assessment. "A girlfriend could make a big difference, but he's picky about who he'll date."

"Riverton has much less to offer than Chicago or Ann Arbor. And even if he found a girl, she would need to take charge. I have trouble seeing him move in for a kiss. And I am certain he is still a virgin. Wil is much too churchy for sex before marriage."

Geri knew of Wil's sexual adventure with his Chicago girlfriend, but sharing that confidence with his mother felt out-of-bounds. She wondered whether the failed romance in Chicago was the reason for his insecurity and trouble finding the right gal. "Now that you mention it, he does seem stuck in the past. Other than that photograph of the three of you at his graduation from Michigan, Wil's not changed Clayton's desk a bit, almost like he's waiting for him to come back and take over."

Ramona swiveled in Wil's chair and looked at the desk area, as if seeing it for the first time. "He is not decisive like Clayt, for better or worse. I see the insecurity of my father in him. The Depression almost crushed that poor man. It was a good thing he married a strong woman.

"I am so jealous. You see more of my son than I do. I had hoped Wilson and I could be close again, like we were when he came home during freshman year."

Geri could not recall Clayton saying much about the episode. "I'd forgotten about that. What was the reason … health?"

Ramona pulled back her skirt and crossed her legs. "It was early in 1946. It might have been mono, but we will never know. Doctor Owen prescribed nerve pills. If there had been a psychiatrist in town, I would have sent him."

"A psychiatrist? Really?" Geri feared what Ramona would say next. Psychiatry ranked high on the list of taboo subjects, even in private conversation.

"A psychoanalyst would have been better, but Wyoming pretends Sigmund Freud never existed. It is primitive to blame a person for neuroses and psychoses and tell them to pray or 'get with it.' There are new treatments and drugs for those conditions now."

Geri wondered whether Ramona was on any of these medicines. "Really?"

Ramona leaned forward and used her cigarette as a pointer. "We need to do better for people with those problems than hide them away in sanitariums."

Geri tapped her ash into the tray and held it out for Ramona. "Do you think Wil had a … that kind of problem?"

"Please keep it to yourself, but yes. Something happened in Michigan that troubled him, but only he knows what it was. We talked a great deal that winter. In fact those were probably my favorite conversations with Wilson. We talked about books and music, and *Look* magazine even made him curious about fashion. We still take the *Look* quiz to see who scores highest. He thinks I cheat. But he kept something to himself back then, a secret neither Clayt nor I ever found out."

Geri imagined an only-child syndrome, if there was such a thing, self-contained and private. She wondered whether her constant presence in the office stymied his dating. He had no way to make a private call from work. "I do remember him spending time here that summer. He had changed. Not a high school student but … I'm not sure what exactly."

Ramona switched her cigarette to the other hand and lifted the coffee mug. "After graduating from Michigan, working at the newspaper in Chicago, and then starting graduate studies in that anthropology program in the summer, I expected him to be more mature. But he reminds me a little of that time in freshman year, but without the sickness."

Ramona slid her chair close and stubbed out her cigarette. "Geri, this has been a pleasure, but I have to run. I am lunching with Emily Engstrom, and she likes a cocktail or two before eating."

"I'm glad you stopped by. I'll let Wil know you were here."

Ramona stood and smoothed her skirt. "Please, please, do not. He will think I am meddling or conspiring with you. But we need to do lunch soon."

Geri rose and held open the half door. She wondered what revelations the woman would make in a social setting. "That would be fun. Let me know what works for you."

"Since I am confessing, I was jealous of all the time you spent with Clayt. It kept me away from this office and getting to know you. I hope we can put Wilson on the right path."

Geri breathed easier when the widow confessed to jealousy instead of accusing her of adultery with Clayton, although she had reasons to be suspicious. Geri smiled as Ramona made her way past and toward the front door, heels clicking on the hardwood floor. Ramona turned and winked before leaving. A stiff drink sounded good to Geri too, but there was too much work to do. What more would this day bring?

CHAPTER 6

"Who is it?"

"Deputy Al Nelson, Fremont County Sheriff's Department."

Gretchen Simpson did not know a Deputy Nelson or why he was at her door. "What do you want?"

"Is this where Corky Freeman lives?"

What would the sheriff want with the tenant of their basement apartment? "Yes, but he's not here now. He's probably working."

"I'm not looking for Corky. Can you open the door?"

Her husband, Delmar, did not like strangers in the house when he was away. "You should come back when my husband is at home."

"I need to come in and look at Corky Freeman's room."

"I'd need his permission."

"Corky Freeman is dead, ma'am. I don't think he'll mind."

Gretchen opened the door before she realized it and found a tall man in uniform, with a gun. "Did you say …?"

"Can I come in? I need to see his room and look at his things."

Gretchen nodded her head, unable to speak. The deputy opened the screen door and waited; she was blocking his way.

"Are you going to be okay, ma'am? Do you want me to call someone?"

Gretchen stepped back, turned, and walked into the kitchen and down the basement stairs. She heard the deputy shut the front door and follow her. At the bottom of the stairs, Gretchen took three steps inside Corky's apartment.

"Was he a problem tenant? Making noise or not paying his rent on time?"

Hands clutched together at her chest, Gretchen shook her head no.

"I'm just going to look around. You can stay if you want."

The deputy poked his head into the kitchen; inspected the living room, including the small desk; and looked back at her before going on to the bedroom. The urge to keep him out of the bedroom was strong, but she stayed in place. Gretchen held her breath at the sound of drawers opening and closing.

The deputy's voice echoed from the bedroom. "Does he have any other place to store things?" He appeared in the doorway as he finished his question.

"No. Well, maybe in the utility room, but ..."

"Can you show me?"

Moving from her spot felt impossible. Gretchen pointed toward a door, next to the bathroom. She watched as the deputy checked the bathroom and then disappeared into the room with the furnace, hot water heater, and washing machine. After only a moment he was back in the apartment.

"Did he ever bring friends over? Girlfriends?"

Gretchen moved her mouth to say no, but no sound came out.

"Was he a loner? Kept to himself?"

A whisper was the best she could do. "I guess."

"The sheriff might want to talk with you and your husband. I didn't get your name."

She took a quick breath and straightened her posture. "Gretchen Simpson. My husband is Delmar. We own this house."

"Looks like a nice place. Sorry your renter died. Anything you want to tell me about him?"

Gretchen shook her head no, sensing tears ready to spill down her cheeks.

"Thanks for your help, ma'am. I'll make my way out the back door."

The deputy put on his cowboy hat, tapped the brim with his index finger, ascended the stairs, and stepped out the back door. He was handsome in an outdoorsman way.

Gretchen used a handkerchief to dab at the tears before moving farther into the basement living room. The first chore was to wash the sheets in his bedroom and search there, and then she would check the living room. She wanted to be done before Delmar came home from work.

+ + +

The Riverton substation of the Fremont County Sheriff's Department was a block off Main Street in a two-story red brick structure originally built as a bank in the mid-1920s. The banker had envisioned a Romanesque marvel with grand arches, but a narrow lot and modest budget had forced compromise. Seven steps led up to an arched single-door entrance capped by "State Bank" carved into a red sandstone frontispiece, the only distinctive feature.

State Bank became a casualty of the Depression, and throughout most of the 1930s, the building had stood vacant. Unpaid property taxes and lack of a willing buyer had made Fremont County the reluctant owner. After the war in Europe and Japan ended, Grayson had begun looking at buildings in Riverton large and solid enough for a temporary holding facility; the department needed a place for city and county prisoners on their way to the county jail in Lander. The old State Bank building had become the solution.

Sheriff Farmer's office sat just off the small front lobby, which allowed him to respond to telephone calls and foot traffic into the substation and monitor radio transmissions. He was seated at his desk when Deputy Nelson returned to the station.

"I went to where Freeman lived."

"What'd you find?"

Nelson worked the Stetson around in a circle at his waist, eyes down, leaning against the office doorframe. "I didn't find nothing, Sheriff. Some clothes and stuff but not much else. I didn't poke through the desk. The landlady, Gretchen Simpson, was watching."

"She tell you anything?"

Nelson stepped into the room and stood behind one of the wooden guest chairs. "Not really. At first I thought she was going to faint and then cry. The news shocked her. I might've been rough on her, but she didn't want to open the door with her husband being gone."

Grayson frowned. Another dead end. He had plenty of questions but no answers or suspects. Earlier he had talked with the Riverton chief of police, only to discover Freeman was just another citizen to that department too. "Go talk to the newspaper people. Find out about Freeman. Dodge promised cooperation. Follow who and where their answers lead you."

Nelson frowned, made brief eye contact, and looked at the floor.

"Keep this to yourself. Just you and me. Nothing to Bud."

The deputy looked up for a moment and then back down.

"You got an idea, Nelson?"

"We'll want to talk with the Simpsons ... and maybe their neighbors. And Wil Dodge, of course."

"I'll sweat young Dodge, after we get some background on this Freeman."

"Is Wil a suspect? He acted shocked when I told him. Got pale like he was gonna throw up."

Grayson stretched his neck to the right and then the left. "Just questioning. But he's a possible." At this point, who was not a possible suspect? The Freeman kid had no local family ties or history and no criminal record. And there were no clues at either the spot where he was found or his apartment. But people did not die for no reason.

+ + +

As Deputy Nelson walked to the *Wrangler* offices, he considered questions for Corky Freeman's coworkers—friends, enemies, arguments, alibis. He had never seen the back room of the newspaper and figured it would be interesting. But his mission involved questioning and not sightseeing.

Mrs. Murphy would be his first interview. Nelson knew her as a widow, and she was older than him with a sprinkling of gray throughout her short dark hair, but he always thought of the woman as appealing. She dressed better than the women in the library and had a figure that could compete with any of the younger girls at the bank. And Geri had a sense of humor, but he doubted she would go on a date with him.

Al checked his watch; his meeting with Larry Jacobsen still two hours away. When the candidate for sheriff had asked to meet, Al thought the day after Labor Day would be good, since Sheriff Farmer should be in Lander. But that was before Corky Freeman.

Sheriff Farmer had treated him fairly, but Farmer might not be boss much longer. Best to hear what Larry had to offer. A highway patrolman and a deputy talking from their cars at the airport should not attract much attention. Al hoped Farmer would not hear about the meeting.

CHAPTER 7

"Good of you to drop in, or did you forget we've got a newspaper to get out? I'm not going to do all the social news."

Wil tiptoed past Geri to his desk, taking a letter from the Shoshoni basket.

"And don't tell me you've been at Gordon's all this time, because I called him."

The sounds of tapping keys, carriage returns, and the end-of-line bell competed with the muffled racket from the pressroom. When Geri stopped to light a cigarette, Wil swiveled in his chair. "I was at Mountain View."

"The cemetery? What for?"

All the thoughts about his father had pushed Wil to visit his gravesite. "It's a good place to gather strength and sort out your thoughts."

Geri tucked an elbow into her body, hand extended forward, the lit cigarette resting between her index and middle fingers. "So you were at the cemetery, getting strong, gossiping with God, and I got to entertain Ramona. Too bad we couldn't have traded places."

"Ramona was here? In the office?"

"Shit, I wasn't supposed to say anything, but ... She waltzed in with her sunglasses and going-to-lunch clothes. She confessed to being jealous of my time with you—and Clay. She's worried about you. Mentioned that time in college when you came home, first year."

Wil grimaced, squinting his eyes. "What'd she say?"

"How she cherished that time with you. Not in those words, but close. The *Look* quizzes. And how she still doesn't know what happened at Michigan."

"It's a long story."

Geri inhaled on her cigarette and held in the smoke before blowing toward the ceiling. "Give me the headlines."

"Boy in strange place in panic over nuclear war. Has crisis of faith. Seeks shelter in psychosomatic symptoms."

Geri fingered a flake of tobacco off her tongue and tended her ash.

"Just before I left for Ann Arbor, we dropped the bombs on the Japs, right? I got there, and all the talk in the dorm was about winning the war and the atom bomb and World War III. I tried to throw myself into studies, but there was no escaping it. Seminars and prayer vigils."

She tapped her cigarette against the ashtray. "I'm glad you survived it. Mrs. Ames called in to report that the head of the Wyoming civil defense told the local committee that with the Russians having the bomb, they've got Fremont County targeted."

"What?"

"My reaction too. Truth is, he said if the plane can't make it to their main target, the closest town will do, including Riverton and Lander. Since you're past that, it shouldn't keep you from helping with the social news. Smoke break's over."

"Wait. Gordon said Corky was working on a project for the paper about the Boysen Dam. You know anything about that?"

Geri shook her head no and turned back to her typewriter.

"And he said Corky had a lot of girlfriends. Why didn't I know that?"

"Corky liked you, Wil, but he thought you were a square. Thought you'd disapprove. He liked to flirt, and the gals liked him."

Wil did not know which bothered him more, a civil defense scare, being thought of as a square, or learning his friend was a womanizer. And how did Geri know this when he did not?

Geri turned her head, cigarette between her lips, and waited for Wil to make eye contact. "Deputy Nelson was here, asking about Corky. He said Gray Farmer will want to question you."

+ + +

By midafternoon Wil and Geri had typed up every scrap of social news, including the fresh batch from the post office. There were few interruptions, as if the usual callers knew to leave them alone with their grief. Deciphering and transcribing the minutia of daily life served as a consuming distraction to fill the time.

Wil delivered the newest stack of copy to the linotype operator for conversion to lines of hot lead. Bernie stopped proofing a page and asked for Wil's thoughts on a few layout issues that Corky would have handled. As he retreated from the clatter of the linotype, Wil hesitated at the darkroom door. Gordon had mentioned Corky taking photos of Boysen Dam. Before he could turn the doorknob, Wil realized all the paper's photographic equipment sat in Corky's car and needed to be retrieved before it was stolen. He hollered his plan to Geri and headed for the rear exit.

A Jeepster pulled into a parking space as Wil walked to his pickup from the dock. A woman Wil did not recognize, dark-haired with hat and sunglasses and bright red lips, climbed out. She looked cute, but he had a bad angle. He hesitated on the sidewalk to see where she went, admiring the swing of her hips in a light gray fitted skirt and red high heels. When she opened the door to the *Wrangler*, he searched for an excuse to go back inside, but duty called. And Geri would share the details on this visitor later.

Wil backed his 1949 Chevy pickup out of the diagonal space and turned onto Main Street headed west, flipping down the visor to block the midafternoon sun. He crossed the railroad tracks, downshifted into second gear, and pushed the foot pedal, rising out of the downtown valley floor onto the broad plateau of Riverton's west side.

A lone mechanic worked in the garage at Thurlow's. Corky's two-door Studebaker Starlight rested along the back fence with the other wrecks, looking south toward the Wind River mountain range and down toward the banks of the Wind River. To call the car with the four-panel wraparound rear windows a wreck struck Wil as false. The windshield did not show so much as a smudge, and the fenders and bumpers were dent-free.

Wil sat in the driver's seat, hands on the steering wheel, wondering what circumstance could have brought Corky's life to an end. The absence of damage to the car and the unbruised body at the morgue created doubts about Albert's one-car accident explanation. Wil spotted the office door key on the ring of keys in the ignition and removed it. The other keys looked like a house key and a padlock key. Wil fingered the latter, decided it could be for the office, and spun it off the ring.

Camera bags filled the floor behind the driver's seat. Stepping out of the car, Wil pushed the seatback forward and transferred the press camera and supplies to the cab of his pickup. Popping the trunk lid, he found a blanket, some motor oil, and a toolbox.

Wil approached the mechanic as he lowered a black 1951 Packard from the hydraulic lift. The man was not at all interested when Wil told him about taking the items in the backseat. When Wil asked if the Studebaker was in drivable condition, the mechanic shrugged, the hiss of the descending Packard echoing his indifference.

+ + +

"Natee Saylor. What brings the county clerk to my house?" Geri had thought Ramona's appearance would be the only surprise visit of the day.

The young woman set a manila envelope and her purse on the countertop. "These were on my desk. I forgot to mail them Friday, and today is your deadline. Am I too late?"

Geri opened the envelope containing minutes from the commissioners' meeting and a listing of detailed disbursements for the newspaper's legal section. "The boys can usually fit these in, but our layout man's out."

She watched Natalie's expression shift from strictly business. The younger woman's eyes widened, and her lips tightened. The reaction passed in an instant. "I heard Corky'd been found this morning."

Geri saw tears push at the boundary of her visitor's eyelids. "It's like I've lost a son. I can only imagine how his mother … Wil had to identify him."

"You do what you can to protect family, but …"

Geri felt a tear forming and took a deep breath, willing herself not to cry.

"Was that Wil just outside?"

"My stars and garters. You've not met Wil yet? He'll come back with forty questions if he saw you."

The hint of a smile offset Natalie's tears. "I might have a few questions of my own."

"But how do you know Corky?"

Natalie's smile faded, and a tear slipped down her cheek. "We were friends. Good friends."

Geri suddenly had forty questions. "Good friends or *good* good friends?"

Natalie opened her purse and removed a handkerchief, formed a point, and dabbed at her cheek. "Friends."

"How'd you meet?"

"It's a long story, Geri. I thought you knew."

Why was today the time for long stories? First Wil and now the county clerk. "Corky had more secrets than I ever imagined. I suspected there was someone special, but he only hinted at it. I never would have guessed it was you, but then …"

The town gossip about the county clerk included her interest in younger men. Even though Natalie had to be pushing thirty, she commanded the interest of men of many ages, single, married, and divorced. The thought of Corky and Natee intimately involved seemed within the realm of possibility, especially to a widow who read romance stories in magazines.

"Not me. I know what you mean about a special gal. He danced around the edges, but even when questioned, or tickled, he wouldn't say a thing."

The "tickled" comment neither confirmed nor denied her suspicions about Corky and Natee. She looked for a hint of jealousy in the watery eyes of her guest but saw only sadness. "Does Gray Farmer know about you two? He sent Albert Nelson over to ask questions about Corky. You do know Albert, right? Gray will want to talk, though."

Natalie dabbed at her cheek again. "I checked in his office at the courthouse this morning, but he wasn't there. Maybe he's here, in town."

"So can I tell Wil you'd be interested in a drink or dinner? He'll want to know."

A frisky smile lit up her tear-streaked face. "What do you think?"

CHAPTER 8

Dallas nibbled on his tongue, an almost unconscious habit. His nephew had just finished reporting the details of his visit to the morgue and Gordon Blakeslee. Wilson had asked if Corky was on assignment for Dallas, in search of a context for his Boysen information.

"As I told Sheriff Farmer this morning, I could not have selected Mr. Freeman from a group of three strangers. Other than your call this morning, the name Corky Freeman means nothing, although you may have mentioned it before."

Wil moved to the edge of the padded guest chair. "So the sheriff was here? Asking about Corky?"

"Yes. I assured him the *Wrangler* staff and my office would cooperate fully. He'll want to interview you."

"What'll he want to know, and what'll I have to tell him?"

Dallas saw Wil's agitation and spoke softly, hoping to calm the boy. "The sheriff may believe the death was suspicious. Freeman wasn't married, was he? No, I thought not. So Gray will want to talk with people who knew the man … find out about friends and enemies." Dallas extended a finger for each of the two likely topics. "And he'll want to know of your movements last night and early this morning."

"Should I tell him about Boysen Dam?"

"This is a possible murder investigation, Wilson. The important thing is to tell the truth. If you know something about the dam project, say so now. Otherwise, merely repeat what you heard from Gordon Blakeslee."

Wil remained motionless, as if in shock. "Murder. How …"

For a college man his nephew seemed slow-witted at times. "A possible murder. What do you know about the dam project?"

"I don't know a thing about the dam. I saw Corky's car, though, getting our camera and supplies, and it didn't look like it'd been in any accident. What does the sheriff think really happened?"

"Perhaps Gray will tell you, but probably not. And he'll not want to read the details of his investigation in the *Wrangler*."

"So what's he going to want from me?"

Dallas gently bit his tongue. "Did you and Corky have any arguments? Was there a problem with any of his coworkers? Did he have a drinking or gambling problem?"

Wil held eye contact with Dallas before looking away. "Nothing like that, at least that I know."

"If Gray thinks this is murder, he needs a suspect. But he may be getting ahead of himself. Ray Winslow needs to determine the cause of death. The important thing for you is to tell the truth, as you know it."

Wil's posture stiffened. "Winslow's just a mortician. He buries people, like Dad. Did he ever figure out why Clayton died? The only answer I've heard given is 'medical problems,' whatever that means."

Dallas rocked in his chair, teeth working at his tongue twice as fast. "No need to go there." He knew the reply contained the hint of a scold, and the lowered-head reaction of his nephew confirmed it had accomplished its purpose. Dallas had no desire for either Wil or the sheriff to ask questions concerning his brother's death. "If there is no reason for Gray Farmer to make you a suspect, you have nothing to worry about. Just answer his questions like an honest and intelligent young man. Anything else?"

Wil thanked him and left the office, refusing the offer of a cocktail. Once Dallas was certain his nephew had left, he instructed Virginia to invite Bob Thornton for a drink at the Wind River Hotel after 4:30 p.m.

+ + +

Grayson stood when he heard the front door to the substation open. Hand on revolver, he moved from his desk to intercept the intruder-visitor.

"Hello? Grayson, where are you?"

Natalie Saylor? What was she doing in Riverton, and why was she in his station? "Hi, Natalie. Come on in."

Grayson's first encounter with Natalie dated back to his time as a deputy, when she was a high school student. Though she had not been the wildest girl in her class at Riverton High, Natalie's spirited adventures had often crossed the path of city and county peace officers. As the daughter of a prominent rancher, she had been treated more gently than classmates in similar situations.

He stood and waited for her entrance into his office. "Did I forget to sign something? If I did …"

"I looked for you at the courthouse earlier. I was in Riverton on an errand, saw what looked like your car, and decided to stop."

Grayson motioned to one of the wooden guest chairs. Having graduated high school and college, Saylor now occupied the office of the county clerk. Since her election two years earlier, Grayson had made it a point to develop a courthouse friendship, a gesture his wife viewed with suspicion. "Sit down, unless you want the tour."

"I need to talk to you about the death this morning. Corky Freeman." A look of sadness filled her eyes. "Corky and I were friends. We'd get together once a week or so."

"When'd you see him last?"

"Saturday. We drove up to Louie Lake for a picnic. He wanted to take some pictures, and I was happy to be in the mountains."

"I'm not sure how to ask …" Grayson stopped, hoping she would know the question.

"He spent the night at my place and left Sunday afternoon."

"So you were …" This time Natalie did not quickly fill in the gap. He watched her measure a reply.

Natalie established eye contact. "Corky and I were close friends."

He settled for the answer. "I have to ask. Did he leave on good terms Sunday?"

The beginnings of a snarl formed on her normally pleasing lips. "Yes."

"So there wasn't a fight? Or a breakup? Anything unpleasant?"

"He wasn't my boyfriend or fiancé, just a good friend. Anything more than that is none of your business." Natalie's jaw was set, and she held his gaze for a good two seconds before looking away.

Grayson saw only anger in her eyes and no sense of guilt. Time to change directions. "He have any enemies?"

"He was too gentle to have enemies. I tried to get him to stand up for himself, but it wasn't in his nature. I thought this was a one-car accident."

"We're doing preliminaries. There may be some doubt. Was he going to see you Monday night?"

"No. I spent the day at the ranch with my folks."

"Know what he was doing Monday?"

"We didn't keep track of each other, but I think he was at the Riverton Labor Day affair for the newspaper."

"What do you know about other women friends?" He looked for an emotional reaction to the question but saw none.

"He had them but never named anyone. There was one special gal. She could be married or … he didn't talk marriage to her, if that's what you mean."

"Here's my problem. This boy ain't from here. I know he worked for the newspaper and was your … friend. I don't know much else. I'm looking for something to grab on to. If you think of anything … let me know."

The sadness returned to her now watery eyes. He hoped the questioning would not damage their friendship, but he saw no alternative. "Since you're here, I could use some help. My reelection campaign needs a push. You got any ideas?"

The change in subject brought a new intensity to her face. "Do you know who's supporting Jacobsen?"

"Cops don't like questions to questions."

The earlier snarl returned along with anger in her eyes. "I thought we were done with the cop part."

"We are, but …" Grayson looked at his desktop, unsure how to fix the situation without apologizing.

"We're playing my game now, and you need help. Do you know who is supporting Larry?"

Grayson felt the heat from her dark-eyed stare. "No."

"Do you want to?"

"That'd be useful." He saw a speck of impatience and knew he should stop being difficult. She was helping him.

"I'll ask around. Larry's trying to connect himself with Ike, just like every other Republican up for election. I believe Larry lives in Shoshoni, and I don't think he grew up in Fremont County. I'd remind voters you are a local boy, with a history of solving local problems."

"I'll put that in my weekly ad. Any other—"

"Maybe a press release of some kind. Get your name in the paper as accomplishing something. It wouldn't hurt to name another police department. Something like the formation of a task force to fight gambling. The Bible folks'll like that." She was offering advice he could use, unlike the smart talk of Dallas Dodge.

"Sounds good. I'll think on it and talk to you first."

"I'll check on Larry. And if I think of anything to help with Corky, I know how to find you."

Grayson walked her to the front door and watched as his first suspect climbed into her Jeepster.

+ + +

Deputy Albert Nelson adjusted the squelch on his countywide radio. By his watch Larry Jacobsen was already eight minutes late, and the longer he sat in the airport parking lot, the more likely Sheriff Farmer would hear about it. Al looked at his watch again and decided to give the highway patrolman another five minutes.

With a minute to spare, Jacobsen pulled off Highway 26 and onto the dirt road leading to the airport terminal. Al thought the man drove like a little old lady or a sugar beet farmer out looking at his fields. The deputy took a deep breath and put on a half-smile as Jacobsen pulled alongside his radio car.

"Deputy Nelson, lovely September day, isn't it?"

Al saw the smugness on Jacobsen's face, a trait his friends with the Riverton Police Department had mentioned. "Sun's shining, but it's been a busy day. Had a dead body this morning just up the road."

"I heard about that, Al. Don't suppose Gray made it over, did he?"

Al did not know if Jacobsen's question was intended to extract embarrassing information or just reflected curiosity. He remembered the sheriff's instruction to keep his mouth shut. "He drove over this morning, and I 'spect he's still at the substation if you want to go visit."

Jacobsen smiled, poked his head out the window, and spit into the space between the two cars. "You have any suspects?"

Al had no idea what Jacobsen hoped to discover. "Nope. Guy twenty yards off the highway, sitting in his car. No sign of a passenger. No weapon. No bullet holes or cuts or nothing."

"Sounds like a heart thing. Or suicide."

Al scanned the area out his windshield. "Coroner's job to decide that."

Jacobsen gave a knowing nod.

Al had prepared only one question and saw no reason to prolong the conversation. "So what changes would you be making?"

"None involving you, unless you're looking for a change. Can't say that about everyone, though."

Al wondered whether the cocky attitude came from highway patrol training or there was another reason Larry acted like the election winner without a single vote cast. "No, I'm content."

"Good, I hear you do good work. But there's some problems in Lander at the jail."

Al resisted sharing dirty laundry with an outsider. "Other than dropping off arrests, I don't get by the jail much. North part of the county is our area. Bud might know more; he likes making that trip with prisoners." Al spotted the disappointment on Larry's face.

"Is Bud a good partner?"

If Larry and Bud were pals, Al's lead deputy position could vanish. And Al would also lose respect for Larry. "Mostly we work alone. Bud has his own style."

"Deputy Nelson, I don't want to put you on the spot. I just want to let you know I take care of my people. And I would be counting on you." Jacobsen relaxed the smug pose, as if taking Al into his confidence. Al figured either Jacobsen was a poor poker player, or the level of his observation skills had sharpened with all the recent interviews. Sincerity was not a characteristic Larry conveyed effectively.

"Thanks for taking the time, Officer Jacobsen. I appreciate it."

"If you have any questions or need to talk, let me know. Life can get strange during an election. 'Specially when there's a dead body found just weeks before the vote. If you need tips on the investigation, I'd be happy to share my thoughts. Off the record, of course. Always willing to help out a brother peace officer."

Al touched the brim of his hat with his left index finger, and Jacobsen winked in response. The highway patrol car pulled away as cautiously as a grandmother driving to church.

As Al eased the radio car toward the highway, he pondered how the election would impact his future. The unfavorable first impression of Jacobsen left Al feeling insecure. Gray Farmer might not be the best boss, but he deserved loyalty, though not to the point of resigning if Farmer lost the election. There were cop jobs all over the state, but he liked living and working in Riverton.

Al pushed aside thoughts of his uncertain future and an election beyond his control. There were a few more girls Freeman had known who needed interviewing.

CHAPTER 9

Wil pushed open the door to the *Wrangler*, the press camera in one hand and a bag full of flashbulbs and film magazines slung over the opposite shoulder. Geri hopped up and held open the door to the back room as he step-shuffled down the narrow passageway, making sure not to bang the camera or the gadget bag against the cabinets and half-height paneling.

"How'd Corky's car look?"

Wil moved through the printing area door, set the camera on a counter, and hollered over the metronome beat of a printing press. "Not a scratch on it. Who was the girl that came in after I left?"

Geri let the pressroom door close, and Wil quickly followed her into the office. "You probably didn't hear me, but I asked who the gal—"

"Red high heels and light gray skirt? Is that who you mean? I'm surprised you noticed her."

Wil spotted Geri's tease. "I would have spotted her seven blocks away."

"That's the county clerk. Took office two years ago. Need any more hints?"

Wil took a step toward the front door, still needing to retrieve a second camera bag. "I should know the name, but … it's not coming. Is she a Riverton girl?"

"She went to high school here. Even taught. But she lives near Lander and spends most of her time there. She's only a little older than you. Give up?"

Wil raised his hands to shoulder level, palms forward. "Uncle."

"Natalie Saylor. Her dad's got a ranch out north of town. Want to know if she's available?"

Wil stepped to within an arm's length of Geri. "What I want to know is, if she's available, why you've not told me about her sooner."

"My sources say she'd go out with you, but she might not be a good match. Natee isn't exactly the marrying kind."

Wil slowly stepped backward. "What kind is she?"

"Go get the rest of the camera gear. I need to leave before the governor of Wyoming or Miss America comes through that door. The boys in back need help with cutlines and have some questions. And you're going to need to figure out Natee on your own. I've done my duty, period."

Upon returning with the second bag in tow, Wil stopped on the way to the back room. "You think Corky might have some newspaper equipment at his apartment?"

"Wouldn't hurt to check. Gordon called about a funeral service. I boxed the details on the front page. And her number at the courthouse is on your desk."

Wil asked Geri to lock the front door when she left the office and pushed his way into the pressroom. Using hand signals, he found who had a question, stood almost cheek-to-cheek to listen to the problem and possible solution, and gave a thumbs-up to go ahead. Bernie presented the photographs needing a caption, and Wil jotted down names or descriptions.

Wil moved the camera bags and equipment into the darkroom. Although the dedicated photography room was not insulated, the irregular staccato of linotype machine and ca-chunk ca-chunk of a press sounded noticeably quieter than in the large open space. Wil switched on the red safety light and waited for his eyes to adjust. Bulky shapes transitioned into developing trays, chemical bottles, enlarger. Strips of developed 35-millimeter film, four-inch by five-inch negatives, and contact sheets were clothespinned to the heavy strings stretched across the length of the tiny room. Wil collected the printed photos and returned to the front office to inspect them at a small light box with the magnifying loupe.

There were both posed and casual shots from the park and the ice cream social. Wil put names to most of the people shots. He circled over a dozen photos on the contact sheets to be enlarged for possible inclusion in the Labor Day follow-up next week. The promising large-format prints would need to be rechecked before any final decisions were made.

Back in the darkroom, Wil inspected the camera bag for film holders containing exposed negatives, found none, and added more flashbulbs. The darkroom inventory for chemicals, film, flashbulbs, and print paper was adequate. Corky had kept the area clean and well stocked.

A wire basket held more contact sheets and prints. Wil took the entire batch to the front office, hoping to discover the Boysen Dam pictures Gordon had mentioned. He found a variety of photos, many connected with news stories from August. Wil tried to recall the procedure for archiving these prints from his high school days but drew a blank. Geri would have the answer tomorrow.

Corky's apartment topped the short list of possible places for the Boysen Dam photos. Wil returned to the darkroom, turned off the red light, and collected the pages of Bernie's proofs for review and approval.

+ + +

Dallas added two ice cubes to the bourbon and sweet vermouth and then stirred the mixture with his fingertip before adding the bitters. As a major investor in the Wind River Hotel, with a suite of rooms on the top floor, he made daily use of the small private party room for his late-afternoon gatherings. Since Bob Thornton would be his only guest, he served as both bartender and host.

He felt warm in the wool sports coat, but a business meeting required proper attire. Shirt sleeves were fine for talking with the sheriff in his office, but not for this. As a silent partner in Thornton's construction and car dealership businesses, Dallas exercised leverage only when it served or threatened his other interests.

The words of his younger brother, Clayton, came to mind as he tested the manhattan. "Be careful with Bob Thornton. He won't make a good partner." Clayton had never explained the basis for the comment. The irony of Thornton dating Clayton's widow provoked a weak chuckle.

"Bob, what can I get you to drink?"

The strut of the short Hudson-De Soto car dealership owner and aspiring politician stuttered as Bob glanced around at the empty room. "Am I early?"

"Just you and me, Bob. Scotch and water, or have you switched?"

Bob slid the knot on his necktie closer to the collar and glanced back over his shoulder before he advanced to the small bar. "That'll be good, and a little ice."

Dallas filled a cocktail glass with ice and added more scotch than water. "How's your campaign coming?"

"Good. Good indeed. Spoke at the park yesterday, and there's a house party at your sister-in-law's tomorrow. Any chance you could introduce me?"

Setting the fresh drink before his guest, Dallas raised his manhattan. "First today. I didn't know Ramona was interested in politics. And yes, I'd be honored."

Bob touched glasses with Dallas and took a taste. "She isn't. I asked if she'd get a few folks together, as a favor to me. She's got such a great place out there. The driveway and yard are perfect for a few cocktails. You going to let me build some houses on that stretch of land you've got out there?"

Dallas set down his drink and nodded, thinking a visit to Ramona's could be useful. "In time. That spot is not ripe yet, but it will be soon. How is business? Any problems?"

Bob took a half step back and brought his other hand up to hold the bottom of the glass. "No, you heard something I should know?"

Dallas worked his jaw, nibbling on his tongue. "Sheriff Farmer visited me today. It seems one of the employees from the *Wrangler* was found dead out west of town. Corky Freeman. That name mean anything to you?"

Bob moved his head back a fraction and wagged it back and forth in a negative reply.

"Seems Sheriff Farmer believes Freeman was working on something involving Boysen Dam. Is Pioneer still on that project?" The Bureau of Reclamation dam project was reported as nearing completion, but he suspected Bob's Pioneer Construction Company remained active at the site.

Bob squinted for just an instant. "Yes. We're near the end, but we've got cleanup to do."

Dallas picked up his glass, sipped, and watched Bob mimic his movement, passing the Virginia Response test. "We going to make any money on that one? Boysen?"

"Not as much as I'd like. But it's a government job, so we'll do okay."

Dallas lifted his glass and paused. "Maybe I should review the books on that one. Don't want any problems coming back on us from a government job."

He thought it a good thing Bob did not have a mouthful of scotch at the moment, or else the spray would have covered him. "No need for that, Dallas. A big pile of official forms. Of course, if you want to spend a day or two pushing around paper, I'll tell the bookkeeper."

Dallas observed Bob to see whether he was still drinking. Perhaps the Virginia Response involved different manifestations. Dallas raised his glass. "To profits." He watched as Bob struggled with just a sip of his scotch. "If I'm going to introduce you, I should have a few details about your life. You grew up in Riverton?"

From experience, Dallas understood the importance of family history to the early settlers of Fremont County and knew that Bob would easily talk for ten minutes as he spun a tale of parents, wife, and children. The Thornton family had failed to make the list of family names to file a claim in 1906, but Dallas expected Bob to stretch the truth, and he did. Dallas always found the lies a person told more useful than any truths.

Bob stopped for a refill, and Dallas lightened the blend, his guest adequately primed. "I came to Fremont County long after you, Bob, but always wondered what it was like in those early days."

"There were four of us boys and two sisters in my family, and growing up, I don't ever remember not being hungry. There was always plenty of chores, even with the four of us. I figured then I didn't want to work the land. And I never wanted to be hungry."

"You've done well for yourself ... would make your parents proud. And you've got two fine girls."

Bob smiled and nodded. "Putting them through college has been an expensive proposition. And Helen's sickness was ... well, it cost a lot and ended bad."

Bob's wife had died within a month of Clayton, after a prolonged hospitalization. "Losing Helen had to be tough for you, and the community. She was a good woman." Dallas decided to change the subject before Bob became sentimental. "Didn't Reclamation bring in a new fellow? What's his name?"

Bob froze for an instant. "Winter. Jack Winter. Says he's going to take it to completion. Jim Haefner, the fellow they had before, was needed in South Dakota. Another part of that Pick-Sloan water deal. Wish we could've bid on more of that, but we ain't got the capital or the equipment."

Dallas smiled and reassured his partner. "There's always the next time. You can count on Washington to keep spending money."

"We got the federals squatting all over the state. Warren Air Force by Cheyenne and national parks up in Yellowstone and the Tetons. Interior's got Forest Service and Geological Survey and Reclamation. And the BIA for those damned injuns. But we don't see any of that money."

Dallas resisted the impulse to remind Bob that federal employees bought cars and pickups from his dealership, rented his apartments, and made down payments on his newly constructed houses. And most of the Indian tribal allowances went into the local economy as well.

"I'll feel better when we get a Republican in the White House. My fear is Truman's going to bomb Russia and China and start another world war before the election—not that we don't need to fight them Communists. I just want a general and not a hat salesman from Missouri leading our boys."

Dallas needed to bring Bob back to his agenda. "Any chance I can meet this Winter? Maybe at Ramona's?"

Bob scowled and angled his head to look at Dallas. "I suppose. But what for?"

"Men like Winter travel around to a lot of places. I want to extend a little western hospitality. Civic duty, you know."

Dallas could see the irritation on Bob's face. The mention of Corky Freeman had not bothered Bob, but Jack Winter touched a nerve. But Bob could not refuse his request.

"I'll invite him, but can't say he'll make it. Anything else on your mind?" Bob gulped the rest of his drink.

Dallas slipped into his courtroom face, void of emotion. "Not really."

Bob set his scotch on the bar. "We've talked before about converting your interest in my companies. Are you still interested?"

Dallas took a breath and gnawed at his tongue. "I've got an amount in mind, if that's what you are asking."

"I'm short on cash but wondered if maybe a swap of land might do."

Dallas resisted a grin, familiar with Bob's obsession for holding cash. "You have a parcel in mind?"

"I've got acres here and there."

Dallas set his drink on the bar. He knew all the Thornton land in Fremont County recorded with the Register of Deeds. "I'd love part of the Thornton family homeplace, but that may have too much sentimental value ... unless you'd consider it."

Bob wagged his head back and forth. "Nope, that's been in the family too many years. Let me check the books and see what I can find. I'm busy with the campaign and other meetings until Friday. I'll find a spot, and we can meet there."

"I do expect to recoup my investment and a good bit more."

"That's a tall order."

Dallas lifted his cocktail glass and frowned. "I could always sell my interests to someone with cash. That is part of the contract."

Bob stepped back. "I'll call you on Thursday ... let you know what we'll be looking at. I've got another meeting about the campaign, but thanks for the drink."

Dallas saw Bob to the door and watched the little man cross into the lobby. His intuition had been correct. Bob might not know anything about the Freeman death, but his partner was keeping secrets about the Boysen project.

+ + +

Grayson turned onto Federal, heading south to Lander and the courthouse. He accelerated around the curve near the armory, drove past the drive-in theater, and headed toward the bridge across the Wind River. His passengers were the collected facts and unanswered questions from his day in Riverton.

Dr. Owen had called in a report of his findings concerning the Freeman boy. The gist was a broken neck that had killed him instantly. Owen had the fancy medical words to describe it, but Grayson had chopped it down to the basics. The doctor had mentioned seeing similar injuries from vehicle collisions and sharp blows to the back of the head. There was no evidence of bullet or knife wound, insect bite, or punctures of any kind. Lab tests had been ordered on blood and stomach contents, but the doctor did not expect to find much.

Based on Owen's report, Winslow could not declare Freeman a "natural causes" death. Dr. Owen's report presented opportunity and danger. If Grayson could make an arrest right before the election, he could point to the accomplishment as solving a local problem, as Saylor had said. But failing to crack the case would give Larry Jacobsen ammunition to talk of Grayson's failure.

Grayson downshifted to climb the rise from the Wind River lowlands onto the flat plain of sage and rabbit brush stretching toward Hudson. His suspects included young Dodge and Natalie Saylor—and just about everyone else in Fremont County. Nelson's report included mention of a project of Freeman's, something about Boysen Dam for the newspaper. That lead would need a follow-up.

The thought of driving back to Riverton again tomorrow, just to interview Dodge, had no appeal. Like most lawmen, Grayson distrusted reporters and their claim of constitutional privileges.

Another day of Nelson digging up more facts about Freeman would be useful in questioning the newspaperman. Nelson should make contact with people at Reclamation too and get some names for interviews, just in case.

"Base to Sheriff 1, over."

Grayson snatched the microphone and pressed the "send" button. "Sheriff 1 here, Base. Over."

"Jail is asking about you, over."

He checked his wristwatch: 5:35 p.m. "Sheriff 1 returning to Base by eighteen hundred. Over."

"Ten-four that, Sheriff 1. No other messages. Base out."

Grayson returned the microphone to the post mount on the dashboard and sighed. His long day in Riverton had probably put Janet in a bad mood, again. If she had heard of Saylor's visit, then fireworks awaited him. Living in the courthouse, with Janet in charge of meals for the prisoners and jail staff, put a strain on their marriage.

Suspicion, jealousy, and complaints had changed the cute and easygoing girl he had married. Janet could be the biggest threat to his reelection, since she openly hoped Jacobsen would take over the sheriff's office. If he lost the election, she would need to find full-time work, along with a new place to live. His employment options were limited. The role of a deputy, or even town cop, would not be part of his future. Maybe Janet would not be part of it either.

He slowed for the hard curve coming into Hudson, intending to drive on through without a reason to stop. The cars parked on the street were few, with one restaurant closed for remodeling. By nightfall the second-floor operation would be open for business, though, crowding the street parking.

And what had Nelson's parting words been? "Going north of town to interview one of Freeman's girlfriends." His deputy had said it to the floor and not made eye contact when Grayson kidded him about having rough duty, talking to all those pretty girls. Instead of getting red-faced from embarrassment, the bachelor had just nodded his head and studied the floorboards. He was hiding something.

Janet wanted him to lose his job. Nelson was keeping a secret, and the other Riverton deputy was lazy and dumb. And now there was a killer in his county.

Grayson understood the wedding vows with Janet and the unspoken agreement of duty to his deputies, but he feared all of them were letting him down. Grayson wondered if every county sheriff in Wyoming had problems like his.

+ + +

Wil turned onto Agate Lane, Corky's street, and saw the house numbers. Nearly identical houses stood on both sides of the two-block-long dirt road. The color of the shingle siding, fencing or lack of it, and model of car or truck in the driveway were the only features differentiating one house from another. Wil parked across the street from Corky's address and looked at the white picket fence and dark gray siding. The front door faced north. Corky had lived in the basement, with a Mormon couple on the main floor.

A six-foot-tall gaunt man with tired eyes answered the door, and Wil introduced himself.

The tall man opened the screen door. "I'm Delmar Simpson."

Once inside, Wil scanned the living room. The condition of the furniture looked better than in his apartment, but the room was not much larger—enough space for a sofa, console radio, and wooden rocking chair. "Nice to meet you, even if the situation is sad."

"Too bad 'bout Corky." Delmar's monotone did little to make his words sound convincing. "You know what happened?"

"One-car accident is what the sheriff's saying. Out on the road to Dubois. We're having trouble at the newspaper figuring out why he would be on that road early in the morning."

The husband considered the problem for a moment and shrugged his shoulders.

So far Wil was giving rather than collecting information. "I understand he has a girlfriend, but I've not met her. Do you know her?"

"None I knowed." Delmar turned toward the kitchen. "Honey. My missus, Gretchen. This here's …"

Gretchen's entry into the living room instantly brightened the space. A turquoise-blue dress contrasted well with her shoulder-length blonde hair, and the belted waist accented the flair of her hips. Wil guessed her to be near his own age, at least five years younger than Delmar. She was full-figured, bright-eyed, and cute.

Wil straightened, sucking in his stomach. He cared little that Delmar had forgotten his name as his attention focused on the wife. "Wilson Dodge, with the *Riverton Wrangler.*"

Delmar put the girlfriend question to his wife.

She made eye contact with him, but Wil saw little emotion or friendliness. "He never mentioned anyone. And he never had anyone over."

Delmar moved closer to his wife. "No, he didn't. We tried fixin' him up with a gal from church, but he'd little interest."

Wil's knowledge of Mormons pointed to the female as subordinate to the male, particularly around outsiders. Wil alternated eye contact between husband and wife and noticed the skin of Gretchen's neck slowly turn burgundy. The flushing signaled something, but all his undergraduate classes in anthropology and psychology did little to explain the reason.

"His people been told?" Delmar's question sounded more like curiosity than concern for the family.

"The sheriff takes care of that. I was planning to call them tomorrow. There are plans for a funeral service."

"I'll be outta town startin' tomorrow, but maybe Gretch …" Delmar glanced at his wife, who lowered her head. Wil followed her gaze and saw matching turquoise high heels.

He took a deep breath and focused on Delmar. "I'll let you know the details and if the parents will come and get his things or not."

Gretchen turned to go back into the kitchen, heels click-clacking on the linoleum floor. The husband nodded, looking past Wil toward the front door.

"I was hoping to see if there was any newspaper property in his rooms."

Delmar led Wil through the kitchen and down the stairs to the basement. The piney scent of cleaning solution led Wil to suspect the apartment had already been searched and cleaned, no doubt by Gretchen. Observation of single men in college dormitories had given Wil enough evidence to know that this amount of housekeeping was beyond the scope of any unmarried man.

Wil started at the desk and sifted through the items sitting atop it, including letters in a wooden holder, a dictionary, and a stack of photography magazines. The bottom drawer contained notebooks with detailed photographic information, consistent with Gordon's description. The top drawer held writing supplies, paper clips, rubber bands, a pocketknife, and scissors. Wil set the notebooks on top of the desk. The remainder of the living room included a couch, a square wooden table and two chairs for dining, a floor lamp, and a radio on a small table.

The kitchen, crammed with near-miniature appliances and shallow open cupboards, gave barely enough room to move. The bedroom included a double bed, chest of drawers, and closet. The space beneath the bed lacked luggage, boxes, or dust. The closet contained clothing, shoes, and two empty cardboard shoe boxes on the top shelf. The stacked contents of the top drawer of the chest looked a little too neat but included nothing of interest.

"I want to take these notebooks. They have his photographic records. If there isn't anything of use to the newspaper, I'll return them."

Delmar frowned. "We got no use for 'em."

"I thought he would have his photographs up. The walls are empty."

Delmar looked around as if seeing the apartment for the first time. "Gretchen wanted somethin' for the walls, but ..." Delmar's voice trailed off, and he looked toward the stairs.

"Can I use the bathroom before I go? I stopped at the diner, and ..."

Delmar pointed to the bathroom.

Wil used the toilet and flushed. The sound of rushing water masked his peek into the medicine cabinet, which contained only a few toiletries. He was not sure what to look for, except that he had seen such inspections in detective movies—prescriptions perhaps, but he found none.

As he washed his hands, Wil examined the reflection in the mirror, the mirror Corky would have used every morning. It felt odd knowing that face would never appear in this mirror again. As he dried his hands, he noticed that the towel beside the sink felt unused.

Heading back up the stairs, Wil stopped in the kitchen and wrote down the Simpsons' telephone number. The coloring of the wife's neck had faded to a pink tint. From brief eye contact with Gretchen, Wil felt certain she was concealing something, but he knew not to pursue it in front of the husband. He thanked them and promised to keep in touch.

Twilight neared surrender to night as Wil crossed the road and approached his truck. A figure shorter than Wil advanced from the shadows of the house beyond the pickup and asked Wil to identify himself. Wil gave his name, looked across the hood of the Chevy, and felt the skin along the back of his neck tingle.

"What you doin' botherin' the Simpsons?" In the low light Wil made out shaggy hair and an untrimmed, thin beard. It was difficult to tell his age through the mask of facial hair.

Wil moved slowly forward, sensing anger in the tone of voice. "Visiting them about a friend."

"You ain't got no friends with them!" The man raised his chin, adding a snarl to his taunt.

Wil shifted the ledgers to his right arm and removed the keys from his pants in case he needed to jump in the truck.

The man took a step toward the front of the truck. "You're not from the church. I'd know ya if you was from the church."

"No, I'm not. What was your name?" Wil asked only to give himself time to get closer to the door of his truck.

"Orrin. Orrin Porter. Not that it's any b'iness of yours. You got no reason to come round here. Best you stay away. Mark my word." The man pointed up with the index finger of his right hand.

Orrin's stone-cold stare caused Wil to quickly hop inside the truck. He offered Orrin a wave, but the man stood still, eyes locked on Wil. Pulling into the Simpsons' driveway for a three-point turn, Wil directed the pickup back toward Federal. Driving away, Wil watched in the rearview mirror as the silhouette of Orrin, standing in the middle of the street backlit by fading twilight, disappeared into the darkness.

CHAPTER **10**

Wil entered the dark pressroom from the dock and flipped on the overhead light switch. The silent printing machinery gave his ears a reprieve, but the smell of paper, ink, and lubricant competed for dominance in his nostrils. He zigzagged to the darkroom, slipped inside, and waited for his eyes to adapt to the red light.

Wil started with the lightproof film vault, where he looked for prints or negatives at the bottom of each shelf or taped inside the door but found nothing but unexposed film. He repeated the search in the photographic paper safe, even going so far as to look inside open packets, hoping to find prints. No prints or negatives of any kind.

Making sure the paper and film containers were sealed against light, he turned the knob on the sixty-watt regular lightbulb. Compared to the red safelight, the bulb was blinding in the compact space. Wil squatted and looked at the shelves below the counter and then stooped over to check the underside of the surfaces. The only discovery was dirt on the floor.

Standing in the middle of the darkroom, he turned in a circle and inspected the ceiling and top of the walls, in search of a hiding place. He repeated the process, working his way down. As Wil completed the last rotation, he grabbed the countertop to steady himself, the walls now revolving about him. The effort had proved useless.

Wil turned off both the white and red lights before leaving the darkroom, stepped into the pressroom, and asked himself where Corky could have hidden the photos Gordon had mentioned. There were plenty of drawers in the workroom, but any of the crew of press workers could access them without arousing suspicion. There was nothing in Corky's car, his apartment, or his restricted work area. The film archives in the basement, the only other option at the office, presented the image of a needle in a very large haystack. And what did the padlock key fit?

He could honestly tell Sheriff Farmer, if he asked about a search for the photos, of his failure to find them. Would the sheriff believe him or want to look for himself? Wil decided he should talk with Dallas in the morning about how to respond to such a request.

Wil checked his wristwatch and saw it was past the time Ramona expected him. He turned off the overhead lights and locked the workroom door from the dock.

As Wil walked to his pickup, he wondered whether Corky had lied to Gordon about the Boysen Dam project or whether Gordon had failed to share everything he knew.

+ + +

Wil turned into the wide driveway of his mother's house at the western edge of town and pulled in behind Ramona's Hudson Hornet, safely beneath the carport. Peggy Lee bragged about "Them There Eyes" as he slipped into the kitchen through the side door. He found Ramona sitting in the sunken family room looking out its south-facing wall of windows, with a cigarette in hand and a martini glass on a glass-topped end table.

A barefoot Ramona stood, wearing her gold suit, and crossed to the record player to lower the volume. "I started without you. There is food in the refrigerator and bread on the counter."

Wil kissed her on the cheek, smelling gin on her breath and smoke from her cigarette. "Can I get you a refill?"

"I can have one more martini. You know the way I like it."

Wil found two paper-wrapped bundles in the refrigerator along with a container of celery stalks in water, two apples, and bottle of bluish-colored milk. He transferred slices of roast beef and Swiss cheese onto a plate and tore off a section of French bread, scattering crumbs on the clean countertop. As he returned the meat and cheese bundles to the refrigerator, it took only a moment to discover a jar of mustard but no mayonnaise or horseradish.

He set the plate on the end table before moving to the bar. "You should feel honored. I've already turned down two invitations for drinks today."

"You would have been forgiven. That business with your camera boy was so sad."

"Corky Freeman. Dad hired him. He was from Idaho, the son of a farmer."

"Did you know him well?"

Wil poured gin into a shiny metal shaker along with dry vermouth and ice, pressed on the lid, and shook. "If you would have asked me that yesterday, I would have said yes. Today I learned Corky thought I was a square."

He strained the clear contents into her martini glass, added an olive on a toothpick, poured a bit of olive juice into the glass, and handed the dirty martini to his mother.

"It could have been much worse, you know. I do not think of you as square at all. Make your drink so we can toast."

Wil poured whiskey and sweet vermouth with a few shakes of bitters for himself.

Ramona raised her glass. "To those we love and loved."

Wil touched her glass. "And those we've yet to love."

"Does this mean you have met someone?"

Wil took a cautious sip. "Do you know the county clerk? Saylor, Natalie Saylor?"

"She has subbed a few times for bridge. Smart girl. Went to college in New York, I think. One of the better schools. When did you meet her?"

He took his seat near the end table and tore off a corner of the sliced Swiss cheese. Wil told Ramona about seeing Saylor outside the *Wrangler* office and about her willingness to go on a date, according to Geri.

"I like her style. She may be the best-dressed young woman in the county."

"No, Mother, you have that title."

Ramona stubbed out her cigarette and rolled up a slice of beef. "I said 'young woman.' But thank you, dear."

"The curious part about the day's been how often Dad has found his way into my thoughts. Even Gordon Blakeslee mentioned him."

"If we are going to talk about Clayt, the two-martini rule may need breaking."

Tearing off a bit of bread, Wil smeared on mustard and topped it with meat and cheese. "That's your rule, not mine. At least you're eating something. Have some bread."

"You are. Contractions are for the working class. Next you will be tossing about 'ain't' like the cleaning lady."

"Between you and Geri, I'm surrounded by frustrated English teachers."

Ramona took the olive from her glass. "Please do not let me fall asleep in this chair."

"I'll prop up your feet and cover you in a blanket, like you used to do back in freshman year. I must have slept twenty hours a day then."

"Be sure to take this food home with you."

"How long was it after you and Dad met that you were married?"

Wil knew the story of how they had met by heart: the young newspaperman sweeping the department-store seamstress off her feet at a store fashion show, his taking her to dinner that night followed by a dance the next evening, their first kiss on the dance floor and how she knew he was the only man for her.

"I wanted to be a June bride. But Dotty was getting married on Valentine's Day, so we made it a double ceremony." Aunt Dorothy and Ramona were twins, although different in almost every way. Dotty was plump, maternal, and more interested in laughing than looking sophisticated.

"That's right—twins married on the same day. I remember seeing the clippings. You were all so young."

"Story with photograph. Our preacher thought he should be paid double, but …"

"Did you quit your job?"

"Dotty did, but I stayed at Brown's. Gus and Dotty lived at our apartment, so I moved in with your father. We were saving for a house."

Wil could see that she was momentarily lost in memories. "Then why was it you moved to Riverton?"

Ramona set down her empty martini glass and lit a cigarette. "That is a story for another day. When are you going to see Natalie? Soon, I hope."

Earlier, Dallas had deflected Wil's question about the cause of Clayton's death, and now Ramona was changing the subject about the move from Denver to Riverton. He knew how much she had loved Denver and Brown's, compared to the stale culture and social life and the small number of fashion shops for the women of Fremont County.

"I'm not sure. I was thinking drinks and dinner. Any suggestions?"

"Chicago, Denver, Cheyenne."

"This is a first date, not a proposal."

"Maybe Hudson, or that new place in Lander. I have heard good things, but getting Bob to leave town before the election is hopeless."

Wil finished his manhattan, picked up Ramona's martini glass, and stood. "I'll leave you to your beauty sleep then."

"No need to rush off, but if you are going, take the bread and cheese and roast beef."

"Won't the celery get lonesome?"

Ramona stood, taking Wil's plate, and kissed him on the cheek on her way to the kitchen. "Everyone knows celery is introverted."

+ + +

Gretchen nestled against Delmar, his arm over her shoulder and hand on her side. Reflected moonlight filled the bedroom and allowed her a view of his face. She stroked his chest and slipped her leg over his thigh.

After the prayer, Delmar liked to sort out the chores for the next day before sex. They had talked about needing to rent the apartment as soon as possible. "Call the paper tomorrow."

"Same rent as last time?"

"Five dollars more?" He made it a question, but Gretchen had no intention of challenging his wisdom.

"I'll pack Corky's things so we can show it."

"Let's try to get a married couple this time. Corky was a good renter, but another woman in the house would be company for you."

The mention of Corky's name had not changed Delmar's expression a bit. His eyes had remained on the ceiling, his breathing slow and steady.

"That'd be good." The major source of tension between them involved Delmar's frequent absences, and he was leaving again tomorrow. Gretchen wanted to ask when he would return home, but she remained silent. Mother had taught her never to complain or argue in bed.

"If you need any help around the house while I'm gone, Orrin can give you a hand."

She thought it a good thing Delmar was not studying her since the mention of Orrin produced a frown. Gretchen did not trust Orrin, even though he was a Mormon and a friend of Delmar. The neighbor had helped her with a problem she had concealed from Delmar, but Orrin would come to the door whenever Delmar was away. She could see the desire in his eyes.

One of the reasons Gretchen had fallen in love with Delmar was that when they met, he just smiled at her. He did not engage in the usual attempt at impressing her like boys her own age. She knew he would be a good provider and father for their children. He was seven years older and more mature. Of course, she had known the lustful stares of older men the same as any pretty girl, but Delmar was different.

Delmar turned onto his side, kissing Gretchen on the forehead. "Who's my sweetheart?"

Gretchen rolled onto her back, and his hand rubbed her breasts before pulling up the nightgown. His words were as predictable as the brief rubbing between her legs, and then he was atop her. She wanted to find the courage to be on top but feared Delmar would wonder how she had learned of that position, just as she wanted him to caress her until she was aroused and wet with anticipation.

She watched his tightly shut eyes, just like when he was praying. As Delmar increased the pace of his thrusts, she grunted and panted and then sighed as he finished. Kissing his cheek, she told him it had been "so good" before he rolled off her and onto his side, his back to her. Gretchen pushed the nightgown down and cuddled behind him, closed her eyes, and hoped to fall asleep as quickly as Delmar.

She would need to put another quilt on their bed tomorrow. The breeze from the open window cooled the room. Even if Delmar were not leaving in the morning, she would need the added warmth. Wednesday was wash day for bedding, but with Delmar gone, she wanted his scent in their bed.

She thought back over the day and how by late afternoon she had finished cleaning the apartment and had been through Corky's belongings. His suitcase would hold most of his things. A cardboard box in the basement could hold the rest. The towels and sheets went with the apartment, along with the kitchen basics. Uncertainty filled her about what to do with the leftover bottles of beer in the refrigerator. And there was the one thing she had looked for and not found.

Delmar snored softly. Gretchen wished she could fall asleep as easily. But she was troubled, wondering whether she was responsible for Corky's death.

CHAPTER 11

Wil switched off the headlights and engine, pulled the parking brake and released the clutch, and looked at the back of the apartment court from his parking spot. The drink and snack with Ramona had been a good change of pace for his day, even though his list of unanswered questions now included one more about his parents and why they had moved to Riverton.

The back porch light of the apartment next to Wil's went on, and Cecil stepped out onto the small porch. Wil slipped out of the pickup. "Cecil, how're you tonight?"

"Mary, Jesus, Joseph, and all the saints. I'm glad to see ya."

Wil had never heard his neighbor speak in biblical terms. Cecil looked to be in his fifties, and his wiry body displayed all the merit badges of a working cowboy: sun-reddened skin, stiff hip and knee joints, and a face crosshatched with creases and wrinkles unable to conceal a life's worth of aches, pains, and injury.

Wil walked toward his porch steps. "Good to see you too."

Cecil worked his way down the porch steps, one at a time. "I knowed you left early this morning and then heard on the radio a newspaper person was dead. I was crying in my beer, but then they said it wasn't you."

Wil moved to the top step of his back porch. "Think we both need a beer." He went inside to retrieve and open a pair of bottles while the retired cowboy waited outside.

Cecil took the bottle offered to him. "So what happened?"

Wil took a seat on a porch step and repeated the details of Corky's death but withheld mention of his visit to the morgue.

"Sorry 'bout that. Means more work for someone. He sickly?"

"He just turned twenty-two. Seemed healthy to me."

Cecil took a swig from his bottle. "Been a time since a townie been kilt here 'bouts. Mostly sickness and gettin' old. Bandits, ya think? Forced 'im off the road, maybe?"

Wil sat on the bottom porch step and could see the wrinkles and creases on Cecil's weather-beaten face lit by moonlight. "I wish I knew, Cecil. I hope the sheriff can figure it out."

Cecil stuck a thumb into a belt loop of his jeans. "Lawmen oft' make a bad thing worse. Cowboy justice works better."

Wil guessed at Cecil's meaning, not certain he wanted it spelled out.

Cecil pointed his index finger at Wil. "If these bandits that kilt your hired man come round here to hurt you, I'll have buckshot waitin' for 'em. Best you keep a good eye out."

Wil could not imagine ever needing a gun to protect himself. The wild west had been tamed, even if the old cowboys like Cecil acted like a gunfight could break out at any moment.

+ + +

Wil rinsed and spit into the sink, dropped the toothbrush into the glass, and then closed the door of the medicine cabinet. The mirror offered back the same image as the one in Corky's apartment. He stared at the face and wondered how much longer his reflection would remain with this particular mirror. Days or months? Not years. Wil's plans for a house would happen sooner than that. For just a second, he thought, *Or I'll die trying*, but the common phrase produced a bitter aftertaste unknown until today.

What could Corky have been doing twenty-four hours ago that led to his death? Was he doing a job Wil just as easily could have done? Something for the newspaper? They had started the morning together at the Labor Day rally—marches performed by the high school band, speeches, singing. Wil had taken notes for his front-page article, and Corky had pressed the shutter release.

He remembered planning to ask Geri her opinion about Bob Thornton's pledge to require a city employee loyalty oath if elected to city council. But that was before Albert Nelson had altered his day. Wil pushed his fingers through the short hair along the left side of his head and kneaded a tight spot at the back of his neck.

After the rally Corky had taken people shots at the ice cream social at the VFW. Wil had scanned the photographic prints and seen faces he could name. Had Corky captured something embarrassing, or perhaps suspicious? And what about the Boysen Dam photos? Where could those be, and what could they reveal?

Wil pulled down the lower lid of his right eye and studied the tiny blood vessels in the mirror. Had Corky lied to Gordon? But lying was not part of the Corky he knew. But then the Corky he had known would not have thought him a square. Or was Gordon confusing Boysen Dam with another photo project?

The Studebaker had not been in a crash. The cause of Corky's death was as much a mystery as Clayton's. And Gretchen Simpson had a secret. Maybe Geri could get the girl to talk. But the sheriff, or Raymond Winslow, needed to come up with an answer as to what had caused Corky's death.

As Cecil had said, someone had "kilt" Corky. Most likely, that someone lived in Riverton. But his Riverton was supposed to be a town of churchgoing people who loved their neighbors and community.

He had studied primitive cultures and their creation of a beast or intruder to explain unexpected death. The professor had called it "externalizing the threat"—a way to maintain the integrity of the tribe or community but still acknowledge the presence of evil.

Wil turned off the bathroom light and stepped into the bedroom. He turned off the reading light too, ready for sleep. But how could he rest peacefully without knowing the truth about Corky's death? Tomorrow he would look at the VFW photos again, closely. The face of the person responsible for Corky's death could be in one of those shots. Gordon would get another visit. And Grayson Farmer needed to supply some answers as well.

Day 2

Wednesday
September 3, 1952

Chapter 12

Wil surfaced and resurfaced, neither asleep nor awake, pursued by featureless faces. He rolled away only to land in another chase; he fled around corners, through tunnels, and down winding paths. Sweaty and breathless, he swung legs off the edge of the bed, feet to the floor. The radium-painted tip of the big hand pointed at the two, the little brother angled at four. Sleep offered no rest. The face he sought had features, possibly caught on film, and awaited detection.

By 6:30 a.m., Wil had spent over an hour in the darkroom enlarging prints and thirty minutes inspecting photographs with a magnifying glass. The discovery he had felt confident of finding the night before simply was not there. Wil struggled to convince himself that a single person in Corky's pictures was capable of any harmful action.

Once the printing crew started to arrive, Wil slipped out for breakfast.

Wil took his customary stool where his mug of coffee waited. He watched as Rose approached the counter. "Cynthia, what about oatmeal?"

Rose wrinkled her nose with a frown. "Alfred, fall is three weeks away, and only horses eat oats before then. Besides, I already put your order in."

Wil did not care for the Alfred label, which he let rest in the pile of other rejects from their morning ritual. Rose refused to explain the reason for a new name each day, but he liked the game. Wil had created a simple rule: be spontaneous in selecting a name for Rose, like the reaction to a psychiatric inkblot test.

He needed that kind of a snap-judgment approach, free of logic and reason, to study the photos. Yet he realized the problem might be one not of method but of viewpoint. He thought like a newspaper reporter and not like a detective, suspecting everyone. But how did a regular person develop that trait?

Wil had seen his share of detective movies with Dick Powell as Marlowe, Humphrey Bogart as Sam Spade, and Joseph Cotten as the writer in *The Third Man*. He preferred the other Powell, teamed with Myrna Loy in the *Thin Man* films, as much comedy as detective story. The back-and-forth word play between star and leading lady had formed Wil's image of a perfect marriage. Other than the verbal fencing with Geri, his breakfast banter with Rose was the closest he came to that ideal. Wil loved both women, but not romantically.

If the answer to the puzzle of who killed Corky Freeman rested with those photographs, he needed help. Many of the people he had looked at in those images were likely to attend Ramona's party for Bob Thornton tonight, and as bartender, he could observe and question them. But what would he ask? Myrna Loy would know.

Rose slid the plate of eggs, bacon, and potatoes in front of Wil. "I'll get a dish of oats for you, just to prove I'm right."

Wil lifted his mug for a refill, but Rose raced off to the booths. Every few forkfuls, he glanced toward the entryway, as if expecting Albert Nelson to track him down again this morning. But Corky could die only once, like his father. And why did Clayton appear every time he thought about Corky?

That he was sitting at the same spot he had shared with Clayton was a partial explanation. His memories of the Round-Up were strong, even though their breakfast and lunch outings had ended when Wil started high school. The casket image of Clayton had arisen after his visit to the morgue. Could repressed memories of his father need resolution? Could transference between Corky and Clayton explain it? Or were psychological concepts just distractions? A way to avoid facing the challenge of finding Corky's killer?

"More coffee, hon?"

Wil accepted the coffee but declined her offer of oatmeal. He needed to get back to work and make a push to put out the Thursday edition. The last batch of enlargements should be dry enough to examine. Would Geri be able to find the face he could not?

After twenty minutes with the guys in the pressroom, Wil settled at his desk along with the new enlarged prints. Photographs of different sizes covered his desktop. Wil looked at the faces and backgrounds of the new photos, wanting a story to emerge involving deceit and suspicion. But the latest batch was no different from the others and failed to serve up the face of a killer.

"Geri, what kind of man could've killed Corky? I've looked at stacks of photos from Monday's ice cream social. The last person to see him alive might be in these pictures. But I can't find a single guilty face."

Geri started the coffee percolator and stepped to her desk. "What makes you think it was a man? And when did you become a cop?"

Wil leaned back, eyes closed. "I don't think there is a single woman in Riverton, or in all of Fremont County, who could kill."

Geri looked over her shoulder at Wil. "I hope you're on the jury if I ever get charged."

"What does that mean?"

"Women can kill just as easily as men. Or lie or cheat or steal, especially cheat. If I had a dollar for every married woman involved with another man … I could go on a shopping trip to Marshall Fields with Ramona."

Wil rocked forward, shaking his head. "It takes a man to lead a woman astray with promises and lies. I don't approve of cheating, but blaming the woman—"

"For a guy who claims to be religious, you're forgetting Genesis and Adam and Eve. She was the temptress who led Adam to disobey, remember?"

Wil raised his index finger, as if making a point to a class of students. "Eve was tempted herself, by a snake, who lied. You don't have to be Sigmund Freud to know the symbolism of a snake. Women are predisposed to obey and surrender to the more powerful man and his snake, from the earliest of times on."

"That's what you got from all that college? It's no wonder the girl in Chicago put you off women. You've no idea … Like I said, I hope you're on my jury."

Wil grabbed a pile of photographs and shoved them at Geri. "Look at these and tell me what man or woman is capable of killing someone. I dare you."

She inspected the first dozen and tossed them back to Wil. "There are at least four men or women in these involved in hanky-panky. And I'd bet half of those could kill a person under the right conditions. How does that fit into your theory?"

Wil looked at Geri's pictures, able to name just about every person. Picking the unfaithful spouses was as elusive as finding the face of a killer.

He wanted to be right about no one in Riverton being able to kill, but then how had Corky died? A person had to be responsible for the death, and he felt certain it was a man. But who? And why?

Geri tapped the nail of her index finger on the desktop. "You still didn't answer my cop question. Why?"

"Last night when I got to my place, Cecil came out to meet me. He'd thought I was the one found dead. The more I thought about it, the more it bothered me. It could've been me in that car. Crazy as it sounds, I'm trying to solve my own murder."

The tormentor from his dream symbolized his obligation to discover the truth of Corky's death. If only he could drink and joke his way to a solution, like the *Thin Man*. But that was the movies and not real life.

+ + +

"Is there a problem, officer?"

The manner of the man in the blue suit and blue tie with tiny white polka dots asked the question made him sound like he was from England. Al instantly knew he was not from Wyoming.

Deputy Albert Nelson identified himself and explained he was conducting routine questioning concerning a suspicious death. The Bureau of Reclamation man introduced himself as Jack Winter and led Al down the hallway. As the riding heels of his boots thudded down the hall, Al felt sponginess in the flooring of the prefabricated structure, reminding him of military barracks—cheap and easy to build, but not meant to last.

"Mr. Winter, Sheriff Farmer has me working on a possible lead in the death of Corky Freeman. He was the photographer for the *Wrangler*. Do you know about our local newspaper?"

Winter sat behind his desk and offered an affirmative head bob in answer to the question.

Al stood behind a gray armless metal chair, curious whether the man would stay sitting. "Did you know Mr. Freeman? Did he take any photos of you for the newspaper?"

Winter made eye contact and then looked away. "Was he a chunky redhead? No? I have become acquainted with very few people in the area, other than those directly connected to the project. My attention the past few months has been on completing this project on schedule. There's been little time for socializing."

Al decided Winter was not from England. The way he pronounced his words, fast but with each syllable distinct, just made him sound odd. "We believe Freeman was taking photographs out at the construction site, around the dam. Is there anyone working out there I might talk to, who might've been in contact with Freeman?"

Winter rubbed the tip of his nose. "I can take you out there and introduce you, but we're nearing completion. There are a few construction workers cleaning up, and the generator installers, and as many as four others are in and out at site headquarters, but that is it. It may be a waste of your time, but Uncle Sam wants to cooperate."

"Any chance someone in this office might know him?"

Winter stood and pulled at the lapels of his suit jacket. "We can ask Diane in the front. She keeps track of the staff with offices here."

Back in the entry area, Winter posed Al's question to Diane. Al took a closer look at the young receptionist with short curled hair and very little makeup. She looked like the sort of girl he remembered from the high school typing and shorthand classes.

"I cannot say for certain, but I doubt it. One of my girlfriends went out with Corky a few times. Would you like her name and number?"

Al winked at the girl, getting a smile in return. After taking the slip of paper from Diane, he put on his Stetson, tapped it with the left forefinger, and returned her smile. She had nice teeth. He thought a little lipstick could take Diane a long way.

CHAPTER 13

The short night of sleep and the hypnotic rhythm from the pressroom pulled at Wil's eyes. The jerk of his chin dropping snapped him awake. He stood, stretched, and resurveyed the photographs from the rally and the ice cream social, looking at possible shots for the two-page gallery in next week's edition. Editing four pages of pictures down to even three seemed impossible.

These same photos were not getting him any closer to finding Corky's killer. The only other clue to follow was Gordon's comment about Corky's work on a Boysen Dam project.

"Did Clayton have a file on Boysen Dam?"

Cigarette snared in the corner of her mouth, Geri angled her head in his direction. "No idea. Right-hand bottom drawer."

Wil eased open the heavy desk drawer packed with manila folders, descriptions penciled on the tabs. He had scanned them when he started, intending to do a detailed inventory, but had never found time. Since the files were not in alphabetical order, he thumbed through them, searching for Boysen. There was a possibility Clayton had assigned Corky to research Boysen Dam, and the photographer had never bothered to mention it to him.

A thin folder with "Boysen" on the label contained a clipped article, two enlarged photos, and a sheet of contact prints, plus a listing of names of people associated with the project. A Bureau of Reclamation press release on the project completed the file.

Farther back, a fat folder with "Hiroshima" inked on the tab caught his attention. Bringing the file onto his desk, he opened it to reveal clipped editorials and cartoons from other newspapers and magazines starting in August 1945. Clayton had noted the date and source publication for each.

A copy of a *New Yorker* magazine with cover art of a picnic in the park was the largest item in the file. Wil knew the entire issue of the magazine contained a single article by John Hersey, titled "Hiroshima." Upon Wil's return to Ann Arbor in the fall of 1946, one of his anthropology instructors had spent the first month of class using the issue to examine the Japanese response to the atomic bombing.

Toward the back of the folder were typed and edit-marked editorials Clayton had written each August starting in 1945 and ending in 1950. Wil scanned the 1945 version but felt too exhausted to concentrate. He thought it odd that clippings of the printed editorials were missing from the file. Clayton had died in early August 1951, and Wil wondered whether his father had written about Hiroshima that year as well.

Wil slid open the pencil drawer and looked for paper clips or rubber bands to separate the different sections of the file. There was an order to the collection he wanted to maintain. The oblong spot in the compartmentalized tray where Clayton had placed paper clips was almost empty. Wil opened the drawer further and found a cardboard box with a drawing of a paper clip on top.

He opened the box, expecting to restock the bin, but instead found a half dozen earrings. He tilted the container; it appeared none of them matched. Why would his father have women's jewelry in his desk?

"Did you find a file for Boysen?"

Wil swiveled his chair toward Geri. "Yeah, but there's this thick one about Hiroshima. Have you read this *New Yorker* issue?" Wil held out the magazine to Geri.

She glanced at the cover and shook her head.

"It's an amazing bit of writing. I had no idea Dad even knew about it."

Geri pulled a cigarette from the pack and used the one she had been smoking to light it. "The bombing of Japan shocked everyone. You mentioned it yesterday, how it was a big reason you left college that first year. But with the war over, soldiers were coming home. People were getting married, having babies, and worrying about finding and keeping their jobs. But ..." Wil waited as she inhaled deeply and a long spindle of smoke seeped out her nose. "That was a long time ago. Those memories ..."

"Did Dad do an editorial on the bombings in 1951? There are markups from '45 to '50, but no '51."

Geri stubbed out her half-smoked cigarette. "That was a tough month. I don't remember."

"I can look in the bound books and see. It was the month he died."

Geri stood and brushed ash and flecks of lint from the front of her skirt. "Yes, you can, and yes, it was."

Wil watched as she walked to the back of the office toward the restroom. Something remained unsaid about Clayton, and it had to do with the Hiroshima file. Why did Geri want to avoid talking about Clayton's death, just like Dallas?

+ + +

Al followed Winter's car with US government license plates east out Highway 26. The drive was a familiar one all the way to Shoshoni, the last decent-sized town between Riverton and Casper— level irrigated fields bounded by fences, awaiting harvest or covered with yellowed cut stubble; abundant stretches of rock-strewn hills and valleys with dried-out grass and brush gripping soil and sand; and in the distance, the ridgelines of mountains with names like Copper and Lysite and the Bighorns farther east.

The route north out of Shoshoni, on Highways 20 and 789, generally meant trouble in the form of car and truck collisions. The road through open range quickly approached the imposing Owl Creek range. Erosion had carved a gap through the layers of geological time that formed the Wind River Canyon, a major road and railway connection between central Wyoming and the northern tier of the state.

The narrow and twisting part of the Wind River Canyon fell within the jurisdiction of Hot Springs County. Most of the car and truck accidents occurred along that section of highway, although Fremont County deputies often controlled access at the southern end of the canyon for serious accidents, giving tow trucks and rescuers a work area free from the threat of high-speed traffic. Al liked the easy pace set by Winter and the sightseeing it allowed, as opposed to the high-speed, rotating red-light, siren-blaring dash common on this road.

The construction site headquarters squatted near the mouth of the canyon, where Al met the middle-aged version of Diane, thirty pounds heavier and the hint of a moustache on her upper lip. She had not heard of Corky Freeman, and none of her friends had dated him. Two engineering types looking at schematics told the same story.

Al accepted Winter's offer to show him around, and they took a battered GSA pickup truck. After coasting to the base of the earthen dam to the concrete bunker for the power-generating equipment, Winter gunned the truck with worn-out springs back uphill and onto a primitive dirt road, roughly parallel to the railroad tracks around the eastern perimeter of the reservoir. Winter talked nonstop, pointing out features and asking questions, but the jostling of Al's insides by the bumps, dips, and tilting ground made any reply impossible.

Between bumps and turns, Al noticed the accumulation of water in the broad hollow spaces of what would become the reservoir. Winter described a larger body of water than Al had expected, suitable for a variety of recreational activities. Al had heard rumors of a state park but dismissed them as wishful thinking by Shoshoni store owners.

By the time Winter turned back onto Highway 20, Al was thankful for the paved roadway. Winter offered to show him the western side of the reservoir. Al declined, apologizing for taking so much of his time, and the whine of tires on pavement carried them back to the headquarters area.

Winter waited for Al to get out of the pickup before slamming his door, a hollow metallic whoop. "This death ... was that the car accident I heard about?"

Al paused, surprised the question had taken so long to be asked. "Yeah. Out west of Riverton."

"Was he a young guy?"

He nodded. "Twenty-two, I think."

"Too bad. You didn't say how it connected to the dam project."

Al adjusted his hat, expecting Winter to ask for details on how the Freeman kid had died. "We're not sure. Just a possible lead. We hoped you knew the guy and could fill in the blank spots."

Winter shook his head. "Most unfortunate."

Al waited for the question not asked and then thanked the man for the tour. Before leaving the site, Al drove up the dirt road past the headquarters hut and found demolished temporary storage and housing no longer needed for work crews, along with scraps of leftover building supplies. He saw a dump truck with Pioneer Construction painted on the door and two workers loading trash and building materials into the box.

Al turned the radio car around and eased his way south, back to Shoshoni. He could report to the sheriff about interviewing and surveying the area, but not much else. The stretch of land the reservoir would occupy had belonged to the Shoshone and Arapahoe tribes. Winter's rough and dusty tour had shown that the land was like much of the reservation, unsuitable for growing a crop or grazing livestock. Maybe Freeman had figured out that Reclamation had paid too much for this stretch of desert.

+ + +

After lunch, Wil met with Bernie to make the final layout and headline calls for the Thursday edition. The first run of papers would be individually wrapped and labeled for mailing to out-of-town subscribers. Before the street edition press run, changes or corrections would be made from a pressroom floor proofreading. If the equipment cooperated, Bernie figured his crew would make it to the supper table with their families.

In the office area, Wil focused on narrowing the choices of the Labor Day photo pages for next week. He had determined that

Geri did not want to revisit the Hiroshima topic, or the topic of his father. Wil did not want to aggravate her, but he still wanted her help, so he tried to ease into his request. "Did you hear about Bob Thornton's pledge to require city employees to take a loyalty oath if he gets elected?"

"It doesn't surprise me, but when did he make it?"

"At the rally in the park, on Monday."

Geri swiveled toward Wil and pulled back her lips, baring her teeth. "Bob Thornton is a horse's ass, using Labor Day, a time to honor working people, to trot out that crap about a loyalty oath for city employees. Workers died so Bob Thornton could have a federal holiday to give his silly –"

"What workers died?"

"The Pullman workers, around the 1890s. The Pullman Company cut hourly wages, but not rents or food prices in the company town. The workers went on strike. Union railroad men wouldn't switch any Pullman cars on trains in sympathy. Eventually the government brought in troops, and workers were shot and killed. Upset a lot of working people. Grover Cleveland and Congress declared Labor Day a national holiday to quiet public outrage."

"Why haven't I heard anything about ––"

"A college graduate and you don't know the history behind a federal holiday. Of course the politicians don't want to talk about such things."

Wil frowned, not sure where to go next except to ask for her help. "Geri, will you come with me to Ramona's tonight? I've got to figure out if Corky's killer is there, and I need a woman's eye."

She took a deep breath, relaxed her posture and narrowed her eyes. "I don't want to give Ramona the idea we're pals. We kept our distance while Clay was alive, and there's no reason to change that. And besides, Gray Farmer is the sheriff, not you."

Wil stood and stretched, drained of energy but far from the end of his day.

Geri turned back toward her typewriter. "You need to go home and take a nap. If the boys in the back have a problem, they'll figure it out. And a bath wouldn't hurt either."

Wil angled his nose down and took a sniff. Geri was right; he smelled sweaty.

"Call Natee Saylor if you want a partner tonight. She likes politics. Let her mingle, and she'll have more gossip than the gals at Friday night Bunko."

The idea of inviting Miss Saylor to the party was perfect. He should have thought of it. "I'll just do that. Anything else I should be doing?"

"Clean up that mess on your desk." The ring of her telephone interrupted any further orders. "*Riverton Wrangler.*"

Wil turned back to his photographs, planning to make one last pass before calling it a day.

"Wil, Sheriff Farmer on the phone for you."

Wil punched the blinking light on his desk set and offered a greeting.

"Mr. Dodge, you need to come see me. Tomorrow at 9:00 a.m. Riverton station."

Wil met Geri's inquiring look. "Sure thing, Sheriff. I'm hoping to interview you about the Corky Freeman investigation, for next week's newspaper."

"I'll be asking the questions."

"Can I quote you on that, Sheriff?" The line went dead.

Geri opened a new pack of cigarettes. "What was that about?"

"Farmer wants to see me tomorrow at nine, in his office. When I asked about the investigation, he gave me the 'I'll be asking the questions' reply." As he quoted the sheriff, Wil lowered his voice, teeth together in a bad imitation of the sheriff.

"It's too late for you to run for sheriff, Wil."

He smiled at the observation. "But it's not too late for the *Wrangler* to endorse a candidate."

She tapped a cigarette against the desktop and lit it. "We've never endorsed a candidate."

"If Grayson Farmer wants to act like a tough guy, I'll fight back in the one way I know how. We might not endorse his opponent, but the reporting of his investigation will be Chicago-style, rough and tough. Who's he running against?"

"Larry Jacobsen, highway patrol. He can be a prick too."

Wil had heard Geri use off-color language before but liked correcting her, as she had with his junior high grammar. "Mrs. Murphy, there's no need for that kind of nasty talk."

"Those Friday night Bunko gals must've corrupted me."

Before he left the office, Wil called the county courthouse to invite Natalie Saylor to Ramona's party. She was out of her office, so he left a message. Although it was not really a date, he thought it a good start.

On the drive home, he considered stopping to see Gordon but feared what he might find. Discovering him with a glass of whiskey before lunch the day before had shocked Wil. Retirement and losing his wife, and now Corky, might be too much for the old guy. Going early tomorrow morning, before Gordon had time to start drinking, would make better sense.

CHAPTER 14

Gretchen wept in the basement darkness on the bed she had slept in with Corky. Her entire body ached, worse than cramps. While packing his belongings, she had searched for the photos again, ashamed of the pictures even though pride had filled her at the time, in poses unthinkable for a married Mormon woman. Now she was more alone than before, husband out of town and boyfriend dead.

She prayed the pictures were never found—hidden in a secret spot or torn to tiny pieces, anyplace except where her husband could find them. But she had looked at them with Corky in that very room. Delmar must have found them.

Forcing herself to the bathroom, she blew her nose and closed her eyes, sensing Corky standing behind her, kissing her neck, fingertips meandering over her skin. She could detect his scent. She felt his touch on her breasts.

How could an unmarried man be so good at sex? She recalled the sincerity of his words, the way he was never in a rush to get into her, how he even let her on top. She did not love him the same as Delmar, but he was better at sex.

Mother had reinforced the teaching that "relations other than making children" was a sin. Having a child with Corky had been out of the question. But Gretchen doubted her mother had ever been with a man like Corky.

She wished there was another woman to talk to about these thoughts and feelings. Gretchen imagined being a part of the group of neighbors, having coffee, but Delmar did not like people visiting when he was not at home. And coffee was forbidden along with

Coca-Cola and alcohol. Was she cursed with the desire for things her faith did not permit? Was that the reason for Corky?

She had made the first move on a May evening when Delmar was out of town. Wearing the satiny pajamas Delmar had seen only once and then forbidden her from wearing again, Gretchen had knocked on Corky's door, saying she needed to get items in the laundry room. After collecting a few dried pieces from the basement clothesline, she had returned to his living room, let a piece fall, and asked for help. When Corky stood from picking up the item, she had closed her eyes and parted her lips. He had known what to do.

That was their first night together in his bed. She crept upstairs before he awoke, and when he tried to kiss her in the kitchen the next morning, she told him he did not belong in that part of the house. She was giddy the entire day, recalling what they had done the night before. The next night, she prepared to sleep in her marriage bed, but once the lights were out, she slipped down the stairs.

Separating her life between the upstairs world of her husband and downstairs time with Corky helped Gretchen deal with the guilt of being unfaithful. She worried Delmar would notice a difference when he came home that first time. But he acted as if nothing had changed. When Delmar went away again, she slept in their bed the first night but spent the next downstairs with Corky. She repeatedly prayed for strength to resist temptation but memorized the way down the stairs in the dark.

Now she was in his bathroom, alone with her memory of Corky, nipples tender from rubbing against her undergarments. Gretchen looked in the mirror. Her neck was blotchy red just as it had been Tuesday night, with nose and eyes to match.

What if Delmar had found those photos and hurt Corky? Had the visit from the deputy and then the newspaperman frightened him? If Delmar had run away, afraid of getting put into jail, what would happen to her? She had never held a job. How could she keep living in her home? Moving in with Mother and Daddy was the best she could expect unless another man would take her. She was still pretty, but if the reason for the failed marriage became known, then finding a decent man would be impossible.

+ + +

Deputy Albert Nelson pulled into armory parking lot on the south end of town. Earlier that morning, he had left a message asking Officer Masin to meet him at the location. An officer in a blue uniform shirt and jeans stood beside a Jeep with the tribal police insignia on it. Al stopped near the Jeep, slid out of the patrol car, and scanned the surroundings. Late-afternoon sun put a yellow tint on the buildings, and a golden hue blanketed the parched ground-hugging vegetation.

Al gave a half-hearted salute with his right hand. "Howdy. Al Nelson."

"Tom Masin."

Al pushed back the brim of his hat with his left hand. "Were you the officer that reported the dead man earlier this week?"

The uniformed officer gave a gentle bob of his head, twice.

"I was hoping you could help with the details. Anything you saw and could tell me 'bout the car and dead guy would be appreciated."

Masin took a short step closer. "The car on the side road was driven from the east. A person, probably a man, got out and pushed a bicycle back to the road. Most likely, the bike was in the trunk since it was not latched shut. I don't know if it went east or west, but I would bet back to the east. He, or maybe she, was wearing cowboy boots. No distinct markings. Size 7 to 9. I'd be surprised if it was an Indian."

"Why's that?"

"An Indian would have been more careful with his tracks ... covered them."

The deputy considered the information. "Unless he wanted to make it look like it wasn't an Indian."

Nelson could not detect any reaction from Masin, except silence.

"You notice anything special about the car? Any damage?"

"Nothing out of the ordinary. But I didn't look at it that close."

"Why'd you stop?"

Masin raised his boot onto the front bumper of his Jeep and leaned on his thigh. "The car was not ... not close enough to the road, or the cabin. Just looked wrong."

"You have any idea if the tribal police are gonna pursue this?"

Masin looked toward his right and then back at Al. "The dead man was not an Indian, and there is no evidence an Indian was involved. My superior has little reason to be interested."

"Were you in the military?"

The tribal policeman made eye contact with Al. "Marines."

"I was in the army. MP. Worked with a Nez Perce. Taught me a lot."

Expressionless, Masin maintained eye contact. The deputy had hoped his mention of military service and another Indian would create some common ground between them. When Masin looked down, Al figured his effort had failed.

"Thanks for talking with me. If you remember anything else … or if there's anything I can ever do to give you a hand, let me know. The dispatcher can usually find me, day or night."

"You are welcome, Deputy Nelson." Officer Masin climbed into his Jeep and drove off.

Al made a quick note about the bicycle in the notebook he kept in his shirt pocket. He liked this tribal cop, although Masin had not been very friendly. At the same time, Larry Jacobsen had acted friendly, but Al disliked the candidate for sheriff's cockiness. Local attitudes about the reservation left little doubt about the inferiority of Indians, but Al thought he would like a chance to work with Masin.

CHAPTER 15

"Who's coming to this?" Wil hoped there would be a few familiar faces at Ramona's corralling of local voters.

"Bob, of course, and some of his friends. And friends of mine. People you know."

The tables for snacks and the stand-up bar were set up near Ramona's home, leaving the twenty-five yards of concrete driveway and front lawn for mingling. Her dream home, a blend of ranch style with a concealed front door, plentiful windows, a modestly pitched roof, and exaggerated eaves, was set back from the road. The mown grass lawn looked out of place next to the desert scrub on either side of the property, but it was only a matter of time before other homes were built on the western edge of town. The setting was perfect for an early-evening social, and with no neighbors nearby, the drinking and laughter would not attract attention.

"I invited Natalie Saylor."

Ramona continued crimping the edges of foil on the trays of snacks. "She might inspire you in unexpected ways."

Wil ignored her response and directed his attention to the boxes of liquor. He pulled out a rum and a tequila, along with multiple bottles of gin and Canadian whiskey and a few of scotch. The selections were all common brands, with a Seagram's and Johnnie Walker that Ramona hoped to send back, unopened. They had tonic, club soda, Coca-Cola, Squirt, 7 Up, and two washtubs with bottled beer on ice. He would not be able to make any fancy drinks, but this was Wyoming and not a suburban Chicago country club.

Wil looked to fill an empty ice bucket. "Ramona, you have any more ice?"

"The beer took all I ordered. Would you run over to the VFW?" She kept a running tab with the VFW and at least three other catering outlets.

"How much?"

"Tell them it will be for forty—make it fifty people. They will know."

By the time he returned, six guests had helped themselves to beer and were hovering around the food. During the next half hour, a steady flow of invitees appeared, wanting a blend of beer and mixed drinks. Wil knew many of them either as friends of his parents or as advertisers and printing service customers. From churchgoers to bridge club wives and Chamber of Commerce husbands, the guests displayed a consistency in their attire, casual yet dressy western outfits.

Gin with tonic won the popularity contest, and Wil could not help but notice the volume level of the conversation increase along with a disturbing amount of flirtation. As he watched and listened between drink orders, Wil recalled Geri's words on infidelity. Yet he could not see anyone capable of killing another person.

A man Wil recognized from church approached. He thought the last name was Anderson but was unwilling to risk being wrong. "What can I get you?"

"Wilson, good to see you. Marg needs another gin, and I think I'll have some scotch. Tonic's hard on my ulcer."

As he poured the drinks, Wil saw Natalie Saylor arrive and stop to greet Ramona. She had traded the business suit and high heels for a denim skirt, flannel shirt with a tied red scarf at the neck, and cowboy boots. "Water with the scotch or soda?"

"Water and ice. Sad news about your fella that died."

Wil filled a glass with ice and more water than scotch. "He'll be missed."

"Jeannie Tilmann over there was in my class. Still looks good, don't she? I always wanted a little of ... heh, Benny. Good to see you."

It upset Wil the man from his church felt at ease openly coveting a married woman. He considered the man as a suspect but only for a moment. The combination of middle age and a soft, pudgy body felt wrong. Wil envisioned Corky's killer as lean and hungry, filled with menace.

Natalie headed his way, her hair no longer pulled back into a bun; a ponytail bounced as she walked. She was much prettier than he had expected. "And what can I get you, Miss Saylor?"

"Natee, please. Gin looks good, but what kind of scotch do you have?"

Wil pulled an unopened bottle up from a cardboard box. "For you, we have Johnnie Walker."

"Just a little water, no ice. Thanks for the invite. This should be fun."

The woman drinks like a man, he thought. Or was it just a prop? "Any chance we can compare notes later?"

A flirtatious smile flashed across her face. "I know just the place."

Wil listened to the next person's drink order but watched as Natee joined a group not far away. His plan to observe and question the guests had sounded good, but making drinks was taking both his time and his attention. It caught Wil by surprise when Dallas slipped in behind him, dropped to one knee, and surveyed the liquor bottles.

"Dallas, I didn't know you'd be here."

"I'm introducing the guest of honor. This Seagram's the best whiskey you got?"

"Best I saw. I don't have any vermouth or bitters."

Dallas took the bottle and stood, removed the cap, and accepted the glass Wil offered. He poured himself three fingers and set the bottle back in the box. "Just a cube'll do."

"Sheriff Farmer wants me to come to his office tomorrow morning. He hung up on me when I asked about the investigation of Corky's death. I'm worried he's going to want to search the office for Corky's photographs."

Dallas leaned close and spoke just above a whisper. "Meet me for breakfast at the hotel at eight. They prepare a decent eggs Benedict and ... Bob's here. Don't worry about the sheriff."

Wil bent over to screw the top on the Seagram's bottle in the cardboard box. He hoped the party would go well to offset Ramona's disappointment over buying both bottles of expensive liquor.

He lost track of Natalie, with a steady run of guests looking for free drinks. Bob's arrival meant a speech was coming, and this crowd understood the wisdom of a fresh drink in hand before the start of any formal remarks.

+ + +

"You must be Mr. Winter, from Reclamation. Welcome. I'm Dallas Dodge and am pleased you could join us."

Winter looked the odd man out in his business suit and blue polka-dot tie, compared with the casual western attire of the other guests. "You are the host then?"

Dallas chuckled, noting the man's crisp diction. "No, my sister-in-law, Ramona Dodge, is the one having the party. But I'm glad you could come. I wanted to make sure you experienced a little Wyoming hospitality during your time with us."

Winter forced a smile. "In a month I'll most likely be in another state. I do not want to experience a Wyoming winter."

Dallas chuckled again and reached out and touched Winter's elbow. "I never had a chance to give my farewells to Jim Haefner. He didn't get sick or have a family emergency, did he?"

Winter took a deep breath. "We needed him at another Pick-Sloan site. The only reason they brought me in to fill his shoes was my engineering background. All that remains is installing and testing the generators and then the completion ceremony."

Dallas could tell this was a half-truth. The man might be an engineer, but the manner in which he repeated the standard reason for Haefner's sudden departure smelled wrong. "What generating system are you using?"

"Westinghouse, along with turbines from Newport News Shipbuilders—efficient and reliable. With minor maintenance and periodic upgrades, the project will generate electricity until the end of the century and beyond."

Dallas had expected technical jargon and not just the names of equipment manufacturers. "Plus the benefits of the water-retention projects."

Winter shrugged and looked toward the bar. "That's not my area."

Any senior staff working with Pick-Sloan projects would know the gospel of water conservation. "I see you've spotted the bar. My nephew Wilson, from the area newspaper, can accommodate you. So if I called your office tomorrow, could you get me Jim's new address? I want to drop him a letter."

Winter looked Dallas in the eye and hesitated a little too long before answering. "Sure thing. I'll tell Diane to expect the call. If you'll excuse me."

Dallas felt certain the story of bringing the project to a finish was a half-truth, at best. Getting caught off-guard about Haefner had produced in Winter an involuntary display of a policeman's eyes. Dallas guessed former military or big-city police force background. His original hunch about the abrupt departure of the gregarious Haefner looked to be correct. Jim Haefner would not have passed on the opportunity for a good-bye party.

Dallas had not lied to Winter about Jim Haefner. The man had been to a few of his Friday afternoon cocktail gatherings, and Virginia would send a cordial letter to the address provided.

He looked about for Bob, hoping his words with Winter had been observed. Plus, he needed to check on whether Bob had details on the exchange of land for his interest in Thornton businesses. The timing of that transaction could not be soon enough.

+ + +

Wil saw his uncle talking with the man in the suit and then wave toward the bar. Unless Ramona's social circle had broadened, he either had come with someone or had been specially invited. The short talk with Dallas led Wil to suspect the latter. The man headed straight from Dallas to the bar.

"Evening. What can I get you to drink?"

"Some scotch would be good."

Wil liked the blue tie with the polka dots. Not the sort of fashion choice men in Wyoming made. "Would you be drinking that with a mixer or ice?"

"Just an ice cube, thanks."

Wil lifted one of the short glasses. "We've got Johnnie Walker, or if you are interested in Canadian whiskey, we've got Seagram's."

"Walker will be good. You uncle says you're with the newspaper. Is that right?"

Wil poured a stout measure into the glass and added a cube. "Yes, I'm the editor. Took over from my father when he died unexpectedly."

"Sorry to hear that. Earlier today I told a deputy sheriff a lie, that I did not know your photographer."

Wil held his breath, not sure what to say.

"I had a drink with him downtown Monday night. He said there were some photographs I should see. He agreed to drop them off at the office on Tuesday, but that was before ..."

Wil glanced left and right and then leaned forward. "Why are you telling me this and who are you?"

"Jack Winter from Reclamation. I'm supervising the Boysen Dam project. I was hoping you may know where those photographs are and how I might get a look at them."

He noticed a pair of men approaching from across the driveway. "I don't, but I'm looking for them. If I find them, how do I reach you?"

"Call the Reclamation office over on Park Street. Like I said, name's Winter, Jack Winter. Thanks for the drink."

Wil took a deep breath and blinked a few times. He remained ignorant about who had killed Corky, but the man walking away could supply missing puzzle pieces.

CHAPTER 16

"Pabst, please."

Wil recognized the face but did not have a name to go with it. He removed the bottle cap and handed the beer to the young fellow with an athletic build. "What'd you think of Bob's speech?"

"Short and to the point. We haven't met, right?"

Wil relaxed, pleased his memory had not failed him. "Wil Dodge. I'm Ramona's son."

"Larry Jacobsen. I like to support other Republicans and meet new folks. A friendly group here."

This was the candidate for sheriff Geri had called a prick. Wil turned and dropped the bottle cap into the trash. "You're running for sheriff. Glad you could come. The turnout's bigger than I expected."

Jacobsen's eyes brightened when Wil made the election connection. "Food's mostly gone, but glad there was at least another beer."

Wil wondered whether the candidate had an agenda or just needed to practice pointless small talk.

"You're with the *Wrangler*, right?"

Wil looked for both Natee and Winter but mainly saw guests leaving in twos and fours. "Yes, I'm editor. I took over when my dad died last year."

"Wasn't the fella found dead yesterday from the *Wrangler*? I hope Gray Farmer can figure out what happened. He uses old-time methods like busting bones and knocking heads. He's a bit sap-happy, if you know what I mean."

Wil understood the intent of Jacobsen's message but not the word "sap." "You said 'sap,' right?"

"Yep, grown-up version of Mrs. Hampton's ruler from third grade. Some leather with lead shot sewn inside. Hurts like hell but don't leave a mark. That's the trouble with these small-town sheriffs—they don't learn new approaches to getting answers."

Over Jacobsen's shoulder, Wil watched Winter follow a couple to the end of the driveway. "We'll be doing a comparison of all the candidates next month. I look forward to talking with you and getting your thoughts on newer methods."

"Hope Gray finds who done it. If you're looking into his death for the paper and need some help, let me know."

Ramona's heels on the concrete signaled her arrival from behind Wil, and he turned in anticipation. When he gestured back to introduce Jacobsen, the patrolman had vanished. Ramona told Wil those wanting to stay would be moved indoors. She asked him to bring in liquor and mixers and assured him the gals from the VFW would clean up the food and collect the cocktail glasses.

+ + +

"So why didn't you tell me that you're the one that dated Freeman?"

Diane brushed her cheek and met his eyes. "I've dated some guys at the office and didn't want them to know."

Al could not help but stare at the tops of Diane's breasts as she rested them on the tabletop of the booth in the bowling alley snack bar. The front of her sweater was low-cut, and he had been right about her looking better with lipstick. "Tell me about Freeman."

"Corky was what I'd call a gentleman. He knew how to treat a woman. He wasn't a husband kind of man, but he made you feel special and was a darn good kisser."

"Why wasn't he husband material?"

"I'd have married him, but he wasn't looking for a wife. What about you? You looking for a wife?"

Al raised his eyebrows. "It takes the right kind of woman to marry a cop, don't you think?"

"I suppose. Hadn't thought about it until meeting you. Are you a good kisser?"

The plan for a simple question session and a Coke with Diane was slipping out of control like all four wheels sliding on loose gravel. His face felt flush with embarrassment. "Did Freeman have any enemies you knew about? Someone who would've wanted to see him dead?"

The question wiped a flirty smirk off her face. "Didn't he die from a car accident? You act like he was killed."

"The sheriff just wants to know about friends, like yourself, and enemies."

Diane leaned back, crossing her arms in a manner that pushed up her breasts. "We dated and kissed and fooled around, but that's all. Small talk. There wasn't any heart-to-heart true confession."

Al liked it better when she was flirting. "How long have you been with Reclamation?"

"Not quite three years. Good pay and benefits, and the work's easy." She started to relax again.

"It looked lonely there to me. Just you and that Winter guy."

Diane reached for her fountain drink and stirred it with the straw. "I've got guys coming and going all day. Winter's there a lot more than Jim Haefner ever was, but Jim had lots going on."

"Did you date Jim too?"

Diane took a sip, tonguing the end of the straw before and after. She was making him wait, flirting again. "A few times. Drinks and dinner, on nights he wasn't meeting someone. But he's off to another project, I guess. But I didn't see any transfer paperwork."

"Do you miss him?"

Diane fingered the straw. "Jim and Corky were alike. They weren't looking for a wife. I think Corky might've looked up to Jim, as an idol or something."

"Why's that?"

"Before Jim got transferred, Corky would ask about him—who Jim was meeting with or having dinner with. I kept his calendar, so it wasn't a big secret."

"When was the last time you saw Corky?"

Diane cradled her chin in her hands, elbows on the table. "Last Thursday night, he took me out to look at the stars. He had this good place for that. I could show it to you. Tonight's good for me."

"I've got a few more questions."

She sat up straight and cocked her head at an angle. "You are off-duty, right? You're not wearing your uniform, so I figured … well, I hoped …"

Al knew it was his turn. Curiosity about Jim Haefner exceeded his interest in Diane. She was appealing, in her own way, but he wanted a girlfriend a bit cuter and more docile. And the girl should not suggest going to a spot to park. That was a man's job.

But if he expected to learn more about Jim Haefner and Reclamation, the direct route involved Diane. As Diane reached for her purse, he quickly slid out his side of the booth and extended a hand to the girl.

"I like the strong silent type too."

CHAPTER 17

"I came here during high school. Most boys wanted to stay in the car, but a few would walk with me." Natee had driven Wil to Mountain View Cemetery in her Jeepster and had hopped out once the parking brake was set.

Wil quickly grasped that she had used the spot for necking, but for him it held a different meaning. "I came here too. First on my bike and later in my car."

"What brought you? A funeral, or just biking around?"

He thought of taking her hand as they walked, wanting intimacy with this sophisticated woman, but it seemed forward. "Just found it with a buddy. I liked the view of the mountains. And all these graves make it a holy place, like a church, a good place to pray. Does that sound odd?"

"A little."

Wil led them toward the western edge of the cemetery, near the highway leading to the airport, the same road where Corky had been discovered. The near-full moon, still below the eastern horizon, colored the snowy ridgeline of the distant Wind River Mountains in a bluish tint. Only the lightest of breezes cooled the night air, a gift on a hillside often pounded by strong westerly winds, with pines trained to lean east.

"I hope you didn't feel I abandoned you back at the party. Making drinks took more time than I thought."

She slipped her hand through his elbow and pulled him close. "You're the introvert, not me. I felt like a butterfly sampling nectar

105

from all the flowers. You can invite me to these kinds of gatherings anytime you want."

Wil doubted another opportunity would arise anytime soon but hoped he could find another reason to get together. "So what did you learn among the flowers?"

"The friends of Bob also like Larry Jacobsen. But I don't know if they share contributors. One of my missions was to learn where Larry's getting his campaign funds from, since he's spending more than a highway patrolman can afford. Bob Thornton might be one of Larry's contributors, but Bob's tight with a buck."

"And what about those who aren't fans of Bob?"

"Mostly Democrats and convenient Republicans."

Wil stopped and turned toward Natalie. "What's a convenient Republican?"

"Convenient Republicans are like convenient Christians. They don't really believe in the party or the church, but belong for business or social purposes." She pulled at his arm, the way a rider coaxes a horse with a kick to the ribs. The concept of convenient Christians was one Wil had decoded without knowing the term.

"What other missions did you have?"

"I was hoping to find out more about Wilson Dodge ... see if he remembered me from junior high square dancing."

Wil stopped in his tracks. "I remember going to square dances starting in grade school, but I'm not sure I ever saw you there."

"I was older than you and a little tall for my age. We never danced, but you always stared at me."

He smiled and took short steps forward. There had been an older girl he found appealing, though he lacked the vocabulary or insight to identify her as seductive. "I do remember ..."

"Tell me what it was like with Ramona as a mother."

"She isn't a homemaker. Taught me to boil water for hot dogs, but that's about it. At college I had to send my clothes out to be washed and pressed, but I could bid and play bridge as good as anyone. And she taught me how to make a number of the drinks in *Old Mr. Boston Bartender's Guide*, so if this newspaper thing doesn't work out, I can always pour cocktails and serve beer."

"And if Clayton hadn't died, what would you be doing now?"

"The plan was graduate school at the University of Chicago, but it wasn't a good fit. Maybe I would've stayed with the *Chicago Daily* as a reporter, but Chicago's an evil town. What brought you back?"

"I graduated from a women's college in New York City and took a job. Chicago could learn a trick or two from New York about heartlessness. A woman can easily get lost and forgotten there. My heart belongs in Wyoming, where a gal can get respect."

"And here you are, the county clerk."

She stopped and turned them back toward the east and the dots of lights marking Riverton's western boundary. "County clerk today, something better tomorrow. We were supposed to be comparing notes. What did you learn, young Mr. Boston?"

Wil had decided even before she asked the question to confide in Natee, although he knew little about her. "I met who could've been the last person to see Corky Freeman alive—Jack Winter, from the Bureau of Reclamation."

"He was the suit and tie, right?" Miss Natee did not miss much. Winter had been at the party less than thirty minutes, but she had spotted him.

"That's the guy. He had a drink with Corky Monday night. Said Corky wanted to show him some photos."

"Not too surprising since he was a photographer."

"But Winter never got to see them. Corky was going to deliver them to him yesterday. But he was found dead before …"

Natalie swung Wil around like a gate and headed back toward her Jeepster. "Do you think his death had something to do with them?"

"Maybe. I'd have a better idea if I could see them. I've looked but not found."

Natalie stopped in front of the Jeepster and turned Wil so that his back rested against the bumper and grill. She leaned forward, kissed him on the lips, and pushed her hips against him. He worried the kisses and closeness would make him hard, but there was no room to retreat.

"Don't try being a hero, Wilson Dodge. It's not easy for a girl to find a guy who'll walk with her in the graveyard."

+ + +

It was almost ten o'clock by the time Wil parked his pickup behind the apartments. He had grabbed beers, ice, and a bucket along with the Johnnie Walker after Natee dropped him at Ramona's house. Wil wanted a few drinks with Cecil before bed, although his neighbor would not be able to keep Natee Saylor, and her lips and hips, out of his thoughts for long.

The light was on in Cecil's kitchen. A holler of his name was all it took to bring Cecil from the one-bedroom. The slender frame and the shine in Cecil's eyes reminded Wil of a well-used but highly polished spring, taut with an appetite for action.

Moonlight bathed the picnic table in the patchy grass on the southeast corner of the apartments. Wil set the bucket of iced beers, the scotch, two glasses, and a bottle opener on the flat wooden surface. Different tenants used the picnic table during the day, but in the evening Cecil and Wil claimed control of the spot to sit and talk.

Cecil opened a cloth tobacco pouch. "What's the celebration?"

"Leftovers from a party at my mom's."

"Thank ya, Missus Ramona Dodge, on behalf o' dry cowboys everywhere." Cecil raised his beer bottle and clinked it against Wil's. "And what kinda hooch you got?"

"Scotch."

The cowboy wrinkled his nose as he sprinkled tobacco flakes onto a rolling paper. "The taste reminds me of a campfire. Always wondered how they got that smoke in it."

Wil poured a fat finger into the glasses and recapped the scotch. Cecil licked the seam of the hand-rolled cigarette. They sat for a moment looking at the night sky, taking in the quiet. A fresh breeze from the southwest carried a hint of cooler fall air. Leaves rustled in the nearby trees, and Cecil took a couple short sniffs.

"Deer down by the river. Smell 'em?"

Wil turned toward the south and the Wind River. "Nope."

Cecil sparked a wooden match using his thumbnail to light the cigarette. "You spend enough time outdoors, you pick up the smell of deer, elk, coyote, bear. Most times, the cattle smell it 'fore you and get restless. Gotta talk to 'em, sing a lullaby, keep 'em relaxed. Let 'em know they're safe."

The description reminded Wil of the stories he had read by Louis L'Amour of cowboys on the range. "Suppose so."

Cecil leaned closer to Wil. "Cattle ain't like people. Don't have any thoughts to spook 'em. The smell of 'nother animal'll do it though. And just like people, one skittish cow can set the herd a'movin'."

They sat watching the moon and stars, drinking beer and scotch, sometimes talking, sometimes not, until around midnight when the beer ran out.

Cecil spit into the grass. "I'm gonna sleep good tonight. Cool September air and a belly full of pain med'cine. Hope my snorin' don't wake nobody."

Wil chuckled and drank the last bit of his beer.

"One of the sheriff's boys came by today, askin' about ya. Asking if you's home Monday night. I told 'im."

The revelation surprised Wil, and he wanted to remember to tell Dallas. Even though his uncle had said not to worry about the interview with the sheriff, he felt vulnerable—the same way he felt insecure when it came to Natee Saylor.

"What do you know about my dad's death?" The question squirted out, unplanned.

"Been 'bout a year ago. Saw him out walkin' maybe a week 'fore he died. Acted lost in his thinkin'. Hadn't been in the hospital I knowed of. Not sure I ever heard what he died of." Cecil poured a little scotch into the empty glasses. "Good man, your dad. Pro'ly worked too hard. That's what some people say kilt him."

Cecil raised his glass. "To good men who died too young. 'Cause the sons o' bitches just live forever."

DAY 3

Thursday
September 4, 1952

CHAPTER 18

Alone in the office, again, with yesterday's cold coffee, a half-empty pack of cigarettes, and no Wil. It was only Thursday but the second time this week Geri had arrived to a dark and empty office. And Monday had been a holiday. Coming to work meant talking and teasing with Wil. It was her reason for getting out of bed.

Since Geri's husband had passed, months before Clayton's death, the companionship of the workplace had become the antidote to her nights of sorry solitude. The conversation of the office was still a poor substitute for her best friend, who had listened and cared about and loved her. Clayton had cared but had his own family—and girlfriends. Solitary confinement could not have been worse than the days after Clayton's death and before Wil's arrival. Too many cigarettes, too much gin, and an open pit of dark thoughts.

Geri did not consider herself superstitious, so she pushed the troubling premonition aside, an echo of the news Wil had carried in about Corky Freeman two days before. Raised a Catholic, with a mother ready to find fault and assign blame, she found guilt from impure thoughts to be a constant threat. Geri's mother might be dead, but her voice could still be heard.

"God, grant that Wil comes by the office before seeing Grayson Farmer. Amen."

Geri glanced at the open manila folder on Wil's desk, surrounded by photographs. Why had he left it out for her to see and be reminded? She shoved the Hiroshima material and folder into his file drawer, toward the back, just like a year earlier. She never wanted to see it again.

Throughout July 1951 her officemate had picked through the folder, often leaving the *New Yorker* open-faced on his desk. Curious, she had read where he left it lay and then was sorry she had. The anniversary of Hiroshima had been a time of torment for Clayton. He had struggled with his 1951 editorial on the bombing, started but discarded and, like the others, never published.

Ramona had been wrong the other day, worried about Wil growing up. Geri had done more than her share to protect the boy's innocence while Ramona raised him in a world of restaurant meals and magazines. But once he was away from home, neither had been able to shield him. Was Wil's breakdown in the first year of college her fault? Or had Wil become as obsessed with and guilt-stricken over the atom bomb as his father?

The four short rings of her telephone broke the spell of loss and guilt. What emergency could there be today?

+ + +

Dallas finished adding cream to his second cup of coffee as Wil arrived at the Wind River Hotel's private dining room. The swirling spoon created a caramel-colored vortex within the ivory of the china cup. He enjoyed his morning coffee almost as much as the first manhattan of the day.

"Did I see you leave with Miss Saylor last night?"

Wil smiled but said nothing, snatching the linen napkin from the table as he took his seat.

Dallas raised his coffee cup, cradling the bottom with his left hand. "What did you think of Bob's speech?"

"Bob Thornton might be dating my mother, but I think he'd be a terrible city councilman. Just because he knows how to make money doesn't mean he's smart or a good person. I thought we were going to talk about my meeting with the sheriff—figure out what to do if he wants to search the files."

Dallas savored the flavors before swallowing. The trouble with china was it cooled the coffee too quickly. "Gray would need a warrant to search the files, and no judge in this part of Wyoming will sign it without checking with me. And Gray is not that thorough."

"So I don't need to worry."

"Saw you talking with Larry Jacobsen. Did he make you any promises?"

"No, but he said Gray Farmer was old-fashioned and something about a sap. Do I need to be worried about getting beat up?"

Dallas smiled reflexively and set the china cup back on the saucer. "I hope not, but you might prepare yourself to witness his desk get a solid thumping."

The waitress appeared and filled Wil's coffee cup from a polished shiny silver pot. "I've already ordered for us, but if you want juice or fruit, tell Marian."

Getting no instructions, Marian left the room. Wil raised the cup of coffee and blew across the top. "I saw you talking to the guy from Reclamation, Winter, before he came over for a drink. What do you know about him?"

Dallas chewed his tongue for a moment. "Says he is an engineer sent to finish the Boysen Dam project. Why?"

"When he learned I was with the *Wrangler*, he talked of lying to Deputy Nelson and having a beer with Corky on Monday night. My photographer promised to deliver some photographs. But then Corky was found dead, and Winter wondered if I had them."

"Do you?"

Wil shook his head and leaned forward. "That's not the point. Do I tell Farmer about Winter? He might've been the last person to see Corky alive."

The swinging door from the kitchen whooshed, and Dallas set to nibbling on his tongue as he cataloged this new fragment of information. He watched as Marian set the plates with eggs Benedict and fried potatoes onto the table. Dallas knew her departure would be quieter than a whisper.

"As I said before, tell the truth. Report your conversation, but try not to speculate. And let Gray figure out for himself the importance of Winter. Did anyone overhear you?"

Wil looked at his plate and then up at Dallas. "No, but I told Natee about it. How do you eat this?"

"I like to cut it into pieces, although I have known some to treat it like a sandwich, but not gracefully. Be sure to tell him about Miss Saylor if he asks, but you are under no obligation to mention our discussion or this meeting. We are protected by attorney-client privilege."

Dallas cut a swath from the yellow-sauced concoction and bisected it into a bite-sized piece. Leaning forward, he pocketed a morsel in his mouth and chewed. "The Hollandaise does not compare to the Brown Palace in Denver or even the Plains in Cheyenne, but it is decent for Riverton."

Wil duplicated his uncle's sawing actions. "Tastes like an egg sandwich with bad butter. The Atomic's got this without all the butter and ... and lemon."

"Perhaps, but privacy there is impossible, and I doubt the eggs are poached."

Wil stabbed another piece and held it over his plate, sauce dripping. "What else'll Farmer want to know? And how do I get him to tell me how Corky died?"

"No need to ask. It seems Dr. Owen examined your man. Mr. Freeman died from a blow to the back of the head, as reported to Raymond Winslow. Grayson may ask if you have Freeman's photos or where you think they may be."

Wil scraped the buttery sauce off the top of the poached eggs and moved meat, yoke, and egg white onto the potatoes. "I don't, but what if I find them?"

Dallas let the flavors blend as he chewed, closing his eyes momentarily. "I thought you might enjoy this treat. Your father was quite fond of eggs Benedict. If you discover those photographs, if they exist, it would be best to bring them to me. As for his questions, he'll want to know your movements Monday night."

"He already sent Nelson to the apartments, asking my neighbors about that night. I had a drink with Ramona before she went out with Bob, then a sandwich at the Bluebird on Federal, about the only place open other than the VFW. And a few beers with Cecil before going to bed."

"Anyone to confirm that after, say, midnight?"

Wil studied his plate. "Not unless Cecil had trouble sleeping."

The men continued their breakfast, Dallas enjoying the Hollandaise and Wil appearing content to mix potatoes with the eggs and meat. Marian, as if she had been waiting for a pause in conversation, appeared and refilled the coffee cups. Wil asked for jam to spread on the orphaned English muffin.

Wil set his elbow on the table and raised his index finger. "Can Farmer figure out who killed Corky?"

Dallas creamed his coffee and studied his nephew. "He may not discover who or why it happened, but that does not mean he will not make an arrest. It's an election year."

"Which reminds me, is there a reason the *Wrangler* shouldn't endorse a candidate for sheriff?"

"Your father had the rare urge to support someone on the pages of the newspaper but usually saw the wisdom in merely collecting fees for advertisements. Picking a side can make a short-term friend but a long-term enemy."

Wil set his fork on the plate and slid back his chair. "Did Farmer investigate Clayton's death?"

Dallas kept chewing, keeping his expression indifferent. "No, but that's a conversation for another day."

"Can you at least tell me what medical condition he died from?"

Dallas matched the stare of his nephew and silently counted to three. "As I said, a conversation for another day."

Wil placed his napkin on the plate and slid his chair back farther. "That day needs to come soon, or I'll be calling Ray Winslow myself."

+ + +

"Where were you Monday night? From ten o'clock on?"

"Probably the same place you were."

117

Grayson watched the eyes of the Dodge boy. "I was in bed with my wife."

"Me too, except your wife wasn't there."

He saw the hint of a smirk on the kid's face. Grayson grabbed the exposed tail of his sap from beneath a stack of papers and slammed it on his desk, watching Dodge flinch. "This ain't no joke!"

"Larry told me about your sap."

The mention of his election opponent caught Grayson off-guard. "Larry Jacobsen? When'd you see him?"

"Last night. But to answer your first question, home in bed, alone."

Grayson's hand relaxed on the leather grip of the sap. "So you got no alibi."

"My neighbor may be able to confirm my story. His name's Cecil. But a deputy's already been around to talk with him."

Grayson made a note of the name. "When'd you see Jacobsen? And who else?"

"Last night. I tended bar for my mother. She had friends over to meet Bob Thornton. He's running for city council, but you probably knew that. There were maybe forty or fifty people, but I don't know all their names. My uncle was there too; you could ask him.

"You should know about one guest. The supervisor of the Boysen Dam project, Jack Winter, told me he'd had a drink with Corky on Monday night. Said Corky was going to show him some photographs."

Grayson had planned to ask about Boysen Dam based on Nelson's interviews, but Dodge seemed one step ahead of him. "He say anything else?"

"Winter wanted to know if I had the pictures, but I don't. In fact, Gordon Blakeslee thinks Corky was working on a project about Boysen Dam for the *Wrangler*, but I don't know a thing about it."

Grayson asked when the reporter had talked with Blakeslee, and Dodge told him about visiting Blakeslee Tuesday morning, before Nelson had interviewed the man. Was the Dodge boy a suspect, or just a nosy smart aleck? "Anyone else know about that?"

"I did tell Natalie Saylor."

Grayson reached over and slammed the sap on the desk. "Why'd you do that?"

"She was at the party, and we talked afterward."

"You tell anyone else?"

Grayson saw the boy hesitate before he shook his head no. This latest information moved the county clerk from a possible suspect to a likely one. She had almost admitted having sex with the dead boy, and now she knew of his connection with Winter. "Who else did Winter talk to?"

"I was too busy making drinks to see."

"You know a James, or Jim, Haefner?"

Puzzlement appeared on Dodge's face for the first time. "No. Who's he?"

Grayson resisted the impulse to show his authority with another rap of the sap. "I'm asking the questions."

"I don't want to tell you how to do your job, but Winter might have some useful information on what Corky Freeman was doing late on Monday night."

Grayson fixed his gaze on the reporter. "There's a problem with that. Got a call from highway patrol a little bit ago. They found him dead. In his car. Partway down a dirt road."

The puzzled expression returned to Dodge's face. Grayson raised his hand to signal "stop" before the boy could start asking questions. "That was off the record. Federal Bureau's going to investigate. Try asking them your questions."

Grayson nurtured his suspicion over how Larry Jacobsen had just happened to find Winter—Jacobsen, his opponent, who Dodge said had been at the same party as Winter the night before.

Dodge leaned forward and tilted his head to the side. "Out west of town? On the same road as Corky?"

"I shouldn't tell you, but no. East of town."

He watched as the Dodge kid worked at fitting the new information together.

"Tell me what you know. I can't help you once the feds get here."

Dodge held his hands up, as if surrendering. "I've told you everything. And why would I need help?"

"Two men dead, both connected to you."

Dodge sat staring at the desk. Grayson waited, knowing the boy had not been entirely truthful. Best to let him speak first.

"This is a waste of time, yours and mine. I need to get back to … but I want to hear what you say caused Corky's death. And I should probably know how Winter died, for the newspaper."

Instinct told him to use the sap and loosen the boy's tongue. But Dodge did have a good point; he needed to meet Nelson and Jacobsen east of town before the FBI man appeared. Any other suspect would spend the next half hour in a holding cell, smarting from the kiss of leather and lead, sweating out the next question session. But this was the nephew of Dallas Dodge, and he would have to let the boy go. He waved the kid away and refused to offer any more information.

CHAPTER 19

"FBI on the way, ETA one hour, over."

Deputy Albert Nelson sat in the driver's seat of his radio car and depressed the button on his microphone. "Ten-four, Base. North Deputy 1 over and out." Al had arrived at the scene within ten minutes of the dispatch and identified Winter from their meeting the previous day. His radio call into base had started the notification of the Federal Bureau of Investigation.

Highway patrolman Larry Jacobsen leaned on the doorframe of Al's car, looking south toward Riverton. "Guess we've got some time. This one same as the other?"

Al knew Jacobsen was fishing for information on the Freeman death. As the first person on the scene, Jacobsen had every reason to stay and answer the questions of the FBI agent. But as a deputy sheriff, Al needed to keep the area secure, and an hour was too long to play the strong silent type with the man who might be his boss in a few months.

"This guy was shot. Freeman didn't have a scratch on him." Winter's shirt was the color of dried blood, making it look like a gunshot wound, although neither officer could define the location of an entry or exit. Jacobsen had wanted to get a closer look, but Al had insisted they leave the car and occupant untouched until the FBI appeared.

Larry ran his tongue over his upper front teeth, as if loosening a bit of trapped food. "That's odd, shooting one but not the other."

"And there ain't any bike tracks. Out west there were boot prints and bicycle wheel tracks. Don't see that here."

Larry squinted and bobbed his head. "We got big old boot tracks. I'd guess maybe a twelve. You saw how they aren't the same, right? Heel deep on one print but not the others. Like they was too big."

Al had reached the same conclusion as Jacobsen, having examined the impressions in the loose dirt earlier. He suspected Sheriff Farmer would have been just as observant. "You ever have a case with the FBI?"

"Not a case, but I've met the guy from Casper. Not the sort you'd want to have coffee and shoot the bull with."

"You ever think of joining the FBI?"

Jacobsen pushed back from the door. "Nope, not my kind of life."

"I always wondered what it'd be like with WHP. Seems like you guys have a lot of freedom and nobody looking over your shoulder. Or do I have that wrong?"

"There's paperwork, like any cop job. The problem is the patrol's ladder up the ranks is short, and there's lots of guys with more seniority."

Al swung both legs out of his car and stood. "What's the appeal of being sheriff? Living next to the jail ain't for me. And I'm not sure Mrs. Farmer thinks much of it, cooking for the prisoners and deputies."

Jacobsen removed his hat and patted along his brow with the cuff of his uniform shirt. He looked toward the car down the dirt lane. "Do you think the guy that killed this fellow's the one that did your boy? Freeman, right?"

"I'd leave it to the sheriff to sort that out. He's the one going to be quoted in the newspaper."

Jacobsen set his hat back in place and flexed his chest forward, hands at his hips. "Are you saying Gray doesn't ask your opinion about such things? I'd want to know what my chief deputy thought."

"I'm just sayin', a sheriff's got to decide where to point the investigation. And Winter don't belong to either of us, but the FBI."

"Thanks, Chief Deputy Nelson, you've given me an idea."

Al feared he had unintentionally lit a firecracker and wondered if it would go off in his hand.

+ + +

"I don't know if I should kiss you or slap your face. I got a call about another person found dead, and you weren't in the office. Why didn't you stop before seeing the sheriff?"

Wil rested his forearms on the paneling that lined the path to the printing work area. He explained oversleeping and the breakfast at the Wind River with Dallas. After learning of Winter, he had rushed to the office to share the latest development.

"What in the hell is going on? Who's Winter?"

"In-charge guy at Boysen. I met him at Ramona's party last night."

Geri grabbed her pack of cigarettes. "I thought Jim Haefner was head man out there."

"So that's who Haefner is. Farmer asked me about him, but I didn't know the man. The odd part is they found Winter almost the same as Corky—alone in his car, down a dirt road off the highway."

Geri tapped a cigarette on the glass of her desktop. "I thought you were being melodramatic the other morning, talking about solving your own murder. And then the call and ..."

Wil envisioned front-page coverage of Winter's death. "We should put out a special edition about this, a four- or six-pager. This can't wait a week. We can update the articles on Thursday with any new facts. And we'll need comments and photos. How many ads would we need?"

"At least a page. But we'd need to work the weekend, and there's Corky's funeral on Saturday."

Wil moved to the open space between the front door and counter. "Call Jan and get her going on the ads. Tell her two pages. I'll interview Farmer and Winslow—and the FBI agent if I can find him. Do you know any of the gals at Reclamation who'd tell us something about Winter?"

Geri stood to face him, unlit cigarette in her left hand. "Why can't we wait for Thursday?"

"A special's the only thing that makes sense. Gray Farmer hasn't a clue on how to solve either murder. Jacobsen told me he'd help if we wanted to investigate. And we can insert a story on Corky's funeral."

Sparking the lighter, Geri lit her cigarette. "At least let me call Dallas and see what he says."

"See if you can get some quotes from him. I'm going for photos of Corky's car, and then I'll see if they'll let me shoot Winter's car. In between I'll stop by Gordon's place."

Wil moved to his desk and picked up a fresh steno pad and then headed toward the pressroom.

"What'd you think of Natalie Saylor?"

Wil stopped and spun to face Geri. "She's something else. Why didn't you—"

"Be careful, Wilson Dodge. Natee's broken a lot of hearts."

Wil grinned, recognizing that the mention of Natee sent a surge of energy through his system. "Thanks, Mom. Gotta go."

+ + +

Grayson pulled to a stop north of Riverton on Highway 26, thinking the party could now begin. Nelson's Ford from the sheriff's department and a highway patrol Chevy, pointed nose to nose, blocked the one-lane dirt path, with a parked car in the distance. A black Ford with US government plates sat on the opposite shoulder, pointed toward Riverton. A station wagon from the Winslow Funeral Home was parked behind Nelson's car.

Grayson joined the four-person cluster around Nelson's car. He introduced himself to the FBI agent, who barely gave him a glance; the agent was busy making notes, using the hood of Nelson's car as a desk.

The sheriff turned to his deputy. "Nelson, you tell 'im about the other body?"

The other men looked at the deputy. "We hadn't got to that yet. Special Agent Oakes just got here from Casper."

The FBI agent remained focused on his notes, confirming Grayson's suspicion that he would not like the man from Casper. Grayson turned his head and spit toward the pavement. "Tell 'im."

Nelson shifted his attention to Special Agent Oakes. "A couple days ago, one of our deputies found a fella dead in his car, off the road just like this. Out west of town."

The FBI man straightened up. "Not a federal employee, I hope."

Grayson looked at the agent's eyes, shaded by the brim of his businessman's hat. "Newspaper fellow."

Nelson sidestepped closer to Grayson. "Photographer. He wasn't shot, though. Broken neck. Have to wonder if they're connected."

Grayson felt the gaze of the special agent and turned his head and spit.

Agent Oakes picked up his notepad and turned to Jacobsen. "You were first here, right? Show me what you found."

The FBI man in his dark suit and street shoes followed Jacobsen down the lane toward the car.

The teenager from the Winslow Funeral Home moved to the spot the agent had left. "Are you going to want me to drive the body to Casper?"

Grayson looked toward the men walking to the car. "Don't know. You wait in the car till we sort this out." Grayson turned to Nelson. "Winslow been called?"

Nelson waited until the kid reached the Winslow station wagon. "I didn't call him, but I'd bet the operator let him know."

Grayson watched as the two other men neared the parked car. "Curious Larry should find the guy."

"Why's that?"

"Jacobsen was at a party last night. Same as Winter. Did you say he was shot?"

Nelson turned toward Grayson. "Larry walked me down, and we looked at him, without opening the doors or anything. We could see his shirt was all reddish-brown. Looked like dried blood."

"Better radio for Winslow to get out here."

Grayson watched as the agent and Larry circled the car. The FBI man would probably want a workroom and interrogation space

125

at the Riverton sheriff's office. The thought of a federal agent in his station displeased Grayson, but at least he could keep track of the man. There were limits to his willingness to cooperate, especially with the number of federal offices around town.

The agent motioned for Grayson to come to the car. Walking down the lane, Grayson decided that having the FBI in the substation meant he would need to spend part of every day in Riverton. Janet would not like that. But there had been no pleasing her lately. At least Winter was not his problem.

CHAPTER 20

Wil knocked on Gordon Blakeslee's door, concerned about the condition of the retiree. Two days before, Gordon had been drinking whiskey before noon. He knocked again.

The door opened, and Gordon gave him a quick glance. "Don't want any."

Wil stood on the porch as the closed door, confused about the reception. He knocked again. "Gordon, it's Wilson Dodge. You told me to come by."

The door opened again, and Gordon had a half-smile. "Wil, didn't recognize you. Come on in."

"Thanks for letting Geri know about Saturday. It'll be on the front page."

The older man gave a nod, but his facial expression seemed flat.

"We were talking about Corky the other day."

"He ain't been here yet, and I'm hungry. He's supposed to come for dinner and supper. But he's not been here."

Wil looked for the glass of whiskey but saw none. "Gordon, can I get a glass of water?"

"Help yourself."

Wil walked into the kitchen, followed by Pudgie, and saw a clear table and a few dishes in the rack beside the sink. The food and water dishes for the dog were empty. He filled the water dish, and Pudgie lapped at it.

"Is it okay if I give Pudgie some dog food?"

"I suppose. Corky does that. Are you going to make dinner?"

Wil lifted the empty bowl, and Pudgie moved beside a lower cabinet door. Inside Wil found a lidded can and scooped dry food into the bowl. "We're going out to eat. How's a roast beef sandwich sound? With gravy?"

Wil helped Gordon to his pickup and drove toward downtown. "We're going to the Atomic Café. You been there lately?"

Gordon nodded. Wil noticed the retiree closely inspecting the houses and yards along the way, as if seeing them for the first time. He thought it odd Corky had never mentioned the routine visits to Gordon's and wondered whether Geri had heard of the practice. At the Atomic, after he had settled Gordon into a booth, Wil ordered two hot beef sandwiches and glasses of milk from Rose.

"Gordon, when was the last time I talked with you?"

The older man twisted his neck around and looked toward the counter. "About a week ago. Maybe two."

"Did you read the paper last week?"

Gordon half-closed his eyes. "Yes."

"What did you think of the election coverage?"

"Pretty good. Why?"

It had been a trick question. The last election report had run after the primary in May. Gordon clearly suffered from memory problems. "How long you had trouble remembering things?"

Gordon nodded, looked about the table, and then looked back toward the kitchen. Wil could see Rose on the way with plates. The mission to ask again about Corky's photos had taken a detour.

+ + +

When Geri called the Reclamation office, a young woman named Diane answered. When the pair discovered Geri knew the girl's mother, Diane gave the office version of the sudden death of Jack Winter. Geri filled two pages of notes as the girl gushed about Winter and the upset it had created. Diane reported two long-distance calls from Washington, DC, and said they were sending an official to town.

Diane agreed to call back with any breaking news without the least bit of persuasion. Although the girl had not asked Geri to keep her identity a secret, Geri planned on a "little bird" as her source if Wil asked.

Jan had jumped at the assignment of selling advertising for the special, and Bernie had reluctantly agreed to look for volunteers to work part of the weekend. Dallas had mentioned libel three times during their phone call but had voiced no objection to a special edition.

The immediate list of duties completed, Geri shuffled through Wil's pile of photographs on his desk, looking for people she did not know at the VFW ice cream social. If Winter had been there, then Corky might have captured him on film.

When the front door opened, she looked up expecting to see Wil but instead recognized Larry Jacobsen from his campaign ads. The highway patrolman removed his hat and approached the front counter.

"You're Larry Jacobsen, running for sheriff, right?"

The young man puffed his chest out and smiled. "Yes, ma'am, I am."

"The photo in your ad doesn't do you justice. I'm Geri Murphy. Nice to meet you."

Jacobsen raised an eyebrow. "Maybe I should have you manage my campaign. Is Mr. Dodge around?"

Geri stepped to her desk and took her seat. "He's out working on a story. Can I help you?"

"I spoke with Mr. Dodge last night, about the fella they found dead, Freeman. And this morning, I found another one out east of town. I shouldn't be telling you, but an FBI man from Casper's come to investigate."

Geri put on her most sincere expression, even though Larry had not reported anything she did not already know. "The radio didn't have any details. What happened?"

"I was going to Dubois and saw this car just parked out in the weeds. When I got there, I saw it was a road of sorts. Just two ruts. But I 'membered hearing about Freeman the other day, so I was careful going to look it over and found the dead fella. Radioed in, and Deputy Nelson came out. Identified the dead guy as working for Reclamation—Winter, I think."

Geri waited for her silence to prompt him to reveal more, but Larry seemed content with the few brief facts. She thought empathy might prime the pump. "Tough way to start your morning."

"I don't have the p's and q's of that other death, involving your picture taker, but I have to wonder if they're connected. Seems odd, two deaths close together, both found in cars like that."

Geri leaned forward and gave the hint of a pucker, Larry giving her his complete attention. "What do you think, Larry?"

The patrolman's eyes widened at the question. "If I was sheriff, I'd be deciding if the two are connected. Sheriff Farmer's the one with all the information, and he's working with the FBI."

"Can I quote you on that?"

A quick grin appeared on candidate Larry's face. "I suppose. I'd be making a statement about it, if I were sheriff."

Geri made a note on her pad and cleared her throat. "But what happened? What'd you see? Did he drive off the road and roll over? Was it murder? Or suicide? Or …"

Larry squinted for a moment. "The car was fine, just driven down the lane a piece. Don't quote me on this next part, but I think Winter was shot. Didn't see a gun inside, but doesn't mean there wasn't one. So maybe murder, like the one a couple days ago."

Geri nodded, scratching a few more steno-symbols on her pad. "Larry, I think you're right. Mr. Dodge may want to talk with you, and he needs to get a statement from Gray Farmer and this FBI man. You catch his name?"

Jacobsen frowned and shook his head no. "Say, I still need to get to Dubois. Ma'am." The highway patrolman rolled his hips as he walked to the door, in what Geri considered a swagger. He positioned his hat before turning toward her with a grin and a wink, and then opened the door.

Geri thought to herself that Larry would not make a very good reporter. How could he not remember the name of the FBI man? She took a cigarette from the pack and lit it. "Larry may not be a reporter, but he knows how to plant a story to embarrass his opponent. Maybe on the front page with a photo."

CHAPTER 21

Wil braked the pickup at his usual parking spot behind the apartments and tapped the horn twice. Cecil poked his head out and then hobbled down the porch steps one at a time. Wil waited until his neighbor was beside the cab before speaking. "How are you with two-leggeds?"

Cecil set a foot on the running board and rested a hand on his thigh. "Depends on how young or how old they are. Why?"

Wil explained his discovery of a memory-impaired Gordon and the need for some companionship as well as help with meals. He did not believe Gordon required any overnight monitoring, just daylight work.

"I never did much chuck wagon duty, but if he ain't a picky eater, I'll be good enough."

He told Cecil of his plan to stop at the grocery store for supplies and said he hoped Cecil could begin duties that afternoon.

"Is he good bein' alone till then?"

Wil chuckled. "I took him out for a hot beef sandwich and ice cream. Both Gordon and his dog are taking a nap. I forgot to mention Pudgie."

"A biscuit in the pocket'd be useful for makin' friends with the four-legged. Maybe you could get a few."

Wil depressed the clutch and slipped into low gear. "I'll pay you for your time, so think about what you'll need."

"You can buy me a beef sandwich one of these days; otherwise, this here's missionary work." Cecil stepped back and slapped the side of the cab.

Wil eased onto the dirt street and turned at the corner to head to the Wyoming Market on Main. Halfway to the store, Wil realized bringing Cecil along would have been a good idea since he did not cook. The boys would have to make do with the items Gordon had on hand plus whatever he added.

Wil was glad Cecil had not asked how long the missionary assignment would last. He recalled that Gordon had a brother in Iowa, but he had no idea of other family. For all Wil knew, the brother could suffer from his own memory problems or be dead. A call to Dallas might be a good idea.

After gathering the groceries, Wil picked up Cecil, and they found Gordon and Pudgie on the front porch. The dog sniffed at the stranger before taking Cecil's treat and settling in the shade to crunch on it.

"Gordon, this is Cecil, and he's going to help you with meals."

Gordon nodded and rocked on the metal chair on the porch. "What about Corky?"

"I was here the day before yesterday, the day the radio said he was found dead in his car out west of town. Do you remember that?"

The retiree stopped rocking, and tears slipped down his face. "Guess I forgot. Terrible thing."

"I should've stopped yesterday and checked on you. I'm sorry. I know Corky was the star pupil of the Blakeslee School of Photography."

Gordon nodded and restarted the back-and-forth of his chair. "Terrible thing."

Wil and Cecil exchanged a glance. "We brought over some groceries. We'll put 'em away in the kitchen."

Cecil took the paper bag, Wil the cardboard box, and the pair separated the items between shelves and the refrigerator. The temporary cook spotted a few missing items, and Wil started a list.

Back on the porch, Pudgie had taken a position beside Gordon. Cecil walked down the steps and along the front of the porch, hopping up to sit on the other side of the dog. "You like pancakes?"

Gordon leaned forward and nodded. "Scrambled eggs and pancakes. Yes, sir."

Cecil caught Wil's eye. "I think we've got supper figured out."

"Gordon, did Corky leave anything with you he wanted me to have?"

Gordon leaned forward again. "Is it time for cocktails?"

"Almost, but not quite yet. Did Corky leave a box with a padlock here for me?"

The older man slid back on his chair and grinned. "That was you had a beef sandwich with me. Yes, that box. Down in the darkroom. You know where that's at?"

"I did have a beef sandwich with you, and you ate some ice cream too. I'll get that box then."

Wil climbed the steps back onto the porch and slipped inside, where he took the stairs down to the basement and Gordon's darkroom. He hoped this was not a wild-goose chase. At the door of a small enclosed space, he found the switch for the safelight, and a red light went on over the door. Wil entered, shut the door, and pushed past the blackout curtains.

The low-wattage bulbs of the basement made the visual adjustment to the red glow of the safelight short work. The oblong room featured more length than width and permitted side-by-side work at the enlarger on one side and the developing counter on the other. He checked beneath the counters first, but no box. The shelving above the counters contained equipment and chemicals. Wil had just about given up when he spotted an odd angle jutting out above the homemade film and paper vault at the far end of the little room.

Wil found a wooden yardstick and lifted the corner of the object enough to slide it over. The end of a box appeared, and he coaxed it forward far enough to get a grip on it. He debated whether to open it now or wait. Instant gratification won when the padlock key fit the lock in the hasp, and he lifted the lid.

A stack of enlargements lay on top, and he immediately identified Bob Thornton with another man. He flipped through the pile and saw more of the same, including one with his uncle. Beneath the photos were negatives and more printed enlargements. Wil closed the box, clicked the padlock shut, and exited the darkroom.

Back in front of the house, Wil found Cecil standing, talking with Gordon. "Gordon wants to know if it's cocktail time."

Wil checked his wristwatch. "My watch says it's one thirty. Seems a little early to me."

Gordon pointed at Cecil. "He wants a drink too."

Wil moved beside Gordon and placed a hand on his shoulder. "I saw some lemonade in your refrigerator. How about you have a glass of that now and wait until, say three thirty for the cocktails. Show him where you keep the liquor, and Cecil'll probably make you a drink. And you should show Cecil where the food for Pudgie is too."

Gordon looked up at him. "Lemonade would be good."

"Anything I need to get for you?"

Gordon returned to rocking back and forth.

Wil wagged his head up and down in rhythm with the back-and-forth of the chair. "Cecil, anything you need when I come back? If you think of something, just call the newspaper office."

He moved down the stairs, wooden box tucked under his arm, and then on to his pickup. He waved, and the two men returned the gesture. A part of him wanted to cry over Gordon and his broken memory. The quick-witted man who had taught him about photography had been replaced by a person dependent on others.

+ + +

Special Agent Oakes dropped the handwritten interview and crime scene reports on Grayson's desk. "Is this all you've got?"

Grayson did not like the FBI man's tone. "Need to add Wilson Dodge. Newspaper editor. And the county clerk, Miss Saylor. She knew Freeman socially."

"What'd the paper guy say?"

Grayson looked up at Oakes, standing with his hands on his hips. "Claims your man talked with Freeman. Said Freeman had photos to show."

"What's on 'em?"

Grayson frowned. "He don't know, and neither do I."

"Where's he now, Gray?"

Grayson rose from his chair. "My friends call me Grayson. You can call me Sheriff Farmer."

"Where's he now?"

The sheriff raised his left arm and pointed. "At the newspaper, maybe."

"What about the clerk?"

Grayson looked at the reports on his desk, not wanting to say much about Natee. "At the courthouse. In Lander."

"What'd she say about Freeman?"

"They dated."

"Either of them know Winter?"

Grayson made eye contact, angered by the way Oakes bossed him around in his own office. "Dodge met him last night. Party at his mother's. Miss Saylor was there too."

"So you don't know—"

"I thought you were investigating Winter's death."

"I'll need to interview those two."

Grayson fought a sneer. "Nobody's stopping you."

"Let's go to the newspaper."

Grayson frowned. "I ain't your boy to be orderin' around. I got my own work to do."

Oakes raised his right hand and pointed a finger at Grayson. "J. Edgar Hoover expects—"

"Hoover ain't the sheriff here. If you want to ask questions, you go ahead. But people round here deserve to be treated with respect."

The agent clenched his jaw. "I need … to make … some phone calls."

"Good. You go find some federal telephone to use. But don't come back here till you're civil. I got enough problems of my own."

As the special agent left his office, Grayson realized his right hand was tightly wrapped around the grip of his holstered service revolver. He relaxed and told himself to calm down. Shooting an FBI agent might get him reelected, but serving time in a federal prison was not a good way to build on his career.

+ + +

At the *Wrangler* office, Wil ignored the boys in the pressroom telling him Geri had asked for him and headed straight to a worktable. He unlocked the padlock and opened the box from Gordon's basement. As he shuffled through the enlargements in normal light, he noted several with a small red X in the upper right-hand corner. Almost all of them included Bob Thornton.

It took Wil only a few moments to find the negatives associated with the red X photos, and he took the box and negatives into the darkroom to make enlargements of the dozen or so pictures. He made two sets, one to show Natee and one for Dallas. Wil figured these were the pictures Corky had planned to give to Jack Winter, but without knowledge of the context, they were just more puzzle pieces to Wil. He hoped Natee or Dallas could fill in the blanks.

After hanging the developed and fixed prints to dry, Wil went to the front office. If Corky's wooden box had led to his death, then anyone who knew of it could be in danger. Perhaps he could use it as bait to bring out the killer, although that would put him in danger. There was no reason to tell Geri until later.

"You missed today's surprise guest, your pal Larry Jacobsen."

Wil stopped outside the enclosed desk area and leaned on the paneling. "What'd he stop for?"

"He thinks Gray Farmer needs to say whether Corky's death and Winter's are connected. And since the two of you are such good friends, he nominated you to get Gray to make it official—in print."

Wil frowned. "I served Larry a beer last night and talked with him for two minutes. Period. So what's this about?"

"Larry's the one that found Winter this morning. Said he thought gunshots were the cause, either murder or suicide. Said if he were sheriff, he'd be saying if Corky's and Winter's deaths are connected, telling it to the newspaper."

Wil nodded, suspecting Jacobsen wanted to put his opponent on the spot. But he also recalled Jacobsen's disappearance around the same time that Winter left Ramona's party.

"Larry's got a point, Wil. If we're doing a special, that would be a good lead story with a photo of Gray and the FBI agent, whose name Larry forgot."

He took a breath, wanting to calm himself and not say too much. "Why don't you go over to the station and interview Farmer, get a comment? He's not going to tell me anything, but refusing you'd be rude. Besides, Winter isn't the only problem. Did you know Corky was going to Gordon's at noon and suppertime to fix his meals? Gordon isn't himself. His memory seems shot."

Geri had been shaking her head no until the mention of Gordon. "Gordon Blakeslee? Corky did what?"

"I stopped at Gordon's on the way out to see Winter's car and found him confused and hungry. He'd forgotten about Corky being dead and said Corky'd not come to fix dinner. So I took him over to the Atomic."

Geri stood, moving to the swinging half door. "Corky never mentioned any of that to me."

"I've got my neighbor Cecil at Gordon's. They're going to have scrambled eggs and pancakes if you want to see for yourself. I'm not sure who to call or what to do."

Geri crossed her arms. "If Gordon's got memory problems, then adding another face isn't going to help."

Wil took a breath and frowned. "You're probably right. Just wanted to let you know, in case."

Geri glared at him. "In case of what?"

"I don't know. Did Jacobsen say he doesn't think Gray can solve the case?"

She pushed through the half door and took a step toward the pressroom. "Larry's a sneaky little turd who'd push his mother down the stairs if he thought it'd get him somewhere. Gray may not be perfect, but … it's his job to do, Wil. Not yours."

Wil gritted his teeth and sucked in air, knowing Geri was right about sticking his nose in this business. At the same time, in a little over forty-eight hours, two men had been killed. He could not just look the other way. "Corky was killed by a hit on the head, and Larry says Winter was shot. Gray's got to make a statement. Can you call him?"

Geri pointed an index finger at him. "You're supposed to be the reporter. I'm just the office girl."

"I need to go to Lander. Natee Saylor might have seen something at Ramona's that could bust this thing open."

Geri pointed to the telephone. "Phone not good enough for you, or is there another reason?"

"Before Dad and Ramona moved to the new house, we had a party line. I remember Ramona listening in on the neighbor's calls. I don't want anyone at the phone company, or the courthouse, listening in on that conversation."

Geri took another two steps toward the pressroom. "I'm not going to put together your special edition while you run around playing sheriff."

"I'm spending all day tomorrow writing up stories and getting photographs and following up with interviews. Promise."

CHAPTER 22

A white catalog envelope in hand, Wil wandered the hallway of the Fremont County Courthouse until he found the offices of the county clerk. When she emerged from the office vault holding a large green ledger, dark hair pulled back in a bun, Wil held his breath. He saw a sudden smile with tiny lines in her cheeks, pleased she was glad to see him. Her navy suit, the skirt snug at the hips and the jacket tailored to accent her waist, looked both professional and fashionable. He did not know her that well but after that smile he trusted her completely.

He asked to take Natee to coffee, and she accepted. She needed to make a phone call before they left, which gave him a chance to observe that her personal office lacked a door. A private telephone conversation at work was just as impossible for Natee as for Wil, with Geri at her desk. The combination of long-distance charges and lack of privacy tainted the convenience of the telephone to arrange a dinner date. But a fifty-mile round-trip offered a poor alternative.

As they left the office, Natee turned her head to look at Wil, who followed closely behind her. He noted the interested stares as they walked through the courthouse. He did not recognize any of the faces but detected the envy of a few of the men.

"What's in the envelope?"

Wil moved beside her and kept his voice low. "Something of Corky's."

She looked him in the eye but did not miss a step. "You're cute; that's working for you."

Wil pushed open the main door of the courthouse. "I thought you were supposed to be the cute one."

"Only cute? You can do better than that, but I prefer being the smart one."

Wil looked over his shoulder, making sure they were alone. "Have you been listening to the radio? Jack Winter, from the party last night, was found dead in his car, east of town."

Natee angled down the steps, away from the in-and-out traffic of the courthouse. "Winter, the business suit, right?"

"Yep, Farmer told me."

"Where's your truck?"

Wil waved the envelope at his pickup, and she grabbed his elbow, leading the way. "Hope you don't mind going to a bar. The coffee's not that good, but it's private."

"I'm not sure you should see these, except I need help with names for some of the faces."

Natee lengthened her stride and tightened her grip on his elbow. "If you don't show me what's in that envelope, there might be a third body found in a pickup."

The privacy of the bar on the west end of town was as advertised. Three men sat clustered at the bar, and Natee guided him to a distant booth where they ordered coffee. She took the envelope and glanced at all the photos.

"Do you recognize any of the faces in these?"

She moved to his side of the booth. "Most of these are of Bob Thornton, but you know that, and Jim Haefner."

"The guy in charge of Boysen, before Winter? Show me."

Natee pointed at Haefner on three different photos. "And these other guys look like they work for Bob. He owns Pioneer Construction. You can see the truck off to the side."

"Do you know Haefner?"

"Well enough to talk at a cocktail party or a meeting. He's a talker and a flirt. Why?"

Wil leaned closer, even though no one was within hearing distance, and lowered his voice. "You smell good. This morning Farmer asked what I knew about Haefner."

"Maybe he's a suspect."

"Maybe, but Winter told me he'd been on the job for a few months, meaning Haefner is someplace else."

"Doesn't mean he's not a suspect. Gray had to have a reason for asking."

Wil rubbed his temple. "But what?"

"His investigation could have pointed toward Jim."

Natee made a good point, and now he had a second reason for seeking out Farmer for comment. "Did you see who Winter talked to at Ramona's party?"

"Not really. He didn't stay long. Here comes coffee."

They put the conversation on hold as the bartender delivered the mugs, taking his time to inspect Natee before retreating to the trio at the bar.

Wil slid the mug to the side. "Did you see if anyone left with Winter?"

"I had to use the ladies' room, and when I came back, Winter was gone. By the way, I want to get a better look at Ramona's house."

"That can be arranged. What's Bob doing with his hand on Jim's chest, like he's going to push him?"

Natee leaned closer and checked the picture that showed Bob poking Haefner in the chest, another man in the background, and a shack in the distance. "Don't know. Where was this taken?"

"No idea. There are a few others with Haefner and Bob."

Natee lowered her voice to a whisper and placed a hand on his thigh. "Do you think Haefner's the reason Corky and Winter are dead?"

Once again, she had asked a question Wil could not answer. "I don't know enough to even guess. Larry Jacobsen thinks the two deaths are connected. Do you want to have dinner tonight and go over everything, and some of the other photos?"

Natee claimed a prior commitment and countered with a proposal for dinner the following night. They agreed on meeting in Hudson. Wil hoped the dinner would be more of a date than this coffee break.

+ + +

Deputy Albert Nelson stopped after just one step into the Riverton substation. Sheriff Farmer stood in the lobby, his service revolver out of the holster, pointed at the brick exterior wall. The sheriff replaced the handgun, bent his knees, and drew the revolver again.

"Sheriff Farmer, have you seen Agent Oakes?"

The sheriff straightened and reholstered the gun. "How often you practice your draw?"

Al took another step forward and closed the front door. "A couple times a week. Why?"

Grayson turned toward Al. "Used to practice my draw an hour every day when I started. Had a gun belt rig, like yours. Now I holster at the waist. Not as fast."

Al nodded, uncertain why the sheriff was telling him this. He also wondered about the flat, emotionless tone of Grayson's voice.

"Nelson, you know how many times I've drawn on a man?"

The sheriff had never shared any stories involving a gun battle. "No, sir."

"Never. All that practice and never used it. Almost drew on that FBI man, right in that office."

Together they looked toward the door of Grayson's office.

"We had words. I told him to get out. Once he's gone, I looked down, and there was my hand, gripping the gun, ready to draw."

Al waited, giving his boss time to continue the story. Since entering the lobby, Al had held his hands palm forward, out and away from his body. Slowly Al removed his Stetson, dropped it on a wooden chair in the lobby, and crossed his arms.

"If the marshals come for me, figured practicing my draw's a good idea."

Al thought a gun battle between US marshals, the FBI, and the sheriff in the Riverton station sounded crazy. "I hope it don't come to that, Sheriff."

The sheriff drew and reholstered his gun twice more. "FBI man thinks he can come be boss in my town. Ain't ... gonna ... happen."

Al nodded, ready for Grayson to explain. "What's he done?"

"Talked smart about the Freeman death. Like he can solve it by talking to three people. I told him to go do it and don't come back."

Al unfolded his arms and took a few steps forward. "I could use some coffee. You want some? Maybe fill me in?"

"Better keep practicing."

Al stopped a good four feet from the sheriff and took a deep breath. "I think you've got it down, Sheriff. Coffee?"

"Half cup. Don't want to get jittery."

Al collected two mugs of coffee from the kitchen area and met the sheriff in his office. Grayson sat in his chair, stared at the corner of the room, and with little prompting gave a detached report of his morning, starting with the Wil Dodge interview.

Al saw Grayson's eyes narrow, as if he were staring down someone in the corner. He wondered if Agent Oakes had stood there earlier that day. Al coughed to get Grayson's attention. "Winslow saw the body and sent that kid with it off to Casper. Guess they'll look it over. And a tow truck came from Casper and took Winter's government car away."

Grayson rocked back and forth, shifting his focus back to the corner. A squawk from the county radio system gave Al an idea. "Sounds like they need you at the jail, Sheriff. I'll take care of things here until you get back tomorrow morning. I think you need to get to Lander."

Grayson stopped rocking for a moment and then resumed his steady rhythm. The only other occasion Al had seen this type of thing was as an MP in the army. Most of the time he and his partner had dealt with drunks, but there had been a few encounters with soldiers suffering from shell shock, or battle fatigue. Grayson was acting just like them.

Grayson stood, moved to the hall tree, and took his hat. "I need to get to Lander." The sheriff unholstered his revolver, opened the cylinder and checked his bullets, and then snapped it back in position. "You check outside. Make sure there ain't no ambush."

Al led the way to the front door, opened it carefully, and looked outside. Swiveling his head right and left, he danced down the steps and then stopped at the bottom and scanned the street and sidewalk. Slowly, he walked to the sheriff's radio car, opened the driver's side door, and inspected inside.

Grayson huddled inside the front door until Al gave him a wave and then dashed down the steps and to his car. Al stood clear as the sheriff backed out the car, ground the gears as he shifted into low, and sped away. He watched the patrol car make a sharp turn toward Federal and the road to Lander.

Al stood on the sidewalk, thinking he was the loneliest man in Riverton. His boss was acting crazy, but who could he tell? He did not trust Larry Jacobsen, Agent Oakes, or fellow Deputy Bud Yost. The worst thing he could imagine was Grayson going berserk in the courthouse or at the jail. And there were other scenarios just as dangerous. But who could he tell?

He still needed to inform Agent Oakes that the government car and Winter's body were on the way to Casper. There might be a chance to explain the pressures on Sheriff Farmer and hope the FBI man understood. He noticed the Ford with the government plates parked in front of First National Bank, meaning the agent should not be too hard to find.

+ + +

"How was your date?"

Wil stood at the front counter, knowing the interrogation by Geri could not be wished away. "It wasn't a date. I needed to ask her a few questions. I didn't tell you about Ramona's party, did I?"

"You're changing the subject, but no."

"Remember how you said there were husbands and wives involved in adultery?"

Geri grabbed her cigarette pack. "Being unfaithful? Yes. Why?"

"I saw so much flirting going on at the party. Maybe it was the booze or being outside at a party or you talking about it. One guy confided that he wanted to be with a woman from his high school class. I won't mention a name, but he goes to my church."

She sparked her lighter and lit a cigarette. "I can guess. Flirting's fun; you should try it."

"So my folks' friends were flirting and being unfaithful all along, and I never noticed it?"

Geri shrugged her shoulders. "I can't say because we weren't part of Clay and Ramona's social crowd. Before Bill died, we had a group of friends, and there was flirting and … While you were going to school, I did what I could to preserve your innocence. But you're grown up and need to know and see what's going on."

Wil did not know whether to thank her or not and wondered what else she had not told him. He walked around the counter, through the half door, and to his desk. "We need to work on the special. Help me with the milestones. We've got Corky killed Monday night or Tuesday morning out west of town."

"Not exactly. Corky's body was found in his car out west of town Tuesday morning. He could have died at a different spot."

Wil grabbed a sheet of typing paper and made notes. "Right. And he didn't have a scratch on him, and his car wasn't banged up. And his apartment had been cleaned before I got there Tuesday night. The wife knows something. Have you called her about the funeral? She might need a ride."

"Not yet, but I will."

He remembered taking Corky's record books. They might give dates and locations for the photos of Bob Thornton and Jim Haefner. "Wednesday night was Ramona's party, where Winter and Jacobsen both showed up. This morning Jacobsen finds Winter, and the FBI is called in. What'd I forget?" The list of events seemed too short.

"There's the people involved. Albert was asking questions about Corky, and Gray interviewed you. Have you got Corky's landlords on the list?"

He added each of the names to his list along with Bob Thornton and his uncle Dallas. "I still need the name of the FBI agent."

"Oh, that reminds me. I called Corky's parents in Idaho, to make sure they knew about the funeral. It seems Gordon invited them to stay with him tomorrow night. From what you say about his memory, I'd guess he's forgotten, and they could be in for a surprise."

Wil scribbled a note on his grocery list. "That will give Cecil and Gordon something to do tomorrow. I've got a silver dollar that says Gordon has no recollection of it. Who else?"

"I called Gray Farmer and asked about Corky and Winter, but he wouldn't give me an answer. I tried pushing him but … didn't even get a chance to ask about the FBI. He sounded funny. Not ha-ha funny, but funny. Maybe you should talk with Albert."

Wil put a star by Albert Nelson's name as a reminder. "Did Dallas give you anything we can use?"

"Not to me. He did mention libel three times, though. Is there enough for a special? And what was this business with Natee Saylor?"

"I needed to ask about what she saw at Ramona's—who was talking with Winter, if anyone left with him, that sort of thing."

"And?"

Wil looked past her toward the front door. He was lying by not telling her about Corky's photos and needed to avoid eye contact. "She had to use the bathroom, and when she came out, Winter was gone. And he wasn't there very long. So I don't know much."

Geri stubbed out her cigarette and crossed her legs. "Natalie Saylor says she used the bathroom at Ramona's house. I'll raise your silver dollar with another that says she fibbed."

"Why?"

Geri folded her hands and bobbed her crossed leg atop the knee. "Women are part camel when it comes to holding our water. At a party we'd be afraid of missing something. And the idea of using the toilet at another woman's house is unthinkable. How many drinks did she have?"

Wil frowned, not certain whether Geri was teasing or revealing a feminine secret. "I made her a small scotch."

"No reason to visit the powder room there. She may've missed Winter's leaving the party, but the girls' room wasn't the reason."

He wanted to change the subject, not comfortable with the idea Natee would lie to him. "She told me about Jim Haefner, too. I mentioned that Gray Farmer asked about him. She knows him socially and wonders if he's a suspect in Corky's death."

Geri uncrossed her leg and turned toward her typewriter. "Corky never mentioned him to me. He was interested in girls. Are you sure there's enough for a special?"

Wil believed showing copies of Corky's photos to Dallas would get a response, especially the one of Dallas with Thornton and Haefner. There had been no reason to show that one to Natee. "After I talk with the sheriff and the FBI guy tomorrow, there should be plenty to write about."

"What if they don't talk?"

"I'll tell them what I think they're hiding and see if that gets a reaction."

Geri crossed her arms and looked confused. "What are they hiding?"

"I don't know yet, but I'll think of something. I'm going to see Dallas. He might have an idea or two."

CHAPTER 23

Gretchen sat at the kitchen table and wondered what to fix for supper. Even though it was only four-thirty in the afternoon, fixing supper was the only chore she had left to do. But she was lonely, not hungry.

She understood why some housewives smoked cigarettes, those without children in particular. With a baby, her day would be filled with nursing and taking care of a son or daughter. Why were they having so much trouble getting pregnant? Was she being punished for having sex with Corky? Was Delmar staying away longer than usual, or did it just seem that way?

When Corky was around, Gretchen had not minded Delmar being gone for more than two nights. The fear that Delmar knew of her betrayal and had left her would not be silenced. He would have been justified in killing Corky. If he had, she wanted to believe it was love, or mercy, that had spared her from death.

She sprang out of her chair at the sound of the back screen door opening, thinking it was Delmar. The knock on the interior door stopped her. Delmar would come right in. Gretchen opened the door to find Orrin, her neighbor.

"Delmar home yet?"

It was a silly question since their car was not in the driveway. "No, but he'll be here soon."

"You need anything? Milk from the store, maybe?"

Gretchen looked at the boy near her own age with the thin raggedy beard. "I've got milk and bread."

"Delmar said to help out if you need it. Just trying to do the Lord's work. Love thy neighbor."

She wondered if the Mormon boys from her high school in Sheridan had grown up to look like Orrin. Finding Delmar had spared her from a life with boys like that.

"Happy to help any way I can, like I did with that elder."

Gretchen wanted to forget about the church leader who had taken an unwanted interest in her when they moved to Riverton. He had tried to "lay hands" on her more than once, for one reason or another, and bumped against her, the hardness in his pants pressing against her thigh.

The elder had come to visit while Delmar was away once, and when he tried to get into the house, she screamed. Orrin ran him off. She had thanked Orrin and asked him not to mention it to Delmar, unwilling to make trouble at church.

Since then, when Delmar was away, she would see Orrin in his mother's yard, across the street, watching her house. Gretchen wanted to think of him as an uncle, looking after her. But she feared he had a hardness in his pants that wanted her just like the elder.

"I thanked you for that, Orrin. It was neighborly, what you did."

"Miss Gretchen, I'd do anything for you."

"I'm a married woman, and my name is Mrs. Simpson. Good-bye."

Gretchen closed the door and thought of turning the skeleton key in the lock but decided against it. If Delmar came home and found the house locked, he would be upset. She prayed Delmar would come home tonight and not go away again. She had learned her lesson. She wanted to be a good wife and mother. How else would she get into heaven?

+ + +

Dallas sent Virginia home early when his nephew stopped by the office. He assumed the large envelope Wilson carried contained the Freeman photos. Since a late-afternoon cocktail hour at the Wind River Hotel had not been scheduled, Virginia's final duty of the day involved setting out cocktail glasses and ice in the combination library and meeting room.

He kept Wilson waiting in the meeting room while he made a phone call. This business with Corky Freeman and now Jack Winter had prompted a developmental shift in his nephew. The insecure young man with simple pleas for advice and a willingness to obey had begun to think and act on his own. By requiring Wilson to wait, he hoped to reestablish his dominant position.

Dallas opened his office door and entered the library, walked to a bookcase at the far end of the room, and released a latch to reveal a display of liquor bottles. A limited selection of bottles rested on two glass shelves, what he liked to think of as the good stuff. "It's my cocktail hour. What can I get you? I'm having a manhattan."

"Some scotch and water would be good. I liked the Johnnie Walker from Ramona's party."

Dallas selected two glasses and set them on the narrow counter beneath the bottles. He took a bottle, uncorked it for a sniff, and poured a modest measure. Then he mixed the bourbon and sweet vermouth for his manhattan, adding bitters and then ice.

The first glass in one hand and the water pitcher in the other, he walked over to the seated Wilson. "This is a good sipping scotch. I'll let you add the water. It's best without ice or much water. What's in the envelope?"

Dallas walked back to the bar and collected his drink before pulling back a chair near his nephew. He waited as Wilson added water to his drink and then tasted it.

Wilson slid the envelope to him. "Some of Corky Freeman's photos. Take a look. I think you'll find them interesting."

Dallas opened the envelope and inspected the photos until he came across the one showing him with Bob Thornton and Jim Haefner. He slid it across the table toward Wil. "That was taken last October. Jim gave Bob and me a tour of the project. We're in front of Jim's offices."

Dallas looked at a few more before spinning a second picture, showing Bob touching Haefner's chest, toward Wil.

His nephew tilted his head to see the image. "Were you around for that one? Any idea what Bob was saying to Jim or where it was taken?"

"No, I wasn't. Looks like some of Bob's boys were there, though. No idea of the location. What do you surmise from it?"

Wilson tapped his index finger on Jim Haefner's image. "Looks like Bob's threatening him. Keep going."

Dallas shuffled a few more enlargements and stopped at one of Bob handing Haefner an envelope. He flashed the image at Wil. "This the one you wanted me to see?"

"Something tells me Bob isn't delivering a letter from his mother. It looks like Bob's dealership in the background."

Dallas looked at the last few photos and then placed them all back into the envelope. "I'm not going to ask where or how you collected these. Can I keep them?"

"Yes, I've got other prints. Gordon Blakeslee pointed me to them. Remind me to get back to him."

Dallas gnawed at his tongue. "It would be best if I kept these and the negatives in my safe. Have you shown them to anyone else?"

"I've got those, and some others, in a safe place. I showed Natee Saylor a few, to learn who Haefner was. Thought I'd get your advice before showing them to Farmer, not that I trust him."

Dallas leaned forward in his chair and turned the stemmed manhattan glass. "What makes you suspicious of our sheriff?"

"I don't think he killed Corky or Winter. But I'm not sure he wants to find out who did either ... or will share what he knows."

"What's the issue with Gordon?"

Wil sighed and set his palms flat on the table. "I told you about seeing him on Tuesday. When I went by this morning, he had no memory of Corky's death. Plus, Corky came by twice a day to feed him. I've got Cecil helping out, but that can't go on forever. I'm hoping you have some suggestions about his memory problem."

"We'll get back to him."

Wil nodded and tapped the table.

Dallas closed his eyes and nibbled his tongue. "Hear me out before speaking. In a courtroom, these photos could be interpreted a number of ways. The person who took them is dead. The individual who possessed them has an unreliable memory. And one of the people in the photos has supposedly moved away, and his replacement is dead. But none of these photos have necessarily captured a crime. They may be used in evidence, and maybe not.

"This could all be coincidence, or it may be connected. And neither of us, you or I, knows the entire story."

Wil sat silently. "So what's your advice?"

"As an officer of the court, I have certain obligations. But as your uncle, there are family and moral duties equally as serious. These photos may be the reason Mr. Freeman is dead. As long as you retain possession of these photos, you may be in danger. I am prepared to do almost anything necessary to ensure your safety, but you have to let me."

Dallas looked for the obedience he expected from his nephew but saw only doubt. He instinctively knew there was nothing more he could say to convince Wil, and he calculated the options, gnawing at his tongue.

He stood and moved around the table to the bookcases lining the back wall. "Since you insist on doing this alone, at least protect yourself." Dallas reached into the bookcase and pressed a release, freeing two of the floor-to-ceiling units to swing open.

Wil stood and took a step closer. "I suppose there's a trapdoor someplace in this room too."

Dallas pushed the bookshelves farther open to reveal a large double-door safe. "No, just a safe. If something should happen to me, the combination is your father's birth date. There's a trick to opening the bookcase, but Virginia knows that. The left side is where I keep part of my gun collection. The right side is filled with another kind of explosive."

Wil picked up the glass of scotch and sipped as Dallas unlocked the safe and opened the left-side door, selecting a sleek, browned leather rifle case.

Dallas pulled a gun from the case. "This shotgun belonged to your father. Twelve-gauge Parker model BHE. Double-barreled. I'd get buckshot if I were you." Dallas broke the breech, displaying the side-by-side empty barrels, and handed it to Wil.

"How'd it end up here?"

"Ramona wanted it out of the house. It's too fine a gun to just sell, and I thought one day you might want it."

Wil glanced at the engraving on the metal, locked the barrels into place, and lifted the dark polished wood stock to his shoulder. "You guys used to shoot flying clay things, right? This was the gun he used?"

Dallas grunted a reply as he bent to remove a compact box from the safe and placed it on the table. "His cleaning kit. If you'd feel more comfortable with a handgun, there are a few I can recommend."

"Since it belonged to Dad, I'll take it. Not that I think I need it."

Dallas closed the left-side door. "As you can see, I have a secure spot to store those photographs and the negatives. If you change your mind, let me know."

"They're safe for now."

Dallas set the leather case on the table, alongside Wil's cocktail. "As your attorney, let me suggest you share prints of those with both the sheriff and the FBI. Make sure to include the one with me in it."

"I might be able to put dates with these, but it'll take a little digging. Corky kept detailed records. You said the one with you was in October?"

"Early October, I believe. If you need a date, I'll have Virginia check my book."

Wil slipped the shotgun into the case. "Aren't you going to lock that?"

Dallas glanced over his shoulder at the safe. "I'm going out to look at some land tomorrow morning. Given the recent homicides, a little firepower seems prudent. Maybe I'll sight in my antelope rifle. The season starts a week from Saturday."

"Any other advice?"

Dallas moved around the table and picked up his manhattan. "As always, tell the truth and protect yourself. Watch your back."

"I'll let you know what the sheriff says about the photos, which reminds me—you have any ideas how to get Gray Farmer to talk?

Maybe suggest something he's hiding? And the same with the FBI guy."

Dallas drank from his cocktail and smiled. "The FBI will not be a problem. Hoover loves to see his name in print, even a small-town newspaper. As for our sheriff, a reminder he has an election coming up is a start."

"Jacobsen came to the office, and Geri has a couple quotes from him. He thinks the two killings are connected. I'll mention that."

"Grayson was in this office the other day and appeared rather vulnerable. A frightened animal pushed into a corner can be unpredictable, if you catch my meaning."

Wil nodded and picked up the glass of scotch. "I'll be careful. What about Gordon?"

"Is there any family? His side or the wife's?"

Wil shared the information about a brother in Iowa. Dallas agreed to make some calls and ask around. The action appeared to satisfy his nephew for the moment.

Dallas had always known the day would come when the details of his brother's death would need sharing. Over the months he had considered possible approaches to revealing the facts and presenting his confession. "If you're not doing anything after church on Sunday, why don't you come up to the lodge, south of Lander. I'll tell you about Clayton's death."

The offer created the reaction Dallas had expected from his nephew: stunned silence. Even though Wil presented a new independent facade, the foundation of avuncular trust could still be tapped. He hoped that trust would survive the confession he intended to offer.

+ + +

Al found Agent Oakes coming out of the post office. The main floor of the building handled the US mail, but the second floor housed a grab bag of smaller federal offices, while Agriculture and Reclamation each maintained independent office space. Al treated Oakes like a respected dignitary, giving him the officer treatment with a "sir" this and a "sir" that. Just like in the army, it mostly worked.

The FBI man scowled at the mention of the sheriff during the report but lost a little of the hostility when Al mentioned the stress of the upcoming election. That contest really did not matter to Al any longer since he had decided to apply for the next Riverton Police Department opening. No matter who won the election for sheriff of Fremont County, his days in the department were counting down.

The report on Winter's body and car complete, he retreated to the substation. The Corky Freeman murder case still needed his attention, and he planned to cooperate on the Winter murder as well. There was no evidence to link the two deaths other than Wil Dodge's report to the sheriff of Winter's meeting with the photographer, even though the Reclamation man had said nothing about it during his interview. Grayson suspected Dodge but Al rejected the idea, the newspaperman lacked both the courage and a motive to kill Freeman.

The sound of the front door opening and the click of heels on the flooring pulled Al out of the sheriff's office. He crossed his arms and leaned against the doorframe. What was Diane doing here?

"Hi. The operator said I might find you here. I called your apartment, but there was no answer." Diane wore a white shirt buttoned to the top and a lavender sweater, without the bright lipstick and eye makeup from the night before.

"Miss Diane. You've probably had a busy day."

"Yes, with the FBI man and calls from Washington, everyone with questions. But I had time to think about you ... and last night."

After they left the bowling alley, the questions had stopped, and kissing had led to lying in the front seat, Diane grinding her pelvis on top of him. Self-conscious about the memory, he felt his face flush. "I've been thinking about you too."

She moved closer to him, and he sniffed the scent of her perfume. "I was hoping we could go someplace and eat. And talk. And ..." The look in her eyes and facial expression matched the night before, after all the grinding.

Al felt defenseless, aroused, and a little protective. "I got a little more work to do before my shift ends. I could pick you up, or we could meet someplace."

Diane looked at his left hand resting atop his right arm. She ran her index finger along his fingers and looked up at him. "When I'm with you, I'm not afraid."

Al let his arms fall and pulled her close. She rested her head on his chest. "There's no need to be afraid."

"I could come to your place, and then you can drive my car. That way it won't look like I'm your prisoner. Is six thirty too early?"

The thought of Diane at his apartment filled Al with anticipation and fear. Diane had not known he existed just the day before, and now she was showing up where he worked. The last time a girl chased him had been in high school. Thankfully, Diane had resisted the temptation to plant a hickey on his neck.

"I can be ready by then. I'm in unit 6 at the Mountain Top Motel, on West Main."

Diane stepped back and smiled. "I'll find it. Do you know if Jim's in trouble? Jim Haefner? His name keeps getting mentioned."

"I've not heard anything, honest. I'll see you in a bit."

She took his hand, kissed it, and was out the door.

CHAPTER 24

Gretchen sat in the bright light of the kitchen, knitting another doily as a gift for her mother. She took little pleasure in needlework, especially embroidery, but found the repetition helped pass the time. Mother would say she should work on a baby quilt or afghan, but she was not pregnant.

Any hope of Delmar coming home today had passed. The sun had not completely set, but she knew it would be another night of sleeping alone, another night of wondering whether he was ever going to come back to her. She tried blinking away the tears and reached for her hankie.

The knock at the back door had to mean Orrin was back again. She thought of ignoring it but knew he would not go away.

The fading twilight lit one side of Orrin's face on the other side of the screen door, darkness behind him worked at swallowing the back yard. "Ma said for me to bring you some o' her chicken soup. She thought you'd like it."

Gretchen opened the screen door, and Orrin carried the towel-wrapped serving dish up the stairs into her kitchen. "You'll have to thank her for me. I'll have some tomorrow for lunch. By then Delmar should be back."

Orrin looked around the kitchen, not meeting her eyes. "So you gonna be renting the basement again?"

Gretchen unknotted the towel and took a sniff. "Smells good. Delmar wants to rent it to a married couple."

"Hmm. Mind if I see it? I could tell people 'bout it."

Gretchen turned and put a hand on her hip, locking the elbow. "Delmar don't like people being inside when he's not around."

"I'm just trying to help, that's all."

The hurt look of a little boy having been scolded melted her resistance. "I suppose this once. But don't tell Delmar, or he'll be mad with both of us."

Gretchen flicked the light switch on for the basement and led the way carefully down the steps, even though she knew the route by heart. The memory of her nights with Corky followed her as she moved down the stairs. She walked into the living room and turned on the floor lamp. "This is the living room, and the kitchen's there."

She watched as Orrin looked into the kitchen and then at the larger room. Gretchen walked to the door to the bedroom, unable to suppress the remembered images and sensations from her nights in that bed. "There's only the one bedroom, but it'll work for … a couple."

She turned and backed into the room, afraid to look at the bed. Orrin cautiously followed and reached out and flipped the light switch. Orrin moved to close the gap between them and reached out to touch her.

"I'm a married woman. You shouldn't be doing that … this is wrong."

"I'd do most anything for you, Miss Gretchen. Most anything."

Gretchen turned to step around him, but he matched the movement. She leaned in his direction and pushed her hips in the other, shuffling quickly to get past him and out of the room. "You've seen the apartment, and now you need to leave. Delmar won't like us being down here."

"I had a revelation we belong together."

She turned off the living room light and marched toward the steps. "I'm a married woman, Orrin. That can't happen."

"God's will be done. We're bound for time and eternity. Revelation, I say."

Gretchen quickly climbed the stairs to the landing, opened the back door, and took the three stairs up to the kitchen. "Don't come around again with that kind of talk. I'm a married woman."

She listened to the slow footfalls on the stairs, impatient for Orrin to leave. He stopped when he reached the landing and stared at her until she looked away.

"I will always protect you, Miss Gretchen."

When she heard the screen door close, she darted down the steps, closed the back door, and turned the key in the lock. If Delmar did not come home tomorrow, she would call Mother.

+ + +

The pressroom had gone silent for the day by the time Wil finished his article on the death of Jack Winter. Unlike the night before, the production crew had joined their families for supper on time or claimed a stool in a bar. He wondered how the demands of the Thursday edition played out as Wednesday rituals for the wives and children. Did they wait to eat until Dad got home, or was there an empty chair at the normal feeding time?

The article on Jack Winter needed work. Sheriff Farmer had provided few facts about the case, and Wil had been unable to locate the FBI agent. Highway patrolman Larry Jacobsen had served up the limited factual basis for the piece, but getting confirmation from another source such as Deputy Albert Nelson or the FBI topped the list of tomorrow's chores.

He wanted to wait until after six thirty to stop by Gordon's to evaluate the wisdom of making Cecil the supervising adult of the household. He allowed for the possibility of finding both men passed out from too many afternoon cocktails. The preferred outcome involved a meal, cleaned dishes, and conversation. Wil wanted to believe part of Gordon's condition related to his isolation from others. But that explanation might be overly optimistic.

Wil stopped by the darkroom to pick up the padlocked box before leaving the *Wrangler*. He had made additional enlargements for the lawmen and planned to inspect the other photos and negatives beneath the Jim Haefner and Bob Thornton collection, but after Geri left the office, the solitude had opened a flow of words at the typewriter.

The final gasps of dusk surrendered as he pulled in front of Gordon's house. A light shining through the front screen door gave him hope that the worst-case scenario of two drunken old-timers had been avoided. Cecil bounced up from a living room chair and held the door as Wil climbed the steps.

Wil shoved his hands into the pockets of his jeans. "How'd it go?"

Cecil pointed toward the kitchen. "One o' my better batches of flapjacks. Too bad you missed it. I'm gonna get me a box of his brand. Just add an egg 'n' some milk, and you got it."

Pudgie pranced into the living room from the kitchen and shoved his nose into Wil's hand. Gordon followed at a slower pace. "Wil, you missed supper."

"Thanks, but Ramona has something planned for a little later."

Cecil bent forward and rubbed Pudgie's hips. "We're a good team. I don't mind cookin' but hate washin' up. Gordon's got the big belt buckle for handlin' the kitchen."

Wil smiled at the former cowboy's rodeo reference. "I got some chores for you fellas tomorrow. Corky's folks are coming for the funeral and need a place to stay. We're hoping they can bunk here with you tomorrow night, Gordon."

Gordon moved farther into the living room. "They could use the spare bedroom."

"Then you and Cecil can plan on getting ready for that. I'd expect them in the afternoon sometime. They'll have to drive over the mountains from Idaho."

Gordon nodded, and Wil wondered whether he would remember the details by tomorrow morning.

Cecil scratched at his ear. "Maybe I can do a big pot o' my trail stew for 'em. I'll need meat, 'less Pudgie can get me a cat or two."

"If I know Ramona, she might have something to contribute. Gordon, can I take Cecil with me? I'll bring him back to help out tomorrow morning."

Gordon took only a moment to consider the question. "Sure. Pudgie and me'll be fine."

Wil looked at the dog for confirmation. "How early? Do you need help with breakfast?"

Gordon glanced at Cecil and then wagged his head for no. "Just coffee and cereal for me. Don't need the stove for that. I've never had trail stew before. Is it good?"

Cecil grinned and added a wink. "If Missus Ramona's doin' the meat, we won't need much ketchup. A few taters 'n' roots, maybe biscuits and honey. A good trail stew's better'n almost any mess o' beans. See ya in the mornin', partner."

The cowboy led the way onto the porch, Gordon and Pudgie out the door last. Wil touched Gordon on the arm, told him to sleep well, and joined Cecil on the sidewalk. As they drove away, Cecil gave a wave, and Gordon returned it.

The cowboy reported in his unique style how it had taken Gordon some time to warm up to him, or else the man had lived alone so long that the "doin's of talkin' ain't easy." Wil asked him to work Boysen Dam into the conversation the next day, hoping to stir up details on Jim Haefner.

At the apartments, Wil asked Cecil to hang on to the wooden box while he visited Ramona, and he took the shotgun and leather sleeve from behind the seat.

Cecil pointed at the long gun case. "Got a saddle buddy, looks like."

"It was Clayton's shotgun. Dallas thought I should have it."

Cecil stopped at the bottom of his back door steps. "Gonna need some shells for that. What gauge?"

Wil reached in and pulled the gun from the case. "You tell me."

Cecil set down the box. "Mercy, but that's a fine gun. Can I hold it?"

Wil passed it to Cecil, who cradled it with the care of a parent holding a new infant. He opened the breech and exposed the side-by-side barrels. "I'd say twelve-gauge, maybe ten."

"Dallas might've said twelve. I can check with him."

Cecil looked up and smiled. "No need. If you got a minute, I got some shells inside we can try."

Wil moved toward his back door. "I need to get to the outhouse. Be back in a shake."

He felt pleased with the short-term solution to the problem with Gordon and thankful his neighbor had willingly jumped in to help. The unanswered question concerning Gordon involved the long term. Just as Cecil had performed his role, Dallas would need to pitch in with alternatives for the retiree.

When Wil got back outside, Cecil was waiting for him on the porch with the gun case and a small cloth bag. "I'as lookin' at this here gun, and it's a Parker. Only seen but a few of 'em and none as nice as this. Mighty fine gun. There's some shells in the bag, in case you need 'em. Bird and buckshot."

"A Parker, huh. I'd bet Dallas gave it to Clayton for his birthday, maybe. Or Christmas."

"You take care o' that one. Some skunk sees it, they might try'n take it."

Wil nodded, thinking he would need to lock the pickup. "I didn't take all your ammunition, did I?"

"Mercy, no. Got my six-shooter too. Varmints come sniffin' round here gonna get bit good."

+ + +

"Would you make me a martini? The leftover gin from last night is on the counter." With the paring knife she was using to peel a pear, Ramona pointed at the counter next to the refrigerator. Wil did not need to confirm the claim since he had placed the bottles in that very spot the night before.

"How late did they stay?"

"Goodness, until after ten. I thought they would never leave, but Bob seemed pleased. I hope he will make up the difference from the allowance he gave me. The alcohol bill was higher than I expected."

Wil glanced at his mother, interested in her thoughts on Bob. "I've heard Bob is cheap. I hope you're not paying for his campaign."

"Bob watches every penny and is terrible at tips. I'll let him be seen with me until after the election; then he is on his own."

Happy with her revelation, Wil watched her quarter and peel another pear, with a green apple standing by. "Speaking of the booze, I took the Johnnie Walker, but one of the guests requested it by name. And Dallas opened the Seagram's. Maybe he'll chip in."

"Wilson, gin martini, please."

Wil left Ramona in the kitchen and took the few steps down into the family room and over to the liquor cart. He carried a tray with martini glasses, vermouth, and the shaker back to the kitchen. "Tell me this isn't your supper—apple and pear."

"I had a big lunch today, with the bridge club girls. Ruby refuses to host in her home, so we always go out. There is cheese to go with the fruit."

Wil dosed the shaker with gin, dry vermouth, ice and then put it down to settle and cool. "Did you hear there was another dead man discovered this morning?"

"The girls at bridge mentioned it, but I do not know the man."

Bridge club explained her dark blue suit with the Eisenhower-style short-length jacket and three-quarter sleeves. The string of pearls looked good against the red blouse. Wil shook and then poured the strained liquid into the martini glasses. "He was at your party last night. Olives?"

Ramona took a jar from the refrigerator and handed it to Wil. "Was he the one you were talking with when we moved inside?"

"No, that was Larry Jacobsen. He's running for sheriff. Winter was the one in the suit, alone."

Ramona squinted and looked at the ceiling as if searching for a cobweb. "I saw him. Good-looking, but he did not stay long."

Wil poured olive juice into Ramona's drink. "Talked with Dallas a little, but you're right. He arrived late and left after Bob's speech."

Ramona picked up the tray with fruit and cheese and walked out of the kitchen. "Bring the drinks, and we'll sit in the living room."

There was no evidence over a dozen people had been in the room the night before. The plush cream-colored carpet was unmarked by footprints, and the ashtrays and tabletops sparkled. She placed the fruit tray on the coffee table in front of the sofa and took a seat, crossing her legs.

Wil set his glass down and then hers, taking his position nearby on the sofa. A large oil portrait of his parents commanded the wall opposite them. He had always thought the artist had been generous in the depiction of his parents. "Remind me when that painting was done."

"After we moved into the new house, your father wanted it— an anniversary present. It took much too long and cost too much, but ... I'm so thankful. We were a lovely couple."

"I like the old photos of the two of you in Denver."

"Your father and I met in September."

Wil knew this story by heart, and they had just talked of their wedding a few nights earlier. He took a slice of cheese and piece of pear but did not want to leave his mother with her memories too long. "So why did you leave Denver?"

"That is such ancient history that ..."

"Don't you remember?"

She looked at the fruit tray and then pulled a cigarette case from inside her jacket. "I remember perfectly. I am just not sure you will want to know."

"I'm old enough to vote and serve on a jury. I wouldn't have asked if I didn't want to know."

She tapped the cigarette end against the case and then lit it. "I had not planned on telling you this, but as you say, you are old enough to understand."

Wil lifted his martini glass and held it out to Ramona. She tapped his, and they each drank. Ramona stretched her neck, as if she needed to make room for the clear chilled liquid to slide down her throat.

"It was the spring of 1930. You were three years old, and we were living in an upstairs apartment in central Denver. I had quit my job at Brown's but did mending and alterations. Your father was with the paper, but money was tight. We tried to save for a house but could never get ahead without something happening and draining our savings." Ramona slid an ashtray beside her martini glass and tapped the cigarette against the edge.

"Your father had been working late most nights starting shortly after the New Year. He was always vague about the assignment, talked of a special story. One night he came home, and I could tell he had been drinking. I put him to bed, and when I was hanging up his clothes, there was an earring in the pocket of his suit coat. It was not one of my earrings."

Wil stood and gulped the rest of his martini. "There's a little more in the shaker."

As he walked to the kitchen, the paper-clip box of single earrings from Clayton's desk drawer tiptoed along the edges of his thoughts. He carried the shaker back and topped off his glass.

Ramona tapped her cigarette on the ashtray. "Are you sure you want to hear this?"

"You shocked me, but yes."

"The next morning at breakfast, I dropped the earring next to his oatmeal and asked him who it belonged to. And before he could answer, I told him to tell the truth because I would know if he was lying. He turned pale and started to speak but could not. Then he lowered his head, saying how sorry he was, over and over. There was a young woman at the newspaper, and they had been having an affair. She knew he was married." Ramona took a deep drag from her cigarette and blew the smoke straight up into the room.

"So what did you do?"

"I never asked for her name because it did not matter. I knew that as long as we lived in Denver, there would always be some younger woman he would seduce, or who would snare him. Your father was a flirt. That is how we met, you know."

Wil had admired his father's ability to effortlessly start conversations. He lacked that kind of confidence, although associating that skill with flirtation and seduction had never occurred to him.

"Dallas had moved to this little town in Wyoming and talked with Clayt about a newspaper for sale, but your father was not interested. The night I found the earring, I decided if we were to stay married, then leaving Denver was a must. I demanded he contact Dallas and find out about the newspaper, or I would leave him. He begged me not to go and agreed to call Dallas. And that is how we moved to Riverton." She picked up her martini, raised the glass toward the portrait, and took a sip.

Wil sat motionless. The story of how Clayton and Ramona had met was so romantic. He was disappointed in his father and sad for Ramona.

"I had no idea …"

"That is only part of the story. I was naive to think he would not be tempted in Riverton. There were other women."

So the earrings in the office represented women he had been with sexually. "Why did you stay with him?"

"Clayt was good for a year, but he enjoyed flirting too much. I would catch him, and he would end it and repent. I looked for another man to have sex with, to get even. But there was no one that tempting."

Wil shut his eyes, stunned at her confession. The thought of Ramona even considering sex with a man other than Clayton shocked him.

"I discovered if I did not say anything, he would get bored with them. And I made it a point of keeping him busy after work. Thankfully, we had a babysitter living nearby for you."

Wil shook his head. "I'm disappointed in Dad. I thought he was a better person."

"Your father was the most thoughtful and interesting man I have ever known. I came to see his wandering as a tiny part of his character. He never talked divorce. He always came home at night. And other than sharing himself with other women, he treated me very well."

"He cheated on you, and that's so sad."

"Spare me. If Dotty were here, she would tell you Clayt had to put up with me too. We truly loved each other. Marriage is not just kisses and close dances. We laughed and fought and cried together. He was a very emotional man. You did not know that, did you?" Ramona speared her cigarette into the ashtray.

On the drive to his apartment, regret over prying into the private lives of his parents troubled him. Wil wondered if his curiosity about the cause of his father's death would lead to more unsettling information. The only good news from the visit was Ramona's lack of romantic interest in Bob Thornton. Wil wanted to tell her about the photos of Bob and Jim Haefner, but the less she knew, the better.

He thought it odd that Corky had concealed his very active pursuit of girls, but so had Clayton. At least Corky had served in the role of guardian angel for Gordon. Wil wanted to believe Corky would have been faithful once he had found a girl to marry. Both men had been more complex than Wil had realized.

The only unfinished chore of the evening was picking up Corky's photographic logs from the office to match specific dates to the photographs he planned to show Sheriff Farmer. The tedium of looking for needles in a haystack might dull his senses enough to help him escape into sleep. If Dallas was right about last October, he had a place to begin.

DAY 4

Friday
September 5, 1952

CHAPTER 25

"You having the regular today, Harvey, or something queer?"

"Does that mean you haven't already put in my order, Minerva?"

Rose pulled the coffeepot away from the mug and scowled. "If you'd called me Minnie, I wouldn't have told you who just got to town."

"Lucky for me."

"Not every day we have both the FBI and Secret Service in town."

Wil scanned the restaurant, searching through the haze of cigarette smoke for men in suits he did not recognize. "Over along the wall? Which is FBI?"

"Brown hair, with his back to us. White hair is Secret Service."

Wil pushed his coffee mug forward, hoping Rose would fill it. "So how'd you find this out?"

Rose poured the coffee and smiled. "Asked."

"How long before they're finished eating?"

She looked over her shoulder and bobbed her head twice. "Next five minutes. Why?"

Wil thanked her, slipped off his stool, and picked a path to the two men at the booth. When the white-haired man noticed him, Wil smiled.

"Excuse me, gentlemen. I'm Wilson Dodge with the newspaper, and our waitress tells me you're with the government. I might have some information for you."

White hair stood and extended his hand. "Roscoe Kemper, Secret Service. This is Special Agent Oakes with the FBI."

Wil shook Kemper's hand and turned to Oakes. "Wednesday night I talked with Mr. Winter at an outdoor party. He mentioned meeting our photographer Monday night and being promised some pictures. But Corky Freeman, the photographer, was found dead Tuesday morning."

Oakes stood and glanced at Kemper. "The sheriff and his deputy mentioned that death."

Wil looked from Oakes to Kemper and back at Oakes. "Mr. Winter asked if I might know about those pictures. At the time I didn't, but since then ... I was planning on sharing them with the sheriff this morning."

Kemper spoke first. "We would like to be at that meeting. Do you have a time to meet with ..." Kemper turned to Oakes. "What's his name? The sheriff?"

Wil did not wait for the FBI man to answer. "Grayson Farmer. And no, sir. I was thinking of going by his office at nine."

Oakes and Kemper nodded, agreeing to the time.

He saw the opportunity to receive confirmation on the specifics of Winter's death. "I'd like to put out a special edition about the two deaths, and I was hoping you could share some information I can print in the paper."

Oakes and Kemper stared at one another, as if waiting to see who would blink first. It was Kemper. "I'm going to brief Sheriff Farmer on the details of an ongoing Secret Service investigation. You're welcome to sit in. Any problem with that, Oakes?"

Oakes grimaced but shrugged his shoulders.

Wil glanced at the counter. "Looks like my breakfast is ready. Good to meet you."

+ + +

Geri smiled when she saw Wil at his desk through the front window of the *Wrangler*. If he had not been in the office, she had half-planned on taking the day off. With her purse slung over one shoulder and the canvas bag filled with mail on the opposite arm, she opened the front door. A third day out of four as the first person into the office would have been too depressing. Never mind the possibility of another dead body in a car somewhere just off a Fremont County highway.

Wil stood and held back the spring-assisted half door. "How's the mail look?"

She placed the canvas sack on the counter beside her typewriter. "Not too bad. We should be able to catch up the town mail."

"I need to go see the sheriff at nine. You're not going to guess who's in town."

Geri opened her purse, took out her cigarettes and lighter, and then set the bag into the bottom desk drawer. "Hopalong Cassidy?"

"Better than Hopalong, Pancho, and the Cisco Kid. A Secret Service agent named Kemper was at breakfast with Special Agent Oakes from the FBI. They're going to meet me at the sheriff's office."

"What's the Secret Service doing here?"

"Kemper said he's going to tell Gray Farmer about an ongoing investigation. I've got no idea what that means, but he said I could sit in. I'm hoping they'll let me put it into the special."

She took a cigarette and tapped in on the glass desktop. He was still thinking of doing a special edition, which meant working through the weekend. "Just remember we've got a regular edition too. It doesn't make sense to print two editions when there's only enough news for one."

"Let's see what happens at this meeting."

She lit the cigarette and inhaled deeply, blowing smoke toward the ceiling. "Dallas have any ideas on how to get Gray to talk?"

Wil took the mailbag from the counter and pulled out envelopes. "I didn't get to that. He told me to be careful and gave me Dad's shotgun."

Geri stood beside Wil, straightening the stack of envelopes to make sorting easier. "Good advice. Like I've said, we already have a sheriff. And you've got a job to do."

"What I'd really like to print is that they've solved both cases."

"Me too. Then we wouldn't need a special. Go comb your hair before the meeting and let me sort the mail."

Wil looked as if he wanted to say something, but instead turned, stopped at his desk, and walked back to the press area and bathroom. Another day of working the mail on her own.

+ + +

Dallas arrived forty-five minutes ahead of time at the spot where he was to meet Bob Thornton. Bob's description had been light on details, but the Register of Deeds in Lander had provided a legal description and verified Thornton's claim of ownership. Dallas had already driven the perimeter of the property, to the extent allowed by county roads.

Just north of Midvale, the parcel formed an odd-shaped rectangle that stretched along the north side of Five Mile Creek. Unlike the cultivated hay fields he had driven past, wild grass and desert flowers and scattered rock covered the uneven ground. The best use for the property would be agricultural, but there was no evidence either Bob or the prior owners had made any effort to tie into the irrigation system or level the land. The only man-made structure appeared to be little more than a log-and-mud grain hut.

Dallas took comfort from the openness of the location—no high point or concealment ideal for an ambush. The hunting rifle with scope and the pump shotgun in the backseat could remain sheathed. But he slipped on the chest holster with the over-the-shoulder strap. The Smith & Wesson Outdoorsman, capable of handling a special handloaded round, was too heavy to carry on the hip.

Dallas walked toward the grain hut, curious about what might be inside. He approached the shed cautiously. The property failed to match his other land holdings, but this was a special situation. He distrusted Thornton and wanted to separate himself from the partnership. The parcel would do, although Bob would need to sweeten the deal with a new car, and not a low-end model. A new Hudson Hornet would probably close the deal.

The grain hut turned out to be a primitive cabin, with rodents as the current occupants. A uniform layer of dust covered a wood-burning stove, a table, and the rotted canvas on a cot frame, all huddled in the low-ceilinged space. Two broken windows and the half-open door enabled the Wyoming wind to push along any odors. Dallas tried to imagine the life of an early settler on the unforgiving patch of ground.

He looked outside for other evidence of a settler but found little. The cabin and the untilled land led him to wonder of the conditions of his Ohio ancestors, who had settled land as fertile as this site was barren. He imagined trees and thick native grass, all needing to be cleared before crops could be planted. His grandfather, the number three son, had become a shopkeeper, leaving farming to the older brothers.

Dallas saw the trail of dust from an approaching car. Most likely it was Bob, a mere ten minutes early. He pulled the gun from the chest holster, checked the cylinder and reholstered. Standing at the front end of his Mercury, he waited.

Bob appeared to be alone in a two-door yellow Hudson Wasp. Dallas held his position behind the Mercury as Bob braked, and then he advanced to greet the driver. He rested his right hand behind the grip of the revolver on his chest and smiled.

Bob slipped out of his car and closed the door. "Heh, Dallas. Out looking things over, I see. You expecting trouble?"

Dallas patted the butt of the revolver. "I had a colleague in Idaho who ran into a bear. Had a small-caliber six-shooter. They found enough of him to bury, but it was a closed casket. I want a fighting chance. Might not find bear here, but there's other predators about."

"I feel safer already."

Dallas made a sweeping motion with his left hand. "So how'd you come by this?"

"Fella was buying a new pickup on time and quit paying. I went to collect, and he offered the property. I already had enough used pickups, so I took the deal. What do you think?"

Dallas looked at Bob and paused. "Most of my property is set up to become either commercial buildings or houses. I'm not sure houses will ever make sense out here. And if I wanted to be a farmer, I'd never have left Ohio, if you know what I mean."

Bob Thornton nodded and moved farther onto the property, kicking at rocks as he walked. "Suppose a person could irrigate and grow hay, like other folks out here. Might be good for sugar beets. I always thought one of the ranches around here would want it one day."

"I was hoping you might have some land on the north side. Or down along the Wind River."

Bob rolled his shoulders back and grimaced. "Like I said before, the only land I got down there's the homeplace. My brother Harlan is living on it and keeps it going. Each of us kids has a share, but we've promised not to break it up."

Dallas knew Bob had told the truth about the family land, but he had lied about other properties. Bob owned parcels of land on Federal north of town and a large plot on the south side next to the Pioneer Construction yard. And there was a spacious pasture area in town, at the north end of First Street. The shoulder roll might be Bob's lie detector, useful knowledge in a poker game.

He joined Bob in shuffling over the ground. "What about mineral rights? Are they part of the deal?"

Bob stopped and looked right and left, as if a clump of sage might contain the answer. "Not sure. Think so, but can't be certain."

"How far does it go to the east?"

"It's between Five Mile Creek and the road up there, and then east to the road and maybe some fences, I think. I tried to rent the ground but had no takers. A fella like you might know someone willing to take a risk."

Dallas rubbed his face with his left hand, the right still resting on his chest. "I'd be more apt to risk it in a card game, but doubt anyone would let it match what I put into your businesses. And I expect to get my money back and then some."

Bob stopped and turned toward Dallas, shaking his head. "I wish I could just write you a check, but cash ... cash is tight."

Dallas studied Bob, seeing the settler's shack over Bob's left shoulder. His gaze shifted from Bob's expression to the hut and back. "I'd need some kind of sweetener for this property to work. Something to make me feel good."

"Like I said, Dallas, cash is tight."

He stared at the settler's hut and gnawed at his tongue. "There is the option to sell my interest to someone for cash."

Bob took a step toward Dallas and pointed his finger. "You don't have to do that. Just be reasonable."

Dallas moved his hand closer to the grip of the revolver. "When I helped you out, you had no one else to go to. You'd been to the banks and the other people with money to invest. That's why you agreed to give me the option to sell off my interest, remember?"

A snarl took shape on Bob's face. "I remember, but never thought you'd do such an underhanded thing. What's it going to take to work this out?"

Dallas chewed on his tongue and looked back at his car. "I could use a new car, Bob."

"Now you're talking."

Dallas raised his eyebrows. "I was thinking a new Hornet."

Bob staggered back. "Dallas, you're bleeding me. That's my best model."

"The other choice is for me to buy out your interest in Pioneer. But I'm a lawyer, not a construction man. I suppose Pioneer could build the new houses on my other land."

Bob threw up his arms in surrender. "Uncle. I'll get you a Hornet. Good enough?"

Dallas let his right hand slip back onto the shelf of his belly. "That should do it. I'll get a title search and a survey, and then I'll draw up the papers."

"Dallas, I said uncle. You got me. Why all the extras?"

Dallas started back toward the cars. "Bob, people pay me good money to advise them on business deals. I'd tell them to do a search and a survey on this kind of a transaction. If I didn't follow my own advice, then it'd be like you taking a car as a trade-in without seeing if it runs."

"I suppose."

They walked along together in silence to the cars. "When I get back to the office, I'll get this going, and we can sign the papers on Monday, say lunchtime, at the hotel."

"I'm not sure why we have to delay this, but it's a deal." Bob extended his hand, and Dallas shook it.

Dallas watched as Bob got into his car and drove off, shooting up another trail of dust. He opened the back door of his Mercury and grabbed the canteen. He took a few short sips of water and turned toward the shack that looked more like a grain hut than a cabin. There was something familiar about it, but he could not place it. And he wondered whether Bob had given in too easily. What did Bob know that he did not?

CHAPTER 26

Deputy Nelson arrived at the Riverton substation before Agent Oakes and his white-haired friend Kemper, who claimed to be with the Secret Service, but after Sheriff Farmer. The arrival of a Secret Service agent had done little to calm Sheriff Farmer's anger from the day before. He looked as if his night had not been at all restful. Al understood how Farmer felt.

His own plan to get a good night of sleep had been derailed when Diane asked to use the bathroom at his apartment after dinner. She had an agenda that included stretching out atop him on his single bed, fully clothed. He finished before her, but she did not stop, leaving him sore. And rather than going home afterward, she had slid off and lain against him in the single bed. She had not snored, but different parts of her body had jerked and moved the entire night, keeping him from sound sleep.

When Wil Dodge walked in the front door of the substation, all Al could think was this situation did not need a civilian. The three men in Farmer's office, all with handguns on their hip, created an atmosphere crackling with danger. But Agent Oakes pulled Dodge into the sheriff's office before Al could send him away. He stayed at the office door, standing, ready to react if necessary.

Kemper rose from his chair. "Mr. Dodge, I believe you know everyone. Sheriff, this young man said he has something to show us."

Dodge moved into the room and stood at the end of Farmer's desk with a brown-colored large envelope. "I've got some photographs taken by Corky Freeman, the newspaper photographer. I believe he planned to show them to Mr. Winter. How do you want to do this?"

Farmer squinted at Dodge. "Where'd you get these?"

"Corky kept them in a locked box that I discovered."

Agent Oakes moved closer to the sheriff's desk. "Why don't you just show 'em and tell us what you know. Will that work?"

Farmer stood to join Oakes and Kemper as Dodge pulled the collection of photos from the envelope. Al stepped forward but did not have a clear view of the enlarged prints.

"Corky kept detailed logs of his photographs—date, location, time of day, subject, and some technical information. This first one was on October 11 of last year. This is Jim Haefner, Bob Thornton, and Dallas Dodge. They are at the Boysen Dam site. The date and location were verified by my uncle."

Oakes cleared his throat. "Any questions? … Okay then."

Sheriff Farmer picked up the photograph Dodge had dropped on his desk, narrowing his eyes as he scanned the image.

"The rest of these are mostly of Haefner and Thornton, with some workmen at the dam, at Thornton's Hudson dealership, and elsewhere. The best I can do on the time frame is from April to June of this year."

The men watched as Dodge laid down picture after picture.

"The last reference to Haefner in Corky's logs was on June 12, with a location listed as north of Midvale. I think these are the photos to go with those entries. I'll let you draw your own conclusions."

Dodge set down three pictures, the first showing Bob Thornton poking Haefner in the chest that Agent Oakes picked up and handed to Kemper. Sheriff Farmer accepted the photos from Kemper and stacked them on his desktop.

Dodge quietly watched as they studied the enlargements, and then laid down a final picture of Thorton handing an envelope to Haefner. "Sheriff, I think these are the photographs Corky told Mr. Winter about the night before he died."

Farmer broke the silence. "I'm going to need everything you got. The box and everything inside."

Dodge took a breath and glanced at the sheriff and the federal men. "I'm happy to provide prints of these photos to each of you, but that's all. Anything more than that will need a search warrant or permission from my attorney."

"I want 'em and—"

Kemper interrupted Farmer. "That's good enough for me. Deputy, can you get a chair for Mr. Dodge?"

Farmer banged the top of his desk. "I'm in charge here."

The Secret Service man pulled his suit jacket back and rested his hands on his hips. Al dropped his hand to the handle of his gun and watched the sheriff's hands as he leaned on the desk.

"Sheriff Farmer, I speak for both Agent Oakes and myself: we'd like you to be part of the joint FBI–Secret Service investigation. I'd like to bring everyone, including Mr. Dodge, up to date on that investigation. But if you don't want to play ball, then Agent Oakes and I are leaving, along with Mr. Dodge. Deputy, a seat for Mr. Dodge."

Farmer looked like he wanted to spit as Al left to grab a chair. The sheriff waited to sit until after Oakes and Wil had taken their seats. Al could feel his heart racing as he moved back to the doorway and tried to remain calm.

The white-haired Secret Service man took a deep breath. "Late in 1950, the Reclamation department asked the Secret Service to investigate possible billing fraud on the Boysen Dam project. Reclamation received an anonymous tip, we think through a former employee, of questionable payment requests. Mr. Winter, with our office, led that investigation, and irregularities were detected. The focus of his efforts became James Haefner, project superintendent.

"In early June, Winter began to coordinate with US marshals to take Haefner into custody for questioning. Haefner disappeared before that action took place."

Farmer looked at Kemper and then Oakes. "So where'd he go?"

Kemper interlaced the fingers of both hands. "When the local office notified Washington that Haefner had not reported for work and was not at his hotel, Jack Winter came out to Riverton and assumed the role of temporary superintendent to find the answer to your question. He created a cover story that Haefner had been assigned to another Reclamation project, to explain his disappearance."

Al knew the next question but let Farmer ask it. "So what'd he find out?"

"Winter's written report revealed Haefner's personal belongings were still in his hotel room. His government car was in the hotel parking lot. None of the Reclamation department vehicles were missing. And the last time anyone remembers seeing him was on the morning of Friday, June 13."

Oakes leaned forward. "The day after the last of Freeman's photos of Haefner."

Farmer pushed his lips forward and leered at the Secret Service man. "So why the hell didn't someone tell me he was missing?"

Oakes sat back in his chair and looked up at Kemper, as if he had the same question.

Kemper took a breath and stared at the wall behind the sheriff. "The Secret Service offices in DC enlisted Justice and the FBI to monitor Haefner's family. His mother and a brother both live near Philadelphia. Neither reported hearing from him; mail and telephone surveillance revealed nothing. We monitored Haefner's bank accounts, and there's been no new activity. Consensus was that Haefner had learned of the investigation and had gone into hiding. Possibly Mexico."

Farmer stood, crossed his arms on his chest, and wagged his head back and forth. "So you lost a suspect. Winter's been killed. And you got your hat in hand, wanting our help."

Kemper held up a finger. "We know the false billings were from Palmer Concrete Company, Riverton, Wyoming."

The sheriff was quick to correct him. "There ain't no Palmer Concrete."

"Exactly. Our agency has tracked the disbursements, and we know they were deposited at a bank in Lander. The account history shows deposits of government-issue checks and several cash withdrawals. The account was closed out in mid-June."

The room was silent as each person digested the information. Al cleared his throat. "Who's the bank say made them deposits? And took out the cash?"

Kemper turned to Al and then back toward Farmer. "We've talked with tellers and bankers, and they all describe a middle-aged woman. The materials given to set up the account include several legal-looking documents that are entirely fictitious. We think the woman was in a disguise to mislead the bank staff. Her hairstyle never changed, meaning it was a wig, and her colored-lens glasses concealed eye color and shape, suggesting deception."

Sheriff Farmer summed up the presentation. "So you're up shit creek then, aren't you?"

Kemper turned toward Dodge and smiled. "This new information from Mr. Dodge gives us a fresh direction. Perhaps Jim Haefner and Mr. Thornton had a personal relationship, as well as a business one. I believe Thornton is an officer of a local construction company involved from the earliest phase of the project. We'll be talking with him."

Sheriff Farmer put his hands on his hips. "Now don't that beat all. The newspaper's in charge of the investigation. Sending white shirts from out of town to harass a solid citizen over some candy they lost. I think you men should move onto Main Street and set up shop at the newspaper."

Al had intended to suggest the men talk with Diane, but given Sheriff Farmer's comment, speaking up felt wrong. Maybe he could talk with them later, away from the substation.

Dodge slid forward on his chair and turned to Kemper. "How much of this can I print?"

Farmer answered first. "None of it. All police business. Just courtesy."

Kemper looked at Dodge, ignoring Sheriff Farmer. "You can mention the joint investigation between the sheriff, FBI, and Secret Service, concerning Mr. Winter's death. You can also report the investigation of possible billing irregularities at the Bureau of Reclamation. It would be best if you did not mention Haefner or Thornton, for obvious reasons."

"I'd like to get quotes from each of the agencies for the story. Is that a problem?"

Kemper nodded. "I'll have a statement on behalf of Reclamation to you this afternoon."

"Ditto for FBI."

Farmer frowned. "No comment. Show's over. Get out of my office."

Kemper rubbed his hands together. "Sheriff, I'll get you a copy of the Reclamation statement. This could be good public relations for your department and your reelection."

Farmer's head snapped toward Kemper at the mention of the election. "Nothin' good about two people being dead."

Agent Oakes bowed his head. "Amen to that."

+ + +

Wil slipped into the *Wrangler* building from the dock entrance off the alley. He stopped at the darkroom and pulled down the last dry set of Corky's photos. For now, Kemper and Oakes could share this set, but he would need to get the negatives from the padlocked box in his pickup to print another batch. One of the federal agents planned to stop after lunch to collect the pictures.

A tower of smoke rose from around Geri's head as he walked into the front office. "I've got a confession to make. The reason I went to see Farmer was I found Corky's photos, the ones that might've gotten him killed."

Geri swiveled her chair toward Wil and watched him push through the half door and cross to his desk.

"At the sheriff's I learned that Jack Winter was with the Secret Service, and there's been embezzlement going on with the Boysen project. And Jim Haefner, the main suspect, has disappeared or is dead like Winter. So that's what I'll be working on for the special edition."

"So what's the confession?"

Wil tossed the set of photos onto her desk and took his seat. "I showed these to other people, like Natee and Dallas, but not you. I hid them because I was afraid it might put you in danger. But now that the sheriff and FBI and Secret Service have seen them, I hope it's safe."

Geri picked up and scanned the collection. After shuffling through the batch, she handed them back to him.

Wil leaned forward and made eye contact. "I thought you'd be mad I didn't tell you earlier."

She stubbed the cigarette that had been dangling from her mouth. "We've all got secrets. If you thought me not knowing would be safer, I understand. But now that the FBI and Secret Service are here and know everything you do, can we abandon the special edition? That's why you wanted to do it, to get attention for the investigation."

Geri had a point, even if he did not want to give up on the idea of a special. "I've already got copy—"

She held up her hands, palms forward. "It'll keep till Thursday. There's only two of us. And we've got a funeral tomorrow. Remember?"

Mention of the funeral reminded Wil of the arrival of the Freemans and the need to call Corky's landlady. "What about the gal that rents to Corky? Have you talked with her?"

"Dotted the i's and crossed the t's. I'm picking her up a good half hour early."

He remembered the Simpson woman's flushed throat. "I still think she knows something about Corky's death, but I've got no idea what. Maybe you can do some girl-on-girl magic."

Geri tilted her head to the side and gave a look he knew from high school, the sort of expression that communicated how little he knew about women. She swiveled back to her typewriter and started clacking the keys.

If the special edition was not going to happen, then he had free time on his hands. Time to think about his dinner date with Natee Saylor. Time to talk with Cecil and tell him the latest. And time to share the news of the Secret Service man with Dallas, even though his uncle was probably aware of Kemper.

Wil opened his desk drawer, removed the paper-clip box with the earrings, and emptied them onto his desktop. "Are these a secret you've been keeping from me?"

Geri picked up her cigarette pack and turned toward him. "What're those?"

Wil recounted Ramona's story about the single earring she had found in Denver and his conclusion the lesson his father had learned was not that cheating on his wife was wrong, but that getting caught was the problem. As he told the story, he held up each earring for inspection before returning it to the box.

She tapped the end of her cigarette against the desktop. "I didn't know for sure, but I suspected. But it wasn't my place to … Hearing it from Ramona … oh, I don't know. You were so, so … what? Indignant? I guess that's as good as any word. So indignant, about husbands cheating on wives, I thought telling you would be hurtful and mean."

Wil closed the lid on the box of unmatched earrings. "You know about Chicago. I'm not proud of that, but it doesn't excuse Clayton."

Geri flicked the lighter and lit her cigarette, sending a stream of smoke sideways. "I understand."

Wil looked up at her. "The sad part is how Ramona just accepted it. She thought about cheating on him but couldn't find anyone that interesting. She just decided to live with it. That's the sad part."

"Maybe your generation will move beyond the double standard, but I doubt it. A man is excused for it, but the woman suffers—not that women aren't just as bad as men. But a gal with a bad reputation has no true girlfriends. You can't trust a woman who'd try to steal your man. But guys admire the fellow who fools around."

Wil doubted whether his generation would see things differently. Since returning to Riverton, he had heard stories of married men from his high school class who were unfaithful. He thought less of them but felt he was probably the exception.

Chapter 27

After Dodge left, Grayson chased Oakes and Kemper out of his office. Nelson acted as if he needed direction, so Grayson sent him off to keep track of the movements of the federal men and report back.

Until yesterday and Nelson's report from talking with Reclamation, the name Jim Haefner had meant nothing to Grayson. He could not give the name a face or a place in Fremont County. But then this morning, young Dodge slaps a photo down and identifies Haefner, with Bob Thornton and Dallas Dodge.

Now that he had seen the photo of Bob Thornton and Haefner arguing, and heard of the Reclamation man's disappearance in June, the details fit together like a key into a lock. The door it opened only meant trouble for Grayson. He was probably safe as long as Haefner remained officially missing. But there could be more photographs, and unlike dead men, they could tell a story.

Kemper suspected Haefner had gone into hiding or left the country. The likelihood of the federal men doing enough police work to find Haefner's body was slim. For that matter, even he did not have a clue about the final resting place.

Finding and destroying any incriminating photographs made the most sense. But there was a risk in that sort of action. Since young Dodge had produced the Haefner photos, his office, pickup, or apartment seemed the obvious choice. But that kind of search could arouse suspicion. And he could not assign that job to one of his deputies.

+ + +

After lunch at Mezetti's, Wil pointed the pickup to Gordon's to check on the progress of preparations for Corky's parents. Before leaving for breakfast that morning, he had supplied Cecil with Ramona's leftover sliced roast beef from earlier in the week. The cowboy had refused Wil's offer to be driven to Gordon's nearby home, saying he wanted to get some air.

Geri's earlier talk of a double standard and sex distracted Wil at the stop sign on Main. The well-spaced parade of cars and pickups heading east and west let his thoughts drift to the limited sexual experience with his ex-girlfriend in Chicago. It had happened the weekend her roommate went to St. Louis for a wedding. Wil had planned to remain celibate until they were married. But that night, when he went to her apartment, their kissing had turned to rubbing and then much more.

A honk brought Wil back to the moment, and he checked traffic again before he crossed Main and headed south. The sensations he had felt through his entire body that night, naked and in contact with a woman, had caused a painful self-awareness. The second time, after the movie, he had felt more in control, although she had acted disappointed.

He learned she owned a diaphragm that night. Up to that moment, he had not known such a contraption existed, much less that she used one. About a week later, Wil discovered her sexual entanglement with another man. That ended his plans for marriage and became another reason for returning to Riverton. He had not thought less of the other man, but she was clearly a tramp.

But why had Chicago come up? Wil thought he had moved beyond that bittersweet failed romance. Maybe his dinner date with Natee Saylor had something to do with it. His thoughts about the woman he had kissed in the cemetery included sex, but that was clearly just wishful thinking.

Natee had taken him to her high school necking spot. He could not help but question whether she had imagined kissing one of her old boyfriends instead of him. Wil believed he had been too good for the girl in Chicago, but doubted he was good enough for Miss Saylor.

Wil pulled in front of Gordon's house, shut off the engine, and stared through the windshield. "We're just having dinner and talking. No reason to think she likes me enough to have ..." He was able to think about sex, but saying the word aloud felt like a sin. Still, he was not the kid from Sunday School people remembered him as, but a man who had tasted life. Chicago and working for the *Daily* had exposed him to murders, corruption, people living in poverty, and sex.

He made eye contact with the image in the rearview mirror. "Grow up. Riverton's got murders too. There's nothing wrong with having sex if you love the person." The words spilled from his mouth, but the voice in his head still called it a sin.

Wil did not know if he loved Natee, but he recognized her as the first appealing single woman he had met since returning to Riverton. He needed to think and act like a smart and confident man, and not an insecure, fumbling junior high boy. "Grow up."

He pushed the cab door open and slid from his seat to the ground. At least the guys were not sitting on the porch, having a drink. As he approached the front door, he could hear the sound of a vacuum cleaner. Pudgie came to the screen door to meet him.

+ + +

Dallas held the photograph in his right hand, steered with the left, and headed north along Tunnel Hill Road. He gnawed at his tongue, mentally cataloguing the events and players. Jack Winter and the Freeman boy were dead, and Jim Haefner was missing. And the discovered photos connected Bob Thornton to Haefner.

He slowed at the bridge over Five Mile Creek. The significance of the settler's shack had registered earlier that morning when Thornton had pointed at his chest. During the drive back to his office Dallas remembered the photo of Bob poking Haefner's chest. Dallas wanted to find the spot where Freeman could have taken such a picture.

Neither ranch nor county road went east after he crossed Five Mile Creek. Dallas drove north along the western edge of the Thornton property, beyond the spot of the morning meeting. He found a pickup pulled halfway onto the shoulder and the owner of the survey company, Eldon, stooped to look through a tripod-mounted scope. Dallas pulled behind the pickup, got out, and walked through dried-out wild grass toward the surveyor. The sand and dust of the afternoon breeze stung his face and neck.

"How's it looking?"

Eldon made a notation before turning toward Dallas. "We'll finish up tomorrow. Odd-shaped lot. Different sort of land for you, Mr. Dodge. Not a good place to build houses."

Dallas grunted. "Glad you could get started so quick."

The surveyor pushed both arms straight up and motioned to a man holding a tall shaft in the distance, who waved back a response. "Looks good, so far. Clear boundaries. Don't think there's any problem with the cement chunks crossing over the lot line."

Dallas looked beyond the surveyor's shoulder. "Cement chunks? Where?"

"Down by the eastern edge. Not far from the creek." Eldon looked at the Mercury parked behind his pickup. "If you want a look I'd advise against taking that car. Need a pickup or a horse to be safe."

Dallas turned to look in the same direction as the surveyor. "How would I get to it?"

The surveyor stooped to the scope. "Suppose you could follow along the river from the pull-in back by that shack, or there's a path worn in on the east end, from dump trucks. We'll be doing that stretch tomorrow morning."

Dallas realized Thornton was planning to unload both barren land and a dumping site used by the construction company. The offered land looked less and less attractive the more Dallas learned. "Let me know if you find anything else out of the ordinary."

"Like what?"

"More concrete. Dumped motor oil or chemicals. Anything that looks like it hasn't been there for twenty years."

Eldon stood up and nodded to acknowledge the request.

"I might see you in the morning."

Head back at the instrument, the surveyor lifted his left arm and signaled to his partner. "Sure thing."

Dallas returned to his Mercury and found a spot in the road to turn back to the south. As he approached the shack, he pulled in and parked. Taking the photograph and binoculars, he found the approximate location of Thornton and Haefner in proper relation to the settler's cabin. The spot was near where he had talked with Bob earlier that morning.

Dallas used field glasses to scan to the south, focusing farther back as he retraced the arc. He saw no obvious location Freeman could have used to capture the photograph.

Back on Tunnel Hill Road, Dallas inched along and looked for a pull-in of any kind. An irrigation ditch path appeared on his left, just beyond the swaying dried grass on the shoulder of the road. He stopped, walked in ten yards, and saw tire tracks. Dallas backed up, turned into the grass, and drove onto the path.

The only landmark Dallas had to work with as he inched along the irrigation ditch was the settler's cabin. When he reached a spot with the correct angle, he stopped, took the binoculars, and focused on the cabin. He compared the photograph to his view and felt certain this could be the spot. And from so far away, Freeman would not have been noticed. At least one mystery had been solved.

CHAPTER 28

"Does it look like Gordon'll be ready for the Freemans?"

Wil moved from the front door to the counter and faced Geri. "That house is going to be cleaner than any maid would make it. Vacuuming, fresh bedding, and a pot of trail stew simmering. Cecil even said Gordon had dusted."

Geri picked up her ashtray and dumped it in the wastepaper basket. "I guess that's a yes. Does that mean he remembers anything?"

Wil nodded. "He remembers seeing the photographs and said there were others—including some of Sheriff Farmer. But I didn't find those in the box he gave me."

"Any thoughts on his memory problems?"

He rubbed at his eyebrow. "I'm still waiting to hear from Dallas, but he should be seen by one of the doctors at the clinic. Maybe they can diagnose him and prescribe pills he can take."

"Have they got pills for that too?"

Wil looked up as if checking for cobwebs. "I don't remember which government agency Gordon worked for, but don't think it was Reclamation. There were a lot of federal employees in the camera club, though. I'd bet Gordon knew the person that tipped off Reclamation about the problems at Boysen Dam."

Geri tilted her head and shrugged her shoulders.

"Did the federal guys come by to get the envelope of pictures?"

Geri turned and looked at the wall clock. "Yup. So what could the photos of Farmer be about? I'm confused."

"Join the crowd."

He moved around the counter to the half door and pushed into the area with the desks. Wil took his seat, opened the desk drawer, and removed the paper-clip box with the earrings. "So there's photos of Farmer. But with who? And where? And there's still the woman that made the deposits in Lander."

"What woman?"

Wil pulled an earring out and rolled it in his fingertips. "Some woman no one recognized made deposits of the government checks to the bank in Lander. And in mid-June, about the time Haefner disappeared, she emptied the account. The Secret Service man thinks she was disguised. She hasn't been seen since."

Geri rolled her chair closer to Wil and crossed her legs. "Did they say how much money?"

"No, but I figure it had to be a least ten thousand dollars. Maybe more. I'll ask Kemper and hope he gives me an answer, but we might not be able to print it."

Geri bobbed her top leg. "Other than Haefner, and the mystery woman, who do you think was involved?"

Wil set the earring back in the box and leaned forward, resting his elbows on his thighs. "If Gordon and Corky were helping the investigation, we know they weren't involved. But that leaves the rest of Fremont County as possible suspects.

"Haefner was clearly a part of it. And maybe someone from his office. That's all it would take. But that's just a guess. It wouldn't surprise me if Bob Thornton was a part of it. And who knows about Farmer. Who's got these other pictures?"

He looked into the paper-clip box and removed three earrings. "If Gordon has any other pictures, he doesn't remember it, for now. I don't have them. If Dallas did, I think he would've told me."

Geri shook her head. "What would Ramona think if Bob was part of it?"

"She told me as soon as the election is over, Bob's on his own. That's the only good news I've gotten this week."

"You going to be in the office for a while? I've got to finish the deposit and take it to the bank."

Wil agreed to stay put and rolled a sheet of typing paper into the typewriter. He had decided to accept Dallas's offer to store the negatives and photographs in his safe. No one had come to steal or destroy the photos before he presented them to Grayson and the federal men. That meant neither Natee nor Dallas had tipped off whoever had killed Corky to prevent release of the pictures. Wil had not liked treating them as suspects but did not want to be a trusting fool either.

He needed to confide in Dallas. The billing fraud information, plus the report of Farmer's possible involvement, could suggest a line of inquiry to his uncle. Wil knew he needed help.

Wil waited for Geri to finish adding up the checks for deposit. "At the funeral, I'll ask his landlady if she found any photographs. But I'd think Farmer or one of the deputies would've already been there. If there are more pictures out there, I want them, whether they put me in danger or not."

Geri slipped the deposit slip, checks, and cash into a canvas zipper bag. "I'm not that afraid. But I do worry about you."

"I'm giving everything I've got to Dallas. He's got a little Fort Knox in his office. You'd have to see the safe to believe it."

She zipped the bag shut and stood. "I'll add it to my list of things to do."

Wil raised an earring and turned it around and around.

Geri brushed off her skirt and jacket and then pushed past the half door. "I wish you'd stop fiddling with those earrings. They bother me almost as much as that Hiroshima file."

Wil placed the earrings back in the box and returned it to the desk drawer. "I don't understand ..."

"They're like hunting trophies, like the head of a deer or elk, not that I ever saw him play with them like you are. It's a part of him I don't want to think about."

"And Hiroshima?"

"Parts of that folder were spread out on his desk from the Fourth of July until his death. Bad association."

Wil wanted to probe with questions but saw on her face a look he translated as "No Trespassing." He hoped Dallas would fill in the details about Clayton on Sunday. "When you get back, I'm going to see Dallas and run some errands. We've had a tough week. Close the office whenever you want."

"In case I forget to remind you when I get back, we've got a funeral tomorrow."

+ + +

Grayson cracked the window vent as he accelerated past the 55 mph speed limit sign just outside Riverton on the drive back to Lander, wanting to make it home by four o'clock. The day had started bad and gotten progressively worse. Dodge's identification of Haefner and Kemper's report of an investigation were the two plus two that equaled Bob Thornton, who had played him as the stooge.

The visit from Thornton at the substation, complaining of threats and pleading with Grayson to set the man straight, had seemed innocent enough back in June. All Grayson had to do was go to a meeting in Thornton's place and confront the man. But at the face-to-face north of Riverton, past Midvale, the man had claimed to be the victim, argued, and acted threatening. Grayson should not have let his temper get away from him.

Thornton had not even contributed to his reelection campaign. Now the car dealer would deny any meeting with Grayson. There were probably pictures of Grayson with Haefner out north of town. There could even be proof he killed the man. And Dodge could have given those pictures to Oakes and Kemper.

He should have disposed of the body himself instead of calling Thornton. Now Thornton could arrange for the body to show up and create questions he did not want asked. Grayson was not about to take the blame for Haefner's death. He would tell everything he knew to Oakes and Kemper, but only if Haefner's body appeared. And Grayson prayed that would not happen.

He had discarded the temptation to call or see Bob Thornton because of the watchful eyes of Oakes and Kemper. His temper had caused the mistake with Haefner, but that was his only involvement. Would Oakes and Kemper believe him?

Kemper's invitation to join them for an early dinner felt like a trap. The Secret Service man had sounded sincere, and Oakes had even smiled and patted him on the back, but they had a plan.

Grayson sped up, wanting to put as much distance between himself and Riverton as fast as possible. Thankfully, tomorrow was Saturday, and he could stay in Lander. Normally, he would attend the funeral of the Freeman boy, to give his sympathy to the family, but not this weekend. Not with Oakes and Kemper and Thornton sneaking around and making plans against him.

+ + +

Dallas already knew a Secret Service man had arrived in Riverton, but Wil's account of a billing fraud investigation had provided a more complete explanation. He had been right about Winter being a cop, even though the undercover agent had lied to him about Haefner. Perhaps Winter had thought of him as a suspect.

"I'd feel safer if you'd keep this. I'll hold on to the key, but what's in the box belongs in your safe."

Dallas visually inspected the wooden box with hinges on the outside. "I'm glad you accepted my offer of safekeeping. I will not even ask about the contents."

Wil shifted his weight back and forth, foot to foot. "Gordon says there're more pictures, including some of Sheriff Farmer. He didn't say who else was in 'em."

Dallas rose from the chair behind his desk and led the way to the meeting room. "Before I forget, can I borrow your truck tomorrow?"

Wil entered the library and half-smiled. "You taking a load to the dump?"

"No, just looking at some property. A little too rough for my Mercury."

"Sure thing. Do you want me to come to your place or what?"

Dallas stood at the bookcases and pressed the release. "I'll come to your apartment, say 8:00 a.m.?"

"Should be good. I'll have it filled up and ready to go."

Dallas opened the swinging bookcases. "Why don't you open the safe? You remember the combination, right?"

His nephew spun the dial as he instructed him to make a full rotation between each set of numbers. The main handle released, and the doors opened. Dallas placed the box into the right-side compartment, shut the doors, and twirled the combination wheel.

"Can I get you a drink? It's about the cocktail hour."

Wil looked down but failed to hide a grin. "No, thanks. I've got some errands."

"How are you and Miss Saylor getting along?"

The grin widened. "I'm meeting her for dinner tonight, in Hudson."

"I will not keep you any longer then, unless you need something else."

"Nope, that was it."

Dallas ushered Wil toward the front door. "Will eight be too early?"

"Nah. I'll be up early, getting ready. I'm giving the eulogy."

Dallas watched his nephew skip down the steps and out to his pickup. He knew Wil would share everything with the girl and hoped that was not a mistake. His nephew lacked finesse with women, unlike Clayton.

"Virginia, would you see if the out-of-town federal men will have dinner with me at the Wind River? Kemper and Oakes. But do not invite them to the cocktail hour."

"What time?"

"I'll meet them in the bar at six thirty. Have the room ready for dining by seven."

Virginia picked up the telephone, and he headed for his office. The Friday cocktail hour with a standing invitation to at least thirty guests was approaching, and he needed to develop a strategy with the federal lawmen. At least Wilson had taken his suggestion, deferring to his older and wiser uncle.

CHAPTER 29

Natalie Saylor stood on the sidewalk by her Jeepster in a sleeveless black dress and the red high heels she had worn earlier in the week. Trying to act more casual than he felt, Wil stepped down from the pickup cab and walked toward her, debating possible greetings.

"I'm cooking. Follow me." She drove off before he could react.

Wil scrambled back to his pickup and caught up just as she turned off the main road a few miles south of Hudson. A cloud of dust rose as they drove through turns and over a bridge of the Little Popo Agie River, stopping just past a stand of cottonwoods near a log cabin. She waited in the front door, holding her purse and black jacket over her arm. The barking sound of a dog carried from the back of the cabin.

By the time his boot hit the ground from his pickup, she had disappeared. He kicked up dust as he hurried to the cabin. At the threshold he stopped and surveyed the small front parlor. The room could have come straight out of one of Ramona's *Sunset* magazines, with varnished log walls, furniture crafted from pine branches, and a large Indian tribal blanket on one wall.

Wil found Natalie just past a short passageway, in the kitchen area, which was flooded with natural light from the west-facing windows. She stood at the counter, chopping vegetables into big chunks. "What do you want to drink? Beer, whiskey, rum?"

Wil took in the functional kitchen counter and dining area, free of frills or decoration. "I'll take scotch, with a little water, if you've got it."

The open living area ran the remaining length and the full width of the cabin and included a secretary with typewriter on the side in one corner, bookcases between windows, and a sofa with pillows and quilt by a wood-burning stove in the other corner.

"Ice? Have a seat." An antique round oak table with matching chairs complemented the light-colored pine logs.

"No ice, thanks. How long you been here?"

"About three years. Daddy wants me to live close to him, but I need my independence."

"How's Art doing?" Wil knew of Arthur Saylor by reputation but not experience.

"Hip trouble. Says he fell off a horse. I think it's arthritis." She handed Wil a glass of liquor, fetched her own, and set both a pitcher of water and her drink on the table. The late-afternoon sun was bright on her left side, and light and shadow danced along the contours of her face. Minor skin imperfections on her cheek did little to diminish her symmetric features.

She sat and crossed her left leg. "I hope you eat deer meat."

"I haven't had venison in years. Dallas and Dad used to hunt."

"If Ramona doesn't cook, what did they do with the meat? Or was it for trophies? I don't approve of that, if you want to know." Wil took a chair facing her and could not help but notice the shiny exposed knee and thigh and the red pump dangling from the toes of her left foot. She raised and lowered the shoe, lines of muscle and tendon winking below the knee and along her lower thigh. Wil had seen Geri make the same motion, without the dangling shoe or the flirtatious smirk.

"The neighbor woman that babysat me also cooked."

Natee nodded at the explanation.

Wil raised his glass in a toast. "To the most striking woman in Fremont County."

She smiled, tapped his glass, and took a shallow swallow.

He turned toward the sun-filled windows. "I heard a dog."

Natalie pulled hairpins from the back of her head and placed them on the table. "You might get to meet him. Depends …"

"I like the quiet here. After a day of listening to printing presses, this is like heaven."

She took a sip and held it in her mouth a moment before swallowing. "Riverton is a lot quieter than Chicago. Or Ann Arbor."

"How'd you know about Ann Arbor?"

She pulled at the unraveling knot of her bun. "A girl has to know who she goes out with."

As she talked about her college time at Barnard and New York City, his eyes focused on the movement of her lips and teeth in the golden late-afternoon sunlight—lips full and colored, the minute vertical lines visible at this distance; lips that guarded her teeth, never open too widely. The kind of lips that he imagined were meant for kissing.

"I need to change and get out of this girdle. Unzip me."

She rose, turned her back to him, and lifted the loosened hair at the top of her neck. Wil stood and clenched his fist, wanting his fingers not to shake. He pulled the tab down far enough to expose a black bra.

Natee reached back and touched his hand. "A little farther."

Wil lowered the zipper to the waist and caught a glimpse of a matching black slip. The exposed bare back and black lingerie caused a momentary paralysis. Just as he moved to run a fingertip down her spine, she stepped away, saying she could handle the rest.

He remained standing and took his drink to the west-facing windows. The light had already begun to fade as the sun flirted with the ridge of the mountains. Wil wondered whether Natee had planned a romantic evening, like he had fantasized. If she had, he wondered whether he could read the clues.

"I've not given you the ten-cent tour."

Wil turned to see Natee in a full-length shiny blue-green robe, held closed by crossed arms.

"This is the kitchen, dining, and living room, plus that little office in the corner. You've already seen the front room. And I need to show you the bathroom."

Natee spun, glanced over her shoulder, and reentered what he assumed was a bedroom. Wil stepped to the kitchen counter, set down his glass, and followed.

"Bath on the left ... and the bedroom."

A matching wood dresser and bed filled the room, with a closet along the wall that separated the bedroom from the front room. Natee uncrossed her arms, and the front of the robe opened to reveal a slice of her naked body from neck to belly button and below. An extended hand was the only invitation he needed.

Wil was uncertain how he became naked and when, during kisses and caresses, they transitioned to her bed. His inner voices were silenced, as if under a spell. Their lips, arms, and legs intertwined, swirled in near-continuous motion. She moved his hands to her breasts, hips, and pubic fleece.

A pungent aroma created a new level of arousal. She rolled atop him and placed her hand over his eyes. "Take a breath and relax." He inhaled and sensed her hovering above him. She repeated the order and ran fingertips about his chest. The muscles of his hips, belly, and legs went slack, and she slipped him inside her.

With her hand off his eyes, he found her smile through the curtain of her hair. "Don't tense up. Breathe and relax." His reward for obedience came in fractions of an inch, until he was fully engulfed. She kissed him on the lips and chin and then rested her cheek on his shoulder and remained still except for tiny squeezes on his manliness. He stroked her hair, letting the muscles of his belly and legs further unwind.

Wil lost track of time and place, sensing only the joined-together single self. He closed his eyes and imagined them floating in a calm lake, her movements creating a gentle wave. The waves became stronger, and he felt himself pulled deeper inside her until he could not stop his climax.

Natee collapsed on his chest, quivered, and leaned sideways to straighten first one leg and then the other. Wil could feel the sweat from her body against his as he held her tightly in his arms, still firm and inside her.

The diffused sunlight from the west side had lit the room when they entered, but now shadow and darkness painted the corners, with only the faintest hint of light at the doorway. Wil opened his mouth to speak but had no words. He closed his eyes and stroked her hair from her neck down her back. A weak sigh escaped from her mouth, followed by a squeeze down there. He moaned and tensed, lifting her hips.

She half-giggled, matching his flexes. He swallowed and took a breath. "I've died and gone to heaven." More giggles.

He felt a tug, pulling him deeper inside her. "Don't you dare die on me."

"I promise."

Wil felt her legs move, and she reached back to pull the top sheet over them. They lay in silence, exchanging kisses, squeezes, and caresses. When he softened and retreated, she arose and wrapped herself in the sheet.

"Stay put."

He watched her glide to the bathroom, saw the light come on, and then heard running water. She returned and climbed onto the bed still wrapped in the sheet, with a small towel in one hand. The towel was warm and wet, and she used it to remove their stickiness.

"You think of everything."

She rubbed his belly. "I hope you're hungry."

He ran his hand inside the sheet and rubbed her thigh. "I didn't know you felt that way about me."

"What way is that?"

"Well enough to have sex with me."

"I was ready Wednesday night. Remember how I talked of using Ramona's bathroom? I didn't need to pee. I was putting on my sombrero."

Wil did not remember her wearing a hat. "You're what?"

"My sex cap to keep from getting pregnant."

He closed his eyes, glad Geri had been wrong about Natee lying to him.

Natee slipped out of the sheet, off the bed, and into her robe. "That wasn't the first time I've done this. And you?"

"Not the first, but … nothing like this."

She leaned against the bed and kissed him. "Let me check on dinner. It'll only take a minute."

Wil listened as she opened and closed the oven door and slammed drawers shut. He pulled the sheet and a blanket around himself. Without the warmth of her body, he felt a mild chill and with it the return of the inner voice. But he refused to feel guilty.

It did not matter that she had been with other men. He was not without sin himself. At least she was unmarried and smart and beautiful. This was the sort of woman he had been looking for since returning to Riverton, but he had wasted a year. Or perhaps he had needed that time to heal and grow from the wounds of Chicago.

She swept into the room and dropped her robe. "We've got a half hour before it's ready."

Wil lifted the sheet and blanket. "And then what?"

"Then you open the wine, and I set the table, and we eat."

Natee dove onto the bed and turned, sliding her back against his front. Wil pulled her closer to him, felt her warmth, and closed his eyes. "What do we talk about until then?"

She wiggled against him. "You've not said a thing about the pictures and the sheriff."

He shared the highlights of the meeting with the sheriff and federal men, of Cecil helping Gordon, and of placing the box of negatives and photos in the safe at Dallas's office. His upper arm and hand moved over her body as he spoke, until she grabbed his hand and shoved it between her breasts.

"I've got a surprise for you, after we eat."

He pushed his nose into her hair, inhaled, and thought of flowers.

+ + +

"I asked the sheriff to join us for dinner, but he wanted no part of it."

Dallas nodded at the Secret Service man's statement and felt the need to provide an explanation. "Grayson and his wife live in the jail, at the courthouse, in Lander. She feeds the prisoners and the jailers.

I've heard a prisoner or two accuse her of trying to poison them, as a way to escape that chore."

Dallas lifted his manhattan, winked at Oakes and Kemper, and took a sip. He had limited his intake to two cocktails during the Friday gathering, knowing of his dinner engagement with the federal officers.

Agent Oakes set his drink on the bar. "He's made no secret what he thinks of us. Maybe having the weekend off will change his mood."

Dallas doubted the situation would play out as Agent Oakes hoped. "He has a murder investigation of his own, plus the one involving your man. Not the kind of thing a man running for reelection wants this close to the vote."

A waitress walked to the end of the bar and gave a nod to Dallas. His private dining room was ready.

"I have a private room for us. Bring your drinks."

The two men followed Dallas to the designated room, with Dallas reciting his declaration of western hospitality to his guests. He had given the short speech so often that he believed it, not allowing an ulterior motive to taint his surface persona of gracious host.

Dallas opened the door to a room with a single table near the center. He motioned them toward it. "If your drinks need freshening up, we have a bar handy. Help yourself to a seat."

He stood behind the chair facing the service entrance, the perfect spot to summon or dismiss the waitress. Kemper and Oakes meandered to the table, slowed by the oil paintings of western landscapes along the walls.

After they joined him at the table, Dallas set down his drink, took his seat, and opened the menu. "The trout are fresh, but I cannot endorse the other fish. The beef is quite good. I'm planning on trout and a steak, unless there is a special."

Dallas gave the men a few moments before signaling the waitress. The only sound of her approach came from the rustling of the starched white uniform with black trim. She guided them through soup or salad, potato choice, vegetable, and entrée, all without the need for a notepad, and quietly disappeared.

He lifted his cocktail and took a sip. "Mr. Kemper, what is your impression of our patch of the West?"

"Gene Autry must've been thinking of Wyoming when he did 'Home on the Range.' But I'm fond of shade trees and a lot less wide open spaces."

Dallas smiled and nodded. "My family was from Ohio, so I know what you mean. But this part of the country grows on you, don't you think, Agent Oakes?"

Oakes talked of hunting and fishing and close access to Yellowstone and the Tetons. The waitress served the first course as they shared small talk. Dallas urged it along until the entrées arrived.

After taking a bite of steak and savoring it, he leaned forward and lowered his voice. "Did you know I visited with Mr. Winter the night before his unfortunate episode? He dropped in on a house party for Bob Thornton, city council candidate. It was at my sister-in-law's house. I asked Mr. Winter about my acquaintance, Jim Haefner, and his sudden departure."

Both men nodded, partially occupied with chewing.

"Winter gave me a story about Haefner being needed at another project. I thought it odd a man as sociable as Jim would disappear without a farewell gathering of any kind. I wish Mr. Winter would have confided in me." Dallas stopped and carved a strip of his trout, slipped it between his lips, and closed his eyes as he savored the flesh. "I cannot help but wonder if it may have saved his life." When he opened his eyes, both men were staring at him.

Oakes glanced at Kemper, who in turn looked quizzically at Dallas. "Could you explain that?"

Dallas set down his fork and drank the last bit of his manhattan. "My nephew tells me Mr. Winter had been investigating Jim Haefner. And he was looking for certain photographs from the newspaper photographer. Had I known, I may have been able to encourage Wilson to speculate more actively on the who and where of them."

He waited for a question or reaction but saw only frowns. "The photos may have proved useful to any theories Mr. Winter had developed. They may have increased his awareness of potential danger and prevented him from placing himself in a vulnerable position."

The FBI agent nodded, as if accepting Dallas's explanation.

Dallas took another bite of trout. "I understand you have examined those photographs and arrived at your own conclusions. My nephew mentioned a fraud investigation by Mr. Winter, but few of the details."

Kemper began to chew again and then sipped his cocktail. "The pictures gave us some questions but no answers. We're still looking for Haefner. He is a suspect in Winter's death."

Dallas made the slightest motion with his head, and the waitress entered the room. "Do either of you need another cocktail? Any problems with your food?"

Oakes turned to the woman. "I'd like some coffee, with cream."

"Please bring cups and coffee for all of us."

Dallas waited until the waitress had returned to the kitchen. "I wanted this private meeting to report on my encounter with Mr. Winter and to answer any questions you may have about Mr. Haefner. I knew Jim socially and received a tour along with Bob Thornton of the Boysen project—although if I am a suspect, questioning should be performed in a formal setting."

Oakes spoke first. "The FBI does not consider you a suspect, at this time."

Kemper concurred with his FBI counterpart and remained silent as the waitress came and went with the coffee service. Kemper then provided a summary of the investigation details presented in the sheriff's office.

Dallas poured coffee, passed cup and saucer to each man, and placed the cream and sugar in easy reach of all. "And now Mr. Winter has been killed, and other than Mr. Haefner, you have no solid suspects, right?"

Both Oakes and Kemper grimaced and nodded agreement.

"If there is anything I can do to assist in your investigation, please let me know."

Kemper sipped his coffee. "Thank you, Mr. Dodge. It was good of you to talk with us."

"Normally, I would offer to drive you around the area, show off the sights, but I have commitments this weekend. Perhaps we could get together for a purely social dinner tomorrow night, same time?"

Oakes cleared his throat. "I was hoping you would let us treat you, at another of the dinner spots in the area."

Dallas gnawed on his tongue. "There's an excellent little place in Hudson you might find interesting. I'll call and make sure they'll have a table for us."

"Do you want us to pick you up, say six thirty?"

Dallas gnawed again. "I'll probably drive on to Lander after the meal. Let me give you a call, just in case. How can I reach you?"

Kemper glanced at Oakes and then Dallas. "I've got paperwork and calls to make, so I'll be at the hotel most of the day."

Dallas gestured to the waitress to clear the table. "More coffee? Or perhaps an after-dinner brandy?"

Both federal men declined the offer of brandy, content with coffee and conversation. Dallas steered them to talk of family and growing up. He noticed the casual questions that would have come up during an interrogation. The food and coffee had offset any loss of inhibition from the cocktails and the possibility of sharing too much information.

It was nearly 9:00 p.m. when he walked them from the dining room and lobbied for a stop at the bar for a nightcap. The evening had gone as planned: an exchange of information in a casual setting and the formation of a relationship. Tomorrow night would further that bond in an entirely social setting.

+ + +

Wil felt the bed jiggle, and his nose detected the scent of cooked meat. He extended his hand, found hers, and planned to pull her onto the bed, but her tug was stronger. As he neared the edge of the mattress, he flexed his knees forward, and sat up on the edge of the bed.

"Time to eat. Put on some pants."

The robe billowed behind her as she left the room, and he began a search for jeans and underpants. A light from the bathroom offered the only illumination, and he discovered his jeans beneath the bed. In the kitchen and dining area, warm yellow light circled the oak table, from an oil lamp with a glass chimney in the center. "Smells great. I couldn't tell you the last time I had a real home-cooked meal."

"It's not often I cook for someone, but it seemed right with you. Can you open the wine?"

As Wil penetrated and then wiggled the cork, he wondered what other men it had "seemed right" with, but he left his question unasked. The warmth of the afternoon sun had passed, and before taking his seat, Wil retrieved his shirt.

He poured wine into the roundish stemmed glasses as she placed a platter of carved meat and vegetables on the table. "Do you want to say grace, or should I?"

The question appeared to confuse Natee for a moment. "If you want to, that's fine, but don't do it on my account."

He recited aloud his short blessing, raised his head, and smiled. "Looks good."

Natee winked in reply and used the serving fork to move a thick strip of venison to her plate. "I could've made gravy but wasn't feeling like that much of a homemaker."

"It's already more than I expected. Weren't your parents religious?"

She cut the meat into smaller pieces. "I was raised a Catholic, which should be enough to make any woman question the existence of a loving God. You can't read early Greek literature without seeing their need for gods, but this is the twentieth century. Science has eliminated the need to attribute this world to the work of divinity. If there is a God, he's an indifferent observer and not the overseer of all, that some believe. But that's not good dinner conversation."

Wil chewed the venison as he attempted to digest her words. The idea that she was an agnostic or atheist had never entered into his assumptions about her. Best to move to another topic. "Good meat. Did Art shoot this?"

"No, this one was mine. The trick is the seasoning and cooking it slowly. But you were going to tell me about your girlfriends."

He took his time chewing the meat and picked up his wine glass. "A gentleman doesn't kiss and tell."

"So how many gals have you had sex with? No names, just a number."

Wil sipped the wine but had to wait a bit before he could swallow. "A few. And you?"

"I asked first."

"Before tonight, just one. A woman in Chicago."

Natee lifted her wine glass, swirled the dark liquid, and drank. "You were planning to marry her, right?"

The fork with a cooked carrot stopped partway to his mouth. "How'd you know?"

"And you thought you'd both be virgins at the altar, but then …"

Wil set the fork on his plate. "Who've you been talking to? Geri? I never told her about being a virgin."

"Just a guess, and a good one. How was it? That first time?"

Wil closed his eyes, lifted his chin, and inhaled. "Nothing like tonight. It was almost over before it started."

"Corky said about the same thing, which surprised me. Usually farm kids know about sex."

The hand reaching for his fork froze. "Corky? You and Corky had …"

"I assumed you knew. Most boys can't wait to talk, and I figured he'd told you. Sorry if I shocked you. No, that's a lie. You're old and smart enough to know the truth."

Wil felt the contents of his stomach attempt to crawl up his throat. He swallowed, hoping to stop the sensation, and took a deep breath. "He kept a lot of secrets, I guess."

She nodded and took a bite of meat.

He picked up his fork with no intention of trying to eat another bite. "So how'd you meet? And why did you and he …"

"I like younger men. Always have. They haven't turned into jerks yet and are open to suggestions. Corky was interesting and fun to be with and accepted my limits."

Wil was uncertain what she meant. "And what limits was it he …"

Natee lowered her chin and gave a half-grin. "Do you always leave your sentences unfinished? That's a bad habit to get into. Confuses people. Limits, as in friends, but not a steady, or a fiancée, or a wife. I've got plans that don't include marriage."

"Like being a senator in DC."

"That and more."

Wil attempted to reconcile the scenario he had entertained alone in bed, featuring Natee as a wife and mother, and some version of her boundaries. He had no desire to assume the role Ramona had accepted in her marriage with his father.

"Did you ever have sex with Clayton?"

She frowned. "I'm attracted to younger men. Your father was handsome, in that mature way, but he wasn't my type."

Wil poked at the items still on his plate, moving them about. At least he would always be younger than Natee, a bittersweet victory at best. How many, other than Corky, before him? And how many would there be after?

"I can cut some fresh fruit for dessert."

"No, thank you."

Natee stood up. "But I haven't shown you the surprise." She moved to the office area and retrieved an item from beneath the desk. When she gave it to him, his surprise was genuine. It was identical to the container he had given Dallas to keep in his safe.

"When you told me about finding the wooden box in Gordon's basement, I remembered Corky left one here, and I forgot about it until you described the other box yesterday."

A padlock, just like the one from Gordon's, held the lid shut. Wil wiggled a hand into his jeans pocket. He pulled out the ring of keys and selected the padlock key. "Let's see if he used the same lock."

He moved his plate aside and set the box on the table. The padlock opened, and Wil removed it. He felt Natee nestle in behind him.

The lid opened to reveal enlarged photographic prints. On the very top was a photo of Sheriff Farmer and Jim Haefner, with two more showing a struggle. The background looked similar to the ones of Thornton arguing with Haefner. The fourth photo featured Gretchen Simpson, naked, with a smile on her face. Wil closed the lid, sorry he had looked inside.

Natee leaned into him, lifted the lid, and turned over the photos like the pages of a book. "I knew there was someone special, but he ... he never talked about ... her. Do you know her?" She displayed a series of revealing images of Corky's landlady, all in the nude.

"The woman is Gretchen Simpson, Corky's landlady, wife of Delmar Simpson. Gordon said there were photos of the sheriff with Jim Haefner. But he didn't mention these."

She flipped the face-down stack back and slowly turned them a second time. "She's cute, but a married woman. That's ... that's ..."

Wil reached into the box for the photos beneath the ones of Gretchen. "Dangerous." He shuffled through the enlargements and did not find any others of Sheriff Farmer but did find portrait shots of different girls, including Natee. At the bottom of the box were negatives in protective sleeves.

She pulled away from the table. "What have I done?"

Wil turned, saw the pained expression, and pulled her onto his lap. When she shuddered, he pulled her head against his, wanting to calm her.

"I could've gotten Corky killed."

He patted her back and shushed her.

"I put him into a situation, by teaching him about women and sex. He may have ..."

Wil put his mouth beside her ear. "Corky was killed because of the photos of Haefner and Thornton and Farmer. Just like Winter. There's no reason to think it had to do with Gretchen Simpson."

"You can't be sure."

Wil patted her back. "Even if it was, you didn't break his neck. His death is not your fault. And it probably had nothing to do with that ... that affair."

Wil rocked side to side, listening to her sobs and feeling the strength leave her body. As her sobs stopped, he slowed the rocking motion and listened to her steady breathing.

He pushed hair away from her ear. "I should probably be going."

"I don't want to be alone. Please stay."

+ + +

Holding his hand against her belly, clasped in both of hers, Natee asked him to talk about Ann Arbor until she fell asleep. Mouth close to her ear, Wil whispered details about the university, the town, and his studies until her breathing slowed.

His restless thoughts filled the hour or so that followed. Wil felt as if he had spent the evening with three different women: the tease who had played "tag, you're it" at Hudson, the seductress with the red shoe dangling from her toes who had steered him straight into the bedroom, and the woman enveloped with unnecessary guilt over teaching Corky the ways of women. Plus the fallen Catholic, the ambitious politician, and a possible sex addict.

Now he could add his former employee's involvement with a married woman to the secrets Corky had kept. The evidence pointed to his spying on Jim Haefner as the reason for Corky's death. What was Wil going to do with this new photographic information? There was no good reason to show the nude photos to Farmer or the federal authorities. But someone needed to see the photos of Farmer and Haefner.

Thoughts of Corky could not compete with the warm body snuggled against him. Wil's attraction to Natee was undeniable. In the time they shared naked in bed, it felt as if they were the entire universe. But her boundaries of not wanting a boyfriend, mate, or husband, sounded genuine. He questioned whether the joy of being with her would justify the misery when he was discarded.

Wil could not imagine a clearer example of approach-avoidance. The concept had seemed simple during introductory psychology. But until this moment, he had not imagined the agony of being pinned between conflicting urges.

The steady rhythm of her breathing offered the only external sound in the room, lit by filtered moonlight. The thoughts repeated, turned back on themselves, and sought an escape route. Closing his eyes or fixing them on a spot on the wall placed him no nearer to sleep.

When the smell of bacon woke him, he was surprised both that he had fallen asleep and that he had not detected Natee's escape from his embrace. He shuffled out of the bedroom and to the kitchen in his jeans and heard the crackle of frying bacon. Natee stood at the stove, an oversized sweatshirt down to her thighs. Her reply to his greeting was a wave of a spatula and the continued tending of the bacon.

In the bathroom he swished water in his mouth and spit it out, taking only a moment to look at the features in the mirror. He found his shirt on the floor, not far from his boots and socks.

"Anything I can do to help? Open a bottle of wine? Boil some water?"

He hoped for a giggle but did not get even a glance. "Coffee's on the table. I'll have eggs and bacon soon."

Wil poured coffee and remained standing, looking through the west-side windows at the early sun lighting up the mountain ridges in the distance. He wanted to know what time it was but decided against asking. The woman at the stove was not acting like anyone he had been with the night before.

She carried two plates with scrambled eggs, bacon, and buttered toast to the table. He bent down, trying to make eye contact, but she refused to cooperate. "Did I say or do something wrong?"

"Dodge, you take yourself too seriously. Eat."

Wil thought of conversation starters but stuffed them all in his back pocket. He finished his plate, said a quiet thank-you, and carried plate and coffee cup to the sink. The thought that this might be how husbands and wives started their day made eating at the Atomic seem like a better choice.

Dressed, fed, and ready to go, Wil stepped out of the bedroom and found the wooden box leaning against the front door. He hollered, "Thanks again," and walked to the door. Box under his arm, ready to open the door, he felt a touch on his back and turned.

Natee looked up at him. "You owe me a dinner, Wilson Dodge. And be careful with what's in the box."

Wil nodded, unable to think of a comeback, and taken by the sadness in her eyes.

She reached up, touched his cheek, and stroked it twice. "Try not to become an asshole."

Wil turned, opened the door, and started toward his pickup. "Maybe I'll see you at the funeral." Without looking back, he climbed into his pickup and drove off.

Day 5

Saturday
September 7, 1952

CHAPTER 30

On his drive from Natee's cabin back to Riverton, Wil decided to entrust the latest wooden box of photos to Cecil until he could inspect them and cross-reference with Corky's notebooks. The next question was whether to tell Dallas about the new photographic evidence when he came for the pickup.

Natalie Saylor, lapsed Catholic, kept popping into his head. Wil had envisioned himself marrying another Protestant, not a woman from another faith. The array of religions in Riverton included the different flavors of Protestant, plus Baptist and Catholic. It was odd that a former Catholic should capture his romantic interests. He refused to consider the larger issue of her denial of God.

Compared to Corky's relationship with Gretchen, the young photographer's involvement with Natee seemed insignificant. Yet Wil could not deny his reaction to the news—shock, anger, disappointment, and jealousy. How could he be jealous of a dead person?

Had he known of that sexual history, would he have gone to bed with Natee? He could not deny he had wanted to have sex with her. Now he felt guilty and conflicted, and at the same time, blessed. Too many emotions.

Wil felt grateful when the drive ended and the free time to consider the same bundle of thoughts that had chased him throughout the night in Natee's bed ended with it. Corky's funeral needed his complete attention.

Cecil accepted the latest guard-duty assignment without complaint. He reported the arrival of the Freeman family the night before and their quiet night after the meal of trail stew. Mrs. Freeman had promised to fix a big breakfast for the men.

Wil quickly bathed and shaved, knowing Dallas would arrive shortly to borrow his truck. His dark suit and white shirt still fit, even though he had not worn them since Clayton's funeral.

The shiny maroon Mercury looked ready for a parade compared to the dust-covered pickup. Dallas, on the other hand, appeared prepared for a day of ranch chores. The blue jeans and the red-and-black box-patterned flannel shirt with rolled-up sleeves looked unnatural on the man. Like the brown work boots, the clothes presented a worn and faded impression that contrasted with the pressed and polished character of his lawyer outfits.

Wil told Dallas about the photos of Sheriff Farmer, as well as Corky's likely affair with Mrs. Simpson, before apologizing for not filling the gas tank. Dallas wanted to place the new information in his safe and suggested Wil could inspect the photos in the privacy of his office library. Wil declined the offer. They traded keys and agreed to meet at the law office at 2:00 p.m. to undo the swap.

+ + +

Dallas felt every bump in the road driving the pickup north of town. The Mercury had floated over these imperfections and gone faster. Trading the Mercury for a sleek Hudson Hornet made sense, yet he wondered whether comfort would be sacrificed for style. Just ten minutes in Wil's truck led him, once again, to question the infatuation with pickups displayed by so many in Fremont County.

He found the survey team at the northeast end of the property, as they prepared to mark the line to the south near Five Mile Creek. An Irish setter barked as he drove up, but the wagging tail gave Dallas confidence to climb down from the truck. The young fellow who held the stick, and apparently owned the dog, offered to guide the way to the reported piles of concrete.

Dallas trailed the other truck from far enough behind to avoid flying gravel and the full force of road dust. He kept glancing to the west, expecting to see the construction refuse, but saw none. The brake lights of the guide pickup flashed, and Dallas downshifted, following a twisting turn up a rise. From this elevation Dallas could see the dump site in a natural hollow.

The stick man turned toward the left, stopped, and began to remove his equipment. Dallas slowed and yelled, "Thanks!" He got a wave in return. The pile of construction rubble rested no more than a quarter mile from the expected property line. He drove along the path left by trucks toward the trash, the setter keeping pace alongside.

Dumped loads of broken concrete, railroad ties, used lumber, and more formed a progression of peaked piles. He drove two-thirds of the way and stopped, got out, and strapped on his chest holster and gun to make a closer examination on foot. The setter ran ahead, stopping periodically to make random sniffs, tail wagging. Dallas judged the length of the waste piles to be over fifty yards. This much construction refuse only reduced the value of the site Bob Thornton wanted to trade.

He had just turned, ready to leave, when the dog barked insistently at a spot near the far end of the dumped loads. Dallas decided to inspect the source of the dog's interest and checked the cylinder of the bear gun in the holster. A need for the gun was doubtful, but Dallas considered a feral animal a possibility.

At no more than five feet from the dog, Dallas discovered the cause of the reaction: a human hand poked out from beneath a pile of boards, cement pieces, and dirt. Scavengers had picked clean the exposed flesh but had lacked the strength to extract the attached arm. Thornton's piles had just escalated from trash to a possible crime scene.

Dallas attempted to calm the dog with little luck. He half-trotted to the pickup and drove to the location of the stick man. The news that his pet had discovered possible human remains provoked a questioning reaction. When the attorney shared his plan to report the discovery to the sheriff's office immediately, the surveyor suggested he "lose the artillery" before approaching any of the nearby ranches to use a telephone.

+ + +

Wil parked the Mercury along the side of the church, leaving the engine running as he listened to the car radio. He decided to get a radio in his next car or truck, since the pickup lacked this luxury. Music may have distracted him from the troubling thoughts from the night before on the trip back from Natee's cabin.

He found camera club members near the front of the church and stopped to listen to stories about Corky. The Jeepster was not in sight, and he wondered whether Miss Saylor had changed her mind about attending, although it was early.

Three pews at the front of the church were reserved for family and participants. The honorary pallbearers had taken the third row. Gordon sat beside the Freemans in the front.

Geri was stationed in the second row, and Wil took the aisle seat next to her. He saw Gretchen tucked next to Geri as he sat. Despite her black veil and hat, there was no mistaking Gretchen's emotional state, red-nosed and sniffling. Geri's posture matched that of a mother bear guarding her frightened cub.

The service listed inside the bulletin matched others funerals Wil had attended. The dreaded portion was titled "Message." Months earlier, Wil had concluded that Pastor Eastman's sermons were nothing short of pathetic, and he doubted today would be any different.

The organist transitioned from preludes to the opening hymn, and the voices of the gathered rose and fell in a restrained Lutheran fashion, except for what sounded like a Baptist or two toward the back of the church. Pastor Eastman offered a brief greeting and an elder read scripture. Another hymn preceded the eulogy. At the lectern, Wil recited the typewritten facts he had collected about Corky's life and added a few stories from the newspaper and one from the men of the camera club.

"Gordon Blakeslee knew Corky better than anyone in Riverton. It is Gordon who has made this service possible. Other than his family, none will miss Corky as much as Gordon, although he was loved and respected by many.

"In some cultures when a person dies before their time, an atonement must be made to return balance, the setting right of a wrong. Our culture does not have such a ritual. We have this funeral service. We will leave today with a deep sense of loss. Our hearts full of sadness for what this life might have been."

Wil stood still and looked briefly at those gathered, before lowering his head and walking back to the pew. Geri placed her left hand onto his and squeezed. Then came another reading, followed by a solo from funeral favorite Sharon Duryea. Taking his time, Pastor Eastman climbed the pulpit for "the message."

Eastman made a feeble attempt to establish his acquaintance with Corky and launched into a tepid retelling of the resurrection of Christ and the promise it offered. Wil's thoughts seized the attention the preacher was failing to capture and hopped from his father's funeral to his session with Sheriff Farmer and then on to Clayton's infidelity and Gretchen's sniffling. Thoughts of Natee tried to intrude, but he shoved them aside.

The standing of those around him signaled Wil the message was over, and it was time for call and response. The Lord's Prayer followed, and the service concluded with a short organ solo, an announcement about lunch in the basement, and the benediction.

The pastor led the procession to the rear of the church, followed by the Freemans, Gordon, Wil, Geri, and Gretchen. As he neared the rear of the church, Wil spotted Natee in a dark suit and red blouse. She made no effort at eye contact, and he wondered whether she would stay for the luncheon.

Once in the church basement, Gretchen quickly disappeared into the ladies' room. Geri motioned for Wil to follow her to an empty corner of the kitchen. He could see a hard edge in her eyes, likely the result of babysitting Gretchen and not wanting to smoke in church.

"I wasn't sure that girl was going to make it through the service. We've got to get her out of here."

"Were you able—"

"She's too upset to talk. I had to stop twice driving here to calm her. Getting her to talk is not going to happen."

"I think I know why she's so upset. Corky and her may've been more than landlady and renter—as in, having sex. There's photos he took of her without any clothes on, and she looked quite pleased with herself."

Geri's hand went to her mouth. "Holy buckets."

"I'm going to take her home and get some answers. I've got Dallas's big Mercury, so she shouldn't have a problem getting in and out. If you want to come along, that's fine."

"No, I'd likely slap her silly. What was she thinking?"

"I'll be outside when she's ready."

CHAPTER 31

Deputy Al Nelson drove to Freeman's street on the morning of the funeral. Tracking the movements of Oakes and Kemper had delayed his planned interviews of Freeman's neighbors. Agate Lane ran a mere two blocks in length with only one way in and out. Al made a left off Federal and drove all the way to the dead end, turned around, and parked a good twenty yards from the Simpson-Freeman house.

The first interview took place through a closed door. The woman of the house was almost as unwilling to talk as to open the door. There was no answer at either of the next two houses, though a dog barked inside one. The residents of the following three houses reported Freeman had kept to himself, had not spent much time at the house, and had not caused any trouble. They all agreed the Simpsons kept to themselves, and two mentioned the husband's frequent absences. Both the Simpsons and Freeman were portrayed as private people.

Sarah O'Hanlon, in the house across the street and down two from the Simpsons, reminded Al of his paternal grandmother when she opened the door. She wore a red bandana over her hair, with dust-covered bifocals, and jeans rolled up almost to the knees. She sat Al at the kitchen table while attacking her oven on hands and knees with a vinegar solution.

"Half this street is Mormon, and the rest is Catholic. Don't even need all of one hand to count the Protestants. You know those Mormons don't believe in the Bible, sending around boys in white shirts trying to make you believe in their book. Christians need to worry more about the Mormons than Communists."

"Yes, ma'am. The young man living in the Simpsons' house, the tenant in the dark gray place on the other side of the street—did you see much of him?"

"He drives a yellow Studebaker, right? I seen him but not that much. He leaves in the morning and comes back at night. I suspect he's a Mormon too, living with them. He's not been around the last few days."

"But you saw him?"

"Oh, sure. That husband living there is away a lot and leaves his wife alone without a car or nothing. She don't have many visitors even though there are Mormons all around her. He must be a traveling salesman."

"I wouldn't know."

"It's a blessing my husband didn't live to see this block taken over by Mormons. It would've killed him. Heart and stomach disease did that. He was in such misery. If he'd known this was going to be a Mormon street, we'd a'moved. But he had no way of knowing, did he?" She backed out of the stove and looked at Al, as if he might offer contradiction.

"Did you ever see the husband and the tenant arguing?"

"Nope. Seen the wife and the neighbor ... not sure if it was arguing, but they weren't agreeing."

"What neighbor is that?"

"The boy across the street from her. He's a hobo Mormon. No white shirt on him going to preach about their book. Got clothes that belong at the dump. She's all proper, dressing up even when her husband ain't at home. No work clothes for her. Dresses all the time. And shoes with heels. Don't she know this is a dirt street she's living on?"

"Does she talk with the neighbor often?"

"He starts it, going to her place when the husband's not around. I might be old, but I'm not blind. Anybody else you need knowing about?"

"No, ma'am. Thanks for your time."

Al walked down the steps, contemplating how to summarize the interview and puzzled over why he had thought Mrs. O'Hanlon similar to his grandmother. Her account agreed with others' shorter versions about Freeman and the husband. The information involving the neighbor was new. He felt blessed that Mrs. O'Hanlon did not live anywhere near him.

Earlier, Al had noticed Mrs. Simpson, dressed in black, getting picked up and driven away. He suspected she was going to Freeman's funeral. Al decided to look around her house, just in case. The property looked clean—no broken glass or visible trash—and the door of a small shed in back was padlocked. A bicycle leaned against the shed. Officer Masin had mentioned a bicycle. The back door of the house, one step up from ground level, was closed.

Al saw the man Mrs. O'Hanlon had described as the "hobo Mormon" as he walked up the driveway to the front of the Simpson house. Five foot eight, 140 pounds, unshaven face, loose-fitting plaid flannel shirt, and worn, brown, stained corduroy pants. Both shirt and pants belonged in the trash, just like she had said. The man stood near the end of the driveway.

"They're not here. You looking for something?"

"Just checking. You would be?"

"I'm Delmar's friend that looks after his place when he's away."

"I see." Nelson did not like the man's attitude. He might be quick, but Al stood almost six inches taller with a forty-pound weight advantage.

"I don't think you should be back there."

"You said your name was ..."

"I didn't, and it's none of your b'iness. This here's private property, and you got no reason to be here."

"Maybe we need to go to the sheriff's office and talk about this." Al reached for the handcuffs on his left hip, hoping that would be enough to change the neighbor's attitude.

"I ain't going nowhere with you."

"You live across the street, right?"

"Woe be unto you for shamin' the ways of the Lord. Understand these things or be smote. The Lord protects."

Al flicked open a cuff, the right hand dropped to his revolver, and he stepped forward. The neighbor turned, dashed across the street, and disappeared behind the house. There was no reason to chase him, other than his being disrespectful. The deputy returned the cuffs to his belt and sidestepped toward the car, unwilling to turn his back in the direction of the neighbor's retreat.

He stood with the driver's side door open, left forearm on the door top, his right arm and hand tense, ready to draw, heart racing. Turning left and then right, Al surveyed the neighborhood. Any sort of gunplay on this street would mean trouble. Too many chances for a bullet to find an innocent civilian. He could not explain the bad feeling he had, but he knew the next time he visited this street, it would be with a pump shotgun.

+ + +

Deputy Sheriff Bud Yost appeared at the site of the exposed hand and suspected semi-buried body. Coroner Raymond Winslow and an assistant arrived ten minutes later in a station wagon with "Winslow Funeral Home" painted on the side. Dallas, Eldon, and the stick man had spent the waiting time talking and looking for improvised digging tools around the rubble.

As coroner, Winslow took charge of the find. "Let's start around the hand and make sure there's an arm in there. If we find that, then there's likely a body. But go slow. Don't want to cause any more damage than necessary."

Winslow's assistant and the stick man, the youngest of the men, carefully but quickly moved small chunks of broken concrete around the hand to reveal a shirt sleeve. The coroner inspected it and gave the order to keep digging. Eldon rolled up his shirt sleeves and joined the excavation.

Dallas edged close to the deputy. "Bud, have you contacted Sheriff Farmer?"

"Not till there's somethin' to report. Ray ain't even sure there's a body there."

Dallas nodded, withholding the fact that he had informed the federal agents staying at the Wind River Hotel of the discovery.

Even with his specific directions, they would get lost before finding the location.

As the digging progressed, the Irish setter in the cab of his master's pickup barked steadily. The stick man took a break to calm the animal, with temporary success. He rejoined the others with a shovel taken from the bed of his truck.

The coroner's assistant shot a look at Winslow. "We've got a body."

Winslow moved close and took a look. "You need to get all the junk on top of it off, but without covering up what you've dug out. Any ideas?"

Eldon cleared his throat. "I've got a tarp, and we might be able to use some of the lumber to make a frame."

"Good idea. Dallas, can you and Bud find some two-by-fours? Watch out for nails. Don't need anyone getting tetanus from this. That goes for you boys too."

Bud stopped at his radio car to notify Sheriff Farmer, by way of the dispatcher, of the development. Dallas waited nearby as he called in, unwilling to let the young deputy escape from helping the effort.

When the mound had been lowered to within less than a foot of the body, the federal agents arrived. Dallas introduced them to Winslow, who shook hands while Bud scowled. Meanwhile, Eldon scrambled to accept debris from the younger men and tossed it aside.

The coroner moved in as the three men continued to remove material. Dallas and the federal agents walked back toward the government Ford. FBI agent Oakes voiced the question on the minds of all three men. "Do you think that's Jim Haefner?"

Dallas turned and looked back at the site. "Maybe. This is part of the property from those pictures of Bob Thornton and Haefner. The cabin in the background's just to the west of here.

"Thornton put up this property in an exchange with me, so I ordered a survey. The guys told me about this trash pile, so I figured to take a look. The dog of the younger survey man found a hand sticking up. That's when I started making calls."

Secret Service agent Kemper stopped. "Odd coincidence if Haefner's body shows up."

Dallas gnawed on his tongue. He explained to the federal men his ignorance of the property until the previous day; he had been interested in Thornton holdings south of town or along north Federal.

Oakes rubbed his cheek. "Convenient the survey crew was out here."

"People pay good money for my advice. I tell clients to get a good title search and a survey when they buy property. Failing to take my own advice isn't good for business. Besides, if I had something to do with Haefner's disappearance, then keeping him hidden would have been the best plan."

Oakes rolled his neck to the right and then left. "I'm not saying you're a suspect, just that the timing is odd."

Dallas shoved both hands into his pants pockets. "So Corky Freeman, the photographer from my newspaper, meets with Winter to tell him about some pictures but gets killed before he can deliver them."

He stopped and looked at Kemper, who pressed his lips together but said nothing. "Then Winter gets killed. I think he must've been getting close to discovering something about your fraud case. If Thornton had not shown me this land, and I had not seen the photographs, then connecting Haefner with this place never would've happened. And if the survey crew hadn't mentioned these junk piles, I never would've come out here. I'm just saying every now and then, you draw to a flush and get your card. Call it luck, fate, or coincidence."

Kemper raised his eyebrows and shrugged.

Dallas pointed back toward the excavation site. "But that body may not be Haefner; it may be someone else entirely. Perhaps my call to you gentlemen was a waste of your time."

Oakes raised his hands, palms forward. "Dallas, take it easy."

Kemper cleared his throat. "Looks like they've about got it cleared."

The Secret Service man led the way back to the excavation, and Oakes settled in at a slower pace with Dallas. As they walked, another sheriff's department car arrived and parked behind the other cars. Dallas turned, surprised that Farmer had arrived from Lander so quickly, but it was Deputy Nelson who climbed out of the car.

Raymond Winslow knelt at the head of the body when Dallas and the federal agents joined the group. "Identification's going to be tough. The bones of the face are broken. Maybe there's some dental work."

Kemper pointed toward the torso. "Is there a wallet?"

Winslow slid forward, resting his weight on one knee. "The skeletal system is a mess, like a broken china plate. See if there's a piece of wood long and wide enough we can slide under him."

The coroner grasped the pants and carefully lifted the fabric enough to access the back pocket. Rather than pull the wallet from the top, he pushed it up from the bottom far enough to get a grip. The wallet in hand, he looked from Deputy Yost to the federal men. "Who gets this?"

Kemper extended his arm to stop Oakes's forward motion. "The local authorities have initial jurisdiction."

Bud took a step back. "Nelson's lead deputy."

Deputy Nelson weaved between Oakes and Kemper and advanced to the coroner and body. He took the wallet from Winslow's outstretched hand and opened the folded leather billfold. "Looks like a US government driver's license. James L. Haefner. Guess he's yours, Agent Oakes."

Dallas noticed Bud turn away and head toward his radio car.

Winslow pointed to the semi-exposed corpse. "Let's get the body moved onto the board. If a couple of you guys will lift up the shirt and pants, we should be able to slide it under. I'm assuming you want me to transport this to Casper, Agent Oakes."

Oakes took the wallet and moved into position to help with the transfer process. "I'm going to need you to wait until Monday to take this to Casper, if that's good with you."

The coroner and his assistant moved the improvised stretcher from the pile of debris and set it on the ground. As the assistant went to the station wagon, Winslow examined the side of the body that had been farthest away.

"Agent, it appears there's a gunshot entry on the side of his head. Take a look."

Oakes squatted to inspect the head. "Looks like powder burns. He was shot at close range."

Kemper moved behind Oakes for his own look.

Winslow straightened and crossed his arms against his chest. "If I was making the report on this, it'd be my opinion the gunshot killed him. He was buried under a pile of heavy material, with damage to most of the major bones, but that didn't kill him."

Kemper moved closer to the body and narrowed his eyes. "How long's he been out here?"

Winslow scanned the body. "I'd say weeks and not days."

Oakes leaned closer to the head. "That's a pretty good hole. Amazing there isn't an exit. At least we'll get a bullet fragment."

Winslow turned toward Bud Yost. "Is Sheriff Farmer coming?"

"I radioed, and he's on the way."

The sound of a car approaching caused everyone to turn. A Wyoming Highway Patrol car drove past the line of parked cars and pulled over at the front of the line.

Winslow checked his wristwatch. "Agent Oakes, any reason to wait until the sheriff sees this?"

Oakes watched as Larry Jacobsen got out of the patrol car. "We've got enough witnesses, but it wouldn't hurt."

+ + +

Wil held the Mercury door open and waited for Gretchen. "Would you like Mrs. Murphy to come along?"

Gretchen turned to Geri. "No. Thank you again, ma'am."

Wil closed the door and glanced at Geri, raising his eyebrows. He walked around the back of the car, took his place at the wheel, and then pulled away from the curb. "How was that service compared to a Mormon one?"

Gretchen directed her answer at the dashboard. "About the same."

Wil drove and debated how to continue. "Do you want to talk about Corky?"

"I want to go home."

The answer angered him. "Corky was more than just some guy living in your basement, and we both know it."

Hands to her face, Gretchen bent forward and resumed crying to the point of shaking. Wil pulled the big sedan over, turned off the engine, and waited for the crying to stop.

Gretchen leaned back and wiped at her tears. "Corky died because of ..."

"Because of what?"

"Me! He's dead because ..."

Wil studied Gretchen, his right hand resting on the sniffling woman's shoulder. "Why do you think that?"

"I did things with Corky a married woman shouldn't do. And when I was packing his things, I didn't find the ... Corky's dead because of me."

"Does your husband know about the two of you?"

"He has to. There were pictures and ..."

"Are you sure? Has he told—"

"He has to know. And if he's left me, I may never see Delmar again."

Wil took a moment to digest the possible flight of Delmar. "What makes you think he killed Corky?"

Gretchen sat up and dropped the hands from her face. "Delmar was in the army before we was married. He don't talk about it, but I think he's killed."

"So you think Delmar killed Corky because you and he were lovers."

Gretchen nodded slightly.

"Are you afraid he'll hurt you?"

She snapped her face toward Wil and glared. "Delmar would never do anything to hurt me."

Wil nodded and gave Gretchen a moment to calm down. "You're not pregnant with Corky's child, are you?"

She vigorously shook her head no.

Wil looked through the windshield, unsure where to go with the questioning.

"I need to go home."

Wil started the car and drove toward her house. "I know where the photos and negatives are."

She sat quietly, head down, until they made the turn onto Gretchen's street, then quickly glanced at him and turned away. "What are you going to do with them pictures?"

"They're safe. I promise."

"I'd feel better if ..."

Wil pulled into her driveway. "They are safe. No one will accidentally find them."

Gretchen nodded and reached for the door latch.

"If you have a problem with Delmar, call either Geri or me. I don't want to see you get hurt."

Gretchen turned to look at Wil. The tension in her sad face relaxed for a moment, and Wil sensed she was about to say something, but just as quickly, Gretchen turned and opened her door.

"Thank you for the ride." She closed the passenger door and began walking to the back of the house.

Wil leaned his head out the sedan window. "I can see that Corky's belongings get to his parents."

Gretchen nodded her agreement and continued walking. Wil stepped out of the car and trotted to catch up with her at the back of the house. As they carried the suitcase and a cardboard box to the car, the neighbor Wil had encountered outside after his interview of the Simpsons stood at the end of the driveway, hands on hips.

Gretchen led the way to the Mercury. "Orrin, we don't need any of your help."

Orrin pointed at Wil. "He's been here afore, and he ain't from the church. What's he—"

"He's from the newspaper. We don't need any help."

"Mark my words, you will. Prophecy revealed." The man pointed to the sky, turned, and walked into the street.

Back in the basement, as they checked for any other belongings, Wil asked about Orrin.

"He's a friend of Delmar's."

"If you don't feel safe here, call the police or a friend. I bet you could stay with Geri if there isn't any other place to go. I'm serious."

"Thank you, but I'm fine here. And thank that lady for helping me this morning."

Wil drove away not entirely pleased, but Gretchen knew the photos were safe. She clearly felt responsible for Corky's death. But what did that really mean? And what was the story with Orrin and the meaning of his talk of prophecy?

CHAPTER 32

"Last thing I need's another death," Grayson thought as he approached the Arapahoe cutoff. Since leaving Lander, he had kept telling himself that the location, north and east of Midvale, had nothing to do with his meeting in June with the man recently identified as Jim Haefner. The repetition did little to convince or calm him.

As he approached the bridge crossing the Wind River, the countywide radio dispatcher called out his car identifier, Sheriff 1. When he responded, the static-laced female voice gave the worst news possible: a preliminary identification of James L. Haefner for the discovered dead body. How could that be? Bob Thornton's boys were supposed to have put it where it could never be found.

Either they had botched the job, or this was an ambush by Bud and Thornton. Bud was supposed to be off this weekend, and had to suspect he would not survive Grayson's reelection. The idea that the laziest deputy in the department had responded to a discovered dead body, on a weekend, made no sense

Grayson lifted the microphone of his radio. "Sheriff 1 to Base. Over."

When the dispatcher replied, he instructed her to contact Nelson's radio unit. He listened to the call for North Deputy 1 twice before getting the report that Nelson had not responded. Grayson wanted to believe in Nelson's loyalty. He would repeat the call in a few minutes.

Grayson slowed as he approached the city limits of Riverton. He thought of driving past the substation and Nelson's apartment, but

234

both were out of the way. As he moved through town on Federal, he looked for a sheriff's car but found none. Just past Sunset Drive, he slowed near Thornton's dealership and looked for Bob's car, but the business had closed for the weekend. Bob was making sure he had an alibi.

Near the turn onto Burma Road, he asked the dispatcher to page Nelson again, with the same result. Dust kicked up behind him as he drove north, and with each passing mile, Grayson became more agitated. "Not taking the blame, not alone. Thornton can just think again."

At the junction to the road west, toward the supposed location of Haefner's body, Grayson stopped the car. He removed the revolver from his holster and checked the cylinder. Then he pulled the snub-nosed revolver from his boot and inspected it as well. If this was an ambush, he planned to make a fight of it and take his chances.

Grayson drove the last mile at a slow speed, not wanting to kick up dust to warn of his approach. He felt certain a trap was waiting for him, but the outcome could end in his favor. As Bud's uncle, former sheriff Homer Yost, had always said, "Better to die fighting than pray for a miracle."

The final segment involved a pair of turns onto a slight incline. As Grayson reached the crest, he spotted the shallow chute between piles of trash and a rise. Grayson decided this was not an ambush but a firing squad as he looked out at a row of over a half dozen vehicles, including two sheriff's patrol cars, the Winslow's Funeral Home station wagon, a dark sedan he figured belonged to the Casper FBI man, the Dodge kid's pickup, and a Wyoming Highway Patrol car at the far end. There was a panel truck and another pickup too, probably Thornton men sent along to help out.

The six bullets in the big revolver and the five in the snub-nose would not be enough. He would need to reload. This many men meant they would try a flanking move. Best to go all the way up front, past the highway patrol car, and use his car for cover.

Grayson gunned the motor and saw Nelson step out from behind the station wagon and wave. The one man he had thought loyal had betrayed him as well. "They can all go straight to hell."

+ + +

Wil pulled into the driveway of the Murphy house, a small one-story painted yellow with flowers along the front. He remembered visiting once when Geri's husband was still alive, but that had been over three years ago. The driveway gravel crunched as he walked to the back of the house, where he expected to find her.

Geri had changed from her black funeral clothes to a floral-print sundress and sat at a picnic table. A wide-brimmed straw hat concealed her short salt-and-pepper hair. An ashtray, a pack of Lucky Strikes, and a can of Hamm's beer, condensation running down the side, topped the table.

"Can I get you a beer? All I've got is Hamm's."

Wil loosened his necktie and opened the top button of his shirt. "At this point I'd drink moonshine. A beer sounds great."

As Geri went indoors, he straddled the picnic bench and thought of what to tell her about his time with Gretchen.

She held open the screen door and navigated down the steps, balancing a tray of crackers, cheese, pickles, and olives in her left hand, the can of Hamm's in her right. "In case you didn't get enough at the church. So what happened?"

"I went at her hard and straight. Made her cry."

Geri used the opener and handed him the can. "Crying's the one thing she does well. Tell me you didn't let her off easy."

"Nope, and I don't feel a bit guilty. She's the one feeling guilty, saying Corky's dead because of her."

"So the husband—"

"She thinks he found the pictures. Said he was in the army and knows how to kill. And she's afraid he's run off, leaving her alone."

"Did you tell her about—"

"I said the photos were safe."

Geri took a cigarette from the pack. "Did she believe you?"

"Not sure there's much choice. Oh, shit."

She had the lighter ready but did not spark it. "What?"

"I've got Corky's belongings in the car. I promised to get them to the Freemans."

Geri stood and swung a leg over the bench. "They were stopping at Gordon's before leaving town. Let's go. We might get lucky."

"What about the beer?"

"It's only six blocks, and we're not going to stay."

They scurried down the driveway and into the Mercury. They raced to Gordon's and arrived just in time. Geri carried the suitcase to the Freemans' Plymouth as Wil took the cardboard box. Mrs. Freeman thanked Geri for being so kind to her son, saying he had always mentioned her in his letters. Mr. Freeman shook Gordon's hand, and Mrs. Freeman kissed him on the cheek. Together the trio waved the Freemans off, telling them to drive safe.

Gordon invited them for a glass of lemonade in the backyard. Geri answered before Wil could, making the obvious observation. "Gordon, you look tired. Maybe you should take a nap. I'll put together a little picnic, and we'll come back, after you've rested."

Tears filled Gordon's eyes. Geri took his hand and led him toward the house, her arm around his waist. At the front porch steps, he wobbled onto the first step, bringing the other foot up before moving on to the next.

Wil turned away and wiped at his tears, the emotion of the day catching up with him. The rush of returning from Natee's, dashing to the funeral, and then questioning Gretchen had distracted him from the tragedy of Corky's death. What kind of man was he?

After helping Gordon inside, Geri danced down the steps and to the Mercury. "So you were telling me about Gretchen feeling guilty, thinking her husband killed Corky. What else?"

Wil leaned back in the driver's seat and closed his eyes. "How did she put it? How her husband could be on the run from the law, leaving her alone. I know she's sad about Corky's death, but some of those tears may be for her ruined marriage."

"What're you going to do about the nudie photos?"

He opened his eyes and grabbed the steering wheel. "They're safe. Eventually, I may give them to Dallas. First I need to look at Corky's logbooks and compare the negatives, just to get a date for when they were taken, as well as the ones of Sheriff Farmer."

"That didn't answer my question."

Wil started the Mercury and shifted into low gear. "Unless there's a reason to show them to Farmer or the FBI, I'll probably burn them. You want to look at 'em first?"

"The idea of looking at a pretty young girl, without any clothes, is not something a woman my age likes to contemplate. Let's get back to that beer, and you can tell me about your date with Natee."

He swerved at the mention of her name. "How'd you know?"

"In a small town a person that pays attention knows a lot. Plus we talked after the service."

Wil nodded. So that was how Natee had known about his attending Michigan; Geri was her source. "It was fun. She cooked venison, and we had a nice talk."

"That's it? Sounds like you struck out."

He felt his face flush from embarrassment. "She told me Corky was having sex with her."

"My stars and garters, that's what she meant the other day. She said something I didn't quite get about them being good friends when she came by the office."

Wil pulled into her driveway and shut off the engine. "There's more than that. She and I, we did more than talk. If I'd known she and Corky … but she had another box, like Gordon. When I unlocked the box and we saw the nudie pictures, she figured she was to blame, teaching him so he and Gretchen could … get together. If I think about it, I just get confused."

He leaned forward, head against his hands on the steering wheel. Geri touched him on the shoulder. "Do me a favor. Come back about five thirty and take me over to Gordon's for the picnic. And bring Cecil, if he wants to come. Will you do that?"

Wil turned to her and nodded, although he was not certain it was a promise he would keep.

+ + +

Dallas and the others watched as the sheriff's car, motionless for a moment, began accelerating down the rise, sending up a cloud of dust as it approached. The car zipped past them and braked hard into a quick right, as if the sheriff were setting up a roadblock. When the dust settled, Dallas saw Grayson Farmer standing behind the car's rear fender, a revolver in each hand.

Nelson stepped forward and walked toward the sheriff. "Sheriff, looks like we found that Haefner guy they's looking for. Come take a look."

Farmer stood still and watched. "I know what you got planned. Ain't fallin' for it or taking all the blame."

Dallas, aware of the gun holstered on his chest, lifted his hands to head height, away from his body, and walked toward the sheriff. "Grayson, we're not planning anything. Just want to know if you need to look at the body."

He could sense movement behind him and figured the others were getting behind the parked cars and trucks. With each short step, heel and toe, he exposed himself to danger and moved farther from the safety of cover.

"Stop right there. I'll admit to killing that Haefner fella, but it was an accident. I was put up to it, and you know who done that."

Dallas took another step. "No one is accusing you of anything. Put the guns away."

"Let my temper get away from me. He sassed me, and I hit him, and then again. It was an accident. Didn't mean to kill 'im."

Dallas detected peripheral motion and glanced left. "Stay put, Larry. Grayson, Jim Haefner was killed by a bullet. If you didn't shoot him, then it wasn't your fault."

"Know that trick. Used it myself. He was dead as can be. But I ain't taking all the blame. Didn't have nothin' to do with Winter. Or the Freeman kid."

From behind Dallas, Winslow called out. "It's true, Grayson, gunshot to the head."

Dallas saw the sheriff sneer at the coroner's comment. "No one said you killed anyone, Grayson. I'll be your lawyer, and we can sort this out in a courtroom."

Grayson pulled back the hammer on the revolver in his right hand. "Ain't nothing getting sorted out in no courtroom, except me getting the blame."

"Grayson, you've got to believe—"

Before Dallas could finish the sentence, Grayson extended his right arm and fired a shot to his right. The sound startled Dallas, and his focus narrowed to the sheriff, who moved as if in slow motion. A second round of gunfire came from the direction Larry Jacobsen had been, followed by another shot from Grayson.

On instinct, Dallas removed the revolver from his holster after the explosion to his left and pulled the hammer back. After Grayson's second shot, the sheriff's eyes moved toward Dallas; the right arm followed along. With his right arm extended and the gun handle supported by his left hand, Dallas aimed at the lawman's upper chest and squeezed the trigger.

The muzzle flash and explosion from the big revolver jolted Dallas and left him blinking. It seemed to take forever to re-aim, but the sheriff was not in sight. Ears ringing, he saw movement going past him as Nelson, Kemper, and Oakes all ran forward, guns drawn. Dallas settled the revolver into the holster and took a deep breath before starting after them.

Grayson Farmer lay flat on his back, blood trickling from the corner of his mouth, a good three feet behind his patrol car. Nelson kicked away the gun in the sheriff's right hand, and Oakes did the same to the snub-nose in the left. The deputy went down on one knee and placed his finger on the side of the sheriff's neck. He looked up and shook his head to indicate there was no pulse.

Winslow yelled from farther back, "Jacobsen's down! He needs a hospital. Anyone else been hit?" Kemper answered that the sheriff had been shot.

Dallas stared down at the motionless Grayson and then turned toward Winslow as he approached. "Why'd he do it, Ray? Why'd he do it?"

Winslow shrugged his shoulders as he moved toward Grayson, and Dallas felt a hand on his shoulder. It was Kemper. "Mr. Dodge, I think we better sit you down for a bit."

"I had to shoot. He would've ..."

Kemper steered him toward the sheriff's car and opened the passenger door. "I know. My gun was out, but you had the better shot. Just sit down ... Can I get some water over here?"

The next ten minutes were a blur for Dallas, with ears ringing and eyes going in and out of focus. Kemper stayed close as Oakes and then Nelson posed questions and talked in low voices with the Secret Service man. Dallas saw Winslow and his assistant carry Jacobsen to the station wagon. Both the surveyors came over, one with a canteen. He took a drink and watched as their mouths moved but could not make out their words. Dallas nodded, not sure what to say.

Kemper bent down, made eye contact, and spoke deliberately. "Think you can walk? I'll drive you home or wherever you want to go. Okay?"

Dallas stood and took a moment to look around. "Never shot a person. Lots of antelope and deer and elk. Leaves you ... dazed."

Kemper took his elbow. "Yes, sir. Which vehicle is yours?"

"Are you arresting me?"

Kemper made eye contact and shook his head. "No, sir. Both Oakes and I agree you did what anyone would do."

He took a tentative step forward. "I'm in the pickup over there. My nephew's. What about Larry?"

Kemper guided him to the truck. "The highway patrolman needs a hospital."

"Why'd he shoot Larry?"

"The highway patrolman had his gun out and raised it. I don't know why."

Dallas kept walking but knew the actions of Larry Jacobsen would be important to remember. "You going to drive? Keys are in it."

The Secret Service man helped him into the passenger side and said he needed to talk with the others before leaving. He saw Bud standing beside his patrol car, looking even more bewildered than Dallas felt. Nelson, Oakes, and Kemper all talked for a minute and then walked together toward the pickup.

Nelson stopped on his side. "Mr. Dodge, we'll need a statement from you, when you can."

Dallas nodded. Kemper climbed into the driver's seat, turned the pickup around, and headed toward Riverton. Dallas decided to go to his office. A stiff drink would do him good, and he could wait for Wilson to come get his pickup. Maybe he would lie down for a little rest.

They rode in silence until reaching the paved highway. Kemper touched his arm. "Just for the report, Mr. Dodge, what kind of gun is that you used?"

Dallas rubbed the bone handle of the nickel-plated revolver. "A Smith & Wesson Outdoorsman."

"And what caliber bullet was that?"

Dallas stared out the windshield. "A .44 cartridge, with extra powder. Guy in Idaho makes special rounds for me."

"Aren't you worried about it being too much for the gun?"

Dallas patted the holster. "Smith & Wesson's N-frame. The normal .38 Special is a K-frame. Plus I've got the long barrel."

"We're going to need that for evidence, you know."

Dallas nodded and pointed out the turn to get to his office. Kemper pulled the pickup to the curb at the law office. Dallas got out and watched as Oakes parked behind them. On the sidewalk in front of his office, Kemper asked if he still wanted to go to Hudson for dinner that evening. Dallas agreed and decided to let the federal men drive him there and back.

CHAPTER 33

Even though Dallas had made a reservation, the three men stood at the bar and waited for the corner booth. The federal men had dispensed with neckties while retaining their starched white shirts and dark suits. Dallas was dressed in his casual cowboy lawyer motif of western shirt, suede sports coat, black slacks, and shiny black cowboy boots. Kemper's white hair added a distinguished note to the threesome.

Kemper picked up an olive from the tray of olives, pickled peppers, and crackers. "Either they think we're food critics, or you're a popular customer."

Dallas glanced at the patrons at the bar as he nursed his manhattan. "More like Wyoming hospitality. It's not like they need to attract more diners."

After trading keys with Wilson at the law office, Dallas had retreated to his suite on the top floor of the Wind River Hotel. A shower followed by a grilled cheese sandwich and change of clothes had revitalized him. The plan for a strictly social outing had been thwarted by the realities of the late morning shoot-out, but his role of gracious local host survived.

Dallas made small talk as they waited, content to keep the evening social as much as possible. A striking petite woman with shiny black hair, dark Slavic eyes, and a colorful scarf around her neck led them to the booth. Dallas squeezed her hand before sliding onto the padded bench, between the two federal men. She handed out menus and promised to bring back wine. He set his menu down unopened.

Oakes peeked over the top of his menu. "Already know what you want?"

Dallas smiled and sipped his manhattan. "You can pick from the menu or let Momma decide. I've never been disappointed in her selection."

Kemper slapped his menu closed. "Was that Momma?"

"No, one of her daughters."

Oakes scanned the list of dishes and then set his menu down. The FBI man leaned toward Dallas. "Do you mind mixing a little business with dinner?"

"Not at all, as long as we all put our cards on the table."

Oakes and Kemper traded glances. "Fair enough."

A waiter with black hair swept straight back and a white towel on his left forearm arrived with a bottle of red wine and three wine glasses, along with a fresh plate of antipasto. Dallas checked with the pair before he announced their order. "We'll have Momma's Choice."

"Excellent, Mr. Dallas, do you need anything more from the bar?"

Dallas requested another manhattan, but the others were anxious to try the wine. The waiter gave a slight bow before striding to the bar.

Kemper poured wine into Oakes's glass and then his own. "You took quite a risk today with the sheriff."

Dallas picked up a round reddish pepper by the stem from the dish. "Not really. I knew Grayson wasn't going to shoot me without provocation. You obviously noticed my hands, high and away from the holster. Grayson is an elected authority. A handful of men in the county represent authority on a different level. I'm one of those men, and Grayson has always been a little afraid of me."

Oakes shook his head. "That first day I came to town, the sheriff threw me out of his office. Had his hand on his gun like he was thinking of shooting me. He acted more crazy than afraid."

Dallas gnawed on his tongue. "The election, federal authorities in his jurisdiction, and two suspicious deaths—good reasons for worry. He arrives to see six cars lined up, with men scattered around, most with guns. Fear in that situation is an appropriate reaction, but the response he chose to enact was not."

Kemper leaned in. "I didn't hear what he was saying."

The fresh manhattan arrived, and Dallas swirled the cherry by the stem in the iced brown liquid. "Something about how he killed him, meaning Haefner, but it was an accident. But that he wasn't going to take all the blame. I think that is how he put it."

The men stopped talking as the waiter passed out bowls of soup with a basket of fresh sliced bread from a large serving tray. Oakes swished his soup spoon in his bowl. "Who did he say should share the blame?"

Dallas looked left and then right. "He didn't get a chance to say."

Kemper tasted the broth and dipped his spoon for a heartier portion. "Any guesses?"

"Even though Agent Oakes isn't making notes, I do not wish to offer an unsubstantiated accusation."

Kemper nodded. "Good soup. Fair enough."

Oakes pulled a slice of bread from the basket and moved the butter dish nearer. "But he did confess to killing Haefner."

Dallas savored a spoonful of soup as he considered his response. "He confessed, but at the same time, I wonder if he did kill the man. There was something about Haefner sassing him, and Grayson hit him once and then again. If the hit he confessed to was a gunshot, meaning he'd shot him, then there would be two bullet holes.

"Grayson is known to favor a sap when he arrests and questions suspects. The medical examiner might find evidence of blows to Haefner's head—although under all that rubble, it may be impossible to discern such a localized impact."

Oakes raised his soup spoon as if to make a point. "But he confessed."

Dallas set down his spoon. "Yes, Agent Oakes, he confessed. But at this point there is no evidence to support it. If you find a bullet, and it matches one of the sheriff's guns, then you have corroborating evidence. You lawmen put too much emphasis on a confession. Just remember, he denied involvement with the Freeman and Winter deaths."

Oakes turned his attention to the soup. The waiter arrived with a bowl of salad, poured dressing over the greens, and mixed before dishing out three plates.

Dallas picked up his salad fork and poked about until he found a strip of seasoned meat. "Leave room for the main course. Momma used to feed coal miners with big appetites, and she's kept the habit."

Oakes slid his soup bowl to the side. "What about the highway patrolman? Any ideas what he was doing?"

Dallas scattered the greens about with his fork, searching for another flavorful morsel. "That would be Larry Jacobsen. You had the better view of his actions. Any news on him from the hospital?"

Oakes sighed. "He didn't make it."

"Until this afternoon, he was the Republican candidate for Fremont County sheriff. Larry happened to be at the party hosted by my sister-in-law, Ramona, mother of Wilson—the same party Mr. Winter visited the night before his death."

Oakes pulled a pocket-sized notepad from his suit jacket pocket. "Interesting. Maybe we should run ballistics on his gun too."

Dallas speared a black olive and slipped it into his mouth. He had wondered if it would be necessary to prescribe such testing and was pleased the special agent had reached the conclusion on his own brainpower.

"That reminds me, who's got my revolver? I'm going to want that back."

Oakes stabbed a forkful of salad. "We gave it to the deputy."

"Which one? The tall one or the short chubby one?"

Oakes, having just placed greens in his mouth, motioned to Kemper to answer.

"The tall one. Does it make a difference?"

Dallas pushed the salad plate away. "The tall one, Nelson, is the smarter of the two. The other, Bud, is the nephew of the former sheriff. Rumor had it Bud would be looking for work if Grayson was reelected."

Oakes made another entry in his notebook.

The waiter returned with a tray and set the used soup bowls onto it. "The main course is almost ready. Do you need anything else from the bar beforehand? Perhaps more salad?"

Dallas topped off the wine glasses of the others before filling his own. "Another bottle of this would be good. Gentlemen, anything else?"

He finished his manhattan as the others took their last bites of salad. "What about the details of how I discovered Haefner's body? You acted suspicious out there."

Kemper waved off the question and pushed his salad plate to the side.

Dallas leaned back against the padded back of the booth. "I learned something today. It may make me a better attorney, and perhaps a better person. I experienced firsthand the shock from shooting another person—and the memory loss. I have no recollection from right after the shooting ended until standing in front of my office with the two of you. That's why I would not place too much value on a confession obtained under the duress of such an incident."

+ + +

Wil spread out Corky's latest photos on the living room coffee table and the logbooks on a couch cushion, everything he needed close at hand. The comfort of the apartment and a cold beer allowed him to carefully go through the logbooks and note his findings.

Dallas's account of the deadly conflict north of town intruded on his concentration. Repeating the story, initially told to him during the exchange of pickup for car, to Geri on the way to Gordon's picnic had helped him mentally organize the sequence. After the picnic he had made a list of the major points at his kitchen table. As he searched the logbook entries, specific fragments of Dallas's report came to mind and demanded notation in the margins. The discovery of Haefner's body and the shooting of both candidates for sheriff, at least one fatally, added another layer of questions.

He began the process of matching photographs to logbook entries with the mid-June log and the Sheriff Farmer pictures. Wil spotted a listing with the initials of Haefner and Farmer on the afternoon of June 13, the day Haefner had been seen last. The book itemized nine entries, but only three had corresponding photos in the box from Natee's.

Log entries for Gretchen did not appear until late July. The photos, negatives, and log of that batch matched. A search of subsequent entries did not reveal additional Gretchen references. He scanned for "NS" references, Natee Saylor, but found none near the Gretchen entries.

The thought of naked pictures of Natee both annoyed and intrigued him. The previous night at her cabin had supplied visual and tactile memories more vivid than any two-dimensional snapshot could offer. Wil initially doubted Natee's willingness to pose naked as Gretchen had but then decided it was possible. The bothersome question involved the physical location of the missing Farmer photos. Did Gordon have more photos? Where else could Corky have hidden them? They also could have been out of focus or over exposed.

He stood to go to the bathroom and kicked over the half-full can of beer on the floor. He retrieved the bathroom hand towel to soak up the puddle on the worn throw rug beneath the coffee table and then tossed it in the kitchen sink. While on his hands and knees with a second towel to blot at the damp spot, he decided to stop the search for the night. The immersion in the photographic detail felt like the forest and trees cliché. A good night of sleep could help him put it all in perspective.

The kitchen clock read nine-thirty as he opened the refrigerator and decided against another beer. In the small living room he closed the scattered logbooks and moved them to the corner of the couch. Wil took the series of Gretchen photos and spread them out on the coffee table. She had a cute face and an appealing shape. He picked up one of the pictures and looked at her facial expression. It reminded him of the way Natee had looked at him in bed last night.

Was this what love looked like? He could not recall getting that kind of look from anyone other than Natee. Or was it just an expression of momentary joy? Wil wondered whether Natee had shared the same affection for Corky on film as Gretchen.

Wil scooped up the Gretchen photos and placed them in the wooden box. He was supposed to be working on finding Corky's killer, not delving into the secrets of love.

The Thornton and Haefner photos had been taken in June, like the shots of Farmer and Haefner. But Dallas said Farmer had denied involvement with the deaths of Corky and Winter. The pictures in Dallas's safe linked the two men but did not confirm the identity of their common killer.

But what if a connection did not exist? What if suppressing Corky's photos had not been his killer's motive? Then Natee's fear he had died because of the affair with Gretchen could be valid. And Gretchen's fear that Delmar had killed Corky and abandoned her might be justified as well.

He remembered that Delmar had left town the day after his visit to the Simpsons' house. In all likelihood, neither Sheriff Farmer nor Deputy Nelson had questioned him and checked on his alibi for Monday night. But Grayson Farmer was dead. Would Nelson have the inclination, or authority, to continue the investigation?

He gathered the photographic prints, placed them in the wooden box, and set them beside the logbooks on the couch. Wil set his notes from the photos and his conversion with Dallas on top of the box.

The obvious next step was consulting Dallas, but he resisted the urge. Wil wanted to resolve the problem on his own. If Corky's murder was not related to the Winter and Haefner deaths, the only other possibility he saw involved Gretchen and her husband, Delmar. A confrontation could be dangerous, both for Gretchen and for himself, but he believed the landlady was the key to solving Corky's murder.

After ensuring the back door was shut and locked, he turned off the kitchen and living room lights and stepped to the bedroom. Memories of the night before delayed sleep as he yearned for the warmth of Natee's body nestled against his.

Wil pulled a pillow against his chest, imagining her, and wondered if there was a future with the woman. Tomorrow meant church with Ramona and then a trip to the family lodge to meet with Dallas. At least one mystery would be solved by this time tomorrow night: how his father had died.

+ + +

"Would you gentlemen care for dessert?"

Groans told Dallas all he needed to know. "Some coffee with cream and sugar, please."

"Certainly, Mr. Dallas. Can I take away any plates?"

The main-course plates of sirloin steak and grilled vegetables, plus side dishes of ravioli and spaghetti, filled the table. The waiter began with the smaller plates and returned with help from the kitchen for the remainder.

Oakes wiped his mouth on the linen napkin. "Dallas, I've never seen a steak that big, let alone tried to eat one."

Dallas sipped the last of his red wine, pleased with Momma's selection. "Glad you enjoyed it. Does this mean you'll be driving over from Casper, Agent Oakes?"

"If Mr. Hoover ever comes out this way, I'll know where to take him."

They all chuckled at the suggestion the FBI chief would leave Washington, DC, for Wyoming. Dallas waited until the waiter served coffee to begin his questions. The talk during the main course had focused on hunting stories, wives and children, and hobbies.

"Can I ask about the status of your investigations?"

Kemper took a deep breath and looked into his coffee cup. "There's not much to go on now that Jim Haefner's been found. He's not going to give us any answers. And I don't have any solid leads to pursue. I talked with my boss, told him what happened. The business of two local lawmen getting shot makes this case, to use his word, radioactive. I'm supposed to wrap this up and be on the plane back to DC on Monday."

Dallas creamed his coffee to a caramel color and added a half spoon of sugar. "So that's it?"

"I'll write a report and send a copy to Reclamation. And it will get filed and maybe even read. Without a solid line of inquiry, there's not much I can do. Agent Oakes'll have to say about Jack Winter."

Oakes stretched his neck and grimaced. "We'll have the medical report on Winter to look at and the ballistics. If the guns of either the sheriff or the patrolman were involved, it'll end there. As much as I dislike federal employees getting killed, Kemper's right. This thing today is radioactive. Justice and Mr. Hoover will want it to just go away."

"So I guess you'll be leaving Fremont County as well."

Oakes picked up his coffee cup and blew on it. "I'll stay around until Tuesday and then head back for Casper."

As Dallas lifted his coffee cup, a short, apple-shaped woman, whose crow's-feet and obviously dyed black hair betrayed her age, appeared at the table in an apron smeared with red sauce. Her smile revealed a gold-colored tooth. "Mr. Dallas, good to see you, and you've brought big shots."

"Momma, let me introduce you to Mr. Kemper, from Washington, DC. And this is Mr. Oakes, from Casper."

A Slavic accent colored her pronunciation but did not overwhelm her words. "Did you get enough? More steak? Or ice cream?"

Both agents reported being too full for another bite.

"I hope you liked and come back. I'll make even better next time."

Kemper leaned forward. "Momma, the only time I expect to eat better than this is in heaven."

"Don't be in hurry to die. You are young man."

Kemper laughed and bowed. "Thank you."

"Friends of Mr. Dallas, friends of mine. On the house."

Both Oakes and Kemper protested, but Dallas knew the truth; he had arranged for this charade when he made the reservations. This was not the first time Momma had delivered these lines.

Momma wagged her index finger back and forth. "Momma say. You talk and drink coffee. Come back and see me; pay next time."

Before leaving she winked at Dallas and told him to come back soon.

Oakes angled his head and peered at Dallas. "Did you know this was going to happen?

"No idea. First time this has happened. Momma didn't say you couldn't leave a tip, though."

Oakes grunted a half-laugh and reached for his wallet. "The odd thing about today was how you were trying to help the sheriff, get him to calm down and put away his guns. And yet you ended up being the person that shot him."

Dallas dropped his hands into his lap and frowned. "If I'd known what was to happen, I never would have let Bud radio for Grayson."

The federal men remained silent as they took sips of coffee and looked about.

"You fellows are lucky. You'll each go back to your office, file your reports, and take the next assignment. We'll have to bury Grayson and Larry. The county will need to figure out what to do about a sheriff, since both candidates are dead. Grayson's wife will be moved out of her home at the jail, a widow.

"In a week's time, we've had four men die of some kind of violence and the discovery of a fifth buried under a pile of rubble. That's a lot for a community to absorb and still feel safe and good about itself."

Oakes nodded and shifted in his seat. "It's getting late. Maybe we should go."

Dallas set his napkin on the table. "Sad way to end such a good meal. Should have kept those thoughts to myself, I suppose."

DAY 6

Sunday
September 7, 1952

CHAPTER 34

Dallas arrived at the family lodge in late morning. As he pushed the hooks from the eyes on the exterior shutters, he noted fresh claw marks. At some point since his last visit, a bear had pawed at this window, and the Fremont County sheriff's office had his bear gun. The Colt 1911 on his hip, with the .45-caliber bullets, was an acceptable substitute, but he preferred his revolver.

He turned to scan the area and then walked to the Mercury and unlocked the trunk. Dallas opened the zippered leather case and removed the Winchester lever-action rifle. The model 1886 held a larger cartridge with good accuracy at a greater distance than the handgun. He inserted cartridges into the feed tube, buckled the ammo belt around his belly, and hoped his nerve held as well with a bear looking for a meal as it had with Sheriff Farmer.

Inside the cabin he removed first the bottom and then the top cross-boards from the interior shutters, opened them, and slid up the windows. A breeze moved about the single room, diluting the cigar smell and refreshing the stale air. The lodge was the one place the Dodge brothers indulged in cigars, but since Clayton's death, he had lost the habit. The thought of Wilson smoking a cigar struck him as out of character.

He took a pair of wooden rocking chairs and cushions out to the front porch along with a stool good for holding drinks. A quick inspection of the wood-burning stove, beds and bedding, and locked cabinet with canned goods showed no change since the last visit. The provisions for today's visit could remain in the closed trunk of the Mercury.

When Clayton was still living, Dallas would find an unmade bed or other evidence of a visit. It was a perfect place for a romantic getaway, but his brother was not diligent at removing trash and locking up. Dallas suspected discarded food scraps as one of the reasons bears took an interest in the lodge.

At the wood and storage shed he found additional new claw marks. A heavy wire screen covered the only window, and the same heavy-duty padlock/hasp combination used on the cabin door secured this entryway. Normally, he would leave the shed door locked, but Wilson needed to see the inside.

Dallas collected the thermos from the car and poured coffee into the lid cup. He settled into a rocker and mentally reviewed his report to Wilson. Disclosing the details would be cathartic, a sharing of a burden.

One of the troubling aspects of the prior day's events was the treatment of Janet Farmer, the widow. As the wife of the sheriff, she lived in the jail portion of the courthouse, feeding the staff and prisoners. An obvious move would be to set her up in a diner or other eating outlet, except for her reputation as a terrible cook. Many of the jailers brought lunch boxes, and no one could recall a request for a second helping.

Perhaps the widow had family outside the county, a sister or brother perhaps. He knew her mother had been at the state mental asylum in Evanston until her death. Since Grayson and Janet were childless, there was no need to provide for dependents. Dallas could not escape feeling partially responsible for her situation. Earlier in the week, he had detected Grayson's level of fear and should have predicted his irrational response. However, his sense of duty to Janet Farmer was subject to certain financial limits.

A visit with a few of the county commissioners about her future could reveal a solution. The other unknown involved the need for a temporary sheriff and the approaching election. His role in creating the situation, even though justified, might limit any influence he could have on that topic.

Given the comments from the Secret Service man the night before, it seemed the investigation into the billing fraud would end. The government's interest in the truth had boundaries, but his did not. A theory was all he could offer, with only circumstantial evidence as support—although helping the government build a case would not enhance a defense attorney's reputation.

Perhaps Oakes and Kemper had accurately described the circumstances as radioactive. He disliked the word but admitted it applied, and hoped it did not rub off on him.

+ + +

Another day of weekend duty, and Al felt his back against the wall, literally. He had taken Diane out for a fried chicken lunch. After eating, she had wanted to go to his place and had suggested a nap. The excuse she gave for taking her dress off was "wrinkles," but the black bra, girdle, and stockings struck him as very planned, as did her suggestion that he remove his deputy uniform, to keep it looking freshly pressed.

Her frame was tucked so tightly against him in the single bed that his shoulders and buttocks pressed at the wall. Al had been thinking about his future with Diane, and the events of the prior day had pushed that issue to the front of his mind. The shooting deaths of his boss and patrolman Larry Jacobsen had served as a reminder the life of a cop involved mortal risk.

"If we were married, then I could iron your uniform. And we could nap however we wanted."

She wiggled her butt against him, but he was not aroused. If he really loved this girl, then they should get married, and quickly. But the attraction had faded, in part because of her frequent need for physical affection and pushy talk of marriage.

She reached back and tried to slip her hand inside his shorts. He took her forearm and moved it back in front of her, holding it against her belly.

"Are you mad at me?"

Al licked his lips. "No, just have a lot on my mind."

"About us?"

257

"I told you yesterday I saw the sheriff and Larry Jacobsen get shot dead."

Her head rocked back and forth.

"But I didn't tell you what else we found. It looks like maybe Jim Haefner was buried out there under a load of cement and dirt and stuff."

Her body stiffened. He waited for a response, but she stayed silent.

"I wondered if maybe you were still sweet on him."

Diane twisted her arm free of his grasp. "We was never as close as I am with you. I didn't love him, if that's what you mean."

Al wished he could see her facial expression as she talked, to determine if he could spot her in a lie. Her repeated questions about Haefner caused him to suspect a degree of deception from this girl who said she loved him. "Did you know that Winter fellow was in town investigating some stealing from the government? And US marshals were about to arrest Haefner when he disappeared?"

Diane twisted her entire body to face him. "You're making that up."

"Winter was with the Secret Service. And the fellow that came to town, Kemper, told that to the sheriff the other day."

She looked into his eyes. "Are you saying that to scare me?"

Al placed his hand on her side and felt the tension in her muscles. "Is there any reason you should be afraid? Was you helping Haefner steal government money?"

Diane pushed away from him and hopped off the bed. "Albert Nelson, you son of a bitch! Is the reason you've been seeing me to find out if I'm a crook?"

He scooted into the center of his bed and lay on his back. "Is the reason you've been chasing me to keep track of the investigation? Or to see if we found Haefner? You keep asking about him."

She stepped forward and struck him on the chest with both hands. "No, no, no."

Al grabbed her arms, and she fell onto him, tears streaming from her eyes. He released her arms and tried to comfort the girl. She spoke, but her words were undecipherable, a jumble of emotion.

"I'm sure Haefner made promises, and he wanted to keep them. Tell me what you know."

He coaxed the story from her, making assurances that sounded genuine. When she finished, he knew Agent Kemper needed to hear the story and ask his own questions.

+ + +

As Wil neared the turnoff to Natee's cabin on his way to the lodge, the idea of stopping to see her crossed his mind. In spite of the cool treatment he had received Saturday morning and the way she had avoided eye contact at the funeral, thoughts of Natee had started his morning and kept returning. Fear he would find another man at the cabin kept his foot on the gas pedal.

He skirted Lander and took the road into the national forest land where the Dodges leased their lodge. The farther he drove into and up the mountainous canyon, the more frequently the red and yellow hints of fall appeared. In a month the road could be snowed in, or it might stay open until Thanksgiving.

Wil downshifted when the pavement ended and drove another four miles before the turn-in to the lodge. The back of the maroon Mercury signaled the end of the trail, and he pulled in beside the big car. Dallas stepped off the bottom porch step and began walking in his direction.

"You have the shotgun with you?"

He opened the driver's side door and slipped to the ground. "Yeah, behind the seat."

"There's signs of recent bear activity. Bring it along, just in case. Buckshot'll be best."

Wil noticed the holstered handgun on Dallas's hip and a rifle on the porch. It was odd to see Dallas in jeans and flannels two days in a row, and he appeared at ease. Wil wished he had accepted one of the invitations to join the hunting trips of his father and uncle when Clayton was alive.

He pocketed shells from the bag after inserting two, left the breech on the shotgun open, and followed his uncle to the porch.

"Wonderful day to be in the mountains. I forget how good it smells. And how quiet it can be."

"It's yours to use as you see fit. I think Ramona has the padlock key. Just be careful with locking up and hauling out any garbage. A hungry bear is never a welcome guest."

Wil thought of spending a weekend with Natee at the lodge, before the cold or snow made it impossible. But that would involve figuring out the relationship possibilities with the woman.

"There's beer and pop in the trunk and some snacks, if you're hungry."

Wil arched his back and twisted his shoulders from side to side. "I was hoping you'd tell me more about yesterday. By the way, I'm glad they haven't arrested you."

"Had supper last night with the FBI and Secret Service. But they're not the highway patrol."

The casual clothes and use of contractions offered a different glimpse of Dallas; this was not the professorial image his uncle maintained in town as a cowboy lawyer. Wil settled onto the cushion of the rocking chair. "You didn't shoot Jacobsen, right? I thought you said Farmer did that. But you were dazed the last time I saw you."

Dallas gnawed on his tongue and rocked in the chair. "You heard Jacobsen didn't make it, right? When we talked I was in a form of shock, I think. It gave me insight into what my clients might experience upon being arrested, especially if they've just witnessed or been involved in a violent episode."

Wil tried to match his uncle's symptoms and description of the experience with a diagnosis or condition he had learned about in psychology classes at Michigan, and temporary amnesia came closest. "I want to hear the entire story, but my big question is, what can I print in the paper?"

"Let me narrate the events, and then we'll talk about what and how to report it."

Dallas started with Bob Thornton's proposed land deal, visiting the surveyors, borrowing Wil's pickup to go back the next day, and finding the exposed hand bones via the dog. Then he described the sequence of arrivals, the excavation, the identification of Haefner, and the appearance of more lawmen.

"So how did Nelson and Jacobsen find out about it?"

Dallas closed his eyes as he recalled the scene. "As I said, I told the federal men. The radio in Bud Yost's car kept squawking, but just the broadcast from dispatch. Nelson and Jacobsen may have followed the radio chat and decided to come out. Actually, I'm surprised the Riverton police didn't find an excuse to join in."

His uncle went on to describe Sheriff Farmer's arrival, their dialogue, and the gunfire.

"But why'd Jacobsen do that?"

Dallas gnawed on his tongue. "Talking about it last night with Oakes and Kemper, we all wondered the same thing. I mentioned to them how Jacobsen had been at Ramona's party for Bob, along with Winter."

"So?"

"The thought that popped up, but I kept to myself, was Jacobsen might've been trying to keep Farmer from saying who put him up to confronting Haefner. The person who should share the blame, as the sheriff said."

Wil connected the dots that led to an obvious question. "So Jacobsen might've been helping someone Winter suspected. But who?"

Dallas rocked in his chair. "We're jumping to conclusions. Perhaps Jacobsen was afraid, and the fear led him to act foolishly. Maybe he thought Farmer wouldn't see him sneaking up since the sheriff was talking with me. Maybe he was trying to show off for the FBI."

"And maybe he shot Winter and wanted to shut Farmer up before he could give a name."

Dallas leaned forward in the rocker. "That's definitely what you cannot print in the paper. And I will resist the temptation to supply a name, although there are plenty of circumstantial clues, because there's no real evidence. The FBI and Secret Service are closing their investigations."

Wil rocked in his chair and puzzled over the clues his uncle had referenced.

Dallas stood, took the stairs down the porch, and turned to Wil. "Sure I can't get you a beer? I've got some food to nibble on."

"A beer sounds good." Wil figured Bob Thornton was the person his uncle suspected. Ramona's party had been for Bob, there were photos showing Bob and Haefner arguing, and the land where Haefner had been found belonged to Bob. If Bob had sent Farmer to intimidate Haefner, he just as easily could have involved Jacobsen. Natee had questioned how the highway patrolman had managed to afford an expensive campaign. Bob Thornton could be the answer.

"I took the federal boys to Hudson last night, and before we left, Momma sent out a bag to take along. Bread, cheese, steak bits, and olives. Help yourself."

"So what can I put in the paper?"

The treats from Momma, other than the bread, rested on a tin foil–covered heavy paper plate. A separate oblong of foil housed the buttered bread. Dallas took a chunk of steak and chewed on it. "You can report the finding of the body under a pile of rubble. There is a tentative identification, but until that is verified, all you can do is report the discovery."

"And what about Farmer and Jacobsen?"

Dallas tucked two stuffed olives and a wedge of cheese into a folded slice of the bread. "They are dead and identified, so that's nothing more than factual reporting. The best approach may be to avoid mention of reason or motive and to say the deaths are under investigation. A comment from the sheriff's office and highway patrol to that effect makes sense, if they'll confirm it."

Wil picked up the beer bottle and the bottle opener from the stool. "I've got a statement from the Secret Service guy about their investigation and Winter's death. It mentions an ongoing investigation."

"You might want to check with Kemper tomorrow before he leaves town. Maybe he'll give you an update."

Wil took a swig of beer and set the bottle on the porch. "And does any of this relate to Corky's death?"

"I suspect Kemper and Oakes view our Mr. Freeman as a Fremont County problem, but you might ask."

Wil took a bit of steak. "Geri talked me out of doing a special edition on these deaths. Now I'm thinking a third section to the Thursday makes sense. There's more going on than I can get in the usual number of pages."

"That, my boy, is your decision."

CHAPTER 35

Dallas jumped as he awoke on the rocker, a branch snap signaling danger. He saw that Wilson had left the porch, and his shotgun was missing. Uneaten snacks sat on the stool between the rockers. He gathered them and his rifle and made a trip to the car. Time to complete his mission and get back to the hotel before the sun set.

The outhouse door barked, and Wilson came round the cabin, open shotgun draped over his right forearm. His nephew backed up against the edge of the porch and hopped up to sit, legs almost to the ground.

"Guess I took a nap."

Wilson smiled and nodded. "You deserve it. Busy day between finding a dead body and running the FBI and Secret Service to Hudson."

Dallas shut the trunk of his car and walked back to the porch. "I promised you some answers about your father. I found him here that day in August, last year. Over in the shed."

Wilson turned his head toward the wood and storage shed.

"But that's the end of the story. The start actually happened in the same month, but in 1945, with the atom bomb getting dropped on Japan."

Wilson bobbed his head. "I found a file folder full of stuff about Hiroshima, including the original copy for his yearly editorials."

"Clayton was never one to over-intellectualize anything. That's why his editorials set well with Wyoming sensibilities. And by the way, those Hiroshima pieces never were published."

"But you saw them, right?"

Dallas put his left foot on the bottom step of the porch. "Yes. And he may have shown them to Geri and Ramona. His reaction to the bombings was emotional rather than intellectual. Clayton saw the threat that kind of weapon could pose, especially if the other side had it."

"From what I read, he supported international control of those kinds of weapons."

Dallas nodded agreement. "Everyone from the scientists to preachers to schoolteachers and newspapermen signed on to that plan. But the military and the politicians did not. There was some compromise legislation, but it was mostly for show.

"I supported Clayton's views and figured with time, reason would replace his emotion. We all had to come to some kind of inner understanding of that kind of destruction, but the war ended, and people wanted to get back to normal—to start families and buy houses and make new lives."

Wilson hopped off the porch and pulled his shoulders back in a stretch. "I remember the GIs invading the campus at Michigan. Not many of them lasted in the dorms."

"I can imagine. Clayton's concern, maybe it was an obsession, with the bomb had lost intensity until the Russians did their bomb test. Truman announced it, and all his insecurities returned. And he began to drink too much."

"And what about the women? Was he cheating on Ramona more then?"

"Wilson, I'm not going to lie about your father. Clayton liked to flirt, especially with cute gals. They didn't have to be smart, just pretty and willing. I don't know if he saw more then or not. It was not something we talked much about."

Wilson leaned his butt against the porch, weight distributed equally. "So he drank too much and worried about the bomb."

"I tried to convince him the fear about a nuclear war was bad for him. Clayton knew that intellectually, but the emotion was too strong. I thought, mistakenly, that seeing a bomb test would take away the mystery. So I arranged for him to be a journalist observer early last year.

"He went on a three-day trip, stayed in Las Vegas at the Flamingo. He witnessed one of the bomb tests—Operation Ranger, I think. And for some reason, they let him see photographs taken after the Japan bombings."

Wilson frowned. "How'd he take it?"

"Instead of it calming him, Clayton came back even more depressed. The test blast was worse than he'd imagined. And he could not get the pictures of the victims out of his head. Like I said, it was a mistake."

"Ramona and Clayton came to my graduation, at Michigan, in January. He seemed in good spirits, but that was before the test, right?"

Dallas took a deep breath, to prepare for the end of the story. "The test was in February. When Clayton came home, he could not stop talking about the bomb. I had Doc Owen prescribe some pills to calm him down, and they seemed to be working. And then late July came around and with it the anniversary of Hiroshima."

"Geri said the file folder was always on his desk, with different articles spread out. She made me put it back in the drawer. Seeing the folder was too painful for her."

Dallas took his foot off the step and straightened up. "That first weekend in August, we planned to come up here. Cigars, some drinks, maybe fishing. When I got here, it looked and smelled like he'd been doing some other entertaining before I arrived. And there was a note on the table. It just said, 'I'm sorry.'"

Dallas looked at the open door of the cabin, turned, and motioned for Wilson to follow him. They walked the twenty yards to the woodshed and into the dark cramped space. "The door to the shed was open. When I got close, there was an odor. I came inside and found your father, the hunting rifle between his legs."

He grabbed Wilson's arm as the boy swayed and led him out of the shed. His nephew leaned against the outside wall of the shed and appeared to be struggling to breathe.

"Take a deep breath or two through your nose. Do it!"

Their eyes met, and Dallas took a deep breath and then another. Wilson closed his eyes and did the same.

Once his nephew had regained his composure, Dallas led them back to the cabin and sat him on the porch steps. "I live with the belief the trip to Nevada led my brother to take his life."

+ + +

Wil checked on Cecil before driving to Ramona's and learned that Sunday afternoon had been quiet at Gordon's and at the apartments. The return trip to Riverton from the lodge had given him time to consider Dallas's words. His uncle had admitted to starting the rumors about trips to medical clinics in Kansas and Minnesota and to feeding them with mention of different life-threatening conditions. Ray Winslow, the Fremont County coroner, had agreed to a vague cause of death, and the sheriff's office never conducted an investigation.

The suicide note Clayton had left behind had been destroyed, although Dallas insisted he knew the contents by heart.

> *D, I'm sorry.*
> *Clay*

His uncle assured Wil the handwriting matched correspondence from Clayton. Dallas had thought the use of his first initial odd since over the years they had consistently used their nicknames from childhood. Clayton's early pronunciation of Dallas had come out "Malice," which turned to Molly and ultimately Ollie, from the Laurel and Hardy films. "Bub" had stuck to Clayton in the neighborhood, at school, and at home.

The rifle Wil's father used had been buried in the same grave as the casket. Dallas never wanted it to fire again and felt certain Ramona would not have objected. And that led to the question of what his mother had been told about her husband's death.

According to Dallas, when she learned that Clayton could not have an open casket, her curiosity over the cause of death disappeared. Ramona had trusted his advice that it was better if she did not know the details. Wil recalled Ramona's remoteness during the funeral, as if she had retreated even further into her own world. His announcement of returning to Riverton had broken through, but only for an afternoon. At the time Wil had thought she might be taking pills, and the report that Clayton had used prescription drugs supported his suspicions.

When he pulled into Ramona's driveway, he was not at all certain what he would share from the afternoon with Dallas.

Ramona greeted him in the kitchen. "Wilson, why are you dressed like … are you a cowboy or a lumber cutter?"

Wil held out his arms in the flannel shirt. "Neither. Dallas invited me up to the lodge south of Lander. That's not a place for church clothes."

Ramona's only wardrobe change had been from high heels into shoes she called "flats." "How is Dallas?"

"Do you want me to fix you a drink?"

She opened the refrigerator, removed a pitcher of lemonade, and asked him to mix gin into hers. He put ice and gin into two tall glasses and added the cold pulpy mixer.

"Dallas told me more about yesterday, but he seems good. Did I mention the body they found was on some property Bob owns? They think it was the supervisor of the Boysen Dam project that disappeared."

"I suppose you will have to report on all this in the newspaper. I wish you would not. I will get calls and questions at bridge. People will think I know something. That can be so embarrassing."

Wil took a large swallow of the lemonade gin, not at all surprised by how Ramona had turned the entire episode around to something that would cause her embarrassment. "What's for supper?"

"A roast you will need to carve and mashed potatoes and the corn soufflé from the Wind River Hotel."

"Smells good. I mentioned to Dallas finding a file folder in Clayton's desk about Hiroshima. Geri said he'd had it out the week before his death. And Dallas thought he might have been depressed."

Ramona opened the oven and used a folded towel to remove a pair of foil-topped containers. "Can you get the roast out? And do not start on the atom bomb business. I see where *Life* is going to publish pictures from right after that bombing later this month. Who would want to see such a thing?"

"So you don't remember his being depressed then?"

She peeled back the foil. "We'll put the meat on a serving dish and use the containers for the rest. I hate to dirty dishes. Clayt depressed? No. We were talking of visiting you in Chicago over the Labor Day holiday. A depressed person does not plan to take a vacation."

Wil removed the roast and cut a half dozen slices, some thin for Ramona and the rest thick for himself. He transferred the meat to a serving plate and carried it to the dining room table, set with the good china for two. He returned to the kitchen.

"If you can put some of the juices from the bottom of the pan in this bowl, I can carry the rest."

The roast was tender, but the flavor could not match the bits of steak Dallas had brought to the lodge. He had forgotten how good the soufflé from the hotel tasted; it almost made up for the egg dish Dallas had served him for breakfast during the week. It was a heavenly meal, in part because Ramona had not cooked any of it.

Ramona smiled as he took a second slice of beef. "I am pleased you like the meat. I will send the roast and potatoes home with you but keep the corn dish. I like it cold, in the morning, with my coffee."

She lit a cigarette as he finished his plate. Half of the roast on her plate and most of the potatoes remained untouched. Wil knew the small mound of whipped potatoes would serve as the resting place for at least one cigarette.

He set the napkin on the table and took a breath. "So how do you think Clayton died?"

She blew a cloud of smoke up toward the ceiling. "I got the impression it involved a bear or some other animal. A wolf perhaps. Clayt was always talking about the wild animals around the lodge. Although Dallas tried to convince people it was a medical condition. Why?"

"So you don't think he committed suicide, or something like that?"

Ramona frowned and tapped ash onto her plate. "Clayt was not the kind of man to kill himself, especially when he had a new girlfriend."

"Why do you say that?"

She licked her bottom lip and rolled the upper over it. "An expensive scent on his shirts, a complex perfume, not the kind Geri would wear. And he checked his appearance constantly in any mirror he passed, as he did only when there was a new little tramp. I bet Geri will agree."

How could he reconcile the scene Dallas had described with the image Ramona painted? Wil understood that different people perceived the same person in entirely unique ways, but they were Clayton's brother and his wife. If his mother was correct, how could the facts Dallas had revealed be explained? Wil might know the where of Clayton's death, but little more.

+ + +

Wrapped in their fuzzy blue wedding-gift blanket, Gretchen awoke on the sofa from crying herself to sleep. She had counted on Delmar coming home today and had fixed a roast and made gravy the way he liked it. The meal was still on the table, meat uncarved and dried out. She had worn the birthday dress Delmar had given her and a tiny bit of perfume. And she had prayed.

Yesterday morning, Gretchen had thought of calling her mother but had decided to wait until today. She had gone to the back door to greet him half a dozen times on Saturday, thinking she heard the car door slam, but he was not there. Instead, Orrin came knocking on the front door once and again later at the back door, offering to take her to church the next day. She did not open the door either time. His talk of being "bound by revelation" made no sense to her.

Now it was Sunday night, and Delmar still had not come home. She had wanted to believe he loved her and wanted her and would not abandon her. But Gretchen was out of hope. She would call her mother first thing in the morning. By tomorrow night, she could be in her old bedroom.

Sadness gripped Gretchen, and she began crying yet again. How could there be any more tears left? Feeling her nose start to run, she searched for but could not find her handkerchief. Tossing off the blanket, she ran to the bathroom and tore toilet paper from the roll to wipe and then blow her nose. As she washed her hands with warm water, she saw a swath of light in the living room at the edge of her vision. Someone had come in the back door and turned on the kitchen light. Hope and fear gripped her. She wanted it to be Delmar but feared it was Orrin. Hands raised in fists before her, Gretchen inched toward the living room. She fell to her knees upon seeing Delmar.

Trying to talk between sobs, she could not get the words out. Gretchen grabbed him around the knees when he came near enough, resting her head against his legs.

"I'm sorry it's so late. I meant to be here earlier."

She clutched him tighter.

"Stand up, Gretchen." She heard the plea in his voice and looked up. Half his face was in darkness, the other half lit from the kitchen light. He stroked her forehead and cheek with his hand. "I'm sorry. Can you stand?"

"I was afraid … afraid you … left me."

"Why'd I leave my sweetie?" Delmar lowered himself to his knees and took her in his arms.

She cried on his shoulder, thinking of what to say. For all the thought she had given to this moment, nothing came to mind.

"You're shivering. Let's get a sweater on you."

"I almost called Mama and had her come get me." She felt him stiffen. "You can beat me if you want, but don't leave me. Please."

"I'm not goin' to beat you. This is my fault, not yours."

She wondered whether he was talking about Corky. If he had killed Corky, she did not want to know. "A deputy came by about Corky. The sheriff wants to talk to both of us."

"Couldn't you tell him what he wanted to know?"

"I wasn't sure what to say. I thought you should be with me."

Delmar patted her back. "We'll go see the sheriff tomorrow then. I'll have to make up the time at work, but we'll see him."

She hugged Delmar tight. "I love you so much."

Delmar pushed her back so that they were facing each other. "Did the deputy say something to scare you?"

Gretchen lowered her head, afraid to say what she feared.

"I should've been here when he came. That's my fault." Delmar rose, bringing Gretchen to her feet with him. He moved her toward the bathroom. "Why don't you take a hot bath, and we'll go to bed. I could fix you some hot cocoa."

"I'm not thirsty."

"Take your bath while I unload the car. Then we'll talk. There's things I need to tell you."

Gretchen started her bathwater, fearful of what Delmar was going to say. If he had killed Corky, she did not want to know. And even if he had, it was her fault.

DAY 7

Monday
September 8, 1952

CHAPTER 36

"Here you go, Calvin." Rose topped off the coffee mug after delivering Wil's order.

"Thanks, Martha. Anything I should be writing about for the paper?" Wil served up the question with an answer in mind.

"Word is a Dodge shot the sheriff over the weekend. I don't see a six-gun, so I guess it wasn't you."

Wil made eye contact before looking back at his plate. "I was at Corky Freeman's funeral when Sheriff Farmer met his maker. Who do they say shot Larry Jacobsen?"

"So it's true about Larry too?"

Wil lifted a piece of toast. "As reported by an eyewitness."

"I'll be back."

If Rose had a finger on the pulse of Riverton, then the news of the weekend shootings was already in circulation. He would have to do better than repeat the common knowledge in his article, but at the same time still refrain from accusation and speculation. Quotes from the eyewitnesses would be ideal, but convincing them to speak on the record could be tricky.

A piece about Corky's funeral also needed to be written. The death of Sheriff Farmer meant no one was in charge of searching for the photographer's killer. He would ask Albert about it but did not expect much of an answer. The way Dallas had talked, all the sins of the recent past would be blamed on Farmer, at least by the FBI.

Wil now believed Gretchen Simpson held the key to solving Corky's death. But in what way? Had the husband found out and killed Corky? Or had there been some kind of argument in which

Gretchen smacked him when Corky's back was turned? Maybe Corky had decided to move out and end the affair. Gretchen might have learned about Natee and become jealous. Or the opposite could be true, even though he found it impossible to believe Natee could be the killer.

Also competing for his attention were the contradictory stories about Clayton's death and the push and pull of Natalie Saylor. He could talk with Geri about Clayton, but sharing his thoughts and feelings about Natee felt juvenile. The best approach with Natee might be to not force a decision.

If Rose had worn roller skates, she could not have slipped behind the counter any quicker. "Curtis, was there really a man buried alive, or is that just puttin' jam on top of jelly?"

Wil stopped chewing and looked up at Rose. "I thought I was Calvin today. Which is it, Curtis or Calvin?"

"You was Calvin until I found out you know more'n I do. Now you're Curtis."

Wil half-chuckled. "The skeleton, or whatever was left, of a dead person was found near where the sheriff was shot."

"Who?"

"The FBI hasn't said yet, and I'm not going to guess."

"Maybe you are just a Calvin. Need anything else? More coffee?"

Wil told her no along with a wink, and fished in his pocket for change to set on the counter. He counted out what he owed and a tip, shoved the rest in his pocket, swiveled off the counter stool, and headed to the *Wrangler*.

+ + +

Deputy Nelson opened the Riverton substation early even though it was his week to work the night shift. He wanted to look through Grayson's desk, although he did not expect to find anything significant. Perhaps the sheriff had left notes on the current investigations, perhaps a memo explaining his odd actions on Saturday, perhaps unfavorable reports about his deputies.

Al's search revealed nothing other than the sheriff's failure to use the desk drawers and a pile of papers on the desktop. There were no files, memos, confessions, or anything of significance. Al had suspected the sheriff disliked paperwork, but now all doubt was removed. The entire contents of the desk could be placed into the wastebasket with no loss of information.

The day-shift schedule called for a 7:00 a.m. start, but Bud Yost did not show up until almost 8:00 a.m. When the junior deputy for the northern portion of Fremont County did arrive, he wondered aloud what had brought Al into the office.

"Just because Gray Farmer is dead don't mean there ain't a sheriff. I'd think the county commissioners are going to appoint his replacement soon, if they haven't already."

Bud plopped into a guest chair. "Suppose you're thinkin' to move up, get a write-in campaign now that both fellas on the ballot is dead."

Al slid forward and rested his forearms on the desk. "No, Bud. I'm not. I expect to get fired, either today or after the new sheriff gets elected. And do you know why? Because on Saturday both of us were out at that spot where he got killed and didn't do nothing about it.

"We didn't help him. We didn't get shot ourselves. We didn't arrest nobody. All we did was collect some guns. At least I got the names of everyone. The new sheriff ain't going to want a pair of deputies who stood around while their boss got shot. That's what I think."

Bud slouched in the chair. "I'm not sorry. I think they'd be glad we're alive, not getting pulled into some of old Gray's foolishness."

"Guess what, Bud? Ray Winslow and Dallas Dodge were out there too. Those two'll have more weight than us in dealing with the commissioners. I don't suppose you saw the way Dodge was buddies with the FBI and Secret Service guys."

Bud set his left boot onto his right knee and sighed. "So what?"

"So they're all gonna say we stood there with our thumbs up our butt, that's what. And that reminds me, what the hell were you doing out there anyway? You had the weekend off."

Bud uncrossed his leg and straightened up in the chair. "Yes, I did, Albert. I had the weekend off, but the telephone operator couldn't find you when Dodge called and said to send out a deputy. So she called me, and when I told her you was on duty, she said Dallas Dodge didn't care who came out, and she couldn't find you. So that's why I was there."

Al figured the call must have come in while he was questioning the Simpsons' neighbors. That was why he had not heard the radio or been at the substation or his apartment to take a phone call. Bud did not need to know those details.

And Bud did not need to know Diane from Reclamation would be speaking with both the Secret Service and FBI later that morning. Al thought he could guess the outcome but decided the problem fell outside the jurisdiction of the Fremont County Sheriff's Department.

Al stood and picked up his coffee cup. "I think my plans to be a lawman in Fremont County, or Wyoming for that matter, died along with Gray Farmer. Maybe I could get a job on the police force up in Gillette or Sheridan, or down in Evanston. But no chance in Riverton or Lander, or with the highway patrol."

Bud leaned back in his chair. "If you're getting coffee, I'll take a mug. I think what I know'd be embarrassing if it got out. Sheriff goes crazy, threatening a bunch of folks doin' their job. Highway patrolman tries an ambush and gets caught. And a pair of federal men just stand and watch. I think nobody wants to hear about that, and it's worth something. That's what I think."

Al heard the front door open and frowned. Could the temporary sheriff already be here to grill them? "One of us may be right, or both of us might be wrong. And I think we're about to find out."

He strode to the doorway to find Gretchen Simpson and a man he assumed was her husband. "Morning, Mrs. Simpson."

The wife looked down, and the man took a step forward. "I'm Delmar Simpson, and we was told to come in and talk to the sheriff."

Al extended his hand and introduced himself. "Deputy Yost, could you come out and see if Mrs. Simpson would like a cup of coffee while I talk to Mr. Simpson? Just have a seat there, and I'll be back in a bit."

The woman looked at him, a plea on her face. "Can't we answer your questions together?"

"No, ma'am, that's not how we do it."

+ + +

"I suppose you're not going to be much help with the letters today."

Wil turned and watched Geri unload the post office box envelopes from her canvas bag. "I've got Corky's funeral to write about and interviews and quotes to get on the dead body and shootings, and I want to update the Winter piece. Too early to ask about Farmer's replacement or the sheriff election without any living candidates."

"Dallas say anything more about Saturday?"

Wil clenched his fists and then waggled his fingers. "Larry Jacobsen died, for one thing. Dallas had dinner with the two federal cops. They're both leaving town and don't want to look back. The deaths of two local cops, especially that way, are too hot to handle. 'Radioactive' is the word they used."

Geri stopped transferring envelopes. "Hard to believe that could happen here."

Wil stood and sat on the corner of his desk. "Dallas talked to me about Clayton's death, and I talked with Ramona as well. I need your help deciding what to make of it."

Geri groaned and lowered herself into her chair. "Is this a one-cigarette story or two?"

"Dallas had me out to the lodge south of Lander and told me the story of how he'd found Clayton there. There was a note on the table in the cabin, and Dad was in the woodshed with his rifle between his legs. Dallas said he killed himself, and it was from being depressed about the atom bomb."

Geri lit her cigarette and focused on the canvas bag. "I told you he had that file out before he died. But I had no idea he was that ... that depressed."

"So at dinner with Ramona last night, I asked if Clayton was depressed and could've killed himself. She said Clayton would never kill himself. Said they were planning a trip to Chicago, and he even had a new girlfriend."

Geri inhaled and held her breath. Smoke seeped out her nose, and then she blew a cloud forward. "What made her say he had a new girlfriend?"

"An expensive perfume on his clothes and something about checking his appearance in mirrors."

A half-smile formed on her face before she took another puff. "I knew about the mirror habit but never connected it with new lady friends."

"So you saw the same thing?"

Geri bobbed her head. "Yes. I just didn't know it was a symptom of a new girl. But affairs can be dangerous and don't always turn out good. I know he was agonizing about Hiroshima and the bomb. But Ramona may be right. Clay and suicide doesn't add up."

"I know he died in that woodshed. There's still dark stains from blood on the wall. If he didn't shoot himself, then who did?"

Geri stubbed out her cigarette in the clean glass ashtray. "I don't know and would just as soon not think about it. I miss him too much."

CHAPTER 37

Gretchen sat stiffly, hands in her lap, as Delmar drove to their home. She wanted to concentrate on packing but knew Delmar would want to talk. It was his place to lead and perhaps even say a prayer. She waited for him to speak.

"Did you say what we talked about?"

It was a simple question with a simple answer. "Yes."

"Did he try to get you to say things you didn't want to?"

She looked straight ahead. "He said things I didn't agree with, and I told him so."

"Did he say anything about me?"

"He asked how you and Corky got along. I told him you weren't friends, and you weren't enemies. Just a renter."

"Did he ask if I killed that boy?"

She felt him looking at her. "No."

"He asked me that. I told him no, and he tried to make me mad, make me say something I didn't want to. But there wasn't nothing I didn't want to say."

She sat silently, wanting to put the visit to the sheriff's office out of her mind. There was something she did want to talk about, but she remained quiet until they pulled into the driveway.

She looked straight ahead, hands in her lap. "Did the deputy ask you about Orrin?"

"No. Did he ask you?"

"He asked if Orrin came around when you was out of town. And I had to tell him yes, because he does. I don't let him in the house, but he still comes around."

"Are you afraid of Orrin?"

"No, but I don't like him coming around."

"I'll talk to him tonight when I get home. You need anything?"

"Can you bring home some boxes? We're going to need them."

Delmar turned off the car and led the way into the house. In the kitchen he said a short prayer, embraced her and kissed her forehead, and promised to be home no later than seven that evening. "I think we're good with the law, but that don't mean they won't be coming back. We need to be ready."

Gretchen gave him a squeeze, and he left for work. She felt guilty about not telling Delmar everything the deputy had said about Corky, though not as guilty as she had felt last night. She had meant to confess what she had done with Corky, but when he finished talking, she felt no need to clear her conscience. And now that Corky was dead and they were moving, she needed to think about the future.

When Delmar had first started talking about sister wives, it upset her. What would Mother say to one husband having many wives? But the idea of helping to raise the children, including the ones she would give birth to, and being part of a large family under the eyes of God made sense. And if Delmar had other wives and had not told her, then she was forgiven for her sins.

If she had wanted to get Delmar in trouble with the deputy, she could have made that happen. But Gretchen was obeying God's law and not the county sheriff's. Corky had been a test of her faith, and she had failed. Gretchen was being given another chance at a life where her husband would not be away from home so much, a chance for her to make it into Heaven.

+ + +

Dallas parked the Mercury in Bob Thornton's car dealership lot on north Federal. He stood and stretched as a salesman came out and then sent the man back in to get the boss. Bob acted as if Dallas had come to pick out the new car to go along with the land deal.

"Did you hear about what happened this weekend?"

Bob rolled his shoulders. "Don't think so."

He could tell Bob was lying, even without the shoulder movement. "Saturday I went up to take a closer look at that land you want to swap. I found a long row of construction trash dumped near the eastern boundary, out of sight from the road running by it. And you know what else I found?"

Bob shoved his hands into his pants pockets, eyes pointed toward his boots. "I never was good at guessing."

"I found a hand sticking out of that trash, chewed down to the bone. And when we cleared away the debris off it, we found a body we think is Jim Haefner, the fellow who was running the Boysen Dam project."

Bob looked to his right, eyes still cast downward. "That's bad."

"What's bad is you tried to trick me into taking property that your boys had loaded up with rubble from who knows where. Add to that the dead body, and that property is of absolutely no use to me."

The car dealer looked up and held out his hands, palms up. "Dallas, be reasonable. I ain't got the cash to pay you. But that land is still good."

"By the way, the FBI and Secret Service were out there, looking at the body. The Secret Service was investigating Haefner on a billing fraud scheme. They were about to arrest him, but then he disappeared."

Bob looked toward the showroom and rolled his shoulders. "You don't say."

"Let's say there were two guys, but I'm just talking a hypothetical situation here. You know what that means, right? Not actual but possible. These two guys become friends, and suddenly one of them needs cash because he's got kids in college, or his wife's sick and there's medical bills, or he just wants more money. Say this someone comes up with an idea with, say, a supervisor or project manager, like Jim Haefner.

"Together these two cook up a plan to steal some money. It's a good plan. And they've got a woman to help out. The plan is working. They are getting checks. But there's a rumor the government has an investigation going on.

"So the project manager wants his cut so he can go into hiding, or else he'll confess and reveal to the law the others involved in the operation. Now, the two are not pals but enemies. There are a number of ways this can go, but one is the manager disappears."

Bob squinted at Dallas and turned away. "That's quite a story. Any reason you're telling it to me?"

"I've been talking with the Secret Service and the FBI. They want to find out where the money went, who killed their man Winter, and how it is Haefner ended up buried under a load of construction trash. J. Edgar Hoover dislikes people who kill federal employees almost as much as Communists.

"And they've got photographs of you arguing with Haefner, on the west end of the property where he was found. And the body was discovered on your land, under a load of rubble dumped by one of your crews. It's circumstantial, but if they start to digging, it is difficult to say what may come up."

Bob looked left and then right and leaned forward. "And you're saying for the right price you can make that go away. Is that it?"

Dallas took two steps back. "No, sir. That would be extortion. I'm saying you may have serious legal problems. And I'm also saying since I found Haefner's body, I'll not be able to be your lawyer."

Bob glared at Dallas and crossed his arms. "Again, why you telling me this?"

"As your partner, I have an obligation to keep you informed of anything that may threaten our business interests. I'd bet the FBI agent will want to talk with you, ask you a few questions, discover where you were on certain dates. Maybe you should get a lawyer. And I wouldn't be leaving town. That would look suspicious."

Dallas watched Bob's eyes zig and zag. The fact the FBI had no immediate plans to question Bob did not invalidate the advice. He would create a memo to file about this conversation, just in case. But the pleasure of watching Bob squirm was priceless.

"The other thing, Bob, is that I still want to cash out my interest. But given recent events, that'll have to wait. Just wanted you to know."

He waited for a reaction. Detecting none, he turned and went to his Mercury. Dallas could not be certain Bob had conspired with Haefner. Perhaps Wilson would discover more photographs to incriminate Bob, or other evidence could surface. And there was still the ballistics reports on Farmer and Jacobsen's guns.

But who had been the female accomplice?

+ + +

Eight envelopes with social news from Shoshoni represented the last of the weekend mail when Wil returned to the *Wrangler*. Geri had emptied her ashtray twice and unplugged the coffeepot. She had taken close to twenty phone calls asking about details from the rumored weekend shooting while he ran errands.

"Hope you found the Secret Service guy because he hasn't been here."

Wil smiled and pushed through the half door to his desk. "I did, and he gave me enough for now. Also said he was staying an extra day or two and to save some room on the front page. That doesn't match the report from Dallas that they're closing the investigation."

She wondered what the smile meant. "And what about the gunfight?"

"Both of them said Dallas did the right thing, and they'd testify to it. I couldn't find Winslow, but it's hard to imagine he'll object."

She picked up an envelope from the Shoshoni basket. "And what about the sheriff's office?"

Wil shrugged. "I tried the front door, but it was locked. There were three sheriff's cars out front. I'll call in a bit."

"So what does the Secret Service think belongs on the front page?"

Wil sat in his chair. "The identity of the dead body, or maybe some arrests. It'd have to be big, don't you think?"

"I think you've got to set a deadline for the front page. There's a dead Secret Service man, two dead local policemen, and another dead man from the Boysen project. How're you going to keep from bumped heads?"

Wil rocked in his chair. "Winter can go below the fold, and the other three'll be combined under the banner. I could leave the left column open for Kemper's news. But you're right about the headlines repeating."

"If Harry Truman were to die tomorrow, he'd have to go on page 3, unless that's full already. You know the wire services'll want this. You've got an exclusive."

Wil stood and pushed through the half door. "Bernie needs to know about this."

"I'm just saying, if any more dead bodies appear, they wait until next week. We've got to have a cutoff."

Wil nodded agreement. "The bad part is I'm the only one interested in finding Corky's killer, and I'm at a dead end. And the sheriff's office has got other problems. The only loose end I can think of is Gretchen and her husband."

"Just because Gray Farmer's dead doesn't mean you can play sheriff. Let Nelson worry about it. Poking around is still too dangerous."

"You're probably right."

She scanned a handwritten note about a visiting sister from Des Moines. "By the way, the more I think about it, Ramona's right. Clay didn't kill himself, and I'd bet money on that."

If Wil heard her, there was no reaction. She heard the sound of printing machines and linotype as the pressroom door opened and closed. She started a fresh paragraph for the Shoshoni letter.

CHAPTER 38

As Wil waited in the pickup, he wished he had stopped by the apartment for bits of the leftover roast from Ramona's. Earlier that morning he had transferred a large portion of the roast to Cecil for his missionary work. He still needed a plan for how to proceed with Gordon.

His watch showed it was past six, and other than half-warm coffee, he had not eaten since lunch. He questioned the wisdom of sitting in the cab of his pickup on Agate Lane, on the chance Delmar Simpson would come home. Was it really worth it?

After driving by the Simpson house and failing to see a car parked in the driveway, he had thought of going home. He had even turned around in a driveway and headed toward Federal but had stopped three houses from the Simpson place. Delmar and Gretchen remained the only lead to Corky's killer, and he believed it would end here, either in resolution or in a dead end.

He questioned whether Corky had made it to his apartment a week earlier. Winter, from Reclamation, said they had met that night, and Corky had told him of the photographs. Wil thought it likely that Corky had tried to return to his apartment, although Corky might have driven to Natalie Saylor's cabin. And if that were true, what did it mean?

The day had been filled with finding, interviewing, and then writing up the stories from Kemper and Oakes, plus a stop at Gordon's house. The promised front-page item from Kemper was an empty half column, waiting for details. Wil realized the intrusive thoughts about Natee Saylor had been absent most of the day.

He vacillated between wanting a simple social friendship and a romantic relationship. Wil could not help but lump her with his Chicago ex and his father with her reported history of casual sex. The desire to avoid Ramona's situation ranked high on his personal priority list. At the same time, Natee exhibited most of the traits he found appealing along with beauty, grace, and style. She was smart, witty, and well educated. If he were to marry, she was the kind of partner he envisioned. Yet he continued to wonder if he was good enough for her.

The pink-orange sunset reflected as glare on a car windshield as a vehicle turned off Federal and onto Agate Lane. Wil stiffened. This could be Delmar. What would he say to or ask him? At his desk this had seemed like a good idea, but fear now threatened his mission.

He watched as the car pulled into the Simpson driveway. Wil slid left against the door, hand on the door handle, and watched. Should he get out or drive away? Unable to move, he sat motionless. For all his talk of finding Corky's killer, he was too much of a coward to act.

Delmar walked to the end of his driveway, and Wil heard him talking through the rolled down window, though he could not make out the words. From the other side of the street, the fellow Wil had encountered twice before, Orrin, strutted out into the dirt lane. Orrin wore a white shirt, a dark vest, and clean pants, although his hair and beard remained unkempt.

Wil watched as Delmar moved forward, still talking, and then Orrin pushed Delmar. More words and another push. When Delmar stepped forward, Orrin moved back and shuffled to the side, lifted something dark, and swatted it against Delmar's head. Wil pushed himself back against the seat, lifted his shoulders, and held his breath. Delmar fell to the ground and remained motionless.

Gretchen ran into the street from her house and knelt beside Delmar. Wil wanted to speak, but his throat was dry and tight with tension. He watched as Orrin pulled her up by the arm and started dragging her toward the Simpsons' house.

Wil pushed open the door of the cab and slid from the seat. "Leave her alone!"

Orrin lifted his arm and a ball of fire flashed, and an explosion sounded. The passenger side of Wil's windshield shattered. Wil reached behind the seat for the shotgun, still loaded from his visit to the lodge. He stepped away from the door, raised the stock to his shoulder, and aligned the sights on an approaching Orrin. Wil fired and the explosion from the shotgun pushed him back. Orrin fired a second shot at the same time.

Wil looked at the wisps of clouds in the fading pink-orange sky. He was on the ground and his left shoulder felt on fire. The open door of his pickup obscured Wil's view of Orrin and Gretchen further down the street.

"Revelation shall be fulfilled, and those who oppose shall suffer."

He saw feet approach. Wil slid his left foot back, sending the knee up, and rolled to his right. His left arm ignored the command to support the barrel of the gun. Orrin came closer.

After another explosion, the pickup door angled half-closed so that he could see Orrin. Wil grimaced, pulled the stock against his shoulder, and raised the barrels.

At the same time, Gretchen ran up behind Orrin. "Let him be, Orrin. You don't need to do that."

The bearded man stopped for a moment and turned to look at her. He said something, but Wil could not hear it. Orrin's temporary distraction gave Wil enough time to aim the shotgun directly at Orrin.

"I got buckshot in this barrel and don't see how I can miss. Cock that hammer, and I shoot. And she could get hurt too. Put the pistol on the ground. Now! Or I'll shoot." He felt the shotgun waver as he watched Orrin. "Do it, now!"

Wil fully expected Orrin to pull back the hammer, but instead he placed the revolver on the ground. He ordered Orrin to lie flat on the ground and the man obeyed. Gretchen turned and ran toward Delmar.

Wil managed to slide away from the partially open door and rise to his knees, shotgun still pointed at Orrin. He took deep breaths and questioned whether the sirens he heard were real or imagined.

His shirt felt wet, and when he looked down, he saw it was dark with blood, his blood.

When he looked back at Orrin on the ground, he could see a car turn onto the street with a rotating red light.

+ + +

Sheriff's Deputy Albert Nelson sat in his radio car outside a liquor store, talking with an on-duty Riverton police officer parked next to him. Al had conveyed the details of his interrogation by the acting sheriff from Lander, concerning the events of Saturday afternoon north of town. The other cop had advised him not to resign on an impulse when his police radio squawked of gunshots on Agate Lane.

Both officers flipped on their rotating lights and sirens and raced to Federal and then north to Agate. Al could see a man waving in the street as they approached, and he stopped behind the Riverton police car. On instinct, Al gripped his shotgun and jumped out of the car.

The waving man yelled as they advanced. "This one's hurt, but the other two're up there."

Al identified Delmar Simpson lying on the ground, his wife kneeling beside him. The man's eyes were open, so Al kept moving forward. The Riverton cop stopped, revolver drawn, and studied the face-down figure in the road. Five yards farther ahead, another person was on his knees, with a shotgun pointed toward the ground.

Al scanned the scene, in search of other shooters. "Keep that one on the ground and cover him. I'll check the guy further on."

The Riverton policeman stepped closer to the man lying in the road and kicked what looked like an old-fashioned pistol to the side.

As Al neared the man on his knees, the deputy recognized Wil Dodge. The newspaperman was leaning to the right, his left arm hanging limply and a dark stain on his chest. The sight of the wound sparked Al's first aid training from his army service.

Al set down his shotgun and then Dodge's, grabbed the good arm and lowered him to the ground. "I need a towel and some blankets—quick!"

A neighbor came with a towel, and Al pressed it against what looked to be the source of the bleeding. "We got to get this guy to the medics."

The police officer hurried over and glanced at Dodge. "What about this other guy?"

A neighbor stepped forward, arms pointing left and right. "Orrin here hit Delmar on the head and then shot this guy. But this guy told Orrin to set down his gun, or he'd shoot. And Orrin did. I seen it all."

The cop looked at the pickup with the windshield shattered on the passenger side. "Al, you could take him in this. Anybody got a blanket? Call the hospital! Tell 'em we got a hurt man coming."

Al kept the pressure on the wound and looked at the Riverton cop. "You better check Orrin for wounds and then cuff him. Make sure he don't have a knife or anything."

The Riverton policeman held his revolver on Orrin, told him to roll over slowly, and frisked him.

Al ordered a neighbor to open the gate on the pickup and then lifted Wil and set him into the bed. He picked up his shotgun and glanced at the face-up Orrin. "I'm going to the hospital. You hold on to that shotgun and this guy's pistol. We'll need 'em for evidence. I'll be back, and we'll take him to a holding cell at the station."

The woman Al recognized as Mrs. O'Hanlon came forward with a blue wool blanket. He threw the blanket over Wil and asked her to jump in the pickup bed, and apply pressure to the towel on the way to the hospital. Al hopped into the cab. He drove forward and braked beside the Simpsons.

"Can you get him in the back? I'm going to the hospital."

Gretchen just kneeled there, stunned, but a neighbor helped raise Delmar to his feet and walked him to the back of the truck. Another neighbor helped Delmar stretch out next to Wil and Mrs. O'Hanlon. Gretchen climbed into the passenger seat.

Al stood on the running board, waiting for Delmar to get settled. "Close that tailgate and step back."

+ + +

Dallas heard a rapid click-click of heels on the linoleum and looked down the hallway of the hospital. He stood as Geraldine Murphy quickly covered the distance between them. The salt-and-pepper hair of the *Wrangler* office girl was disheveled, and instead of a business suit, she wore jeans and a sweatshirt. He could not remember seeing Geri in anything but conservative dresses. Without heels she was shorter than he had realized.

"What happened? How is he? Tell me he's going to be okay."

Dallas pulled her close to him, and she leaned in, shaking. "They're operating on Wilson right now. He's lost blood, but they believe he will make it. His collarbone is broken, and there's bleeding. And there is a fragment in his leg, but it is not serious."

She pushed against him, and he allowed a small distance. "What happened?"

"Deputy Nelson brought Wilson and the couple who rented the apartment to Mr. Freeman to the hospital. It seems the husband had been attacked."

Geri opened her mouth to speak, but Dallas continued before a word could leave her mouth.

"The attacker, Orrin something, started to pull the wife away, and the neighbors said Wilson told him to stop. This Orrin then shot at Wilson but missed. Wilson pulled out his shotgun, and that's when Orrin shot him in the left shoulder."

She fell into him and struck her head against his chest. "I told him to be careful. Damn it, damn it, damn it."

Dallas rubbed her back and rocked back and forth, as much for his own comfort as hers.

She pushed back again. "Does Ramona know?"

"She's down by the operating room, waiting. But she wants to be alone."

"Oh, Dallas, why'd he have to go there?"

He put a hand on each shoulder. "I'm hoping you can tell me what he was doing on that street."

"Wil thought Gretchen was the key to finding Corky's killer. He didn't have any other place to go except to question them. You know the wife and Corky were having sex, right? Wil got the idea her husband found out and might've killed Corky, accidental or not. But I told him not to go. It was too dangerous. And now he's been shot." Tears trickled down Geri's face.

"The husband was struck in the back of the head by the pistol Orrin had. My guess is it will be near the same spot where Corky took a fatal blow. Mormons have thicker skulls, or he was luckier."

Geri gave him a sideways look. "Does Nelson know that?"

Dallas pulled her close again. "Yes, Geri. He knows and will be talking with both the husband and the wife. It seems Mrs. Simpson talked incoherently on the ride to the hospital. But when the neighbors spoke to Nelson, they said Orrin told her she was no longer married and belonged to him. And something about the book. Perhaps Revelations."

Geri pushed away again. "So did Orrin kill Corky? And is he dead?"

"This Orrin is very much alive. And yes, it looks as if he killed Corky. I'm sure Deputy Nelson will be questioning him."

Dallas could not help but compare this situation to the one involving Sheriff Farmer and Patrolman Jacobsen—and for that matter, James Haefner. Dead men could neither answer questions nor make accusations. Earlier in the day, a material witness had surfaced and incriminated Bob Thornton. And now Orrin could be interrogated.

"Geri, the doctors say Wilson will be unconscious until tomorrow morning. Why don't you go home and get your rest? Between taking charge of the paper and visiting Wilson, you'll have a busy tomorrow. Sadly, you already know what it is like when the editor is absent. At least Wilson will return."

Geri tilted her head and stared at him. "Odd you should say that. Wil told me about Clay's awful death. And that Ramona said he'd never commit suicide. I agree with her."

Dallas felt as if she had slapped him hard on the face. "What makes Ramona say that?"

She prefaced her answer with raised eyebrows and tightened lips. "Ramona says Clay had a new girlfriend, who wore expensive perfume. A depressed person's not likely to do much seducing."

"Go home and rest. And let me know if I can help at the newspaper."

She thanked him, straightened his collar, and turned away. He watched as she purposefully walked back toward the hospital entrance. Geri had left behind a contention for him to consider as he waited for news about his nephew. It was going to be a long night, and he had time to tackle a puzzle, even if it did not have an obvious answer.

DAY 8

Tuesday
September 9, 1952

Chapter 39

When he awoke, it surprised Wil to see Natee Saylor sitting beside his hospital bed. He wondered how long she had sat there, his sleep coming and going in irregular doses. The night before had not been restful, with nurses checking his temperature and blood pressure repeatedly.

Earlier that morning, Dr. Owen had told him he was a lucky man. A bullet had likely cracked his collarbone and sent lead fragments into the surrounding tissue. The injury had been made worse by a woman pressing on the bone during the drive to the hospital, turning the crack into a break. Another bullet fragment had hit his thigh, but missed a major artery. As it was, his shoulder would need rehabilitation after the chest bandages immobilizing the left arm were removed.

Natee stood and came to the bedside. "How are you feeling?"

He squinted and focused on her dark eyes, filled with the same intensity he had seen at her cabin. "I'm fine. They're letting me out in a few days. I've got a newspaper to run." He liked the way the corners of her mouth turned up and smile lines appeared in her cheeks.

"Good, because you still owe me dinner. And I'm not done with you."

He tried to sit up, but the wrapping around his chest and arm made it difficult. "Could you raise the bed so I don't have to strain to see you?"

Natalie went to the foot of the bed and turned the crank until he signaled. "What happened?"

"Orrin, the guy living across from the Simpsons and Corky, tried to kill the husband and kidnap the wife. I'd parked near their house and planned to question them about Corky. Truth is, I was so scared I couldn't open my door. But when I saw Orrin grab Gretchen, I must've jumped out of the truck. He shot at me and hit my truck. I grabbed my dad's shotgun, and then he did shoot me. Even though I was on the ground, I managed to get him to put down his gun. I got lucky when Deputy Nelson showed up."

She stepped back to the bedside with frown lines marking her forehead. "Heroic but foolish. You're lucky to be alive."

He wanted her smile to return. "I figure the reason I'm alive is to make you an honest woman."

She half-laughed and took his right hand. "I am an honest woman, and that's part of the problem. I'm not going to pretend to be anything other than what I am. And I'm—"

"How about a wife and mother then?"

Natee squeezed his right hand. "You're lucky you got shot; otherwise, I'd punch you in the arm for butting in when I'm talking."

He wanted to reach out and pull her to him for a kiss, but the tube in his right arm and the chest bandages made it impossible. "So the wife and mother part doesn't bother you?"

Her smirk hinted at playfulness. "Now you're looking for a sock on the jaw. I've told you my thoughts—"

"And now you know mine. Will you marry me, Natee Shepherd?"

Her expression turned serious. "I may have gotten Corky killed, and there are others… You don't want to marry—"

"Yes I do want to marry you. I am a better person when I'm with you."

"Ask me again when you're not in a hospital bed and I'll think about it."

"Am I interrupting something?" Geri stood just inside the door of Wil's room, a bouquet of flowers at her chest.

"I think your boss has had too many painkillers. Thinks he's Romeo, talking romance."

Geri moved closer to Wil's bed. "Romance! I should be so lucky."

Wil pulled on Natee's hand. "Juliet, me thinks you doth protest too much."

Natee laughed. "Wrong play, Willie, but nice try. If both of you are going to take sides against me, I'm leaving. I have to run anyway—commissioners' budget meeting in Lander."

He tried to bring her hand close to kiss it. "I meant it. Come back later. Please."

Natee broke his grip and touched his cheek. "I might, now that I know you're not in a coma. I'm not done with you yet."

Geri stepped back, letting Natee move toward the door. "Do come back. I can't stay."

Wil watched Natee leave, a smile on his face even though the shoulder ached. "Did you call her?"

Geri set the flowers on the bedside stand. "No. I've no idea how she knew about it, unless Ramona told her."

He frowned since there had been no sign of his mother. "Where is Ramona?"

"Both Ramona and Dallas were here on a vigil last night. I suppose she went home after the surgery and the report you were stable."

Wil winced and squeezed his eyes tightly. "If you see a nurse, I could use something for pain. You're making that up about her spending the night, right?"

"Nope. I came by, and Dallas gave me the report. You probably haven't heard about Bob Thornton, have you?"

He took in shallow breaths and blew them out his mouth. "No. What'd he do, propose to Ramona?"

"Hardly. Your friends from the FBI and Secret Service arrested him. Seems Haefner had a girlfriend working at Reclamation who named Thornton as the one behind the billing fraud. She did the banking in Lander. The bank clerks identified her."

"I just asked Natee to marry me. A few days ago I was afraid to hold her hand. I guess getting shot changes a person."

"So that's what she meant by romance. What'd she say?"

Wil tried to twist toward her, groaned from the pain, and fell back. "To ask again when I wasn't in a hospital bed. I've got to get out of here and work on a write up of Bob's arrest for Thursday."

Geri put her hand on his chest. "You're not doing much of anything except recover. But I could look for a girl at the high school to take dictation a few hours a day. Plus she could help you edit the other stories. Sound good?"

Wil nodded his head as a wave of nausea joined the shoulder pain to torment him.

Geri stepped into the hall and returned to his bedside a moment later. "Delmar is down the hall with a few broken bones in his face."

"And Gretchen? Was she hurt?"

Geri moved closer and lowered her voice. "She's fine, but it seems Delmar has another wife in Utah."

"Delmar has … Polygamy? I thought the Mormon Church … Does Gretchen know?"

Geri looked over her shoulder. "On the ride to the hospital she was talking, and Nelson heard her say they were moving to Utah, to be with her sister wife."

A heavyset woman in a white uniform invaded his room. "We need to get you back down, young man. How's the pain?"

Wil raised his head. "Bad. And I feel sick to my stomach."

The nurse turned the handle to lower the bed. "I'll get you something for that too. But quit jumping around in bed. That shoulder needs to rest if it's going to mend. Are you the mother?"

Geri stepped away from the bed and smiled. "Not really."

The nurse checked the spot where the needle in his arm connected to the tubing from the suspended glass bottle. "I'll get you some medication, but you need rest. And you'll need to leave, ma'am."

Wil groaned from trying to sit up. "Just a few more minutes. She's my second mother."

"When I come back, she goes. Period."

Geri retuned to the bedside as the nurse left. "Anything else?"

"Orrin—did he kill Corky?"

She rocked back and forth. "Last I heard, Deputy Nelson was going to question him. I do know they had him behind bars at the Riverton station."

"Call and find out. And get that high school girl. And see if there's a way to get me out of here. I've got a newspaper to run."

Geri touched his hand. "Bernie and the boys say to get well soon. And the radio station's been calling about an interview."

"Not until the Thursday's out. Maybe Ramona will let me stay at her place. Should I send Natee flowers?"

The nurse reappeared with two syringes in her hand. "Time to skedaddle, number two. This one goes in your hip and the other in the IV."

As the nurse lifted his sheet, Geri moved for the door. "I'll come back after lunch. Maybe I'll have a stenographer, Romeo."

"Thanks, Mom … Ouch! That stings."

The nurse swabbed alcohol at the injection site. "I thought your name was Wilson. Is Romeo your middle name?"

He heard Geri laugh as she left the room.

+ + +

The head of the bed had been raised for the evening meal, but with only one arm, Wil felt almost helpless. Geri carved the roast beef into small bites and cut the green beans into inch-long pieces. The mashed potatoes looked dry.

Wil picked up the fork and speared the green beans. "It was good to see Ramona even though she tried to make herself the victim, having to answer people's questions. I could tell she was glad when you two showed up."

Geri glanced at Dallas on the other side of the bed and then at Wil. "Did you ask about staying at her place to recover?"

Wil set the fork down and chewed on the beans. "She wouldn't let me go anyplace else."

Dallas moved a chair closer to the bed and sat. "That is the best place for now."

"I've been trying to piece this thing together. I'm thinking Corky's death got overshadowed by the Bob Thornton dealings. If he and Jim Haefner hadn't stolen money from the government, finding Orrin Porter would have been much easier."

Dallas sighed and shifted his weight on the wooden chair. "You make it sound like an arithmetic problem—a few less entries, and you could solve it in your head. The truth is, if you had been on that street anytime other than last night, nothing would have happened. The situation had to ripen."

Wil set the fork on his plate. "The truth is, I planned to question the Simpsons but was too much of a coward to get out of the truck. If Orrin hadn't tried to kidnap Gretchen, I'm not sure anything would've happened."

Dallas groaned and arched his back. "But all the steps you had taken led you to that spot, at that time."

Geri looked at the plate on the hospital tray. "You've got to eat more than that. Both of you are lucky. Dallas shoots the sheriff and isn't in jail, and you get shot, but it doesn't kill you—although I'm not sure why you didn't shoot Orrin."

Wil lifted a forkful of the mashed potatoes. "After I was on the ground, Gretchen stood close to Orrin and told him to stop. I was afraid she'd get hurt if I pulled the trigger. And if I missed, he could've shot me and the game would've been over. Besides, you told me there wasn't enough space to report any more deaths."

Geri shook her head. "But why'd he kill Corky?"

Wil raised the empty fork. "I think he learned about Gretchen and Corky and thought he had a chance of making her his girl. After he killed Corky, Delmar was just another obstacle."

Dallas grunted, stood, and moved to the foot of the hospital bed. "Bob Thornton is in jail at Lander, waiting for the US marshals to take him to Cheyenne to be charged in federal court. Mr. Orrin Porter confessed to the Freeman killing. Plus there's his attempted murder of one Wilson Dodge. And he is claiming to be Mormon royalty of some sort, the great-nephew of some enforcer, Rockwell, I think. Insanity defense if you ask me.

"Special Agent Oakes tells me a gun found at the home of highway patrolman Jacobsen matched the bullet found in Mr. Winter. My guess is Bob ordered Larry to take care of the nosy Mr. Winter. But Larry cannot confirm that theory. My point is, in one fashion or another all these results were from your persistence."

Geri raised her eyebrows. "How do you figure that?"

"Wilson found the lost photos, showed them to all the investigators, and kept asking questions. And he figured out Freeman's death was not connected to the Haefner-Winter deaths."

Wil dropped the fork on the plate. "But I thought Delmar did it, not Orrin. And without your discovery of Haefner, the Secret Service had nothing."

"But I would not have known a thing if you had not kept me informed."

Geri raised her left hand, as if requesting permission to ask a question. "And what about Jim Haefner? Who killed him?"

Dallas pulled back his shoulders and flexed his chest. "I'm afraid Grayson Farmer's confession is being taken as proof he committed that crime, even though the evidence does not support it. I fear Lady Justice is blind."

Wil thought he saw a spark of romance in the eye contact between Dallas and Geri. "One thing I know is I'm not much of a detective. I thought Delmar killed Corky. Or Gretchen. Orrin never entered my thoughts."

Dallas pointed at Wil. "But you were at the right place at the right time, and did the right thing."

"All I know is I've got this urge to get on with my life. I've been stuck in neutral this past year. If getting shot is what it took to learn that, I'm glad it happened."

Geri glanced at the dinner plate. "Are you done with this? And does Ramona know about your plans with Natee?"

"Yes, and no. I'd just as soon it stay that way."

Dallas glanced at Geri and then Wil. "Plans with Miss Saylor?"

Geri lifted the dinner tray. "Wil asked her to marry him this morning."

"If that's what you meant by getting on with your life, I approve."

Wil gave Geri a sideways glance. "She hasn't said yes, but I'd rather believe she will than worry that she won't. But don't tell Ramona."

Geri took the tray into the hallway and returned. "Mothers have a way of sensing that kind of thing. Don't try to hide it from her too long."

Dallas moved closer to Geri. "I was thinking of offering Virginia's services while you are recovering but Geri says there's a girl from the high school."

Wil nodded, glad for the change in subject. "Beverly Denor, a senior, came by and took dictation this afternoon. And we revised a few stories. Did she get those to Bernie?"

Geri nodded her head. "Yes, and he wonders if you want to look at proofs in the morning."

Wil turned his head to the right, stretching his neck. "No, but if she comes early enough I figure to get out one or two more stories. Are you helping Bernie with the headlines?"

Geri reported the edition was under control when they heard the thump-thump of boot heels on linoleum announcing Natee's arrival. Dressed in jeans, an embroidered western shirt, and cowboy boots, she looked at the different faces. "Am I early or late?"

Dallas shot Wil a quick grin. "Just in time, Miss Saylor. Geri, will you join me for dinner and drinks at the Wind River? Best to leave boy and girl to themselves."

Wil reached out for Natee's hand. "Geri, see if the Denor girl can come by early in the morning. We've got a newspaper to get out."

CHAPTER 40

Officer Tom Masin chewed on a thin stalk of wild grass, pulled from the clump just off the dirt road near the airport terminal. Masin wondered what Deputy Nelson wanted this time. He liked the high open space of the airfield better than the location of their previous meeting south of Riverton.

A faint breeze moved the tops of grass tufts and kicked up small fingers of dust. He watched patiently as the air and earth played with one another like kittens. He heard the sound of tires on pavement and looked toward the road.

As the Fremont County Sheriff's Department patrol car approached, he dropped the stalk of grass and gathered saliva in his mouth and spit, removing the remnants of his chewing. The deputy was alone and parked a good ten feet away.

Nelson climbed from his car and cut the distance between them in half. "Officer Masin, thanks for meeting with me."

"Deputy Nelson, I heard there was trouble in Fremont County this week."

"Yes, we got the man who killed that boy you found. He was loco."

"Loco." Masin nodded and rubbed his cheek. He wondered if Nelson thought loco was an Indian word. "Were you involved, Deputy Nelson?"

"Yes, I made the arrest. He tried to shoot another man and almost kidnapped a woman."

Masin waited for the deputy to continue, expecting to hear about the death of the sheriff. "I am glad you were able to stop this man before he hurt others."

Nelson looked down and then to the west, the late day sun bright on his face.

"The problem with your sheriff and highway patrolman, were you involved in that?"

Nelson continued to look west and nodded his head. "I was a witness. It happened fast, but I saw it all."

"I was sad to hear of this business. But I am glad you were only a witness. Taking a life is a burden you can never escape." Masin could see talking of this troubled the deputy. A gust of wind whisked past and faded. Masin hoped the wind blew away any bad trying to enter when the deputy's guard was lowered.

Nelson grimaced and turned to glance at Masin, and took a moment to gather himself. "I wanted to thank you for your assistance. I'd like the chance to work with you again."

"I'm not sure my superior would approve of this."

Nelson cocked his head to the right. "No reasons we can't get along. Lawmen should work together."

"I hope it will not involve another death." Nelson nodded in agreement.

Officer Masin watched as Nelson tapped his hat brim with the left forefinger, turned and walked back to his car, and then drove away.

The sound of Nelson's tires on the highway slowly faded. There was no breeze. For a moment it was completely silent. Masin closed his eyes and focused on the in and out of breathing. The sound of an approaching car on the highway intruded.

Masin took the spiral notebook from his pocket and noted the date, and then entered "Deputy Nelson." As he returned the notebook to the pocket he knew they would come together again and it would involve death. Masin hoped it would be a long time before the next meeting.

CPSIA information can be obtained at www.ICGtesting.com
Printed in the USA
LVOW08s0354300814

401530LV00003B/3/P